Black Dawn

Blood on the Stars VIII

Jay Allan

system **7**
publishing

Also By Jay Allan

www.jayallanbooks.com

Black Dawn

Black Dawn is a work of fiction. All names, characters, incidents, and locations are fictitious. Any resemblance to actual persons, living or dead, events or places is entirely coincidental.

ISBN: 978-1-946451-09-5

Chapter One

Excerpt from the Log of Captain Jake Stockton

Two months. Two months of endless fighting, of sortie after sortie, with little rest in between. That is what my people have been through...and that is what lies ahead of them, as far as I can see. At least as long as any of us are left to fly.

I would resent Admiral Barron leaving the fleet, heading back to the Confederation while we remained here to fight, and probably die...if I hadn't seen his eyes that day we forced him to go. It took nothing less than the combined threats of all his senior officers to mutiny to get him to leave, to accept that his duty lay on Megara right now, and not in this endless bloody void with the rest of us.

It would do us no good to have Admiral Barron here, to know that he would just die along with the rest of us, far from home and to no purpose. Barron has a chance to rally the Confederation, to prepare our comrades to face what is almost certainly coming, a darkness from the deepest reaches of space, a hell they are utterly unprepared to endure. In that hope, lies something for us as well, for if we must die, I would see it mean something. I would know in my final moments that we expend the last of our strength buying time for our comrades to defeat this enemy.

My pilots have earned their keep. There can be no question of that. The enemy ships are too strong for our battle line to face, their numbers too great. But the enemy doesn't have fighters... and that has cleared the way for my squadrons to bomb their ships again and again. The lack of interceptors does not mean they have no defenses, however, and they have quickly adapted their point defense batteries to an anti-fighter role. The fixed guns are no substitute for their own fighter squadrons, but they have taken a steady toll on my wings. I had selected the cream of the fighter corps for the White Fleet...and now, half of those are gone. We have done all we could to rebuild our numbers, raided the transport ships for replacement fighters, and patched together every battered bird that could still be coaxed to fly.

We have also raided every quarter of the fleet for personnel with flight experience, however slight that may be. These efforts have allowed me to keep my numbers up, for now, but the average quality, both of pilots and craft, is steadily declining. Each battered, patched up old ship in the place of a shiny new Lightning, each green, half-trained pilot replacing a lost ace, reduces our combat power...and brings us closer to the moment when we will no longer be able to hold the enemy back.

Interplanetary Space
Unknown System 18
12,000,000 Kilometers from Inner Gas Giant
Year 316 AC

"Watch the patterns on those defensive batteries. These bastards' aim is getting better, but their fire configurations are a dead giveaway, if you watch for them." Jake Stockton's voice was raw as he shouted into the comm, repeating the warning for the third or fourth time, with increasing frustration at the seeming inability of his pilots to exert the caution he was demanding.

The irony of his attitude wasn't completely lost on him. "Raptor" Stockton had been the wildest, most reckless pilot the Confederation fighter service had ever known...and one of the best, too. But rank and responsibility had caught up with him, as had age. Jacked up, over the top maneuvers didn't just put him at risk anymore...the danger extended to hundreds of his pilots, and that was a heavier burden than he could endure.

"Keep your eyes open, and anticipate where they're going to fire next. You can see it coming if you try." He could feel the hoarseness of his parched throat as he forced the words out. He'd been in the cockpit for almost eighteen hours, and while that wasn't anywhere close to his record jammed into a fighter, it was a damned long time under sustained combat conditions. He was tired, and worn down, and he didn't like to repeat himself, much less more than once…but his pilots were still blundering into recognizable defensive fire patterns. They were getting themselves killed.

Needlessly.

"I've got the patterns, Raptor…you're right, they're not that hard to pick out. It looks like they've got three different sequences going."

Stockton almost winced when he heard the first voice to respond…especially when it turned out to be the only clear answer he got.

Olya "Lynx" Federov was absolutely the last pilot in the strike force he was worried about. Federov was one of his oldest friends, and also one of the few pilots to make it through the war with the Union in one piece. The fighter corps had paid more than its share—far more—for the victory in that last conflict…if the weak, simpering end to that struggle could be called victory. Stockton still had a sour taste in his mouth that all the sacrifices made by so many of his comrades had been thrown away.

None of that mattered now, of course. The Union had just given up its primacy as the greatest danger facing the Confederation. Even if no one back in Union or Confederation space knew that yet.

It was a massive break that the Hegemony didn't seem to have any fighters or other small craft—an advantage Stockton knew wouldn't last long. The last months of sustained fighting had left little doubt in his mind that this new enemy was more dangerous than the last one.

A lot more dangerous.

The White Fleet had been tasked with an exploratory mission, but all it had managed to find was another war. From what Stockton had seen so far, he was willing to bet his pilots—and the rest of the fleet—would be missing their old enemies before long.

"That's right, Lynx…and the rest of you, pay Goddamned attention to what Commander Federov is saying, so you don't get blasted to radioactive bits. Normally, I wouldn't care if you lost focus and got yourselves blown to hell, because that would set an example for your comrades of what not to do. But the nearest replacements for those shiny new Lightnings are a hell of a long way from here." *Not that many of those Lightnings are all that shiny or new by now…*

Stockton knew he was being hard on his people, but he'd always found that going easy on them was a good way to end up with dead fighter pilots. It didn't take more than a fraction of a second's misstep to get into real trouble, regardless of skill levels. Every pilot's match was out there waiting for him somewhere, and Stockton didn't have to think farther than Dirk Timmons to remind himself of that.

"Warrior" Timmons had been his rival as the best pilot in the fleet…but the day he'd met the Alliance ace, Jovi Grachus, in battle, she'd been just that little bit better. Timmons had been lucky that day…if ending up burned over most of his body and minus both legs instead of dead could somehow be characterized as good fortune.

Stockton tapped his throttle and blasted his ship back toward the enemy formation. He watched as the small cluster of icons representing the flight of resupply shuttles receded behind his newly rearmed ship. The shuttles represented a combined effort. He'd come up with the idea of refitting fighters from the small craft, and he'd sketched out the basics…then Anya Fritz had somehow made the engineering work. The process was cumbersome, and it would never have worked against an enemy that fielded its own fighters…but he and his squadrons had made it work against the Hegemony, at least after a fashion.

The shuttles allowed his bombers to refuel and rearm without returning to their motherships…and that meant not only faster turnaround times, it also allowed Commodore Eaton to keep her battleships out of range of the deadly enemy main guns while the fighters engaged the fleet's pursuers. The White Fleet, or what was left of it, didn't have the numbers or supplies for a straight up fight against its Hegemony pursuers, so any way to hold the enemy back and sustain the running pursuit was the clear strategy to pursue.

However hard it was on the squadrons.

Stockton's eyes darted down to the screen on his main panel. He still had hundreds of spent fighters stacked up, waiting to connect to the shuttles, but there were almost two dozen squadrons ready to go back in, their fuel tanks topped off and fresh plasma torpedoes in their bomb bays. That meant it was time to lead in another attack before the enemy could regroup and move in on Admiral Eaton and the battle line.

"All right...all resupplied squadrons, form up on me. We're going back in." He gripped the throttle tightly, his arm tensing as he started to slide the control back and feed thrust into his engines. Then, he paused, and he leaned toward the comm unit.

"And whatever the hell you do, keep your eyes on those fire patterns..."

*   *   *

"Captain Stockton reports his primary strike force has refueled and rearmed. He requests permission to reengage the enemy."

Sara Eaton was still getting used to her sister acting as her aide. The two had been close enough as children, but there had been a lot of years since then, over which they'd seen each other only two or three times. It wasn't lack of desire, nor any animosity that had kept them apart, but two active naval careers didn't mesh well with a normal family life.

"Yes...send them back in." Eaton had to force out the words. She knew how long her pilots had been out there, and while she'd never flown a fighter, she could only imagine how cramped a cockpit got after twelve hours.

Or fifteen...or more...

And that didn't take into account the stress and danger. The inevitable fact was that the harder she drove them, the more worn they would get…and the more of them would die because of fatigue and lost sharpness.

That hadn't been as much a problem in her past battles. Fighters needed to land and resupply between missions, and that had always given pilots a chance to stretch their legs, grab a sandwich, maybe even find a quiet place to close their eyes for an hour. But the logistics shuttles allowed just that kind of extended flight mission, as fighters resupplied two or three times before actually returning to their mother ships. It was a clumsy, complicated routine that barely worked…but in the fleet's current precarious situation, "barely" was enough.

"Yes, Commodore."

Sara listened as her sister relayed the command. The signal would take several minutes to reach the squadrons…and she was also aware that by the time Stockton's wings got back into the fight, they would be all that was left in the system of the Confederation forces. Resupplying by shuttles wasn't the only change the squadrons were dealing with on this campaign.

A quick glance at the display confirmed that her lead ships were less than twenty minutes from transit, and that meant the White Fleet would be completely through the gate within forty minutes.

Except for the fighter squadrons.

Stockton's people would have to break off after they hit the enemy fleet, and race like hell toward the transit point. If all went perfectly, they'd get there before the disordered Hegemony forces and with enough time to get through and land on the waiting motherships…before the fleet located the next exit transit point and moved on.

Eaton couldn't remember the last time everything had gone perfectly.

Flying a fighter through a transit point and making it to the other side was no one's idea of a pleasant or easy task. The heavy shielding that protected ship crews from the strange effects of alien space was not something a small fighter could carry, and that meant the pilots had to hang onto their focus—and their sanity—through their own force of will. It was not a challenge all of them would survive.

She turned and looked down at the roster of Stockton's squadrons. The fighters had been battling almost non-stop for the nearly two months since Tyler Barron had taken *Dauntless*, *Fortiter*, and a handful of other ships on a mad dash back to the Confederation. Barron was bringing back the warning that the White Fleet had found a deadly new enemy, one that was a threat not only to the Confederation, but probably to the entire Rim Sector. Eaton's mission was starkly clear…to survive if she could, but more importantly, to lead the pursuing enemy into uncharted space, away from *Dauntless* and its few companion vessels. To buy the Confederation time to prepare for what was likely coming.

Assuming Barron could get the politicians and others to listen…to *truly* listen and understand the magnitude of the impending danger. Not just the Confederation leaders, but those in the Alliance…and even the Union. Old enemies would have to stand beside each other as allies. Eaton didn't have any real data on the strength of the Hegemony, but her gut told her it was going to take everything the Rim had to have any kind of chance of turning back this new threat.

Eaton liked to think she could get her people, the fleet she'd inherited, through the challenges they all faced, but when she tried to think it through in rational terms, she just couldn't see how. Deep down, she believed they were all doomed, that any success would have to be measured in buying time for their comrades.

Sara Eaton had faced death before, and she'd escaped its grasp more than once. She wasn't ready to give up… at least not yet. There was nothing more important than gaining that time that Tyler Barron needed.

Chapter Two

Report from Agent Marieles to Citizen Villieneuve

I have refrained from reporting for several months, as I did not want to take any inordinate risks so close to the launch of Black Dawn. Now, however, I must take the chance. The operation is almost ready. I am projecting zero hour in just a matter of days, and while this message cannot possibly reach you in that time, I decided you had to know we had begun.

I have all pieces in place now, and things have gone better than I could possibly have expected. While I have found only a moderate amount of outright disloyalty among the Confederation political and bureaucratic classes, the corruption and infighting among them has exceeded all expectations. I have been able to manipulate power-hungry functionaries and long-simmering resentments to create the level of disorder and confusion required.

I must confess that, when you initially sent me here, I considered the mission all but impossible. Now, however, I am considerably more optimistic. I even believe we have some chance of gaining outright control over Confederation governmental operations through the proxies I have put into place, at least for a limited time. Even if we fall short of that goal, it is likely—very likely—that Confederation military and political operations will be thrown into uncontrolled chaos for the foreseeable future, allowing you to take whatever steps you have planned to take advantage of such conditions...and position the Union for the next conflict.

Troyus City
Planet Megara, Olyus III
Year 316 AC

"Our investigative reports have continued to uncover extensive instances of corruption at almost every level of government and the military. Trillions of credits budgeted to pay for weapons and supplies for our brave spacers and soldiers, have been diverted instead into the pockets of industrial profiteers, and their allies in the government."

Marieles stood quietly off-set, watching the reporter speak into the camera. The audience numbered in the billions on Megara alone, and almost beyond count once the transmission was disseminated over the transit point comm network to the ITN affiliates on the more than one hundred twenty inhabited worlds of the Confederation.

"Our network teams have been repeatedly harassed and threatened by agents of both the government and the private interests involved in the misdeeds we have uncovered—even attacked in the streets and beaten when trying to gain information. But the Interstellar Truth Network has no intention of allowing these powerful and corrupt forces to prevent us from bringing you the truth. Whatever the cost."

Marieles had to hold back a smile as the reporter reached up and put her hand on the gauze pad affixed to the side of her head. That particular prop was a phony, but it was true that half a dozen ITN reporters *had* been attacked over the past week. Marieles knew that for sure, both because she'd seen the results—mostly contusions, with a couple broken bones—and also because the assailants had been on her own payroll. It had taken every resource Villieneuve could get to her to complete the takeover of ITN, and now she was determined to make the most of it.

A few battered reporters were useful props to display on the air, though the attacks had also served to fire up the vast majority of the ITN staff that wasn't in on her plan. That didn't surprise her, but what had come as a bit of a shock was how quickly ITN had jumped aboard her largely manufactured crisis with a level of unbridled groupthink. She now had the entire massive operation, the second largest network in the Confederation behind its rival CIN, under her thumb in a way that had exceeded her most fervent hopes.

She had always been a manipulator, even before she'd ended up in a career in espionage, but it still amazed her how easily people could allow themselves to be led. She'd come to Megara because she hadn't felt she'd had any choice except to accept Villieneuve's assignment, but she'd been pessimistic about making any real progress. Now, she was excitedly counting the remaining hours until she put the plan into full operation…and she was expecting some level of success.

"So, stay tuned to our updates, on your vids and on the information nets. The ITN team is at work, and we will bring you the truth, all of it, no matter how upsetting or disturbing it may be." A short pause. "You have my personal promise on that. Raina Maren, reporting from the main studio in Troyus City." The reporter stood stone still, staring into the camera with a look so earnest, Marieles couldn't imagine any viewer not believing every word the woman had just told them.

Marieles walked forward as the warning lights went out, signaling that the broadcast had ended. She smiled and extended her hand toward the reporter. "That was excellent, Raina. With any luck, we'll have some new footage for your show tomorrow." Marieles knew for certain they would…though it would show activities ostensibly occurring later that evening, it was already filmed and waiting in her secure system.

"Thank you, Desiree. This story has taken on a life of its own. Government corruption is one thing, but the reach of this is beyond anything I've seen before." The reporter seemed genuinely happy at Marieles's words. Raina Maren was one of ITN's top assets, their highest rated on-air personality. Marieles found it amusing that, amid all the paid operatives she'd been struggling to integrate into the network, one of the company's pre-existing employees had bought into her manufactured storyline with such unrestrained momentum. She was still stunned that such an obviously intelligent woman could allow herself to be so easily deceived…and could demand so little evidence before allowing her beliefs to rigidly take hold. And a journalist with a wall full of awards, no less.

Of course, her ratings have never been higher. Maybe that's why it was so easy to get her to wear a fake bandage on the air…

"If we get the evidence I'm expecting, tomorrow you'll have your most impactful segment yet." Marieles paused. "I wish I could tell you about it now, but I have to be sure we can back it up before we even risk discussing it." That was all show, of course. The evidence to back it up had all been manufactured already, and it was in place. When the news hit…the Confedera-tion population would go wild.

Assuming we've prepared them enough. Working up anger toward the government was one thing, a far easier effort than turning public opinion against a beloved figure.

Once she set this final series of operations into motion, she would go beyond the point of no return. Black Dawn would be active…and she would be fully committed.

*   *   *

"Well, it costs four times what a beer does on Dannith—and six or seven times what I paid the last time I was on leave on some frontier dump of a planet—but it *is* good, I'll admit that." Hank Bellingham raised the glass mug, still covered with a bit of the frosty sheen it had possessed in such abundance a few moments before, when the very well-dressed waiter had brought it to the table. The Marine guzzled down most of what remained, and set the mug down just a bit harder than he might have two or three beers earlier.

"Leave…when was the last time *you* were on leave? I'm sur-prised it's not ten times what you paid that long ago." Jon Peter-son had a mug of his own sitting on the table in front of him. He'd also found it to be a high-quality brew, cold enough to hurt his teeth when he took a drink, but he was lagging behind his friend in draining it.

Peterson couldn't argue that the prices of things on Megara, and especially in Troyus City, were somewhat of a shock to a Marine who spent most of his time in officers' clubs or base commissaries. Troyus City was the capital of the Confederation, and it was overrun with politicians and with the particularly high-end breed of parasites that fed off of them. At least, that was how Peterson saw them all. He'd gladly have gone the rest of his life without a trip to the capital, or to any of the Core Worlds for that matter. He'd always planned to serve his time and muster out with a couple stars and a quiet spread somewhere toward the Outer Rim. Someplace where he could grow an apple orchard…and go years on end without laying eyes on corrupt politicians.

But something was going on, right there in Troyus City… and Jon Peterson was going to get to the bottom of it. He didn't usually involve himself in political matters, but Gary Holsten was a friend…and Peterson didn't think much of any man who'd abandon a friend in trouble.

"I'm a little worried about the Marines, Jon." Bellingham was Peterson's subordinate, but they were old friends, too…and their current activity was definitely an "off the books" kind of operation. That was enough to put them on a first name basis, at least when it was just the two of them. "We've been letting our pay accumulate for so long, a few expensive beers won't kill us. But Troyus seems like a heavy lift on a private or non-com's pay." The Marines recruited from every Confederation planet, but it was no secret that most of the rank and file came from the poor fringe and agricultural worlds. Not one Marine in twenty had any kind of family money or anything to fall back on except his or her wages…and a Marine private just didn't make all that much.

And they had brought Bellingham's entire first company back to Megara for "shore leave." That was over a hundred Marines, eating, drinking, and spending like only off-duty Marines could do.

"You're right, Hank…of course." Peterson paused for a few seconds. "I suppose we can come up with some kind of small bonus from the division's discretionary fund. Especially since we don't know how long we're going to be here."

Bellingham nodded, but then a few second later his expression turned to a frown. He looked around, and then he leaned forward toward Peterson. "So, what do we do now, Jon? We've been here a week, and we haven't got a clue to where Holsten is being held…and no idea how to communicate with him, or even to find out what it really going on." Another pause. "So, what's next?"

Peterson returned his friend's gaze, his own face morphing into a concerned expression. "I don't know, Hank. I was hoping his arrest would be public, that some kind of open charges would be brought…or something like that." The fact that Holsten was being held in total secrecy only increased the Marine's certainty that something suspicious was going on…but it also left him short on options for how to proceed.

Finally, he looked over at Bellingham and said quietly, "I think we need to find Admiral Striker. As soon as possible."

Van Striker wasn't only the navy's top officer, he was Holsten's close ally…and another senior officer Jon Peterson counted as a friend. And he was the *only* person Peterson could get to right now with enough clout to find out just what was going on.

* * *

"I want some answers, and I want them now, Commander." Admiral Van Striker was frustrated. No, he was past frustrated now, and well on his way toward unfiltered anger. He was used to challenges dealing with the government, the endless jousts he was forced to fight with the Senate and the various layers of politicians that affected every aspect of the fleet's operations. But something stranger than normal had been going on, for the past couple months at least, and he was damned well going to get to the bottom of it.

"Yes, sir…I have made that clear. The Senate has been meeting in closed session for several weeks now, and I can't get past a small group of aides. They told me we would be contacted when the Senate has concluded its current proceedings." Kate Britten was relatively new as Striker's primary aide, the daughter of an old comrade who hadn't made it through the Union war. Striker had put her in the post out of a sense of obligation to his lost friend, but he had to admit, despite her inability to get through the Senate's labyrinthine stonewalling, she was the best aide he'd ever had.

"Well then…maybe it's time for *me* to make myself clear." Striker wasn't the kind of officer prone to throw position and prestige around…unless he really needed to. But now he was going to see if the bureaucrats shoving his aide aside had the guts to pull that shit with the navy's commanding officer.

He sat quietly for a moment, slipping deeper into thought. His natural tendency was to respect the civilian leadership, even when they had their heads buried deeply in an unpleasant place. But he couldn't push aside the concern that something was going on…something *bad*. The fact that he hadn't been able to reach Gary Holsten only increased his concern. He'd written off his friend's disappearance to the operations he had under-way on Dannith, but his concern had grown as the time passed by with no communication of any kind. Something was wrong, on Dannith, on Megara…and probably other places too. He had to do something about it.

"Commander…get my transport ready. We're going to the Senate House. Now."

"Yes, sir." Striker could hear the satisfaction in Britten's voice. Clearly, the aide hadn't enjoyed being pushed aside.

She stood up, just as the room's AI spoke. "Admiral Striker, there is a Marine officer here requesting to see you, a Colonel Peterson."

Striker had been about to stand himself, to head right down to his transport, but now he plopped back into the chair. He knew Peterson fairly well, and he considered him a friend. Apart from his own personal impression of the man, he knew Jon Peterson had a reputation as one of the toughest officers the Marine Corps had ever produced.

He also knew that Peterson and Holsten had known each

other for a very long time…and Peterson's division had been out on Dannith for the past few months.

"Show the colonel in," he said softly. He turned toward Britten. "Why don't you go make sure the transport is ready. I'll see what Colonel Peterson needs, and then I'll go to the Senate House." He generally trusted Britten to stay during his meetings, but he had a feeling that whatever Jon Peterson had to say, he'd want to hear it alone. "And, while I'm gone, you can continue to supervise the search for Gary Holsten."

"Yes, sir." Britten stood up and walked across the room, just as the door slid open and Jon Peterson walked in. Britten saluted, not exactly protocol between the two services, but a show of respect nevertheless. Then she slipped through the door and out into the exterior office.

Striker sat for a few seconds, waiting quietly until the door closed. Then he looked up at Peterson.

"Well, Jon, I know you well enough to guess you're not here just to pay your respects. So, let's cut through all the weeds, shall we? What's going on?"

Chapter Three

"Captain...you've got to come back and land that ship. You can't stay out there forever, flying sortie after sortie. You need rest, and your pilots damned sure do. Don't make me issue an order. Be reasonable. You may be the best we've got, but you're not indestructible."

Stockton sat and listened to Sara Eaton's words pour through the comm as he watched the monitors on his screen slowly tracking the progress as the conduits from the shuttle filled his fuel tanks. He'd already reloaded his bomb bay, and in another minute or two his tanks would be topped off and he'd be on the way back.

Back toward the relentlessly approaching enemy fleet, not to the rest Eaton was urging. For the eighth time.

No...the ninth...

He'd started sending his squadrons back to their mother ships, a third of them at a time...and now he was about to order the first group back for a second time. He had been letting his pilots rearm from the shuttles twice, in a few cases, three times, but after that, he'd ordered them all back to their base ships for a full refit. He agreed with everything Eaton had just said, at least with regard to the pilots under his command.

The shuttles were a brilliant innovation, and one that worked far better than he'd had any right to hope it would. But they weren't a substitute for a battleship's landing bay and the vast crew of engineers and technicians stationed there…and he wasn't about to watch his people fly ships that hadn't received even a cursory inspection after two or three missions, much less the repairs he knew many of them needed.

Except for him, of course.

He wasn't sure if he had truly come to believe he was indestructible, that he was *that* good…or if he just didn't care anymore. It was hard to believe any of his people were going to make it back from this mission anyway, himself included. Not only were they outnumbered, but they were flying off into unexplored space, and the only known way back was through the massive Hegemony forces pursuing them.

Stockton reached out and flipped a series of switches, disconnecting his ship from the refueling brackets. His tanks were only ninety percent full, but that was enough. It was time for him to go back to plant another massive plasma torpedo into the guts of one of those Hegemony battleships.

Regardless of what Commodore Eaton was saying to him. She'd continued on for another minute—more of the same— clearly aware that Stockton was likely to ignore her…and not quite willing to issue a flat out, utterly clear order that he return.

He wondered if that was because, in the end, she deferred to his knowledge of fighter tactics…or because she was afraid he'd disregard even an outright command. That could thrust her into an open mutiny situation that would force some kind of action he was sure she preferred to avoid. He suspected it was mostly that staying her hand, though he wasn't absolutely sure he would ignore a direct order…at least if she worded it carefully enough to leave him no outs.

He wasn't sure he wouldn't disobey either.

Stockton respected Eaton greatly, and he considered her one of the most skilled and admirable flag officers he'd ever known.

But he was where he was for Tyler Barron, to lead the deadly Hegemony forces on as involved a wild goose chase as possible before they realized they were being led to nowhere. Stockton knew Barron needed time, not just to get back to the Confederation, but to rally all its forces—and those of the neighboring powers if possible. He hadn't deluded himself on the prospects when he'd accepted his place remaining behind with the fleet, and he'd promised himself that he and his people would do whatever it took to give Barron what he needed.

Even disobey an order if need be.

He flipped the last of the switches on his control panel, and he felt the fighter shake hard as it detached from the shuttle. He angled the small ship slowly, using the positioning jets to slide far enough from the refueling ship to clear the way to engage full thrust. A few seconds later, he pulled back on the throttle, and he felt the impact of the engine blast slamming him back into his chair.

His eyes darted down to the panel, to the comm unit. He knew he had to answer Eaton. The fact that the admiral was almost six light minutes away had given him some extra time, but now he had to decide what to say. He was fully armed again, and he had no intention of turning back until he planted his plasma torpedo right into one of those Hegemony battleships. But, after that, perhaps he would return. He'd been out a long time, and he could use a break, even a short one, and perhaps even something to eat. He'd been going on supplements and stims since he launched, and, though part of him might have argued the point, he had to accept that he couldn't keep going forever the way he was.

Besides, he could avoid an outright break with Eaton if he told her now that he was only doing one more run. She'd never force a showdown with him over that.

"Admiral…this is Captain Stockton. I'm refueled and rearmed, and heading toward the enemy line now." He was grateful that she wouldn't be able to get an answer to him in less than twelve minutes. He was pretty sure she would accept what he was about to suggest, but it almost didn't matter. By the time she could answer—and he could argue—too much time would elapse to call off the attack anyway. He would be able to complete his run without overtly disobeying her…and then he would return to *Repulse*. If only for a brief rest and a decent refit for his fighter. "I will return to base after this attack run. Projected time until firing range, twenty-four minutes. Given current distance and return velocity, I should be back in…" He stared at the screen, realizing as he tried to run the calculations in his head just how tired he really was. "Two hours, eleven minutes."

He thought that was right.

Close enough.

He tried to clear his head, to push aside the exhaustion closing in on him from all sides. His eyes darted back and forth, checking on his scattered squadrons. He had half a dozen birds with him now. The rest of his hundreds of fighters were all around, their formations hopelessly disordered, their pilots clustering together into whatever small, ad hoc combat groups they could form as they ran their constant attack runs.

Stockton had seen some terrible battles in his day, watched hundreds of fighters obliterated in the fury of combat, but he'd never seen sustained offensive action like what his people were engaged in now. They had to realize how desperate a position they were in, how hopeless a fight it was…but it didn't stop them. Stockton knew the Hegemony would be a terrifying enemy, that their technology and numbers outstripped anything the Confederation could match.

He also knew his pilots would leave a lasting impression. The enemy might invade the Confederation, lay waste to peaceful worlds, start a war that could only end in a holocaust…but they wouldn't soon forget what fighter squadrons could do.

He would make damned sure of that.

He moved his hand slowly, bringing his vector around on a course toward a cluster of nearby enemy battleships. He picked one, for no other reason than his eyes landed on it first.

No, they wouldn't forget what his pilots did here.

*   *   *

"Damn you, Jake…" Stara Sinclair sat at the main station in *Repulse*'s flight control center. She'd spent six years working on the old *Dauntless*'s fighter operations, first as an assistant, and later as the flight deck commander…and for the last several years, she'd had what she could only see now as the misfortune to fall in love with the best—and worse, the craziest—pilot in the fleet. She didn't doubt the intensity or the sincerity of her feelings for Stockton, but that didn't stop her from wanting to hit him with a solid, well-aimed bat at times.

She'd sent a number of…requests…to Stockton, urging him to bring his ship back to *Repulse* to rearm and refit, finally enlisting the commodore to add her own voice to the mix. He'd ignored most of them, and outright refused the few to which he'd even bothered to reply. Sinclair had grown more and more frustrated, but there was nothing she could do besides sit there with her fists clenched under the desk. She had technically had the authority to issue orders to *Dauntless*'s strike force when the fleet had first left Confederation space, but her hurried transfer to *Repulse*, and the rough command structure that had been thrown into place upon Admiral Barron's departure, had left her decidedly unsure of who was obliged to follow her orders.

And even if she'd had a reliable OB, Stockton was the fleet-wide strike force commander, and while she hadn't really considered it, she suspected she'd never had any real authority directly over him.

Certainly, that was the way Stockton saw it.

She wanted to be angry…in fact, she *was* angry. But she also knew that Stockton's crazy fighter tactics were probably all that had kept the fleet from being overtaken and destroyed. Fighters were the one advantage the fleet had over their Hegemony pursuers, and she doubted there was a better man or woman in human-inhabited space to take advantage of that edge than Jake Stockton.

She turned and looked at the display. Stockton had sent a third of his fighters back to the fleet, and another third were still

on the ships, completing their refits and repairs. A quick look
at the status reports told her most of the ships weren't going
to make their schedules and launch on time. The fighters had
flown repeated sorties, refueling multiple times at the shuttles,
and the damage and wear and tear on the craft exceeded what
the flight crews had expected.

Or, more likely, exceeded what they told you. Sinclair wasn't too
surprised. She hadn't believed the figures her people had given
her either.

She watched as the display updated. A small group of fighters were moving toward a forward cluster of enemy ships. There
were no more than a dozen and a half of them in the first wave.
About as many again were just pulling away from the shuttles
behind and following.

It was a weak force, far smaller than should have been attacking even the single group of enemy battleships, but she wasn't
surprised Stockton was sending them in. She was even less surprised when she saw his fighter was at the head of the formation.

As a fellow officer, she respected his courage and his devo-
tion to his pilots. As a spacer hoping to preserve some chance—
any chance—of actually getting back home, she appreciated his
heroics and his unstoppable effort.

As a woman who loved him, she wanted to strangle him.

She knew how tired he had to be…and she was well aware
he was leading in a light attack force because that was all he had
now. She was also fairly sure that the idea of *not* attacking, of
bringing all his ships back to base, had simply never occurred
to him.

She watched as the symbols moved across her screen, coming to within a few minutes of range. She was watching the past,
she realized, looking at scanner signals that had traveled across
more than six light minutes. The ships on her screen appeared
to be two or three minutes from attack range.

The real ships, out there in the darkness, had already completed their runs…or failed to do so. The thought that Stockton
was already dead, that he'd been hit by enemy defensive fire and
the light depicting that reality had simply not reached her yet,

stirred a quick panic in her stomach.

But, as mad as she was at Stockton, she believed in him too much to assume any Hegemony gun turret had bested him.

As much as she worried about him, and as crazy as he drove her, part of her also believed no one could take him down. Stockton and his fighter were as close to a perfect pair as existed…she'd made her peace with that.

No, they wouldn't take him.

Not my Jake Stockton…

* * *

Stockton squeezed his hands tightly, gripping the throttle so firmly, he half expected to see finger indents driven deep in the tempered steel. He'd finished his attack run, planted the plasma torpedo right in the midsection of the biggest Hegemony ship. It was his seventh hit of nine attempts.

But then he'd stayed around too long.

He had brought his ship around and driven back toward the enemy ship just as the rest of his pilots were coming in. He didn't have anything but lasers, and he knew the tiny energy weapons offered limited effectiveness against a behemoth like the Hegemony battleship. But he couldn't bring himself to pull away and head back to *Repulse*, not until the rest of his wave had come through. They would all go back together.

He had fired as he closed, scoring a few minor hits, even taking out what looked a lot like a defensive turret. Three of his ships had streaked in, one after another, planting their bombs almost dead center to where he had landed his own. The third one had set off a massive series of internal explosions, sending huge plumes of radiation and instantly-frozen fluids blasting out into space.

Stockton had allowed his attention to wander, to focus for too long on the damage his ships had done.

His eyes had been fixed on that last torpedo going in…just as one of the target's remaining defensive emplacements scored a hit on his Lightning.

I'm dead.

It was his first thought, one he'd truly believed...perhaps for the longest three or four seconds of his life. Then he realized his ship was still there.

It was spinning wildly out of control, and until the repair bot managed to seal the gap, it had been spewing precious life support into the frigid wastes of space. But it was still there, mostly intact, and he frantically grabbed the controls, struggling to restore the vessel's bearing.

The ship was damaged. Badly, most likely.

But it was still functional...enough that he was still alive. He was willing to take it one step at a time from there.

He reached down and tapped on the comm controls. Active.

"Attention all squadrons...all groups return to base ships as soon as you complete your final attack runs. All supply shuttles, return to base immediately." He'd pushed things as far as he could. If he could get tired and careless enough to get hit, any of his people could. He still had time to get them all back aboard before the fleet transited again and they had to make another trip through the transwarp lines in their tiny, unprotected craft. He still had two dozen pilots in sickbay from the last transit, at least half of whom were likely to face a long and difficult recovery before they were themselves again. He wouldn't put his people through that again unless it was a dire emergency.

Maybe he even had time to get himself back, too. He looked down at the display, at the wavering power monitors.

Maybe.

That would be a good thing, because as far from sure as he was that he could get his shaky, battered ship back to *Repulse*, he didn't figure he had one chance in ten of getting through the jump point if he missed the ride on the mother ship.

And the Hegemony fleet was a bit large to face off against in a single, damaged Lightning.

Chapter Four

Barron stared out from his chair into *Dauntless*'s massive main display. His thoughts were in a dark place, as they'd been since he'd reluctantly agreed to return to the Confederation… while most of his ships and spacers put themselves at horrific risk to cover his escape. It went against everything that made him who he was, every belief he'd ever held. But, in the end, he'd realized his people were right in their insistence that he go. The Confederation was in grave danger—and worse, no one beyond the White Fleet even knew the deadly hazard existed. Someone *had* to get back and warn the fleet, the Senate…everyone. As uncomfortable as he'd always been with his celebrity, he couldn't argue that his voice would likely be taken the most seriously by those he had to warn.

Now, however, his thoughts were elsewhere, out among the planets and the vast empty space of the system *Dauntless* was passing through. His ship had made many transits since leaving the fleet, and was now moving back into the area of space known for the past two centuries as the Badlands.

The Badlands was a haunted region of space, dotted with the

24

ruins of ancient civilization but devoid of any signs of ongoing human life. It was a vast stretch of hundreds of systems, extending out from the Confederation's border into the depths of the unknown.

The Badlands didn't have a set outer border, not one that was universally agreed upon. It was generally considered to extend out as far as any exploratory missions reached, at least until the White Fleet pressed on well past the range of any previous expedition. But, *Dauntless* had returned back to familiar space now…very familiar space.

Seven years before—*has it really been almost seven years?*—when the old *Dauntless* had visited this system.

He thought about it for a few seconds, redoing the calculations in his head and coming to the unavoidable conclusion that it had, in fact, been that long since he'd led his ship into the Chrysallis system. Since he'd faced and defeated a Union fleet that vastly outnumbered his force…and somehow managed to destroy the planetkiller as well, the most deadly and powerful ancient artifact ever discovered by those who dwelled on the Rim.

Almost seven years since he'd met Andromeda Lafarge.

He still remembered the first time he'd seen her. She was tough, as tough as any veteran spacer he'd ever known, and she was smart too. He'd found her irritating, off-putting in the extreme…and at the time, he'd longed only to complete his mission, to prevent the Union forces from gaining control of the artifact…and to say his final goodbyes to Captain Lafarge and her group of frontier bandits.

Things hadn't worked quite the way he'd expected with regard to Andi Lafarge. He'd never been able to get her out of his system—and he'd *tried*—and over the intervening years, they'd reconnected a number of times. He loved her, though it wasn't something he was always willing to admit to himself, and he had a pretty good guess she returned the feelings. But that wasn't enough, not for two people like them. He was a creature of duty, born to it, with obligations that preceded his birth. And Andi had her own irresistible drives: to escape the desperate poverty into which she'd been born, to attain the wealth and privilege she'd seen all around her childhood squalor, and to disregard, disrespect, and otherwise ignore the rules and societal constraints that were such a central part of his life as a naval officer.

She'd achieved all she'd set out to, and more. Barron was truly happy that Andi had attained all she'd pursued for so long. She was wealthy now, her resources almost as vast as those of the Barron fortune around which he'd always lived. He missed her, as he always did when he didn't see her, but she had been part of the reason he'd accepted command of the White Fleet… to give her the time to adapt to her new life.

Time to get over him.

Barron had even considered retiring, leaving the navy and joining Andi in her new home, but in the end, he'd known it just wasn't something he could do. He'd been born into obligation to the navy, his wealth and privilege acting as chains in some ways. Tyler Barron had been destined since birth to lead Confederation fleets, and he knew there was no escape. As much as part of him might want a different life, he could never live with a choice that abandoned his duty.

He'd also considered asking Andi to join him…she'd come close to outright offering to do just that. But she could never have been happy as just the spouse of an admiral. She'd made her own way in the universe, attained a level of success that almost defied comprehension. She had done all she'd set out to do in life, and Barron wasn't willing to lure her away from what she'd spent a lifetime building.

Still, he still missed her, as much as he ever had. Even the misery at leaving so many of his people behind, the tension about what he now knew was facing the Confederation…none of it was enough to push Andi Lafarge from his thoughts.

"Admiral…we're picking up a scanner contact, on the other side of the primary, moving toward our target transit point."

Barron's head snapped around toward his aide's station. Eliot Cumberland was a capable officer who'd been utterly reliable since the fleet had begun its return journey, but Barron couldn't help but miss his previous aide. He knew it wasn't fair, that Cumberland had done no lesser of a job than Sonya Eaton. But Barron still felt the pain of leaving Eaton behind. He hadn't had a choice, not really…not when Eaton's sister was in command of the entire fleet. He'd approved Sonya's transfer request, and he'd wished her the best…but it only made it more difficult to accept what he'd done. For all he tried to tell himself Sara Eaton would somehow lead the fleet through the nightmare to which he'd consigned them, deep down he didn't believe any of them would survive. He hadn't just abandoned them all…he'd left them behind to die.

"On the display, Commander." Barron tried, as he always did, to keep any resentment from his voice when speaking with Cumberland. He was mostly successful, though he suspected sometimes his angst and bitterness slipped through.

"Yes, sir." The officer's tone was crisp, respectful. Whatever Cumberland had perceived of Barron's feelings, he'd never let any of it show.

Barron looked out at the display, watching as the lone symbol appeared. It was a ship, a fairly small one, and there was no question it was heading for the transit point.

Barron had been worried for an instant, as he had been in every system through which they'd passed, that the Hegemony forces had somehow managed to follow his small flotilla. But the ship he was staring at was just a smuggler's vessel, not unlike Andi Lafarge's *Pegasus*, out in the Badlands searching for artifacts.

With a crew that I suspect is none too happy to see a couple of battleships moving into the system…

Private expeditions searching for ancient artifacts were still illegal in the Confederation. The Senate had never pulled out of the international accords regarding Badlands exploration, despite the fact that the Confeds were just about the only signatory who seemed to pay even cursory attention to the treaty's provisions.

At least it did…before *Dauntless* came here…

Seven years before, the Union had come close to gaining a weapon deadly enough to alter the balance of power on the

Rim. The Confederation politicians hadn't taken any action based on what had happened in the Chrysallis system, remaining in the accords despite the clear evidence that their enemy was actively seeking artifacts. But virtually everyone else had, especially Gary Holsten and the agents of his intelligence operation. It had become abundantly clear that ancient technology was a potentially destabilizing factor on the Rim, and that realization had set off an arms race of sorts, one that had led all the way to the formation of the White Fleet. The expedition's purpose had been touted as historical research, but Barron had known from day one, his primary goal was to find old tech…and return it secretly to Megara.

"Should we order them to stop, Admiral?"

Barron sat still for a moment, his eyes fixed on the small ship. "No, Commander…I think we scared the hell out of them, and that's enough for today. They'd just bolt anyway, and they're close enough to make it through the transit point before we can do anything about it." He paused for a moment, still looking at the icon in the display. The ship was a good sized one for a rogue explorer, probably half again as big as *Pegasus*. But there wasn't a doubt in Barron's mind that was just what the ship was. "Just let them go. We've got enough to worry about without chasing down frontier smugglers."

"Yes, sir."

Barron watched for a few moments as the ship blasted toward the transit point, accelerating with what he'd have bet was its full thrust capacity. He wasn't surprised to encounter a ship like that one, especially in Chrysallis. As far as he knew, nothing significant had been discovered in the system since the planetkiller, but it only made sense that the frontier scavengers who prowled the Badlands would return to the area in which it had been found.

Finally, Barron pulled his eyes from the display and stood up. "I'll be in my office, Commander. Keep an eye on that ship until it transits, but don't interfere. Maintain course and speed."

"Yes, Admiral."

Barron walked across the bridge, back to the room to the

rear he used as an office. He paused once he entered the corridor, glancing at the door across from his. *Dauntless* had been designed as a flagship, and it had both a captain's and an admiral's office. He'd been captain of the previous *Dauntless*, and he'd spent six years at her helm. But, as his eyes focused on the door across the corridor, he reminded himself he wasn't this *Dauntless*'s captain, that he never had been. He was only filling in for the ship's real commander, and indulging himself a bit as well. He'd had two promotions since his days as the old *Dauntless*'s commanding officer, and yet, he knew, in his heart he was still a ship's captain. He would do his duty, rise to meet whatever challenges faced him…but he knew he'd never again feel as centered—as at home—as he had, on a battered old ship that had served him so well.

One that he would never forget.

* * *

Barron stepped into the main area of *Dauntless*'s sickbay, as he had each day since he'd led his small fleet back from the depths of unexplored space. He'd spent hours sitting in a small, hard chair next to the pod that kept Atara Travis alive. For days, weeks even, he been waiting for her to die, for word to come to him that her worn and weakened body had given out. He'd tried to prepare himself for the loss of his friend…his comrade, his sister, the one person who'd been at his side during every deadly battle he'd fought. But he'd found there was no way to prepare for such a thing. He couldn't bring himself to give up on her.

And she hadn't given up on herself either. Atara Travis had clung to life for weeks…and then, something unexpected had happened. She began to get stronger.

She was still unconscious, and Stu Weldon had been very cautious and guarded in his assessments. *Dauntless*'s chief surgeon had told Barron in no uncertain terms that there were no assurances that Travis would regain consciousness, even if her bodily functions continued to strengthen. But Barron had sensed the hope in Weldon's voice as well, despite the doctor's cautious words.

"Any change, Doc?" Barron walked up behind Weldon, who was leaning over a workstation, tapping away on a keyboard.

"Admiral…" The doctor turned around and straightened up to face *Dauntless*'s acting commander. "There's been some continued improvement, sir…but no signs of any imminent recovery from the coma. Her brain scans remain active, but…" Weldon hesitated for a few seconds. "I just don't know what's kept her alive, Admiral. She was so weak…she should have died. I can't explain it, but at least now, she seems to be out of danger. Based on her recovery to this moment, I have to believe she'll regain consciousness…" The doctor paused again, an uncomfortable look coming onto his face. "…but I'm afraid we can't be sure if there will be any permanent damage. Her brain function looks good, but there are any number of possible problems that could appear."

"I wouldn't bet against her, Doc. She's tough…and stubborn. I'd wager the missing element in your analysis is pure, unadulterated pigheadedness. She just wouldn't give up…and I wouldn't bet on her doing it now, or at any point until she is back at one hundred percent." As difficult as it was to watch his friend lying in that medpod, Barron realized he *had* become convinced Atara Travis would recover.

Completely.

Chapter Five

"You've waited for this for a long time, Alex. Your rivals have cheated you, kept from you what should have been yours, but now it is your moment." Marieles was lying on her side on the bed, a thin white sheet draped strategically over her. She was looking across at the man she'd chosen to play a key role in her unfolding plan.

And also in her bed.

Admiral Torrance Whitten had come from a navy family as old, and nearly as prestigious, as the Barrons. He had famous ancestors dating back even farther than Barron's…men and women who'd helped to build the Confederation, and to hold it against a century of Union aggression. He might have become the hero of the past war, taken Tyler Barron's place as the navy's rising star, save for one problem.

He was more or less incompetent.

Marieles had come to understand early on that the schemes and plots Whitten resented so much, and about which he whined almost incessantly, were really little more than the manifestation of his lack of talent. She'd also decided that it didn't matter, not enough for her to switch gears at this late stage. She needed a

31

vain man, one easily manipulated, and Whitten scored well on both of those counts. That was more important to her than actual martial or operational ability. And while he wasn't going to win any aptitude contests, he was a hell of a good looking man, and that offered its own advantages, both in terms of presenting him as a charismatic figure…and in terms of softening the drudgery of her own job of manipulating him.

"That's all true, Desiree…but…" She could hear the doubt in his voice, and she knew his confidence needed another boost. He wasn't just a fool. Fundamentally, he was a coward as well. He could talk for hours about grievances and plans to redress them, but he invariably lost his drive when action was imminent.

"There are no 'buts,' Alex, my sweet. You're ready for this, more ready than I've ever seen any man, to meet your destiny." She'd used every trick at her disposal to control Whitten…flattery, sex, planting unexpected supporters to fawn over him and offer their loyalty. She'd even taken to calling him by his middle name to create a sort of bond between the two of them, a level of personal connection he'd bought into hook, line, and sinker.

As far as she knew, she was the only person who'd ever called him "Alex," and she only did it when they were alone. Intimacy was an extremely useful tool, one she employed with ruthless efficiency. She was far from certain Whitten would hold it together and follow through on what the two had planned, but she didn't have the slightest doubt he was loyal to her.

"Yes, I'm ready…but must we go so far so quickly? This is…could be viewed as…treason."

"Treason? To save the Confederation from the profiteers? From the gangsters who control it now? How many spacers died in the war? Trillions of credits that should have bought them better weapons and equipment were stolen…with the help of the very same men who took your birthright from you. What would you do? Continue to reside in comfortable obscurity, cast aside by Striker and Barron and the others? A man of your ability, treated like a fool by officers not fit to polish your boots?"

For an instant, she was afraid she'd poured it on a little too thick…but then she saw the expression on his face.

"You're right, of course, Desiree. It's my duty to rid the Confederation of the traitors, to restore it to the people, as it always should have remained. The nation my grandfather served, that my great-grandfather helped to found."

"Yes," she said, surprised yet again at how effectively ego could be utilized as a tool to control people. "It's not only your destiny…it is your obligation. You owe it to the generations of Whittens who have come before, to the billions of people in the Confederation. They cannot stand against the forces of corruption themselves…but you can. Legions of officers will follow your flag. Men and women who now chafe helplessly under the control of the criminals."

Marieles was far from sure about that last part. She'd done everything possible to line up support for Whitten's coup, and she was confident that some of it, at least, would materialize. The Whitten name was still powerful, and in the cliquish universe of the Confederation navy, there was considerable loyalty to it. But she was far from sure the officer could manage to take control and hold on to what his birthright gave him.

That didn't matter, though. She wasn't trying to take and hold control of the Confederation. That was a goal beyond her resources and the time she had available. No, her purpose was to plunge the Union's main enemy into a whirlwind of chaos and turmoil. If her plan worked, she would see Confederation military forces choosing sides, perhaps even clashing with each other. Riots in the streets, the breakdown of normal services. And an economic collapse of immense proportions.

The Confeds would get through it, no doubt, and they would restore some rational successor to their current government… but they would be weakened, perhaps greatly weakened, and the Union would have time to restore its strength, to prepare for the next conflict. *And I will be back at the side of a grateful Gaston Villieneuve, at the very seat of power.*

She looked across the bed at Whitten. There was almost no projected conclusion to her plan that didn't see the fool of an admiral dead in battle or mounting a scaffold, branded a traitor. That was a shame. She wasn't going to miss him for his ability, certainly, but he was charming in his way, at least when he wasn't bragging incessantly or complaining about how he'd been mistreated. He was about as attractive a pawn as she'd ever played in any of her spy games and, while she'd sacrifice him when she needed to, she almost wished she could keep him. Like a pet of sorts.

She reached over and put her hand on his shoulder, smiling sweetly as she did. She might as well get the most of out him while she still had him.

*   *   *

"Dammit." It was the third time Striker had said it…and from the growing heat of the anger inside him, it didn't seem likely to be the last. Jon Peterson was sitting across from the desk, silent, clearly giving the admiral the time to fully absorb what he had told him.

"I felt the same way, Admiral Striker." Peterson stared right back at Striker as he finally spoke. He looked around, what seemed like an instinctive glance, though he had to realize the two men were alone. Then he said, "To be honest, I was ready to have my Marines arrest the Lictors right then and there."

Striker could hear the anger in Peterson's voice, despite the officer's clear attempt to suppress it. He might have done the same if he'd been there with a group of naval troopers, but he doubted that would have done much good. He'd seen the naked pomposity of Senators before, and for all he had a profound distaste for most of them, he had no illusions about just how powerful members of the Confederation Senate were.

"Better that you didn't, Jon…and, by the way, I'm Van. Let's cut the 'Admiral Striker' stuff right now, especially if we're going to work together to get to the bottom of all this." Striker paused for a few seconds. "At least we know where Gary went. If a whole group of Lictors came for him, that means the Senate is investigating something. Which fits with the fact that the whole body has been in secret session for weeks now."

"Investigating? Gary pushes things to the edge sometimes,

but I can't believe he's done something to justify arresting him and dragging him halfway across the Confederation in secrecy… or even if he did, left a trail anyone could find. Especially two years after the war ended."

Striker nodded. He knew of one or two things Holsten had done that might create an uproar if the wrong people found out about them, but he had to agree. The timing seemed strange… and Holsten *was* too careful to get caught, even when he strayed.

"There's something else going on here, Jon. Gary's arrest is only part of it. There's a lot of unrest. I hadn't pieced it all together, not until now, but I'm wondering if there's something bigger at work." A pause. "What if someone needed to get Gary out of the way? To disrupt Confederation Intelligence and its operations?"

"You think we're dealing with some kind of subversion? Something in the government?"

"Maybe." Striker tried to control the wild directions into which his thoughts were racing. "More likely, some Senator or group of Senators is taking the chance to get revenge on Gary." Striker hesitated, but then he continued. "He's got some pretty extensive files on some of them, and he's used his influence to keep them…let's just say, on the line." Striker knew those words could be taken in several ways, but he was pretty sure Peterson would see them the same way he did, and Holsten always had.

"Whatever it is…you mentioned unrest, and other problems. Do you think there's a link?"

"I just don't know." Striker was frustrated. He couldn't quite separate the various things in his mind…but he couldn't bring himself to imagine some kind of grand conspiracy was going on either. For all the dishonesty and foulness in the Confederation's government, he wasn't sure he believed there was enough raw competence to pull off any kind of significant plot.

Still, the fact that Holsten had clearly been targeted was unsettling. There were few people in a better position to thwart any kind of nefarious activity.

"We have to do something, Van. I owe Gary Holsten…for more than I can quickly recount. I came here all the way from

Dannith to see what happened to him, and I'm not about to go back without finding out…and helping him any way I can."

"I'm with you, Jon…but we have to be careful. If there really is some kind of plot underway, we have to be very cautious who we involve. Who we even talk to." Striker still found it difficult to believe some kind of coup or other activity of the sort was really underway…but he was too concerned to ignore the possibility. As much as he hated doubting any of his people, if there was some kind of power grab brewing, those involved would almost certainly have supporters in the navy.

Striker leaned back and put his hand to his face. "We've got to make a list of people we're sure can't be involved in whatever is happening. I'll vouch for Kate Britten." He paused, feeling a wave of discomfort at how few names were coming to his mind as being beyond question. He had many loyal officers, he was sure of that, but most of the ones he knew best had been sent out on various missions, not assigned to headquarters on Megara…and now, he wondered if some of that hadn't even been the result of someone's planning. Had he been unknowingly manipulated?

You're getting paranoid, Van…

"I might be able to help, Van…with a few bodies at the right place and time."

Striker stared across the desk, a questioning look on his face.

"Well, you see, when I decided to come to Megara and see what was happening to Gary, I brought my second in command, Hank Bellingham, with me…" Peterson paused, looking uncharacteristically hesitant. Then, he continued, "…and my whole first company."

"You brought a company of Marines to Megara?"

"On leave, Admiral." Peterson looked a bit edgy and defensive. "None of the Marines had ever been to the capital…and I heard the museums are a real sight."

Striker almost laughed. Bringing a force of Marines to Megara without orders could be viewed as treason.

But bringing a pack of veteran warriors to the capital on a cultural excursion to tour the museums…no one could argue with that.

                              *   *   *

"Desiree…it has been some time. It's good to see you." Ricard Lille gestured toward the two stewards gathering his bags—they were agents, actually, but Sector Nine personnel didn't exactly stroll around Megara out in the open, and the covers he'd purchased for his group had been expensive ones indeed. "Gaston tells me you've made commendable progress." Actually, the brief message he'd received from Villieneuve had been sketchy, and it had relied heavily upon his ability to read between the lines. Communication was always a danger point on operations of this sort, and there was little to be gained by risking too much back and forth chatter.

"Agent Lille, welcome to Megara." Marieles stepped forward, leaning close to Lille's ear. "This room is secure, but once we leave, we will need to maintain our covers at all times."

"Of course, Desiree. Why don't we keep things simple, and you call me Ricard? I am, after all, here to help you any way I can."

Marieles flashed a smile, but Lille had a pretty good idea of her real thoughts and feelings. The two had never worked together, not on anything significant, and Villieneuve had send her to Megara to lead the Confederation destabilization operation. By all accounts, she'd done a masterful job, and she had no reason to fear for her position, not from him. The last thing Lille wanted was the burden of controlling hundreds of operative, dupes, and purchased traitors…he was happy to leave it all to her. But he was Gaston Villieneuve's closest confidante, so it was only natural for Marieles to see him as a superior come to take control.

"Things are about to come to a head. The Senate is currently conducting a trial against Gary Holsten…using the considerable evidence I have supplied. Through various channels, of course. And the news operation is…"

"Truly, Desiree, I am not here to usurp your position, nor

to micromanage your operation. You are to continue as you have been. I do not need—nor, frankly, want—to be apprised of every detail. Such elaborate missions are not in my chosen milieu, shall we say. I am truly here simply to assist with any… shall we say, particularly troublesome elements that may threaten your success." That was true, for the most part. Lille's specialty was problem removal. He was there to keep an eye on Marieles too, of course, but more because Villieneuve didn't trust anyone than any real suspicion the agent had strayed from her directives.

Marieles stood for a moment, silent, clearly thinking. Then she looked over at Lille. "Well, Ricard…I believe I have most factors in hand, but if there is one person who worries me, it has to be Admiral Striker. He's just too powerful, too connected… and I know he and Holsten are close friends. I've put a plan to discredit him into place…but I'm concerned how he will respond, and what support he will be able to gather."

Lille stood still for a moment, and then he nodded his head. "You're right, Desiree…Van Striker *is* a dangerous man, and a smart one. He has harmed our plans many times. If he gets an idea what you're up to…" He was silent again for a moment. "You see to your final arrangements…and I will make certain Admiral Striker does not interfere."

Chapter Six

Stockton put both hands on the throttle, struggling to keep steady as he directed his ship back across the emptiness of the system. He'd been relieved when the repair bot had managed to seal the breach in the hull before the last of his air escaped into the void, but the life support system wasn't working after all, not completely.

He was weak, and it took most of the effort he could muster just to raise his arms. His vision was blurry, too, and he could feel himself getting more and more lightheaded. He had oxygen…he'd be dead by now if he didn't. But there was something wrong with the air, some kind of contaminant seeping into it, probably from a coolant leak or some kind of engine malfunction.

It would kill him, he was sure of that. What he didn't know was if he'd make it back to *Repulse* before it did.

At least these bastards don't have any fighters…

He'd be long dead by now if there had been any effective pursuit. But he was way out in front of the Hegemony fleet now, far beyond the range of any of their weapons. He knew the enemy ships had enough acceleration to catch him…and the fleet, for that matter. But he was just a lone fighter, and he doubted they were even paying any attention to his battered craft's fight to get back to base.

He knew they had no intention of catching the rest of the fleet yet either, not until they saw where the Confederation ships were going. There wasn't a doubt in Stockton's mind the Hegemony was looking for the path back to Rim nations…or that they could have closed and destroyed the fleet by now if they'd wanted to, despite his constant fighter strikes and the disorder they had caused.

They'd find it eventually, of course, now that they knew it existed, but the fleet wasn't going to lead them there. Admiral Eaton had set a course out into the depths of unexplored space, and she'd dragged the Hegemony forces along with her. The fleet couldn't maintain the flight forever, especially without time to stop and search for sources of fuel and other supplies, but every day, week, and month the Confederation got to prepare was worth another fight.

He glanced at the local area scanner. It was empty, finally devoid of the dozens of his pilots who had clustered around his stricken craft earlier, refusing to leave his side. It had taken orders—from both him and from the commodore—as well as threats, pleas, and finally unrestrained verbal abuse, before he'd finally managed to convince them there was nothing they could do to help him. An escort might have made sense if there were enemy birds on his tail, but he was alone, in the middle of a silent quest to squeeze just enough performance from his tortured instrumentation to make it back.

He looked over now to the longer-range display. *Repulse* was actually getting fairly close now, and a quick calculation told him he was about twenty minutes from landing…assuming he could get enough thrust from his engines to decelerate in time. If his power failed, he wouldn't be able to stop, and he'd sail right by the battleship. That would set off a wild series of rescue operations, all of which he knew would be in vain. He wasn't sure how long his air would stay breathable, but he figured it would be a close enough match to an optimal landing pattern...and definitely nowhere near long enough for rescue ships to launch and match velocities and all the rest.

If he missed *Repulse*, he would die. If he lost too much of his focus, his vision, his attentiveness, he would die. If any of a thousand other things went wrong, he would die.

Any calculation of his chances was inherently a depressing and demoralizing enterprise, save for one thing.

"Raptor" Stockton didn't fail.

He took a deep breath, about halfway, before he decided it was counterproductive trying to get enough oxygen from the contaminated atmosphere of his ship. He reached down, under the seat, fishing around for the emergency bottle of air he knew was there. It was good for perhaps twenty minutes...which should be just enough.

He moved his hand all around...until he felt the smooth, cold metal of the air canister. He felt for the finger holds, and then he tugged hard. The bottle resisted for a few seconds, and then it slid out hard, almost slipping out of his grasp as he pulled it free.

He worked his hand underneath and pulled it up next to him, feeling around for the small mouthpiece he knew was clipped to the top. It came loose with a snap, and a few seconds later, it was strapped across his face, and clean, cool, oxygen-rich air was filling his lungs.

He didn't realize how poor the quality of the air he'd been breathing was until he got a few clean breaths. He realized almost at once that he'd never have made it without the bottled air. His head cleared somewhat, and the headache that had been pounding like a sledgehammer eased up. He still felt like something lying in the gutter on some slumworld, but he'd regained some of his normal sharpness.

"Jake..." He'd normally be called "Raptor" on the battle comm, but he recognized the voice at once, and it explained the first name.

"Stara...I'm inbound. My bird's pretty shot up, but I think I can manage."

"Your power readings are fluctuating pretty wildly. Maybe you should ditch. I can send out a pair of rescue ships."

"No, Stara. That's no good."

"Jake, I know you can land it, but…"

"It's not that, Stara. My life support's blown. I'm on my bottled air now. I can make it back to the ship…just. But if I wait for a rescue ship to match up with me and dock…"

"All right, Jake…then let's get you on the beacon. You'd better start decelerating soon…just in case you have any problems."

He was surprised for a few seconds that she didn't argue with him…but then he realized he shouldn't be. She was often more concerned for his well-being than he was for his own, but she wasn't one to base her actions on pointless worry. Stara Sinclair was a steel-hard veteran flight control officer, and she'd brought countless wounded pilots in with their damaged ships.

And she'd lost enough of them, too. She was deadly serious in situations like the current one…regardless of who was flying in the damaged ship.

"All right, Stara, I'm shifting power to the reverse thrust… now." Stockton held his breath for a moment. His gut told him he had about a 50/50 chance of the engines firing without any problems.

The ship shook, and it lurched forward, blasting at full for five seconds, maybe six. Then the engines cut out entirely.

"Damn…"

"Jake…I'm getting shaky readings here."

"My engines cut out." Stockton wasn't panicking. Well, he *was* panicking a little, but he wasn't about to let anyone see that.

"Have your AI activate the backups."

"I know what to do, Stara." He was sorry immediately for the harshness of his tone, but it didn't stop him from repeating it almost immediately. "I can handle this."

He flipped a series of switches. Nothing. Then, he ordered the AI to activate the backup systems.

"Backups non-responsive."

Stockton wasn't surprised. He figured it was something outside the engines themselves, probably nothing more than a fried series of connections or power feeds. A five-minute fix in the landing bay.

But enough to finish him off out here.

He leaned over to the side, checking a series of gauges. Most of them read normal, or close enough, but the last two were dead. He reached out and tapped them both, and then he had the AI run a diagnostic. No power at all.

"Jake…" Stara had remained quiet for a few minutes, longer than he'd expected, and though he felt an initial burst of anger at the interruption, she had no choice. He had five minutes, maybe six. If he couldn't get his engines back online by then, he wouldn't have time to decelerate.

And if he sailed past *Repulse*, his chances of holding his ship together long enough to come about seemed pretty damned nil…assuming he could somehow stretch his oxygen long enough to give it a try.

"I'm working on it, Stara." He was wracking his brain, but he wasn't sure what to do next. He had as much a working knowledge of his ship's guts as any veteran pilot, but he'd worked through most of what he knew how to do, and none of it seemed likely to help.

"Jake…"

He turned back to the comm, trying to come up with some kind of answer to satisfy Stara. Only, it wasn't Stara on the comm now.

"Captain Fritz?"

"Yes, Jake. Listen to me carefully. We don't have much time. Link your AI to the flight control AI. I want to see every readout and report your system is generating."

"On it." He reached out and punched at the small keyboard on his control panel. Stockton wasn't one to quietly obey instructions, but he knew one thing for certain. If there was anyone in the fleet who could get his ship operational in…four and a half minutes…it was Anya Fritz.

The comm was silent for a time, perhaps twenty seconds. Stockton's edginess was growing, but even the legendary Captain Fritz needed some time to review the data.

"Okay, Jake…I think I know what it is." A pause. "We've got to get you into a hard to reach spot, so get out of your harness…and grab the small emergency toolkit under your chair."

Stockton's hand moved up, punching at the clasp that released the harness. He scrambled out of his seat, reaching down as he did to find the tool pouch.

"I've got the tools…and I'm on the chair, leaning over, facing backwards." Not for the first time, Stockton wished the designers of the Lightnings had managed to squeeze just a bit more space into the cramped cockpits.

"Good. You're going to have to lean down, behind your seat and below the bottom of it. Can you see the T-4 access panel?"

Stockton looked down, his eyes landing on a small access hatch. There was a tiny T-1 next to it.

Shit.

He looked down, past the T-2 and T 3 panels. "You weren't kidding. That's far down."

"It is…and remember, Jake, you're going to have to get yourself back up. If you get stuck or wedged down there…"

She didn't finish. She didn't need to.

He twisted his hips, and he felt himself sliding down lower. He very unsure he was going to be able to reverse the movement.

He reached out, stretching his arms forward. His fingers touched the plate, and he pushed down on the small access control. He half expected it to just sit there, but the tiny door popped open immediately.

"Okay, I'm in."

"You still have the tools?"

"Yes." That wasn't entirely true when he said it. He swung his body to the side, pulling his left arm around—painfully—but getting it just far enough to grab the small pouch.

"Open the pouch and pull out the number four replacement conduit." A pause. "And whatever you do, be careful. Don't drop it. You've only got one."

"I'll try to remember that." Stockton reached his fingers into the pouch, but then he hesitated. His faced was soaked with sweat, and it was pouring into his eyes, making his already blurry vision even worse. His hands were exhausted, and as he tried to hold them steady, he realized how much they were shaking. It would be a miracle if he could manage the repair…and another one if we could actually fly his ship back in both its and his current conditions.

He poked around until he found what he was looking for. It was a small connector, about three centimeters in length. He looked at it for a moment, suddenly uncomfortable that such a small piece of metal would likely determine if he lived or died.

"Got it." He held it tightly, but it still almost slipped away from his moist fingers.

"Good. Now get as close as you can to the panel. There's only one number four in there, so you'll know it when you see it." A pause. "My guess is, it's pretty fried, so it might not look just like the new one."

Stockton poked his fingers into the small cavity in the side of his ship. There were several different kinds of electrical lines going through the box, but at first, he couldn't find the one he was looking for. He couldn't see the chronometer, and he almost asked the AI how much time he had left…but then he decided he didn't want to know.

He picked at a section of burnt circuitry, and suddenly, he saw it. It was fried all right…beyond fried. In fact, he almost didn't recognize it despite Fritz's warning. The lines flanking it looked like they were in pretty rough shape, too, and he almost asked Fritz if just changing the one connector would be enough.

He decided he didn't want to know that either. There was only time to fix the one—if there was time even to do that. If it didn't work…it didn't work.

He pulled his hand back and wiped the sweat off onto his other sleeve. Then he reached back inside and gripped the connector between his fingers. He pulled, but at first it didn't move. He knew it should have come out easily, but he could see where it had melted into the structure around it.

He pulled again, and his fingers slipped off. The stress and fear were really starting to get to him.

He reached in again, and he tightened his fingers…and

pulled as hard as he could. His hands ached, but he put as much force as he could into holding onto the small bit of metal…and then it finally gave way, his hand snapping back, slapping him in the face as it did.

But he'd gotten the conduit out.

He dropped the blackened chunk of metal and heard it slide down under his chair. Then he grabbed the new one, and he extended his hand back into the small panel. He expected it to resist, for the burnt and damaged bracket to give him trouble putting the new connector in place…but it slid right in.

"It's in, Anya." He managed to keep *some* of the fear out of his voice.

"Good…I've got to reprogram your AI's power routing. Meanwhile, you get yourself back in that chair." He was grateful she'd left out, "in case it works," or something of the sort, though he didn't have the slightest doubt she was thinking just that.

As he was…

Then she said, "It's gong to be a rough ride, but you can handle it."

Stockton wasn't exactly a pilot with a confidence problem, but he thought maybe she could have left that last part out, given him a little token encouragement. But Anya Fritz had ice water in her veins. She was the best engineer he'd ever known, but her bedside manner left much to be desired.

He gritted his teeth and swung his body hard, rolling over to the side and reaching out to claw his way back up. He got himself up—just—and he tried not to think about how close he'd come to not making it.

He slid down into the chair, grabbing the harness and pulling it around, slipping the connector in place with a loud snap. The he leaned back and closed his eyes, taking one deep breath and trying to center himself, to get his focus on what he had to do now.

Assuming his hurried repair worked, that is.

As he was exhaling, Fritz's voice came through on his headset. "We're all set, Jake. I need you to power up the engines…

but slowly. *Slowly.*"

He reached down toward the control, grabbing it and pulling back just the smallest bit. For an instant, he didn't think the engines were responding. It hadn't worked. He was done.

Then he felt the thrust, the slightest bit of pressure pushing against him. He pulled his arm back, a bit more...and then more.

The engines were working!

He eased it back using infinitesimal taps...but then his eyes fixed on the chronometer. He was decelerating too slowly. He was out of time.

Even as he was noticing, Stara's voice came through the headset, where Fritz's had been a moment before. "All right, Jake...you need to decelerate a bit faster. We don't have much time left."

We don't have any *time left...*

He'd been cautious, exerted all care he could manage...but now it was time to get back to *Repulse.* Or not to get back.

He pulled back, a bit harder at first, and then, all the way in one hard push. He half-expected the engines to die out, for his thrust to fail...but then he felt the massive wall of force blasting out, decelerating his ship, even as he saw *Repulse* looking large on his monitor.

He watched as the velocity dropped, struggling to turn his head enough to get a view under the massive thrust. His dampeners were down, and he was taking the full force of better than 15g. His entire body hurt, and he could feel a muscle pull in his shoulder, the tissues in his body tearing away from the cartilage, spreading agony down half his body. The pain was almost unbearable, but he focused, gripped the throttle with the last strength he could muster...and then he shouted out, a long guttural cry against the pain.

He tried to calculate, to figure out if he'd decelerated in time, if he could make the landing bay, or if he would sail past, to almost certain death. It was hard to keep the figures in his head...it was hard even to keep from blacking out. But his velocity was dropping rapidly, and his best guess was, he'd made the insertion angle.

Barely.

It was another ninety seconds or so, a minute and a half of unrelenting agony, but then he let the controls go and gasped a breath into his tortured lungs, as the relief of freefall eased the pain he felt almost everywhere. He'd done it. He was on a landing pattern, his velocity down to two hundred meters a second.

He could see *Repulse* up ahead now. At a range of less than two kilometers, the massive battleship covered his entire field of view. He tapped his throttle lightly, angling his vector toward the landing bay, and slowing his velocity further. Even the slight movement of his arm sent pain through his body…and, suddenly, he had a wave of fear, a worry that he was too battered, that he wouldn't be able to complete the landing.

No…this is not how Raptor Stockton dies…

He'd never realized how large a part ego played in the abilities set of a fighter ace. There was training at play now, skill, experience…but Stockton knew the thing that would play the largest part in saving him now was defiance. He was just too stubborn to die, at least not without a dozen enemy birds chasing him down.

He could feel the darkness coming, that last of his vision barely hanging on. He was coughing hard now, and he could feel fluid building in his chest.

The range was under a kilometer now, and he tapped his thrusters, reducing his velocity again, even as the large hatch leading to the landing bay loomed before him.

His ship was shaking hard, pitching in every direction, and he knew it wasn't going to last much longer. But it didn't have to. He held on, somehow, even as the ship slipped past the hatch and into the bay.

He was going a little faster than ideal landing speed, and he fired the positioning jets one last time—normally a no go in the bay—sending his ship down a bit hard to the deck…and then to soft collision with the wall.

It wasn't a pretty landing, not even a decent one. But it was one he'd survived…and without taking out the bay. Right now, he'd take that.

He forced a painful smile, just for a few seconds. Then, the last of his strength slipped away, and he fell into blackness.

Chapter Seven

"No…I'm okay, Vig." There was edge in Andi Lafarge's voice, but no anger, at least not any directed at her loyal comrade. She was sore as hell, and a little shakier on her feet than she liked, but she'd spent as long lying in a bed as she was going to. She had work to do. She had to find out what had happened to Gary Holsten.

And she had a man to find.

To kill.

Lafarge had been working on controlling her temper…for years now. Ever since she'd met Tyler Barron. She knew nothing could ever come of her relationship with the famous officer, but still, she wanted to feel as though she could have lived in his world, given other circumstances. Shaking off her Badlands frontier roughness and acquiring a bit of polish had seemed a good way to go.

Until now.

Wherever she eventually went, if she ended up one day truly enjoying her wealth, choosing china patterns and swirling fine wines around her mouth instead of chugging frontier bar rotgut, she had something to do first, a job that tolerated no veneers of civilization or high culture. She had to find Ricard Lille…and she had to kill the bastard.

Whatever it took.

"Okay, Andi…but take it easy. You shouldn't even be out of the hospital even, yet. You *wouldn't* be if you hadn't 'convinced' the doctor to approve it." Merrick paused, his expression half concerned, half amused. "What did you say to him anyway, Andi? I've never seen a man's face turn so pale almost instantly."

She smiled, though only for an instant. "We just had a… heart to heart." She paused and looked back at Merrick. "And I told him just how many ways I knew to remove his…"

Lafarge looked around the street, her eyes pausing momentarily on the various groups of people moving about. She felt uncomfortable, because she was unarmed—the hospital hadn't allowed her compatriots to bring her gun to her as she requested—and because she suspected Ricard Lille was the one person besides herself who might be sure she would come for him. The Sector Nine operative was an arrogant man, and she suspected he just *might* fail to take her seriously enough. Still, he was no fool, and she wasn't about to do him the favor of taking him for one.

Lille was probably long gone from Dannith by now. The Marines Colonel Peterson had left to protect her had formed a cordon around her room day and night. An operative as smart as Lille would have realized the risks of making a move then were just too great. But now she was out in the open. The Marines had offered—begged almost—to go with her, to maintain their protective vigil, but as much as she would have liked to have the grim warriors at her side, they were far too restrained—by regulations, by honor codes, by orders—for what she had in mind.

Andi wasn't restrained by anything, not now. She was a hunter on the trail of a beast—a deadly and dangerous beast, but a beast nonetheless. Nothing would stand in her way, not laws, not regulations, not foolish concepts like honor.

Not until the man who had tormented her, had almost killed her, who had stripped her of her belief in herself, was dead.

The man who had broken her will. She hadn't told anyone, not Vig, not the Marines, no one, but she'd been ready to give Lille anything he demanded. Anything to make the torture stop. She just hadn't known anything he wanted.

She knew she would never think of herself the same way again. From her youngest days, the abject misery and poverty, she'd always had believed in herself, that she could endure whatever she had to. That was gone now, ripped away from her by Sector Nine's top assassin. She knew she could never recover what she'd lost, never regain the pride she'd once felt in herself. But she could take her revenge on the man who'd stolen it from her, and she'd sworn in her hospital bed to do just that, whatever it took.

"*Pegasus* is fully equipped, isn't she, Vig?"

Merrick looked confused for a few seconds, but then a smile slipped onto his lips. "Yes, Andi…*fully* equipped."

Andi managed a smile, one far more evil than jovial in appearance. She'd long carried a cache of illegal weapons on her ship…an insurance policy of sorts against the types of trouble one could run into on the frontier and in the Badlands. Back in her smuggling days, she used to drop them in a scanner-resistant pod on the edges of the system before landing on Dannith. But that was before she'd brought back a war-winning bit of ancient technology, and won the lasting friendship of both the navy and Confederation Intelligence.

Gary Holsten and Van Striker had given her permanent clearance to land at any Confederation port, without risk of search or seizure…an almost unimaginable luxury. And one that let her keep her cache of weapons secured in Pegasus's lockers, safe and ready for her when she needed them.

Like now.

*   *   *

"There she is." The operative turned toward the small cluster of agents standing around him. They were all dressed as inconspicuously as possible, but Louis Drossier knew every one of them was a trained killer…and fully-armed. They were, perhaps, not quite the equal of the teams he'd led before the Union lost the war, and its government fell. Sector Nine—*no*, he reminded himself, *we're the People's Protectorate now*—had suffered considerably in the upheaval that followed the deaths of nearly the entire Presidium and the rebellion that swept across the Union. Still, they were good enough.

Good enough to hunt down one jumped up smuggler…

Ricard Lille had left coldly specific instructions. He was to kill Andromeda Lafarge, and he was to do it before she had a chance to leave Dannith.

And he was not to underestimate her.

Drossier was having a hard time with the last part. He couldn't imagine some Confed border rat smuggler, even one who'd apparently stumbled on a lucky score and struck it rich, was a real danger to him and his team—and certainly not to Lille. The Union's top assassin was virtually the embodiment of fear, at least to those who knew enough about his shadowy existence to truly appreciate what he represented.

Still, Lille seemed…edgy about this one. The thought of an adversary that unnerved Ricard Lille made Drossier's blood run cold. He wouldn't take any chances. He'd wait, observe, follow…and then, when the moment was right, he would strike.

"Spread out…I want her covered from all angles. We don't let her out of our sight, you understand me? If she goes in a building, we surround it, monitor every possible exit." He paused, and his tone darkened. "Don't be the one who lets her get away."

He put his hand to the side of his head for a second, adjusting the small earpiece while each of his operatives acknowledged his instructions. Then he stood and watched as they slipped away, one or two at a time, drifting into the crowds with the practiced nonchalance of well-trained and practiced killers.

Drossier remained until they were all gone, watching as Andi Lafarge and one of her people—Vig Merrick, he reminded himself from the memorized files—began to slip around the corner. There were just two of them, and on their way from the hospital. She was probably as vulnerable as she was going to be.

For an instant, he considered ordering his people in, finishing the job then and there. Getting away might be difficult on the crowded street, but that wasn't what stopped him. His eyes darted around, looking for suspicious types in the crowd. Lafarge had sent the Marines away, no doubt because she didn't want them to see what dirty business she was planning. But the grim warriors had adopted her in their own way, and Drossier knew enough about the Confederation's elite warriors to bet they hadn't let her go, however it might appear.

His eyes settled on a trio dressed in civilian clothes, two men and a woman. Their hair was cropped short—buzz cuts, almost—and all had deep set, grim eyes. He wasn't *sure* they were Marines, but his gut was too alive with suspicion to order his people in now.

He'd tangled with Confederation Marines before. The warriors were no match for his people in tradecraft, certainly…but if it came to a straight up fight, the Marines were veritable killing machines. And he didn't have the slightest doubt…if they had people following Lafarge, those Marines would be armed.

Well armed.

No…it was smarter to wait, to get a real feeling of the situation, of what he faced.

Then he would give the order. And his people would kill Andromeda Lafarge.

*   *   *

"I think you should stay here, Andi…or better still, let's just blast off and get off this rock. None of us need this anymore."

Lafarge was sitting in one of the chairs in *Pegasus*'s small lounge area. Andi's ship didn't look like all that much from outside, but Pegasus had some bite that wasn't obvious under casual examination. For years, she had poured her profits into improving her vessel and buying the equipment her people needed in their expeditions, a sharp contrast to many of her peers, who squandered vast sums on gambling, drinking, and all sorts of debauchery. *Pegasus* wasn't a match for a navy ship, but the tough old bird had more than one system upgraded well past civilian maximums.

"I can't stay here, Vig. And I'd love to leave, but we've got work to do. It seems like Ricard Lille has either left Dannith or he's gone into deep hiding." For a while she'd thought the assassin was laying low, waiting to finish her off, but as she analyzed it more, she realized Lille would have other responsibilities than tying up one old loose end. Most likely, he had moved on...and that meant he was long gone from Dannith.

But he wouldn't have left her behind unmolested. That wasn't his way, and, while she didn't know how seriously Lille took her as a threat, she couldn't imagine he didn't realize she would come after him.

He's left someone behind to finish the job.

And they're my ticket to finding his trail.

"At least sleep here, Andi. With *Pegasus*'s security systems, no one is going to get in here without you knowing about it." Clearly, Merrick also expected someone to come for Andi.

"Yes, Vig, that's all true...except for one thing. I need them to come for me."

"What?" Merrick sounded horrified. "Andi, don't play around with these people. I know you're as tough as they come, but they're dangerous...and we have no idea how many people he's got after you."

"I don't know where he is, Vig. I have no ideas, no clues, no leads. I need to get some."

Merrick looked back at her for a few seconds, the blank stare on his face giving way suddenly to a terrified expression. "No... Andi. No. You can't set yourself up as bait."

"Why not?" The matter-of-factness of her tone chilled the very air.

"Andi..."

"Look, Vig...I've got to do this, there's just no other way for me. For one thing, he'll come after me and kill me eventually if I don't get him first...but even if that wasn't the case, I *have* to do this. After...what happened..." She paused, struggling to maintain her composure. "…I just can't let him live. I won't." The last two words were spoken with a tone of pure iron.

"I understand." Merrick had looked like he was going to argue further, but then he clearly realized there was no point.

"I want you to go home, though, Vig. You and all the others. I appreciate your coming here and staying with me when I was in the hospital, but now it's time for you all to go back to the lives you've found. This is my fight. Mine alone."

Merrick's expression hardened. "That's enough of that, Andi. We're with you, the whole crew. Until the end…whatever end this all leads to. They're all out there now, working over whatever contacts we've got left, trying to put together some leads. So, we'll follow your orders, we'll do whatever you need us to do…but I don't want to hear any more about leaving you to deal with all of this alone."

Andi felt the urge to continue the argument, to insist again that they all go. But she couldn't. They'd come back to help her, and she couldn't insult their loyalty by trying to send them away, especially when she doubted they'd go no matter what she did.

"Thank you, Vig. I'm very grateful…for all of you." They were hard words for her to say. Lafarge didn't like feeling dependent. She didn't like needing anyone.

But if she was going to get through this, do what she had to do, she was damned sure going to need all the help they could give her.

Chapter Eight

CFS Dauntless
Orbiting Planet Dannith, Ventica III
Year 316 AC

"Absolutely not. No receptions, no parades…honestly, I'd prefer the planetary administrator not even announce we're here, if there's any way you can swing that." Tyler Barron sat on *Dauntless*'s bridge, the expression on his face leaving no doubt as to the intensity of the headache pounding inside his skull. "I'd just like to meet with him alone. Immediately. I'll be taking a shuttle down at once."

"Yes, Admiral."

The light, hazy blue disk of Dannith hung on *Dauntless*'s primary screen, against the far wall beyond the huge 3D display that dominated the bridge. Dannith was a fairly pretty world, from orbit at least, but Barron knew the place far too well to be taken in by idyllic distant views. As far as he was concerned, the place was a grimy pit, and one on which he'd spent far too much time already.

The extensive Spacers' District of Port Royal City was the grungiest dump on the planet, but it was also the only place on the entire pointless rock that offered anything at all of interest. The rest of Dannith's moderately inhabited surface was covered with dense factory blocks producing an assortment of the most boring and unexceptional industrial products for sale anywhere in the Confederation. Barron suspected someone, somewhere, found the variations between viscosities of sealant and the number of different sizes of reactor fittings available to be fascinating, but he wasn't one of them. Almost everything of interest to him—and most everyone else—on the planet originated in, or passed through, the seedy bars and other establishments surrounding the spaceport.

Barron watched as Cumberland followed his orders…and as whoever was down on the surface in ground control clearly argued with him. He felt a flush of anger, and he almost grabbed the comm himself to tell whatever officer was on duty, in no uncertain terms, what he was to do. But he held back and let Cumberland handle it…which he did in significantly more diplomatic terms than Barron would have. The officer down there was just following orders, of course, and Barron's recollection of Dannith's most recent planetary administrator—Walter Cantor, he thought he remembered the name—was one of a pompous ass, someone he couldn't imagine was an easy boss.

He wished he had a better candidate to whom he could give the first report that a new enemy—a new war—was very likely coming, but he had what he had. He'd almost decided to pass by Dannith entirely, or to stop and refit and refuel without giving any hint of why *Dauntless* and her companion ships were there. But Dannith was the first Confederation port of call he'd reached, and also very likely the initial target on an invasion route from the Hegemony. Barron *had* to warn whoever he could there, fool or not.

"Sir…Administrator Cantor will be pleased to see you as soon as you are able to land." There was some satisfaction in Cumberland's voice. He'd been far more pleasant than Barron would have been…but in the end, he'd slammed the ground officer pretty hard. Barron wasn't sure "pleased" was the appropriate word, but he *was* sure he didn't give a damn.

"Very well, Commander." Barron stood up. "Advise the bay I want my shuttle ready as soon as possible."

"Yes, sir."

Barron took a couple steps from his chair, and he stopped.

"I'll take a Marine guard with me, Commander. Ten strong."
He paused. It seemed superfluous to him, foolish even, to
bring guards, to engage in a contest about who was the biggest
bigshot, but Cantor was just the kind to be impressed by such
things, and the sooner he got the imbecile to shut up and truly
understand the importance of what he had to say, the better.
"And tell General Rogan I'd like him to accompany me as well.
All Marines in dress uniforms." A Marine General couldn't hurt
his little show, and as much as he suspected they'd grumble a
bit behind his back, putting his little honor guard in their dress
grays couldn't hurt either.

"Yes, sir." It was clear from Cumberland's tone that the officer agreed with everything Barron had just said. A few seconds
later: "Admiral, flight control reports your ship will be ready to
launch in ten minutes. And General Rogan acknowledges."

"Very well, Commander. You have command while I'd on
the surface. I want the fleet refueled at once and ready to leave
on a moment's notice. Understood? We don't have time to
waste here."

"Yes, sir...understood."

Barron turned and walked across the bridge, trying to deal
with the realization that he had no idea how to break the news
he'd brought...and no idea how to suggest Dannith prepare for
what was coming.

*   *   *

"Admiral Barron, it's a pleasure to see you again, and so
much sooner than expected. We hadn't anticipated your return
for quite some time." Walter Cantor was a large man, both tall
and stocky. Roughly half his once dark-brown hair had turned
to a steely gray. He would have been a good-looking man by
most accounts, at least if he hadn't had the taste he did for gar-
ish—to Barron's opinion, ridiculous—clothing.

"Yes, unfortunately, we were compelled to return because..."

"I do wish you'd allow us to throw you an appropriate welcome, Admiral, a state dinner at the very least. I simply could

not allow…"

"Administrator, truly…there is simply no time for such pursuits." *And if you interrupt me again, you'll be sorry. Didn't you see that I came down here with eleven Marines? Do you know what they'll do to you if I order them to, Planetary Administrator or not?* "There is a situation we must discuss, one that threatens considerable danger." Barron turned his head, looking around the room. "Are you quite sure we are alone…and that no one can hear what we are discussing?"

"Of course, Admiral. My office is highly secure, and I would never risk any breach of privacy with such a notable guest present."

Barron struggled to keep the expression on his face neutral. He really detested the administrator, but there was no place for his personal feelings, not with the Hegemony coming.

"Very well…" Barron didn't really believe Cantor's assurances, but time was just as crucial now as discretion. If the administrator was careless and let word slip, the panic spreading across the planet would be his problem. *Dauntless* would be back in space and on the way to Megara in twelve hours, eighteen max. "Administrator, the White Fleet encountered something, out beyond the Badlands."

"Encountered something? Have you found noteworthy old tech? I knew your mission would be crowned…"

"No…It's something far more serious. Even dire."

Cantor looked back, confusion slipping onto his face. "I'm afraid I don't understand, Admiral."

"I can go into greater detail, but that would serve little purpose now. What you need to know is simply this: we found people beyond the Badlands."

"People? What kind of people? Renegades? Smugglers?"

"Many different kinds of people, Administrator. Large numbers, in fact, likely millions…no, billions. An entire civilization. Other survivors from the Cataclysm."

Cantor looked back, silent, clearly having trouble reconciling with what Barron had just told him.

"We are not the only inhabited worlds to remain after the

Cataclysm. There are survivors beyond the Rim…and they are hostile."

"Hostile?" Cantor still looked confused, but now he also looked scared. "Is this some kind of joke, Admiral?"

"No, Administrator, I'm afraid it's deadly serious. There is another civilization out there, a large and powerful one, with technology as advanced as our own…no, more advanced. We fought two battles with them. They refused all attempts at communication, all offers to mediate any disputes."

"This is terrible, Admiral! What are we going to do? Is the rest of the White Fleet coming back? They have to take position around Dannith and defend us. I will send a communique to fleet headquarters at once. We must have more forces sent…"

"The fleet isn't coming, Administrator. I left most of them behind, to hold back and misdirect the enemy for as long as possible. To buy time. And I'm not staying here either. I must get back to Megara, to warn the Senate and the Admiralty…and help prepare to mobilize the Confederation for war."

"No…you cannot leave! Dannith is right on the border. If an invasion force comes…"

"You'll have to do your best to prepare for that possibility, Administrator. That's why I wanted to see you…and just you. I would not tell you how to conduct your civilian responsibilities, but I strongly suggest you maintain secrecy for as long as possible. Panicked mobs won't help with your preparations."

"Preparations? For what? What can we do if the fleet abandons us?" The administrator was barely controlling his growing panic.

"First, Administrator, no one is abandoning you. *Dauntless* and the few ships with her are not sufficient to mount any kind of reasonable defense, even if Dannith was our only concern, which, of course, it is not. We must rally the entire fleet…as well as the forces of the Alliance and our lesser allies. We must put together a force that can face the enemy that is coming, one that can hopefully display our strength, convince them to discuss peace instead of attacking." Barron paused. "And if that is unsuccessful, to mount a credible defense of the Confederation…of the whole Rim."

"This is terrible, Admiral." Cantor fumbled around his desk as he spoke, so unnerved, he clearly couldn't focus on anything. "I will come back to Megara with you. I will add my voice to yours."

Barron did the best he could to hold back his anger. He'd seen too many courageous friends and comrades killed in his career to suffer a coward presuming to lead an entire planet.

"You will do nothing of the sort, Administrator." He managed to keep his tone even, but that was about the limit of his success in controlling his hostility. "Let me be very clear to you so we do not misunderstand one another. It is utterly beyond me what might have possessed the people of Dannith to elect a creature like you to lead them, but they did it, and you accepted the job. Not only accepted…my mind reels at the thought of the lies and dirty politics it took to lift you from whatever shit-hole you spawned from to the administrator's office. However, you are there now, Mr. Cantor, and I can assure you, you are going to stay on this planet and lead these people in the time of trouble that is coming. You will set an example for them. You may well end up fighting here. You may even die. But you will not abandon them."

"Die? Fighting? Admiral, I must protest this…"

"Yes, Administrator…die. That is what happens in combat, and if you are going to defend Dannith, there is a very strong likelihood that many people—perhaps including you—will be killed." Barron paused and glared at the politician. "Many of the spacers of the White Fleet have died already…more almost certainly will, perhaps all of them. To buy time for vermin like you to do your jobs." Barron's gaze hit a new level of unbridled hostility. "Let me make this perfectly clear, Administrator…if I find out you shirked in your duty, that you boarded some ship to leave Dannith, or that you did anything less than your absolute best to lead your people and ready them for what is coming…I will find you myself. Then, you will wish this new enemy got to you before I did. You have my word as a Barron." He paused, his stare maintaining every bit of its frigid intensity. "Do we understand each other, Administrator?"

The politician slumped behind his desk in shock. He was shaking, and he looked like he might lose all composure any moment.

"Do we understand each other?" Barron repeated.

Cantor struggled to look up, to meet Barron's stare. He never made it, not all the way, but he finally forced out a soft, "Yes."

"Good." Barron was far from satisfied with the response, but he didn't have time to waste. "I'm going to send down some officers to assist in your preparations." The thought of leaving any of his people behind on a planet under the rule of a creature like Cantor sickened him, but he had taken an oath to defend the citizens of the Confederation...and however foolish they'd been at the ballots, there were millions of Confederation citizens on Dannith. "You will listen to them, and follow their advice...do you understand?"

The administrator nodded slowly. Barron was still far from satisfied, but he knew it was the best he could do on short notice. Even if he—illegally—took some action to remove Cantor from his office, something like throwing him in *Dauntless*'s brig, he didn't have anyone to put in the fool's place. And he didn't have time to find someone.

"Dig down, Administrator...every man has a spark of courage somewhere. Here is your chance to excel, to prove that your people didn't make a mistake when they chose you to lead them." Barron didn't believe a bit of it...but he said it anyway.

It was all he had.

Chapter Nine

"We have seen the evidence. There can be little doubt of the defendant's guilt, nor of the staggering magnitude of his crimes. For many years, Garrison James Holsten has been entrusted with one of the highest and most powerful offices in the Confederation…and through that time, he used that position to enrich himself. To add, with almost unimaginable aggression, to his already obscene fortune. Worse, during the recent war years, Mr. Holsten's greed grew unabated, even as the Confederation battled for its survival. How many of our young soldiers might have lived, if the funds this body had committed to equip and provision them hadn't been stolen by the defendant and his cronies?"

Emmerson Tolbert Ferrell had long been considered somewhat of a buffoon, a man who owed his standing, and his fortune, such as it was, to convincing the backward and poorly educated people of his obscure homeworld to elect him as their sole representative in the Confederation Senate. That was an achievement of sorts, and for many years, it had looked to be his last, as he skirted personal bankruptcy and engaged in a senatorial career noteworthy more for its lack of any kind of significant distinction than anything else.

That had all changed now, and Ferrell's position at the head of a group of Senators investigating war profiteering had given him a distinction he'd never had before. The prosecution of Gary Holsten looked to be the crowning achievement of his race to the top. A conviction would place him at the very peak of the Confederation's ruling body, at the head of the largest active coalition, one that controlled no less than forty percent of the Senate's votes.

Holsten sat quietly, watching what he knew was a witch hunt unfold with surprising rapidity. He'd been concerned, of course, when the Lictors had come for him on Dannith, and dragged him back to Megara to face a Senate inquiry, but he'd also figured he could work his way out of whatever problem had arisen. He had extensive files on many of the Senators, a large percentage of whom were little more than sanitized criminals. But whoever was behind this whole thing had handled it brilliantly. He'd been cut off from any of his people, even from reaching his personal AI. He had some safeguards in place, of course, some disclosures set for release if he didn't check in after a certain amount of time, but he'd been hesitant to employ such measures too extensively, for fear he might be captured by the enemy.

Now, he was truly concerned. Especially after seeing the torrents of fraudulent evidence presented against him. He'd assumed his arrest had been related to his aggressive use of intelligence tactics, even blackmail to compel Senators to do what had to be done. He couldn't argue that he'd crossed that line more than once, though he'd never done it for his own gain, and he'd been utterly shocked as he watched endless records entered into evidence, all pointing to his theft of billions of credits during the war. A few of the documents were based on real transactions, but those had been heavily modified. The others were outright fabrications.

He'd demanded on a dozen occasions his right to access his records to prepare his defense, and his right to representation, but the prosecution had objected, arguing that Holsten's position as head of Confederation Intelligence gave him too much power if he had access to any outside staff or data networks.

That much, he knew was true. But it didn't terminate his legal rights. At least, not until the Senate voted to do just that, pending completion of the case. The Senate was a powerful body, but they didn't have the authority to terminate a citizen's basic rights…until it turned out they had effectively just that capability, as long as no one outside the chamber knew about it.

Holsten had tuned out from the proceedings. He'd had enough trouble sitting silently while Ferrell and his band of sycophants lied about him all day. He was an even-tempered man…if Van Striker or Tyler Barron had been in his place, he suspected Ferrell's neck would have been snapped by now. But he was losing his patience, and worse, he was losing hope of getting himself out of the situation. He had a lot of enemies in the Senate, and even those not in on whatever fraud was in progress were unlikely to view him sympathetically. He suspected many of them were perfectly aware how wrong all of this was, but they were just as happy to remain quiet and take the chance to rid themselves of him.

"The defendant will rise." Holsten barely heard the command…and he ignored it anyway. He'd tried to maintain a respectful demeanor at the outset, but he'd long ago decided he was facing a kangaroo court, and that nothing he said or did would make a difference.

Not if he couldn't get word out to one of his allies. He was still trying to devise a way, but so far every effort had been a pointless waste of time.

"The defendant will rise, or the Senate Lictors will compel him to do so."

Holsten sighed. Part of him wanted to continue to resist, but there was no point. If one of the Lictors grabbed him right now, he wasn't sure what he would do.

No…he *was* sure.

He stood up slowly, looking up with a look of undisguised contempt at the raised platform that held the three Senators presiding over the Inquiry.

"Garrison James Holsten, for three weeks, this body has

heard testimony and viewed documentary evidence regarding your conduct as head of Confederation Intelligence, and most specifically during the recent war with the Union. You have been charged with a vast conspiracy against the Confederation and its military services...of indulging in a level of shameless greed that is almost impossible to fully grasp."

Holsten stared back, impressed that he had managed to more or less control his temper. He knew he'd been set up, but he was stunned by the complexity of the whole thing, and he couldn't imagine any of the Senators with whom he'd clashed pulling off something so vast. For an instant, he wondered if it couldn't be one of his own people, some kind of power play to get him out of the way. But he'd carefully selected his closest associates, and as much as he truly trusted anyone, he trusted them. Besides, he'd organized his affairs so that none of his people could move against him without the others being aware of it. So, if he was dealing with a traitor in Confederation Intelligence, his top four or five agents had to be in on it together... and that seemed impossible.

"Do you understand the charges? Do you have anything to say before this body begins to deliberate?"

He almost remained silent. He was being railroaded, and nothing he added to the mix would matter at all. But then he said, "I repeat my demand for legal representation and for access to my files and records to refute these false charges. I am well within my rights as a Confederation citizen in this, and I contest the validity of these proceedings unless I am granted such access. I maintain that no finding of this body, absent the provision of my basic rights as a Confederation citizen, can or shall be valid."

"Your requests have been reviewed already, Mr. Holsten, and denied. Your unique position makes it impossible to grant you the normal rights of a Confederation citizen. Your interests have been protected by Senate-appointed guardians, and a special act of the Senate has authorized this procedure in your case."

"You are not dictators..." Holsten felt his temper slipping

out of control. "You don't have the authority to strip a Confederation citizen of his basic rights. I repeat my demands for
counsel and for access to my records."

"And, pursuant to Senate decree, your request is again
refused. I will ask you one more time only. Do you have anything to say before this body begins deliberation?"

"I contest the authority of this body to deny me my rights as
a Confederation citizen."

"The record will show that the defendant has no statement
to make in his regard. The Lictors are hereby instructed to
remand him to his cell while the Senate begins deliberations.
And may justice prevail."

Holsten felt his stomach flop, and he fought back nausea.
He wanted to fight back as the Lictors took his arms and shackled him, but he knew that would only make things worse.

Assuming they could *get any worse.*

He bit back on his anger and said nothing, the only sign of
visible rage his tightly clenched fists, chained behind his back.

If his career had taught him one lesson, it was that things
could *always* get worse.

* * *

"It's done, Desiree. He was convicted on all counts."
Emmerson Ferrell stepped into the room, looking terribly
pleased with himself, which wasn't surprising. Marieles knew
about the conviction already, of course. In a way, she'd known
before it had happened. She'd put so much bribery money and
so much free press behind Ferrell, even the buffoonish Senator
had been unable to screw things up. He controlled nearly half
of the Senate by rote, leaving making the path to a majority a
fairly short and easy one. And, while Ferrell controlled the Senate, she controlled him.

That was an oversimplification, of course. Ferrell was a
fool, and one who lusted after her to boot, but that didn't mean
she could make him do anything. He'd been gullible enough
to accept as reasonable the fact that a lobbyist had just hap-

pened to also become involved in the takeover of a massive information network, and, to date, grateful enough for her help to do whatever she'd asked. But she saw the limits to her power as well. She could manipulate the Senate to discredit certain individuals—and she was about to move on to the much more difficult target of the Barron clan and the famous Tyler Barron. She could cause disruption, possibly even enough to throw the Confederation's government into disarray. But even Ferrell would see through any attempts to control the Confederation outright, or to obviously throw open the gates to the Union. And regardless, the Union wasn't ready yet for that kind of commitment. Gaston Villieneuve was solidifying his hold on control and working to get the still-weak Union economy back on track. Even a limited invasion of the Confederation or a wholesale attempt to seize vital systems was out of the question.

No, all she could do was thrust the Confederation into a crisis, a political struggle and an economic depression…perhaps, if she was incredibly lucky, somewhat of a partial civil war. If Confeds spilled Confed blood, her success would have exceeded even her greatest hopes.

That would give the Union a few years to get back on its feet and hit the enemy before they could fully recover. It would be a complete enough victory, one that would almost certainly earn her Villieneuve's full gratitude, and a place very near the top in his new Union.

"I'm very proud of you, Emmerson. Those who doubted you are now exposed as fools." She smiled sweetly at him. "You should feel very good about yourself today…both on your own account and as a public servant of the Confederation."

Ferrell returned the smile. "I couldn't have done it—any of it—without your help, Desiree. Thank you."

She just nodded. He seemed truly grateful…but she knew that wouldn't last. Emmerson Ferrell wasn't the kind of man one counted on for extended loyalty. He was basking in the glow of his achievement for the moment, but that would fade quickly as the realities and pressures of being a Senatorial power broker wore him down. His attraction would delay his turning against her, she suspected—though she wasn't sure how much longer she could reject him. One day he would start saying "no" to her requests for action, legislation, help of some kind or another…or he would return his own demands. Every indication was, Ferrell would act very much like a petulant child if she continued to reject him…and that he would lose interest in her fairly quickly if she gave him what he wanted.

Hopefully, before long it wouldn't matter. If Ferrell really became a problem, she had Ricard Lille now. She was wise enough to realize that the deadly assassin wasn't under her command…but she suspected Villieneuve had instructed him to help her any way he could. She'd already requested his aid on one matter…and if Ferrell made an impediment of himself… well, she suspected Lille might be amused by adding a Confederation Senator to his list of…achievements.

* * *

"Your transport is ready, sir." The officer stood at attention in front of Striker's desk, clearly trying not to notice the fact that two grim-looking Marine officers were sitting opposite the admiral.

"Very well, Lieutenant. I'll be down shortly." His tone was friendly, but it also carried an unspoken, 'that is all.'

"Yes, sir." The officer turned and walked about out of the office, the doors sliding shut right behind him.

"Gary's sections chiefs are notoriously difficult to locate. He, of course, always knows where to find them, but it is not easy for anyone else to march into Confederation Intelligence headquarters and ask for one of them." Striker paused for a moment. "I believe I may be able to convince one of his aides to assist me, however. Something is clearly going on, something of grave concern, and the fact that Gary's people don't appear to be aware of it is even more disturbing. I dare not rely on any communications lines…I believe it's wiser to simply go there and see what I can discover."

Striker didn't let himself consider the even more dire prospect that Holsten's subordinates *did* know he was a captive of the Senate, that they were involved in some kind of power play or treachery. He might have believed that if he hadn't known just how carefully Holsten picked his closest aides.

"Perhaps we should come with you, Admiral. As you said, something is certainly going on. Perhaps we should exert additional caution." There was concern in Peterson's voice, and it had been growing throughout the hour since the three had begun their meeting. That wasn't a surprise. More or less everything they had discussed had only increased Striker's concern level, and he doubted it was any different for Peterson.

Despite his own level of concern, Striker almost discounted the colonel's remarks out of hand. But something stopped him. He *was* worried, at least on some level, and the fact that he felt any concern about moving around in the middle of the capital told him just how edgy he'd become. He'd been wondering why he hadn't heard from Holsten for quite some time, but he hadn't been *really* concerned until Peterson and Bellingham came to him with the story about how the Senatorial Lictors had arrested the intelligence chief and brought him back to Megara. Combined with the fact that he'd heard nothing at all of Holsten's presence in the capital, or the details of the proceedings that had clearly been underway for weeks now, he was convinced something very dangerous was going on.

"No, Colonel. I appreciate the offer, but I'm going to have enough trouble getting to Gary's people alone. If all three of us show up, I'm sure we won't get anywhere. I'm just taking a quick ride across town, and then I'll be back. But you're right...we do need to start thinking about security. If Gary could get scooped up without word getting out about it, we all need to be cautious." He paused a moment, and then added, "In fact, perhaps the two of you should stay here until I get back. I don't know if anyone has connected you to Gary, but I don't think we should be taking any chances now. When I get back, we can start to put together a system for keeping track of key personnel...and triggering an alert if anyone else disappears."

Peterson looked uncomfortable, but finally he said, "Of

course we'll wait for you, sir, but…I'd feel much better if we rode to Confederation Intelligence with you. We can stay in the transport when you go in."

Striker hesitated for a few seconds, but then he answered, "No, I'll be fine. I've got my driver and guards." He stood up. "I think it'd be better if you stayed here, maybe put together a plan to get word to your Marines. We may need them after all."

Chapter Ten

CFS Repulse
Unknown System 20
Year 316 AC

The light above Stockton's eyes was dim, hazy. He was groggy, his consciousness fading in and out. He wasn't sure where he was, at first, but then his memory began to return. He was landing his fighter…no, he wasn't in the ship anymore. He was lying on a bed or cot somewhere.

Sickbay?

Did I land already?

"Jake…" The voice was soft, comforting…but he could hear the concern in it as well.

"Stara?" He spoke her name, or at least he tried. His throat was sore and parched, and he wasn't sure how audible it was.

"Yes, Jake, it's Stara." She leaned down, moving closer to his face. "You did it. You got your ship back and landed it."

His memory was still fuzzy, but the scenes inside the cockpit continued to come back…and the final moments as he brought his fighter down into the bay.

"I crashed."

"It wasn't the cleanest landing…but you're going to be fine, and there was no damage to the bay. Considering the circumstances, it was a very successful landing."

"The squadrons…we've got to get them ready to launch

73

again. I've got to get back out." He pulled himself up, rising about half way before vertigo overtook him and he fell back onto the bed.

"You need some rest before you can launch again. The fleet is about to transit, and the enemy is far enough behind to allow us to go through with the fighters in the bays." Stara paused. "Olya Federov has taken charge of the squadrons until you return to duty."

Stockton shook his head, stopping again as the dizziness worsened. "I have to take command…I have to be ready once the fleet is through the transit point."

"Jake, you can't even stand. If you insist on being an obstinate ass, you're going to be in here for a week. If you cooperate, and get some rest…and let the doctor clean out the residue from the overdoes of stims choking your system, you'll be back on duty in two days."

Stockton was about to argue again, but it was pointless. He *couldn't* stand just then, much less fly a fighter. As natural as it was for him to argue and insist he could do anything, he knew Stara and the doctor were right.

Perhaps harder for him to accept was the fact that Federov could fill in for him for two days, that she could lead the squadrons without him…if, perhaps, he told himself, a bit less than skillfully he might.

"I want to see her. Lynx. Before she leads the next wave." It was vanity, perhaps, to believe Federov needed some kind of pep talk from him, but it was one he needed now. Stockton had led his squadrons in many desperate battles, and he'd lost more pilots than he cared to think about, but there was something different this time. This was no battle against invading Union forces, not even a desperate struggle fighting alongside Alliance wings deep in civil war. The fleet was lost in the depths of space, and the only way home was back through a force that vastly overpowered it. His squadrons weren't fighting in combined fleet engagements as one weapon of several as they had for so many years. They were throwing themselves at the enemy alone, struggling to turn the one advantage the Confederation forces had into a chance to prolong the desperate, and ultimately hopeless, flight. He'd never had an easy time sending his pilots to fight without him, but it cut at him more deeply this time, made it nearly unbearable to remain on *Repulse* lying in a bed while he had ships out in space.

"Okay…" Stara shook her head, but there was a smile on her face. "You can obsess over the squadrons, bore Olya to death with a lot of warnings and tactical advice she already knows…as long as I have your word you'll follow the doctor's orders to the letter."

"Fine."

"I mean it, Jake. Your word."

He sighed hard. "You have it. Now, send Lynx down here so I can talk to her…just in case we have an alert before you expect one."

Stara smiled, and a voice called out from just outside the small alcove. "I'm here, Captain." Federov stepped out and walked up next to the bed. She was tall and slender, her long hair tied back behind her head in a haphazard ponytail. Federov had always had a youthful look, one she retained despite all she'd been through. But as Stockton gazed up at her, he could see the years of combat and loss in her eyes. "Stara sent for me. She said you'd want to see me…and I'd been thinking just the same thing when she called." She paused and smiled. "And, before you ask, half the ships are refueled and rearmed, and the others are in the shops right now. I'm afraid more than a few needed considerable repairs after the extended missions."

She stood next to the bed, looking down at him, the smile still on her face. "So, what did you want to tell me that you think I haven't learned flying with you for eight years?"

*   *   *

"Commodore…I'm sorry to disturb you." The officer leaned through the door, peering nervously in Eaton's direction.

"Come in, Lieutenant…come in." She'd been in her office, mostly working, though earlier she'd dozed off for a bit as well.

Stockton's constant sorties had seriously disordered the enemy fleet, at least that was the only explanation she had for the lack of immediate pursuit. The fleet had been through the transit point for nearly eighteen hours, with no sign of any enemy ships following. She'd expected them six hours before, at the latest.

She appreciated the opportunity to give her crews a little rest, especially her exhausted fighter wings, but she hadn't included herself in that. Not until she'd fallen asleep at her desk, right in the middle of reading a series of status reports.

"What is it, Ivan?" Ivan Fensker was just about the last member of *Repulse*'s crew she'd expected to see outside her door. The ship's chief astrogator, she hadn't expected him to have anything material to tell her about the unknown systems the fleet was passing through, except, perhaps, the almost useless data of their positions in actual space.

"Well, Commodore…I'm not one hundred percent sure about this, but I felt it was likely enough that I had to bring it to your attention." The officer paused, looking nervous.

"Ivan, please…you know I respect your ability. If you have something to tell me, out with it." She was tired, and her head ached. She didn't have the patience for foolish games.

Not that Fensker was a game player. In all her time on *Repulse*, and before that on *Intrepid*, the introverted officer had mostly kept to his laboratories, managing science and research operations.

"Well, Commodore…it's about this system. As you know, we haven't yet discovered any transit points beyond the one from which we entered."

"That's true, Ivan, but we're still scanning. You know it takes time to properly survey a system." Eaton had been worried about the same thing. Not panicked yet, though the thought had crossed her mind of the fleet's dire predicament if this system turned out to be some sort of dead end.

If the only way out was back the way they had come…right into the maw of the massive Hegemony fleet…

"Yes, of course, Commodore. But…well, when our initial scans showed no signs of other transit points, I took a look at the local astrogation, and…" He paused again. "…this star is part of a binary system, and its twin is close, at least by interplanetary distances…just over one-twentieth of a lightyear."

Eaton stared at the scientist, uncertain for a moment where he was going. Then, realization dawned. "Are you saying you believe the other transit points are orbiting the partner-star? That they're five percent of a lightyear from here?"

"Yes, Commodore. I'm saying that is a significant possibility."

Eaton leaned back in her chair, and a small sigh escaped her lips. She could bring her ships up to a considerable velocity if they were going to travel in a straight line, twenty percent or more of lightspeed, but it would still take three months to reach the other star.

Accelerating to that velocity and then decelerating would burn most of the fuel the fleet had left. She'd managed to resupply her ships from the tankers and freighters the fleet had brought with it for its extended mission, but she hadn't had time to stop anywhere with a suitable gas giant to mine for emergency fuel supplies. She hadn't had time to stop for anything, not with the Hegemony fleet on her tail.

"So, Ivan…you're saying I have to decide whether to stay here and hope to find a transit point in this local system…or I have to gamble on finding something closer in to that other star, burning most of our fuel to do it." She hesitated and looked up at Fensker. "You know, if we get there and find nothing, we won't have enough fuel left to get back here." Another pause. "We'll be stuck there…unless we can find a place to harvest fuel." *And the enemy leaves us alone long enough to do it…*

"Yes, Commodore, I know." A pause. "I felt you needed to have all the information to make your decision. I can't tell you unequivocally that there isn't a second transit point orbiting this star, however the AI currently projects less than a ten percent likelihood, based on comparison to point layouts in known systems." He was silent for a moment, and then he added, "I will also note that, with pre-Cataclysm anti-matter powered drives, the distance between these stars would not be prohibitive. Depending on the cost of constructing the transit points—and that's something we can barely guess at—it might have been a simple choice to just accept the somewhat larger normal space distance in this binary system."

"Yes, it might have. That certainly makes sense. Or, perhaps the companion system is a dead end."

"We are likely at a dead end here, Commodore. What other choices do we really have?"

Eaton nodded slightly. "Thank you, Ivan. I will consider all factors and make my decision."

"Yes, Commodore." He stood up and turned to leave. Then, he paused and looked back. "Commodore, whatever you decide, time is not an ally right now."

Eaton felt a flash of anger at the officer pushing her, but it only lasted a few seconds…and it was replaced by a sort of grim amusement. "Yes, Ivan…I'm well aware of that. But since a bad decision here could kill us all, I think I can take a few minutes to review all data, don't you?"

"Yes, of course, Commodore." The officer seemed flustered, and he turned and walked quickly toward the door."

"And Ivan?"

Fensker stopped abruptly, just inside the door.

"Commodore?" He turned, and his voice was sheepish. He clearly felt he'd pushed too hard.

"Thank you. Your research, along with your prompt reporting of your findings to me, has been invaluable. Never hesitate in coming to me with anything."

"Yes, Commodore. Thank you." The officer slipped through the door, leaving Eaton alone with her thoughts.

Just make a decision, Sara…don't let the fact that a wrong choice will kill everyone hold you up…

She shook her head.

Any decision will probably kill us. It's a false assumption that there is a right choice, that any way out exists.

If she stayed, and they didn't find a transit point, the enemy would catch the fleet. Her people would fight fiercely, she knew, and they would extract a price. But, in the end, they would all die.

If she made a run for the inner system—assuming her ships proved up to the strenuous journey, and also that the enemy didn't just run her fleet down during the extended period of straight-line acceleration—she could get there to find nothing. Her people could be cornered, and even if the enemy didn't pursue them, they could still be trapped without enough fuel to get back.

Acceleration to the next star would also mean that some of her ships would fall behind, unable to keep up with the others. She would have to abandon them, leave their crews behind to catch up as well as they could…or to be overtaken by the pursuing enemy. She'd had to make those sorts of decisions before, but that didn't make any of it easier.

She wished for a moment that Tyler Barron was there, that the weight of this decision was on his shoulders and not hers. It was easier sometimes, simply to obey orders. She was ashamed that she wanted to push her duties off on her friend, but she couldn't escape the fact that part of her, at least, wanted just that.

She sat for a time, perhaps twenty minutes, but the situation became no clearer. In the end, she knew, she had to go with her gut, make a choice.

And hope for the best.

She reached down and flipped on the comm unit.

"Yes, Commodore?" Her sister's voice came through the small desk speaker.

"Commander…issue a fleet order. All ships are to set a course for the companion star. And I want emergency diagnostic routines in place immediately. We'll be engaging in a protracted period of maximum thrust, so if there are any engineering problems out there, I want them found *now*."

"Yes, Commodore."

Sara tapped the comm unit, closing the line.

She stared at the small screen on her desk, at the bright dot that represented the fleet's destination. And its hope to survive…a little longer.

Chapter Eleven

"I'm leaving a small team of Marines here, Administrator. They're all veterans, and they will be invaluable in preparing your people to defend Dannith, if things come to that." Barron hated leaving his people behind, especially since, if it came to fighting on the ground, that meant the enemy fleet had already crushed the planet's not inconsiderable orbital defenses. He figured it would take a dozen frontline Confederation battle-ships to mount a credible assault on Dannith's defensive grid, though he wondered what the Hegemony railguns would do to static defenses. Nevertheless, whatever force was required to break through the planetary defenses would almost certainly possess considerable ground assault capabilities as well. He wasn't entirely sure what a few Marine advisors would be able to do about that…but he just couldn't leave Dannith's millions of inhabitants without doing something to help them defend themselves.

"Thank you, Admiral." There was anything but gratitude in the administrator's voice. Barron knew Cantor was terrified, and that he would likely have fled from his post on Dannith if he hadn't been just as scared of the admiral's wrath as he was of the heretofore unseen Hegemony. That was a reasonable point of view, since Barron was perfectly willing to shoot the son of a bitch if he shirked from his duty.

"*Dauntless* will be leaving in a few hours, Administrator. We must get to Megara and report on our discoveries. I'm sorry I don't have the firepower to leave here to augment your defenses, but your planetary array is quite potent. I strongly urge you to use whatever time you have to bring your preparations to maximum readiness." Barron felt guilty leaving *Dannith*'s populations in the hands of such a contemptible piece of excrement, but there was nothing he could do. Besides, they'd elected him, and as much as he sympathized, they'd made their own bed, so to speak.

"Good luck to you, Administrator. With any luck, a naval relief force will arrive here before the enemy. Or, perhaps, the enemy won't show at all." Barron didn't believe that, not for a second. He didn't know much about the Hegemony, but what he did know suggested strongly it was not a power that could tolerate the existence of other nations. Whatever happened in the next few months, he suspected the greatest war he'd ever seen was looming out there, heading toward the Confederation like an unstoppable train.

"Yes, perhaps." The administrator's voice was deadpan, somber. "Thank you again for all your help, Admiral." Cantor had little success hiding the sarcasm in his tone.

Barron bit back on his anger, resisting the urge for about the twentieth time to pull out his pistol and relieve Dannith of its mistake. But he just turned, and he gestured toward one of the Marines. "Captain, a word please, before I leave."

"Yes, sir." The Marine snapped to attention, and he followed Barron out of the room.

"Captain…I'm sorry I have to leave you and your Marines here." He paused. "It's no secret that if the enemy appears, Dannith's orbital defenses will likely fall. You will be trapped on the surface, trying to aide an overmatched and unprepared defensive effort." Barron hesitated, wondering if he should be doing his best to demoralize the Marine. But he didn't like lying to his people, and he didn't have it in him to do it right now.

"There's no reason to be sorry, Admiral. We'll do our duty. And if any invasion force lands on Dannith, we'll make sure they regret it."

Barron almost felt a smile trying to surface. He'd always gotten along very well with his Marine contingents, and he never got tired of watching the rigid discipline and dedication to duty of the Confederation's elite warriors. He was leaving thirty-two Marines behind on a planet of hundreds of millions, facing possible invasion by a massive enemy force…and the captain was telling him the insignificant detachment was going to make a difference. Barron wished he could believe the same thing… convince himself that he wasn't leaving thirty-two of his people behind to almost certain death.

But he couldn't.

"Captain Blanth, I want you to listen very carefully to what I am about to say. I am entering exactly what I am telling you into my log, so there is a record of it. You are not to allow Administrator Cantor to leave Dannith under any circumstances. If he attempts to escape, or if, in your sole opinion, he takes any action which jeopardizes the defense of the planet, you are authorized to use whatever force is necessary to place him under control, up to and including summary execution. Do you understand, Captain?"

The Marine had been impassive the entire time, but now just a hint of concern slipped onto his face, the prospect of shooting a planetary head of state shaking even the veteran's innards. But in the end, he didn't flinch, and he didn't delay more than an instant in his response. "Yes, sir. Understood."

"Very well, Captain. Good luck to you and your Marines."

"Sir!"

Barron turned and walked away, trying to hide the increasingly grim expression on his face from the men and women he was leaving behind.

*   *   *

"Admiral on the bridge!"

Barron waved his arm as the officers and crew on *Dauntless*'s bridge began to rise to their feet, gesturing for them all to remain in their seats. He generally hated the pomp and ceremony that accrued to his new rank. At least it still felt new to him, even though it had been nearly two years since he'd first pinned on his admiral's stars.

He appreciated the recognition of his service, and the confidence his superiors had expressed in him with the promotions, but deep down, Barron missed his days as a ship's captain. The captain of *his* ship. *Dauntless*. *His Dauntless*. She had died a heroic death, arguably saving the fleet, and even the Confederation, from defeat, but that didn't do anything to prevent him from missing the creaky old battlewagon with an intensity that had hardly faded. He suspected—no, he *knew*—that those years on her bridge, with a crew he still thought of as family, would prove to be the best of his life.

And now they were part of his past.

He was playacting now, using Atara's incapacitation to buy a little more time at the con, justifying his monitoring the crew and doing the duties of a ship captain…but it wasn't the same. Nothing would ever be the same.

"Commander, are all ships ready to leave orbit?"

"Yes, sir." A brief pause. "Admiral, Commander Globus is on your line. He requests a final word and permission to depart."

Barron turned toward his chair, and he scooped up the headset, slipping it on while still standing. "Cilian?"

"Admiral…I wanted to offer my compliments and my sincerest wishes for good fortune to attend you until we are destined to meet again." A tiny smile slipped on Barron's lips. He'd come to respect his Palatian allies, but the Alliance ethos of honor in battle occasionally led to some theatrics.

"And fortune go with you, my friend. I look to the next day we stand side by side in battle." Palatians weren't the only ones who could lay it on…

"Our course is laid in. With your permission, we will depart now for Palatia."

"By all means, Cilian. You have duty to do, as do I. Give my regards and deepest respect to the Imperator." Vian Tulus was the supreme ruler of the Alliance, but he was also Barron's old comrade from the days of the Palatian Civil War. Barron had led Confederation forces to the aid of Tarkus Vennius in that conflict, and Tulus had taken Vennius's place when the old Imperator was killed less than two years after the final victory.

Vennius was another lost friend, one of many still alive in Barron's thoughts. Too many.

"I shall relay your regards to his Supremacy…along with our combined and fervent request that he act immediately toward our joint defense against the new enemy."

Barron shook his head slowly. Globus would first have to tell the Imperator that a vast and hostile empire existed, far off in an area of space all on the Rim had long thought dead. He didn't doubt his friend's loyalty nor his steadfastness, but he knew perfectly well that Tulus was responsible first and foremost to his own people…and different warriors saw their duty through various lenses. He liked to think a powerful Alliance fleet would come rushing to aid the Confederation, but he was far from sure that would happen, at least immediately…and he had his own job to do as well, to clear the way before his people would open their borders and welcome the arrival of vast forces from so recent an ally.

"You are authorized to depart, Commander Globus." He felt like he'd already as much as said that, but his experience with Palatians suggested that an order could never be too clear or firmly stated.

"Acknowledged, Admiral Barron."

The comm line went dead, and a few seconds later, Commander Cumberland reported that *Fortiter* had broken orbit and was accelerating toward the Volan transit point.

Barron stood where he was for a few seconds, his eyes moving over his chair before he turned toward the back of the bridge. "I'll be in my office, Commander. Please advise all ships we will be breaking orbit in precisely thirty minutes."

"Yes, sir."

Barron walked back to the small corridor behind the bridge leading toward the room that served as his office. As always, the first door he saw was the closed one across the hall.

Atara's office.

He felt a pang for his longtime first officer, now his flag captain. Things looked a bit more hopeful for his friend now, though her condition was obviously still very serious. But beyond the worrying…he just missed her. Her counsel, her advice. Her friendship. She'd been unconscious for months now, clamped in the medpod that was keeping her alive. He wished she was back, because he cared for her, because he wanted her to be okay.

Because he *needed* her…perhaps more now than he ever had.

He stood for a while longer, losing track of the time. Then he turned and walked into his own office, moving swiftly across the room and sitting down hard behind his desk. He'd been there no more than a few minutes when the AI spoke.

"Commander Cumberland is requesting entry, Admiral."

Barron was surprised. He'd just been on the bridge with Cumberland. What would send the officer back here in person instead of using the comm?

"Allow him in."

The door slid open, and Eliot Cumberland walked slowly inside.

"What can I do for you, Commander?"

"Sir…I'm sorry to disturb you…but I came upon something I thought you should know." The officer looked a little tentative.

"What is it, Eliot?"

"Well, Admiral, I stumbled on it by accident. I was connecting *Dauntless*'s AI banks with Dannith's…standard procedure, to update the records and news reports, that kind of thing."

Barron was looking at Cumberland as he fell silent again. "Yes, that is standard procedure. What did you find out of the ordinary?"

"Well, Admiral, I found some unusual traffic, so…well, I'm not sure if I went beyond my authorization, but I investigated a bit further."

"What kind of traffic?"

"There was a very strange docking record, Admiral. A ship with no registry reported, no place on any schedule…no records of any kind. I wouldn't have found it, except a maintenance tech apparently filed a routine repair report instead of disregarding it as he was ordered."

"That *is* very strange." Barron had a few ideas what kind of ship could overrule local regulations. There weren't many. Spy ships, Senatorial craft, very highly-placed military traffic.

"Yes, sir…but there's more. I went a bit further…deeper than I should have, I'm afraid. The ship left shortly after it arrived, and by all accounts, it carried some kind of prisoner."

"A prisoner?"

"Yes, sir. Apparently a very highly-ranked one."

Barron frowned. He'd spent almost an entire—seemingly endless—day with the administrator, and he hadn't said anything about a high profile arrest of some kind. It wasn't, strictly speaking, necessary, but Barron was surprised the fool hadn't mentioned it.

"When was this, Commander?"

"Nearly two and a half months ago, sir."

"Were you able to find out anything more specific?"

"I'm afraid not much, sir…not about this. I was able to piece together the ship's destination. Megara."

Barron stared back at the officer. *Megara. Maybe it* was *a Senatorial ship.*

He thought for a moment. He didn't have time to wait. He had to get back to Megara to begin the work of preparing to fight the Hegemony. Still, it nagged at him that the administrator hadn't said anything. He wasn't *sure* the politician was deliberately hiding something from him…but the more he thought about it, the more suspicious he became.

"Commander…place the fleet departure order on hold. And get Administrator Cantor on my line."

"Yes, sir." Cumberland stood, unmoving, still looking nervous.

"Is there something else, Commander?"

"Yes, sir…after I found these entries, I did a more extensive review." He paused. "I found another departure I thought would be of interest to you. A free trader…a ship named *Pegasus*."

The name hit Barron like a sledgehammer. *Pegasus*? No, it couldn't be. Andi was retired, living on some strip of coastal paradise on Tellurus. What the hell would she be doing on Dannith?

"*Pegasus*? Did you check the registry?"

"Yes, sir. It is her ship. And still registered to her." Cumberland had generally engaged in the same practiced ignorance of Barron's relationship with Andi Lafarge as all of *Dauntless*'s crew, but he and Andi had long been the worst-kept secret in the fleet.

But what was she doing on Dannith?

He couldn't figure it out. For a moment, he wondered if she'd leased out her ship, if someone else had flown the vessel to the frontier. But he knew she would never have done that with *Pegasus*. She didn't need the money, and her ship was the closest thing she had to a child.

"Go get Cantor on my line, Eliot. Now." His voice was cold. "If he isn't available, get Captain Blanth, and tell him he is to find the administrator and get him on the comm…if he has to drag him by his feet. Understood?"

"Yes, sir." Cumberland turned, but then he stopped as Barron snapped out another command.

"When that's done, Commander, I want you to get back to Dannith's record banks, and dig out everything you can find about either departure…or anything else that seems abnormal. You have my authorization to tear through their records without limitation. Do you follow me?"

"Yes, sir."

"Find me all you can, Commander. Now, go get me the administrator."

Barron stared straight ahead as Cumberland turned and left the office. His eyes were blazing with intensity.

What happened here?

And how the hell was Andi involved in it?

Chapter Twelve

"I want you to go back up and stay with Colonel Peterson and Major Bellingham. Give them any assistance they request. Either of them asking for it is the same thing as me asking for it. Understood?" Van Striker walked through the lobby of the Admiralty, snapping off commands to a cluster of aides.

"Yes, sir. I'll see to it immediately." One of the assistants saluted and turned around abruptly, rushing back toward the lifts that led to Striker's office.

The admiral glanced around, vaguely wondering how long it had been since the last time he'd been in the lobby. He didn't usually come in and out through the main entrance. The Admiralty building was located in the center of Troyus City, not far from the Senate building and the other major government centers. The main entrance fronted Grand Boulevard itself, but for security reasons, Striker usually came in and out through the underground levels. He'd received notice earlier that the lower levels were closed temporarily for some emergency maintenance. He'd just been about to find out whose screw up was responsible for the change when Peterson showed up with the news about Holsten.

Striker had forgotten all about the maintenance matter. Who-

88

ever had dropped the ball down there had been lucky enough to do it when something more important was going on…always one of the best ways to avoid trouble for a mistake.

"Stan, you come with me. The rest of you…you've got enough to keep you busy until I get back…so get to it." He turned slightly and gestured to the single aide he'd told to stay with him. "The transport should be ready…" He glanced out through the massive glass walls in the front of the building, his eyes darting around until he caught sight of a Marine, one of his guards, standing in front of a black luxury transport. "There," he said, extending his arm toward the leftmost door along the building's front.

He turned and walked toward the vehicle, the building's massive door sliding aside as he walked through. Stan followed close behind. The Marine by the car snapped to attention, then opened the side entry for the admiral.

There were two Marines from his guard waiting inside—one beside the driver, and the other sitting across from him in the back. Striker nodded at the Marines as he climbed inside and slid across the soft seat covering. He'd spent so much of his life in combat, and on distant postings, the luxury that clung to the navy's commander on Megara tended to embarrass him a bit. He usually just tried to ignore it, and not to admit to himself just how much he enjoyed it.

As soon as the door slid shut behind his aide, Striker began rattling off more orders to him. "Stan, I want you to…" But he didn't finish.

A shot rang out, muffled by some sort of silencing device, but still audible in the confines of the vehicle. Then another. The Marine in the front seat slumped forward, and then the one sitting across from him in the back dropped to his side, onto the seat, staring up with a stunned look frozen in his still open eyes. Striker could see blood pouring from the man's clearly fatal head wound.

He reached down for the sidearm he knew wasn't there. Striker was a combat officer, used to being armed at all times, but when he'd come to Megara and assumed the navy's senior post, he'd found that it wasn't customary for the top brass to go around the capital armed. After some token resistance, he'd reluctantly gone along with the tradition. After all, he didn't really need a weapon on the capital…did he?

Stan, however, did carry a pistol, and even as Striker turned, he could see the aide reaching for his weapon…drawing it about halfway from the holster before he, too, slammed back against the seat, a perfectly-placed wound right in the center of his forehead.

Striker's combat reflexes swung into action, but before he could move toward the front of the transport, the barrier between the vehicle's two compartments slammed closed, leaving him alone in the passenger section with the bodies of his aide and one of his Marine guards.

He dropped low, slipping to the side, doing whatever he could to avoid the shot he expected was coming. But there was no gunfire…only a voice on the vehicle's internal comm as the driver pulled away from the curb.

"There's no need to leap around in such an undignified manner, Admiral Striker. I assure you, I have no intention of killing you…not now. Consider yourself my guest for the time being. Make yourself comfortable. I know many people find it upsetting to sit among dead bodies, but unfortunately, there is nothing I can do about that now, not until we reach our destination. I've never shared that particular view. I've always found death to be a fascinating endeavor. What other factor has more completely directed the course of human history than our efforts at killing each other?"

Striker stopped moving, but he didn't answer. His mind was racing, trying to figure out who had abducted him. He didn't have to think long, though.

"Allow me to apologize for my meanderings, Admiral, and to introduce myself. I'm afraid we've never met, though I am quite familiar with your career…and I daresay, my activities have not been entirely unknown to you." There was a short pause, then: "Ricard Lille, Admiral, at your service."

Striker tried to stay focused, but the name stunned him. He

knew who Ricard Lille was very well. The coldest, deadliest assassin the Rim had ever known.

Why am I still alive?

He had a million questions, and an even larger pool of curses and invectives he wanted to hurl at his now unmasked captor. But he remained silent, his discipline straining to control the rage boiling inside him.

"We will arrive at our initial destination shortly, Admiral. I'm afraid your reception there will be somewhat unsettling. As far as I know, the Confederation doesn't usually implant tracking devices in top naval officers, but I find the possibility a bit too unsettling to ignore. No one knows you're missing yet, but, of course, that will quickly change…and if there are any homing chips or similar gear buried somewhere inside you, well, I'm sure you understand, we simply cannot have that. I have no desire to cause you excessive discomfort, but I'm afraid the process involved in locating such devices is far from a pleasant one."

The voice paused for a second before continuing. "Best we get you through it as quickly as possible, no? Then, maybe we can talk about more interesting matters."

*   *   *

"Senator Ferrell is here as you requested…"

Marieles waved her hand sharply, silencing the executive. He was actually one of her top agents masquerading as a senior manager of the media empire she now controlled. As such, it was safe to finish her phone call with him in the room.

"That's excellent news, Ricard. I must thank you again for your assistance in this matter. We'll discuss in more detail later. Over dinner, perhaps?"

"I'm pleased to provide whatever support is required to see Black Dawn to a successful conclusion. Yes, I believe we should discuss how to utilize—and ultimately dispose of—Admiral Striker. I suggest we meet earlier, however. Perhaps 6pm? I've always found work to be more productive without distractions like meals interfering."

"Yes, Ricard, of course. I will meet you at 6pm, at safehouse one."

"Very well, Desiree. Until then."

Marieles sat for a few seconds after the line went dead, allowing her agent to stand and wait. She'd known of Ricard Lille, in one way or another, her entire career. Nothing detailed, of course. The assassin had always been Gaston Villieneuve's secret resource, his deadly weapon of last resort. This was the first time she'd worked with him, and she found him difficult to understand.

She tended to try to keep those she worked with close to her, both marks and allies alike. But Lille seemed completely resistant to her charms. She'd heard enough rumors to know he had his appetites, powerful ones, the kinds of desires that should have made him perfect for her influence. But he was cold as ice on the job, and he showed no interest in any of her flirtations, or even her efforts to establish a veneer of friendship.

She couldn't argue Lille was a valuable asset, but there was no disputing one other, less appealing fact. He scared the hell out of her. She knew Lille would go to great lengths to help with Black Dawn, but also that the instant he thought it was in his interests, he'd smile at her and put a bullet between her eyes. She'd worked with ruthless agents for years …there were few more ruthless than she was herself. But Lille was something else entirely.

She tried to put such worries out of her mind. The moment she'd been working for was finally at hand. Lille had Striker… and that meant it was time to put Black Dawn fully into motion. She sighed. The first step was meeting with Ferrell, directing the tiresome Senator in how to use the power she'd helped him acquire. It was an inescapable part of the job, but she was sick to death of putting up with the insufferable fool.

"Show Senator Ferrell in," she finally said to the agent, who nodded and turned to slip out the door. A moment later, the familiar form of Emmerson Tolbert Ferrell ambled in, a smile on his face.

"Desiree…I was delighted to hear from you. I had quite a

busy morning, but when I received your message, I cleared my schedule and came right over."

Marieles forced her own smile, the manufactured one she used around Ferrell. Around most people.

"Emmerson, thank you so much." She could see a glimmer of hope in his eyes, perhaps at the prospect that she had sent for him in a social manner. The sooner she cut that off, the better. She needed the Senator focused now, and doing her bidding in the Senate, not daydreaming about...whatever it was he daydreamed about.

She let the smile slip from her face. "I'm afraid I didn't ask you to come here today for social reasons, sadly." She let a somber look take over her expression, one of disillusionment. "It was a tremendous opportunity for me to become involved with the investment group that took over ITN. In my years working in public relations, and then as a lobbyist, I've always considered media and information technologies to be my true interest." She sighed softly. "I never imagined how difficult it would be to be privy to so much information...to know things you wish you didn't."

"What is it, Desiree? I can assure you, Mr. Holsten will receive the punishment he deserves...and he will not be allowed to access his files, to strike back at those bringing him to justice. Have you discovered even more evidence of his corruption?"

Marieles sighed, playing her role meticulously. She was about to present Ferrell with the largest cache of mostly-falsified data she had ever seen, more than she'd even given him on Holsten. Those files would show that, without a discernable doubt, much of the top brass of the navy had been deeply involved in Holsten's—equally fictional—schemes and corruptions. It hadn't been an easy dossier to assemble, and it had taken the efforts of an almost unmatched team of hackers and computer engineers to plant the supporting data. When her team had finished, many of the navy's top officers, and a cadre of Holsten's top agents as well, had considerable assets and hidden accounts, all apparently exposed by diligent investigative reporting. Ill-gotten gains that would now be damning evidence of corruption and illegality.

She knew she couldn't maintain the deceptions indefinitely, but she didn't need to. She just needed it all to have enough impact to throw the Confederation into a political and constitutional crisis…one that would allow Torrance Whitten to step up and "rescue" the government.

Whitten didn't have the ability to truly see a coup through to its successful end. But with her help, he had a good chance of securing the control and loyalty of at least a portion of the fleet. If the Confederation didn't face outright civil war, it would certainly endure a damaging and extended period of crisis…and almost certainly an economic collapse from which it would take years to recover.

"Emmerson…you need to look at these files. When my team here began this investigation, I thought the corruption was mostly centered around Gary Holsten." She paused, pretending the news was upsetting to her. "But as you will see, it goes far beyond that. Literally trillions of credits stolen, and dozens, if not hundreds of guilty parties. This material is a tremendous scoop for ITN, a story of almost unimaginable value… but some things go beyond business. Things like patriotism." She looked up at him, letting a well-placed tear slip out of her eye as she did. "I didn't know who else to bring this to. It is terrible, Emmerson. So many heroes are involved, people the Confederation has come to admire, to adore. Admiral Striker, Tyler Barron…so many others."

She was pleased with herself, and her performance. Ferrell wasn't the toughest target, but even a gullible fool like the Senator would need considerable persuasion to believe such charges against the Confederation's greatest war heroes…and to find the courage to go after them.

"That seems impossible." For an instant, she thought Ferrell was going to argue with her. But he just paused, staring back with a stunned look on his face.

"That's what I thought, Emmerson. It's what I said when this was first brought to me…and I pray there *is* some mistake, even now, though I don't see how that's possible. Review it all, please…and perhaps call Admiral Striker to the Senate to…

explain." She had a hard time holding back a smile. When the Senate summoned Van Striker they wouldn't find him…and nothing else Maricles did would make the admiral look as guilty as his own disappearance.

Ferrell was still for a time, looking something between nervous and terrified. But, finally, he nodded, and reached out to take the box of data chips off the desk. "I'll review it, Desiree… and I'll call you when I have." The Senator looked like he was about to leave, but he hesitated. "I hope this is a mistake, Desiree." She could hear the fear in his voice…and perhaps a hint of something else. Was it anticipation of what he could do with such a scandal, how far he imagined he could take his position if he uncovered such deep-seated corruption…even treason?

She returned his gaze, her expression a combination of sadness, affection, trust—all fake, of course. "I hope so, too, Emmerson," she said, her voice soft. "But once you've read it, I don't think you'll see much hope of that."

It took her a few more minutes to actually get Ferrell out of her office, but as soon as she was alone, she leaned back and let the genuine smile she'd been holding back burst out on her face.

Chapter Thirteen

Free Trader Pegasus
Rhodia System
En Route to Planet Megara, Olyus III
Year 316 AC

Andi Lafarge sat quietly in her chair, dead center on *Pegasus*'s tiny bridge. It was a place she'd always considered home. She hadn't realized just how much she'd felt that way about her old ship until she'd stowed it away and settled down to live the life she'd pursued for so many years. The life she'd wanted desperately.

That she'd *thought* she wanted desperately.

She wasn't in a good state now—and after what she'd been through, she was far from sure she ever would be again—but she still remembered what she'd felt after Gary Holsten had enticed her to leave her new home on Tellurus and return to Dannith as one of his agents.

Relief.

It was only after she'd left Tellurus that she'd realized just how suffocated she'd become by the stifling routine of her life there. She'd tried to convince herself choosing paintings for the north wing study was an endeavor that could keep her interested, but as soon as she'd cleared the planet's atmosphere, the truth had become startlingly clear. The life she'd sought since her days as a homeless orphan was not one she wanted. Not even one she could endure. She'd tasted too much adventure, seen too much of space to content herself with decorating a mansion and lunching at the elite bistros in town.

Now, however, she feared she had a real problem. She'd been tortured, endured suffering like she never had in all her close calls and wild experiences. She hadn't told Holsten all that had happened, nor anyone else. She never would. But the man who'd taken so much from her had given her the one thing she had left, the purpose that kept her going, drove her on with fiery intensity. Vengeance.

She was going to find Ricard Lille, whatever it took. And when she found him, she was going to kill him.

"You really should try to get some rest, Andi."

She didn't say anything, didn't even turn to acknowledge Vig at first. Her long-time second-in-command, a very wealthy man now in his own account, had been watching her since he'd arrived, practically monitoring her sleep, food intake, and the hours she spent staring at the wall with a frown on her face. He'd been annoying the hell out of her. And she loved him for it.

"I'm okay, Vig. I'm not tired." That was a lie. She was exhausted, but she was too twisted in knots to sleep, too focused on trying to deal with memories of the pain that was mostly gone, yet still so vivid. She'd managed to slip into a fitful sleep a few times, mostly to drop into a pit of nightmares that drove her quickly back to wakefulness, screaming. She'd tried to hide as much of that as possible from her crew…but she suspected Vig, at least, was aware of a fair amount of it.

"Andi, come on…" He walked up and slid into the station he usually occupied. There were only three on *Pegasus*'s bridge, and they were close enough to each other that their occupants could reach out and touch the others. "You know you're not okay. I'm not trying to push, but…"

"Then, don't." The harsh words slipped out of her mouth, with a nastiness she didn't want to unleash on her oldest friend. "I'm sorry, Vig…I'm just on edge. We'll be at Megara soon, and it's hitting me now just how little I have to go on."

Andi had ravaged the Dannith Spacer's District with the savagery of a barbarian horde. She'd visited every seedy tavern and backroom poker game, every place where rogues and scoundrels plied their trade. She didn't want treasure maps this time, nor rumors of old tech…she just wanted information. She wanted to know where Ricard Lille had gone.

She'd already had a reputation as someone not to be trifled with, but now, she suspected, that had increased rather dramatically, both in reach and in scale. She'd worked her way through the District, and she'd left behind no small number of its denizens terrorized and beaten.

She hadn't had much success…either those she encountered knew nothing, or they were more afraid of Lille than of her. She suspected it was mostly the former. She didn't tell herself she was more of a threat than Ricard Lille, but she knew very well that a threat standing before someone enjoyed a multiplying factor of fear versus one that was far away. Since she'd shown little hesitancy to put a slug into a leg or slip a blade somewhere non-vital but painful, she'd made the most of that premise.

She'd virtually stumbled onto her one good source of information…one of Lille's agents, who'd help him beat and torture her. One whom, it turned out, he had sent with a pack of thugs to find and kill her. But Drossier's mission hadn't gone as planned. She and her people had discovered what they were doing, and lured them into a series of traps, killing them one by one. All except Drossier himself.

It had taken all she had not to kill the man as she monitored his movements…but she was after a higher mark. She'd tracked him for days, even as he was trying to find her. Lille's agents were highly skilled and not to be underestimated, and she reminded herself constantly to maintain her guard and watchfulness. Finally, she took him one night, after following him to one of the District's higher end entertainment establishments, where he no doubt had a contact he planned to interrogate for information on her.

She'd grabbed him just outside, on the street, a move so

quick that for all his training and experience, he'd never seen it coming. An instant later, he was in the back of an unmarked transport, where Vig and the enormous Dolph Messer proceeded to beat him into submission and silence.

He'd been difficult to break, but Andi had kept at it, finding the experience particularly satisfying when she utilized the tactics her subject had used on her some months before. He'd been in bad shape by the time he'd spilled what he knew, but Andi didn't care.

She didn't care, because she'd had no intention of letting the bastard go. Not after what he'd done.

She'd thrown what was left of him into the reactor of a large apartment block, kilometers from the District, in the most boring part of town she could find. She'd just as soon have tossed his carcass into the street, but she didn't want word of his death to somehow reach Lille. The man was a deadly killer, and a genius at what he did…but perhaps overconfidence would be his downfall. If he knew Andi was coming for him, he would be ready. If she approached quietly, without warning…perhaps she could gain the edge she needed.

And put the piece of shit down for good.

"We found everything we could, I think, Andi. I don't think staying on Dannith any longer would have gained anything."

"No, Vig…you're right. I guess knowing Lille is on Megara *is* narrowing things down a bit. But it's still an awfully large place to look." Andi had been a little shocked to find out that Sector Nine's greatest assassin had left Dannith for the Confederation's capital.

She'd intended to keep her pursuit of Lille to herself—and, of course, her crew—but now she decided she would have to tell Gary Holsten and Van Striker. The spymaster and the admiral had been very good to her, and she considered them both friends. Even in her current state, Andi Lafarge never forgot her few true friends.

If Lille is risking being on Megara, he's up to something big. It had crossed her mind several times that Lille could even be after either Holsten or Striker. The Union agent was an assassin, after all, and both of her friends were high-value targets. That was something else that was weighing on her…the fear that she might get to Megara too late.

She turned back to Merrick. "I'm going to go down to engineering and see if Lex can squeeze a little more thrust out of the engines." She'd been pushing *Pegasus* harder than she ever had before, but her old ship had also enjoyed a serious refit since her last mission, courtesy of her newfound wealth. Now, she needed even more.

"I'll make you a deal, Andi. You go back to your quarters, try to get some rest…and I'll go down to engineering and help Lex get what he can from the engines." Merrick wasn't an engineer of Lex Righter's caliber, but Andi knew he had a good bit of experience working on spaceship engines.

She also knew her chances of getting any sleep were effectively zero. But perhaps she should put on a show, try to make her people think they had gotten her to go to bed. She owed them, at least by her reckoning. They had all achieved the vast wealth they had so long pursued, and yet they had all come back to *Pegasus*'s cramped quarters and the danger of her quest for revenge. Not one of them had pulled out, gone back to the gilded existence they had fought so long to attain.

That was loyalty, and however scarred she was, however damaged and compelled to pursue a possibly ruinous trail, she had long ago sworn to herself she would always repay that rarest commodity in kind.

"Okay, Vig…I'll try. But I'm not promising anything. Maybe Rina can watch the bridge for a while."

"Already here, Andi." Rina Strand was another of Andi's people from the early days. The two had been in more scrapes together than she could count, and they'd saved each other's lives more than once to boot.

"You just like my chair." Andi forced a smile. The darkness inside her was too strong to allow those kinds of feelings to emerge. She wondered if that would always be the case.

Just then, it felt like it would be.

"I do like that chair, Andi…I can't deny it." Strand returned the grin, hers looking authentic. "Just try to get some rest." She paused. "You're going to need everything you've got when we reach Megara...you know that."

Andi nodded at her friend. She did know that. Ricard Lille was no easy target. She *would* need all she had to defeat him.

But knowing that and actually getting some rest were two different things.

Two very different things.

Chapter Fourteen

Sara Eaton was watching three of her ships dying on the display.

Three more of her ships.

Two of the vessels were freighters with damaged drives, abandoned by their crews and left in the control of artificial intelligence units. The third was a cruiser, also a victim of mal-functioning engines. Unlike the freighters, it was still manned by a skeleton crew, one entirely made up of volunteers.

Volunteers doomed to die.

Eaton knew the fact that the nine men and women on that ship had offered to stay, without orders and without any real hope of survival, should have made it easier on her…but it didn't. Not really. They were her people, more of her spacers, about to die, even as the rest of the fleet continued its nearly hopeless flight.

She wondered if it mattered. If in some ways, it wasn't more merciful for the nine volunteers to meet their ends now, rather than continuing on. Her fleet had plunged out into deep space, following long-forgotten transit paths leading to…who knew where? Now, even the hope of continuing that grim journey felt as though it was slipping away. Their chances rested entirely on the hope that there were transit points orbiting the companion star that lay ahead.

She waited, hoping to see the cruiser open fire, to get a shot in before the enemy finished it off…but she knew that was a false hope. The Hegemony battleships massively outranged the Confederation heavy cruiser, and Eaton knew, almost for a certainty, that she would watch her people die without getting off so much as a single shot. She regretted allowing any of them to stay, despite their stated—but ultimately futile—hope that they could get the engines back up to full power in time.

Perhaps the worst part of it all was how she'd withheld what support she could have sent to support her latest three laggards. Olya Federov and Jake Stockton had both requested permission to lead bombing strikes to support the trailing ships. Stockton, particularly, had done so repeatedly. She had refused them both. No number of sorties was going to save those ships, and she couldn't afford to lose more pilots, not when she knew she'd need them soon enough. The enemy forces had taken several days to emerge into the system, most likely because Stockton's relentless assaults had disordered them badly. But now they were pursuing the fleet again, and their thrust levels outmatched her own. They were going to catch the fleet, sooner or later, and she was going to need every fighter she had then.

She saw the indicators on her screen light up. Energy readings. The enemy ships along their front line were powering up their weapons. There was no warning, no demand for surrender, no communication of any kind. Eaton saw starkly just what kind of enemy—what kind of war—the Confederation faced. The Hegemony was brutal, unyielding…and they operated under the absolute certainty that they were superior, that any who opposed them were inferiors, fit only to serve, if to live at all.

She saw a small flash, one of the enemy ships opening fire. Actually, she suspected her ships were already gone, their crews dead even as she watched the projections in the display. The lagging vessels were a full six light minutes behind, and that meant what she was seeing now had happened three hundred sixty seconds before.

She didn't think any of the ships would last that long.

Even as that thought crossed her mind, one of the freighters vanished from the display, followed a few seconds later by the AI report that the vessel had been destroyed.

There were a few quiet gasps on the bridge, but for the most part her people were veterans, and they remained silent. They'd lost comrades before, and while she didn't suspect they'd become any less disgusted by it than she had, she knew they were harder, more disciplined than they had been before the war with the Union.

She waited, watching, counting the seconds. A quick glance at her screen told her it would be almost nine minutes before the cruiser was even within extreme range…and she had a pretty good idea of the odds of the ship surviving that long.

She'd barely finished that thought when the small circle representing the cruiser brightened. A hit.

The ship was still there, but as she continued to watch, the damage reports began coming in. The vessel was hurt, badly, its already diminished thrust completely gone now. She felt a controlled sort of panic, an urge to get some help to the ship, to somehow save her people she knew were about to die. Losing spacers in a battle was difficult enough, but the camaraderie of facing an enemy together somehow made it easier to endure. Watching one of her ships hunted like a wounded animal, a hundred million kilometers from any help, was almost too much to endure.

She continued to watch as a pair of Hegemony battleships increased their thrust and blasted out in front of the main formation. An instant later, one of them opened fire, and the second freighter disappeared from her screen. Now, the desperate cruiser was alone.

She wanted to look away, but she couldn't. She wouldn't let herself. *If you can send them out there to die, you can damned sure watch it.*

She sat still…all of *Repulse*'s bridge was still, silent. Every officer present was watching the display, immersed in the same horror that engulfed Eaton. Part of her wanted the cruiser to survive as long as possible…and part wanted the whole thing to be over. But, whatever she wanted, time was passing slowly, each second seeming to drag out almost to eternity.

Part of her still hoped the enemy would stop, that they would contact the ship, demand its surrender. She knew that wouldn't happen. She didn't know much about the Hegemony, but she'd seen no willingness to take prisoners. The naval officer in her, the strict, hard persona that had fought so many battles, was grateful for that fact. There was guilt, of course, for her relief that her people would die, but she couldn't imagine the intelligence the captured spacers might be forced to divulge.

As much as Sara Eaton, the human being, wanted her people to live, the flag officer, the part of her who had already dared to imagine the war that was likely coming, *wanted* those few spacers to die. Better that than to become the instruments by which the enemy found the Confederation…and killed millions more.

A few seconds later, she got her wish, as the cruiser was hit twice in rapid succession, and disappeared in the fury of nuclear fusion.

*   *   *

"What are you saying, Ivan?" Eaton stared across her desk at Fensker. The astrogation specialist had come to see her for an unprecedented second time in as many months. His first visit had convinced her to take the fleet on a desperate dash across the vast stretch of space between the stars of the binary system.

She'd agreed with him then, but this visit filled her with utter dread.

"I've checked it five times, Commodore, and I've had the main AI review my findings and run its own analysis. I can't be one hundred percent sure, but I'd put my confidence level above ninety percent. Even ninety-five percent."

Eaton looked back down at the images on the large tablet Fensker had brought with him. It was just about the biggest of the portable units, but it was still too small for her to make out the details the scientist was pointing out. To her eyes, the scans just looked like random arrays of stars, with a few highlighted in red or blue…but Fensker had pointed to each of them and stated a specific name. Some were stars she'd heard of before, others were unknown to her. But the fleet's chief astrogator seemed utterly certain of his analysis.

"You're that sure, Ivan, really? This is no time for boasting or exaggeration. I *have* to know."

"Commodore…how long have I served with you? Have you ever known me to state something with virtual certainty…when I wasn't virtually certain?" She could hear the sorrow in the scientist's voice.

Eaton felt like she'd been punched in the gut. Fensker had always behaved in all ways with a strict scientific code. If anything, he was likely to denote a level of uncertainty where, really, there was none. She couldn't imagine him puffing himself up with half-proven assertions.

That meant they had trouble. Big trouble.

"So, you're telling me that we transited into the outer star of a binary system…and that the inner star is a system in the Badlands?"

"Yes, Commodore, that is what I'm telling you. It is reference number Sigma-112, colloquially known as Bellephoron. It's well-documented, if uninhabited."

"How is that possible? How could the point we came through remain undetected for so long?" She knew the answer, even as she asked the question.

"The system is outside the Confederation, Commodore, and the inner planets were of modest value. It has four transit points, making it somewhat of a hub in the inner Badlands. There was simply no reason for any ships to make the extensive journey out to explore the companion star…and, in point of fact, few ships capable of so rigorous a trip would have visited this system. Our own fleet is outfitted to military standards, and yet we are having a…difficult…journey. It's highly unlikely some Badlands free trader or explorer's ship could survive the trip there and back. With no one coming through the other side, until us, there was no indication of a transit point located so far from the primary, nor any reason to suspect one."

"So, after all we've done, the number of systems we've come through, the people we lost…we've managed to lead them back to the Confederation anyway. Is that what you're telling me?"

Fensker shifted uncomfortably, the guilt written on his face. "I wouldn't have put it exactly that way, Commodore." He paused, looking at Eaton. "For one thing…we have led them dangerously close to the Confederation, but not all the way there. Perhaps there is a course we could take, a way to turn about and lead them away from the border. They appear to have pursued us rather doggedly and not scattered their strength exploring other transit points we have passed."

Eaton nodded, barely. She appreciated Fensker's words, and his attempt to give her hope…but the scientist had no idea what the Hegemony forces had done along the route, or just how large their fleets truly were. For all any of them knew, there was a force as large as the one bearing down on the fleet now in every other transit route they had gone by.

"Is there such a route?" Eaton was doubtful. She was no expert on Badlands navigation, but she knew the close-in systems of the dead zone tended to have small numbers of working transit points, and that they mostly led back and forth to other nearby stars. The routes out into deep space were relatively few…and it would take considerable luck to chart a course that would lead away, without going through a system that would raise suspicion. The stars near the border tended to have fairly considerable traffic from smugglers, survey ships, and the like. It would only take one appearing on Hegemony scanners to give things away.

Fensker sighed. "I haven't explored every option yet, Commodore…" She could tell the answer from his tone. "…but it will probably be difficult."

"You mean impossible."

"No, Commodore…not impossible."

"But not within any risk parameters I can accept. Not when leading the Hegemony right to Confederation space is the downside."

Fensker looked down, his eyes avoiding hers. "No, Commodore. Probably not." A pause. "I am so sorry, Commodore. I should have checked this before I counseled you to…"

"That's enough of that, Ivan. There was no way you could have foreseen this."

"Yes, Commodore." She could tell Fensker still blamed himself. She wished she could say something that would ease the officer's guilt…but she suspected she'd feel the same way.

She sat still for a moment, silent. Then she reached out and put her hand on Fensker's shoulder. "Thank you, Ivan. You've done your duty. Now, it is time for me to do mine."

She took a deep breath, and then continued, her voice softer when she did. "As soon as I can figure out what that is."

She sat where she was, thinking she'd dismissed the officer… until she noticed him still standing there, looking uncomfortable, and a little confused.

"That will be all, Ivan. Perhaps you can review your calculations. It's important that we're sure about this." She didn't have a doubt the scientist was right, and from the expression on his face, neither did he.

He nodded. "Yes, Commodore. Immediately." He turned and walked across the room, and out through the door…leaving Eaton with a problem to solve, and one hell of a pounding headache.

*   *   *

Sara Eaton looked out across the bridge, her eyes fixed on the display, at the vast array of Hegemony ships moving even now toward firing range. She had time—maybe—to get her ships out of the system before they were engaged and destroyed. That was what she would have done before…it was what she'd intended to do, and her ships were even now moving toward the targeted transit point. But Fensker's words were still echoing in her mind, the news he'd brought her standing in her way.

She'd known since the day Barron had left to return to the

Confederation that the fleet likely faced destruction, but it was one thing to know that while continuing to fight and flee, and quite another to face the fact that the moment had come. The final fight was upon her.

Her mission had been clear: to keep the enemy confused and occupied as long as possible, to preserve the secret of the Confederation's location. Circumstance had betrayed her, and the course she'd pursued into the depths of the darkness had instead brought her back around, no more than seven transits from the Confederation border itself.

Her mind raced, desperately searching for tactics, ideas, anything. But there were only two options. Lead the enemy back through the Badlands, a hair's breadth from the inhabited Rim.

Or fight here, to the death…and hope the enemy didn't push on farther after her ships were gone.

It was a poor choice, one of the worst she'd ever faced. But, to Sara Eaton, only one of the options was possible.

She turned her head, looking across the bridge toward her sister. "Sonya…issue a fleet order. All ships, battle stations. All squadrons…scramble and prepare to attack." She stared across the bridge, aware every eye was fixed upon her. "We're going to fight it out right here."

Chapter Fifteen

Troyus City
Planet Megara, Olyus III
Year 316 AC

The silence on the street was ominous. Troyus City was usually bustling in the early evening, especially right before a weekend. The streets all through the city center were lined with restaurants, and they were usually packed, as were the venues in the theater district, and the clubs that lined the waterfront south of the main government sector. But tonight, a table could be had anywhere, as could admission to any of the sought-after shows or the hottest clubs. Most of the capital's population was home, watching the newscasts.

The crisis had broken the day before, and most of those who hadn't skipped work to watch the telecasts had raced home early, after, in most cases, a stunningly distracted and unproductive day. The stories had come out in rapid succession, starting two nights before with the announcement that the former head of Confederation Intelligence had been convicted of a vast conspiracy and widespread corruption…and sentenced to life imprisonment on a penal colony in the distant Corvega system's asteroid belt.

The name Gary Holsten was familiar to most of those watching, though only a tiny percentage had known that, in addition to

his role as the heir to one of the Confederation's greatest industrial fortunes, he had also headed the main intelligence agency
for years. That news was as shocking as the revelation that he
had used his position to siphon government funds—worse, tax
revenues targeted to supply the forces fighting the war against
the Union. Megara was a wealthy planet by any measure, and
its people enjoyed a standard of living that most would envy.
Those residing in the vicinity of the capital were also used to
witnessing astonishing, and often revolting, displays of almost
incalculable wealth. For some reason, they were more forgiving
of such conduct by politicians than by industrialists…especially
those, like Holsten, who had inherited great wealth.

The announcement had been made by Senator Ferrell, a man
whom few of the Megarans watching had ever heard of. He
was the lone Senator from a distance world, one so unimportant
that though it was part of the Confederation, perhaps half of
Megara's citizens had never heard of it. They knew Ferrell now,
and as he railed against Holsten's greed and corruption, they
silently cheered.

The uncovering of such vast criminality was upsetting, of
course, but the discovery that an industrialist was corrupt, that
he had bought himself a government post and misused it, was
nothing that rose to crisis levels. That hadn't happened until
the next night…when every network and channel on Megara's
extensive information net broke away for fresh news reports.

The corruption was even vaster than had been initially
reported, the anchors told their attentive viewers, and the list of
those involved had grown to include hundreds more names…
including members of the navy and Marines. *That* was enough
to unnerve most of those watching. The Confederation had
fought four major wars in less than a century, and whatever
political groups its people belonged to, almost all recognized
that they would be Union slaves without the military forces that
had preserved their freedom.

As the networks began to release the names of the accused,
the citizenry of Megara let out a collective gasp. At the top of
the lengthy roster were household names, heroes the people of

the Confederation almost worshipped…and the first two were Admiral Van Striker and Admiral Tyler Barron.

The people had been quick to accept Holsten's guilt, demanding little in the way of evidence to support the claims of the politicians, but all across Megara, howls of doubt now erupted. Billions of citizens clung to their belief in their heroes. But the evidence started to come, a trickle at first, and then a torrent. Documents, extensive financial analysis…and finally, guilty parties, farther down the chain of command, tearfully confessing on the air, sobbing and begging forgiveness…and pointing damning figures at officers like Striker and Barron, who they claimed had lured them into the scheme.

Slowly, fitfully, more and more of those watching began to believe the stories. ITN had been at the forefront, but as the results of Senate deliberations poured out, the other networks joined in, seeking to catch their rival's lead. Competing for viewership, every broadcast entity sought to get anyone on the air who could speak about the scandal…and throw mud at the accused.

"Things have gone better than we could have hoped, Ricard." Marieles had made no progress trying to break down Lille's cold, impenetrable wall, but she was still trying. The truth was, he scared the shit out of her, and she was doing anything she could to keep the killer firmly on her side.

"So far, Desiree…so far." Lille was calling her by her first name as well, but he managed to do it with no sign of emotion or closeness at all. There was no question, his arrival had been a massive assistance to her. Not only was Van Striker out of the picture now, but his disappearance had pumped suspicions about him into overdrive. People had been reluctant, at first, to believe the hero of the last war was a criminal, even a traitor… but his failure to appear before the Senate as summoned, or even to answer the charges, had been damning. As far as the people of Megara—and soon the entire Confederation—knew, Striker had fled to avoid being held accountable for his actions. None of them knew the truth, of course, that their completely innocent admiral was still in Troyus City, in the sub-basement of a very nondescript warehouse on the outskirts of town.

She ignored the touch of restraint in Lille's tone. She was well aware of all the things that could go wrong, but after months of difficult and dangerous work, she was determined to enjoy her success.

"Was your tool in the Senate able to put your chosen officers in place?"

Marieles didn't know the answer to Lille's question, not right then. The Senate was in closed session at that moment, as it had been for almost eleven straight hours. The grounds of the Senate Building had been shut down, and the Lictor Corps had been ordered to keep any but those summoned away. She saw some humor in that…if the Senators were afraid of their own military, she wasn't sure what the Lictors were going to do about it. The last she'd studied tactics, she'd come to the conclusion that pomposity and arrogance didn't stand up well in the field against grim killers with guns. The thought of the Senate's pampered lapdogs actually going up against veteran Confederation Marines was a stark one.

Sadly, from her perspective, arranging a Marine attack on the Senate was considerably beyond her reach. Manipulating the military was the most difficult part of the whole operation. While she didn't think she had much chance of turning them all—or even most—against Striker and Barron and the others, getting some key officers replaced in the forces deployed in the Olyus system seemed doable.

As long as Ferrell came through. And that was never something she liked to count on. Still, the clear edginess—and that was a charitable term—on display by the Senate suggested they *were* worried, and that could only help. Now, if she could nudge worried up to *scared*…

She was trying to think of something to say to Lille that would express a level of confidence beyond what she possessed, when one of her agents came running over. "Word just came in. The Senate has adjourned until tomorrow. They relieved over one hundred officers in the home forces…and Admiral Whitten has been placed in command of all Olyus system military assets."

Marieles smiled and nodded. "Thank you, Tomas." She turned toward Lille, a satisfied look on her face. Inside, the wave of relief she felt told her just how worried she'd been. She didn't have any real faith in Ferrell or Whitten, but the problem with smarter dupes was…it was harder to make them into dupes.

* * *

"It's been five days, Captain Stanhope, and there has been no sign of the admiral…nor of his aide or escort, nor even the transport he left in. We must increase the intensity of our searches…now." Colonel Peterson was standing right next to the naval officer. Too close, probably, and the tone of his voice was, if not hostile, at the very least, frustrated.

"Colonel, we've done everything possible to find Admiral Striker. I don't know what else we could do, and if you have some idea, I encourage you to share it." Stanhope had arrived the day after Striker's disappearance, and he'd more or less taken charge of the admiral's office while the search went on. He'd ostensibly been sent to help find the admiral, but from Peterson's point of view, his effort had been lackluster…if not outright obstructive.

"For one, we can increase the personnel assigned to search duties." Peterson already had his company of Marines looking for the admiral, though that was strictly an informal operation, and one he had told Stanhope nothing about. The resources the captain had assigned to look for the missing admiral were grossly inadequate, and the grizzled old Marine had made that clear on more than one occasion over the past several days.

"Colonel Peterson, I understand that your duties have seen you mostly on the front lines or out on the peripheral worlds. There is nothing wrong with any of that, of course, but Megara is the most cosmopolitan planet in the galaxy. We simply cannot have hundreds of troops bashing down doors looking for a man who, mostly likely, simply doesn't…" The officer paused for a second, and then he finished, his voice lower than it had been. "…want to be found."

"Don't tell me you believe these ridiculous charges? You think the admiral is in hiding, that he's fleeing from the slander laid against him?" The accusations leveled at Striker and the others, and the debate over whether there was any truth to any of it, had been the main topic of discussion throughout naval headquarters. Few had paid any heed at all to the reports at first, but Striker's disappearance, and the inability of anyone to find a trace of him, was beginning to wear away at peoples' faith.

Not Jon Peterson's, however. The Marine had a sense of loyalty that verged on obsessive. He believed in Striker, and until anyone proved unequivocally to the contrary, he would continue to do so. It appeared Stanhope was cut from a different cloth.

"I don't want to believe it, Colonel. But the admiral disappeared from the center of Troyus City, with two hand-picked guards and a personal aide, the day before a massive scandal erupted that involves him deeply, and that appears to be supported by quite damning evidence. I'm not saying Admiral Striker is guilty, that he's gone into hiding…but it is certainly beginning to look like that."

Peterson struggled to hold back the rage building inside him. The Marine knew smashing in the obnoxious officer's face in wasn't going to help anything, but that didn't make him want it any less. "I don't care what you choose to make out of the… evidence…but I know Van Striker well enough to be damned sure he'd never have stolen money earmarked to buy his spacers what they needed."

"There's no point in arguing, Colonel. The Lictors are looking for the admiral now, as are the federal marshals. Whether he is guilty or not, he is now the subject of a massive manhunt, on top of all our own efforts to find him. Wherever he is, however he disappeared, he will almost certainly be found…and then he will have the chance to clear his name." The officer paused, his voice somehow becoming even more grating when he resumed. "Or, he will face the consequences of what he did."

Peterson's hand tightened into a fist, but he managed to keep it at his side…with no little effort. "Very well, Captain. Let me know if you find anything." He turned and walked away, not even waiting for an acknowledgement. He hadn't liked Stanhope from the instant the officer walked through the door, but only now had he realized the man wasn't there to help Striker at all, but to find and arrest him.

Peterson didn't know where his friend had gone, but he was sure of one thing now. His Marines had to find Striker…before any of the others did.

*   *   *

"You are relieved, Admiral. I believe you already received the orders." Torrance Whitten stood bolt upright, the perfect image of a martinet as he stood before the somewhat stunned looking Admiral Reichman. If he'd cared at all what was going through the old flag officer's mind, he might have considered how shocking and rapid the events of the past several days had been. But Reichman was on the Admiralty Board, one of the officers who'd gradually derailed his career until, admiral or not, Whitten couldn't get a command towing ore to the shipyards.

And now it was payback time.

"You're also under arrest, Admiral…effective immediately. These gentlemen…" He gestured toward a half dozen partially armored and heavily armed naval security troopers—an absurdly overpowered contingent to escort a one-legged admiral less than a year from retirement to the Senate to hear the charges against him. Whitten had waited a long time for his revenge, and he wasn't about to let anything interfere with it.

"Admiral Whitten, surely you know all of this is just a pack of lies. I have never…"

"I suggest you save it, Admiral, for the Senate. You'll need a good explanation if you wish to avoid spending your last years mining radioactives on some desolate asteroid." There was a caustic edge to Whitten's tone. He'd carried a grudge for a long time, and Reichman was the first to feel the sting of his retaliation…though he would certainly not be the last.

"Commander Quinn, Commander Callahan…" Whitten turned, looking at the pair of officers standing behind him in the orbital station's docking bay. "…we have significant work to do, so the sooner we begin, the better." He turned back toward the six guards, gesturing abruptly for them to take the admiral away. He didn't say another word to Reichman, and he barely watched as the broken officer was shackled and led to a waiting transport.

"Yes, Admiral." The two officers answered almost as one. Then, they each turned toward a column of security troops waiting behind them, snapping out a series of commands and leading the soldiers toward two waiting shuttles. They had over one hundred arrests to make on the ships of the home system forces…and when they were done, every vessel and orbital fortress around Megara would be under the control of Whitten's loyalists.

Those who had sabotaged his career, who had done him so much harm…they would now endure their own trials.

Chapter Sixteen

CFS Dauntless
Entering Olyus System
En Route to Megara, Olyus III
Year 316 AC

"We haven't received clearance from ground control yet, Admiral." Barron listened as Cumberland's voice crackled through the shuttle's comm speaker. "If you just wait a…"

"I don't know what's going on down there, Commander, but I've got to find out. I'll have a much better chance to get somewhere with that down on the surface in someone's face rather than jousting over the comm with some mid-level officer." He paused, just for a second. "Launch."

There was a brief hesitation, just long enough that Barron knew Cumberland wanted to argue with him but held his tongue. "Yes, Admiral."

Barron turned toward the shuttle's pilot and nodded, just as the launch authorization light lit up a bright green. He should probably have been sitting in the back of the ship, in the far plusher main cabin of the admiral's cutter. But he'd decided to go down alone, or as close to alone as he could get, and he'd always considered the luxury of the cutter a bit over the top. Truth be told, he was far more comfortable up in the cockpit, sitting next to the pilot.

He knew the officer at the controls, at least he was pretty sure he could remember the man's name. Barron had known every crew member of the old *Dauntless*, but now that his responsibilities had moved up the chain of command, he found it impossible to keep track of everyone under him. Jake Stockton usually flew him around, or one of the other aces of the squadrons, but Barron had left them all behind to fight the Hegemony. He fought back the thought poking around the edge of his mind… *you left them there to die.*

The pilot glanced over at Barron for about the tenth time. The young officer was clearly nervous to be flying an officer of such exalted rank, much less the famous Tyler Barron. Barron could see his edginess, and he smiled and nodded, doing his best to ease the pressure.

"It's just a quick trip down to the surface, Lieutenant. The easiest run you've taken in some time, I imagine." Though Barron wondered how many difficult flights the pilot had made. Any at all? He'd left most of the experienced shuttle pilots with Eaton's fleet as well, and if this was the best Cumberland had found to take him down to the surface, there wasn't much in the way of experienced flight personnel left on *Dauntless*.

"Yes, sir." The pilot tried to return Barron's smile, and then he turned toward the forward screen, and he flipped a series of switches, activating the engines. "Shuttle Alpha-One… launching."

Barron could feel the force as the ship blasted down the bay, and then out into the blackness of Megara's orbital space. Normal protocol would be to dock with one of the stations before landing, but Barron didn't have any time to waste. He'd come back home to report a crisis, and when he'd gotten to Dannith, he'd found something that looked an awful lot like another one. The trip to the capital had been an interminable one, even at *Dauntless*'s maximum acceleration, and he'd left behind three of the five ships he'd brought back from the White Fleet. Two because they couldn't match the thrust of the flagship, and one because it was even faster than *Dauntless*…and he'd sent it on a very important mission, one in its own way as vital as his to

Megara.

He didn't know what kind of trouble Holsten had found his way into, but he couldn't imagine it was anything too serious. Or, at least, not something he and Striker couldn't deal with together, combining their clout…and the still quite considerable power of the Barron name.

He did believe that, mostly…but there was a feeling in his stomach that told him he had doubts.

I will get to the bottom of everything…as soon as I get down to the surface…

* * *

"Launch." Whitten stood in the middle of the control center of Megara's largest orbital fortress, known as Prime Base. It was a monument to Confederation industrial might, a twenty-kilometer long bastion filled with fighter bays and bristling with weapons.

"Sir…that's Admiral Barron's shuttle. Are you…"

"I issued a command, Lieutenant, not a request for opinions. Launch at once."

The officer looked uncertain. The ceaseless barrage of news stories about corruption and treason had continued, and the spacers on the station were in various stages of confusion, denial, and anger. Some had begun to resent Barron, to believe the stories that had begun to spread about him, and even his grandfather. But most, like the flight control officer, didn't seem to know what to think. Tyler Barron was a hero…and worship of heroes died slowly.

"Launching, Admiral." He paused for another few seconds, but then he flipped a row of four controls…sending the launch instructions to four separate squadrons, the duty wing…and by almost any measure, overkill to intercept a single, unarmed cutter.

The station was so immense, even the vibration of sixty fighters blasting down the catapults couldn't be felt in the control center. A few seconds later, however, the small clusters of dots appeared on the main screen. Whitten watched, and then his eyes moved toward the single triangle he knew was Barron's cutter, a smile forming on his lips as he focused on the tiny symbol. Barron had never done anything to him personally, but Whitten, too, had been the descendant of Confederation heroes…and he'd had to watch as all the rewards, all the positions and commands that should rightfully have been his, went to Barron. He could barely restrain his glee at the prospect of seeing the navy's beloved darling in shackles, disgraced and under arrest.

He turned and moved back toward his chair, sitting down and watching.

Watching the decline and fall of Tyler Barron.

* * *

"Get this off of me!" Her voice was scratchy, low in tone, but she put more energy into it and shouted again. And then again. A confusing swirl of thoughts and impulses were moving through her mind, but impatience was at the top of the list.

She looked around, uncertain of where she was. She was in some kind of body-sized canister. *A medpod.*

What the hell am I doing in a medpod?

"Get me the hell out of—"

"I'm here…I'm here…" The voice was familiar, but she couldn't quite place it. She was conscious, but her head was fuzzy, and her thoughts clouded. "Atara…my God…Atara…"

A man walked up next to the pod, a broad smile on his face. He was tall, with long brown hair. She knew him. But the name eluded her.

"Atara…please, lay still. I have to check your readouts." The man turned, yelling toward the space outside the alcove, calling for assistance.

"Why am I here? What's happening? Get me out of this thing, now. I mean—"

"Please, Atara…just remain calm. You've been in a coma for almost four months. You're on *Dauntless*, in a medpod. Now, if you'll just lay back and stay calm, I can check you out."

Dauntless…

Yes, her ship. She was on her ship. "Tyler…"

The admiral isn't here, Atara. He's on his way down to the surface." A pause. "We're orbiting Megara."

Travis was silent for a few seconds, absorbing what she'd just been told. *Yes, Dauntless. Megara? No, Dauntless is with the White Fleet. They were…*

Her memories started flooding back, comprehension forming almost faster than she could keep up with it. The epidemic. Her blood.

"Stu…" She recognized the face above her now. Stu Weldon, *Dauntless*'s chief surgeon.

"Yes…very good, Atara. And your vitals are good as well, almost shockingly so. I need to run a complete battery of tests on you, but I'm very optimistic. Your recovery has been nothing short of miraculous." She could hear the gratitude in his voice, and she began to remember everything that had happened. He'd also blamed himself for what had happened to her. He had developed the serum that could save so many of the fleet's people. The serum that had required her blood.

"Not your fault, Stu…" She remembered giving the blood, so much blood…and then nothing. "Did it work? Did we save them?"

"Yes, Atara…it worked. Everyone we treated recovered."

She managed a frail smile. "That's good." She sighed softly, suddenly realizing how tired and weak she was. "Why are we at Megara?"

Weldon hesitated. "Admiral Barron brought us back to report on the Hegemony…to warn the fleet and the Confederation of the new danger."

The Hegemony…another flood of memories returned, and Travis lurched up again. "The Hegemony. Yes…how did we get away? Is the whole fleet here? Have we—"

"Please, Atara…I'll tell you everything, but first let me finish checking out your condition." He paused as he looked at more of the readouts. "It's amazing…you're almost fully recovered."

He hesitated again and then added, "I have to tell you…for a while, I wasn't sure you were going to make it."

"Well, I did." She smiled again. "And this pod is damned uncomfortable, so can you please finish up and get me the hell out of here?"

*   *   *

"I repeat…you are ordered to alter course at once and return with us to Prime Base. If you resist, your vessel will be disabled and boarded."

Barron sat looking at the cutter's main screen, almost in shock. He'd heard the order repeated, and the same words moved through his mind, defying his ability to comprehend them. He wasn't in battle, wasn't at some distant system. He was orbiting the Confederation's capital…and someone was ordering him to surrender.

He looked over at his pilot who, if anything, looked even more in shock. Then he grabbed the comm controls. "This is Admiral Tyler Barron. I have urgent business in Troyus City, and I do not have time to waste. This must be some kind of mistake. If this is about my not waiting for final clearance, I…"

"You are to return to Prime Base with us, Admiral." The officer paused, a hint of confusion and tension in his voice as he added, "There is no mistake, Admiral Barron. Come with us now." Then, a few seconds later, "Please."

Barron looked at the pilot again, realizing almost immediately that the rookie was going to be no help at all. He couldn't imagine what Jake Stockton would have been doing just then, the torrent of invective he would have launched at the wing commander…probably before threatening to somehow shoot down all sixty fighters with the unarmed cutter.

Why would four squadrons come after us anyway? Over a failure to gain clearance? None of it makes any sense. Unless…

For a few terrifying, unimaginable seconds, he wondered if the Hegemony forces had somehow gotten there before him… but that was impossible.

"Who is this?" He wasn't sure if he was trying to get to the bottom of things, or just playing for time until he could figure out what was happening.

"I'm Commander Calvin Dougherty, Admiral. I'm afraid I'm acting on the direct orders of Fleetcom Olyus, Admiral Whitten. I must insist that you comply at once. My orders are very clear."

Whitten?

Barron knew the officer, of course, and his family. *But Whitten isn't Fleetcom Olyus…Irwin Reichman is…*

He sat for a few seconds, staring at the comm unit without words. He'd been worried enough about the people he'd left behind, the looming threat of a deadly new enemy…and then he'd discovered that Gary Holsten had been arrested and taken back to Megara.

Now there were four squadrons of fighters threatening open fire on his cutter. None of it made any sense. If he'd been anywhere else, in foreign space, on a battlefront, he'd have found a way to resist…but he was home, orbiting the Confederation's capital. Resistance would be treason. Defending himself, even if it were possible, would mean killing comrades.

Wouldn't it?

"Admiral, I'm sorry, but you must comply. Now."

Barron sat, watching as the squadrons took position all around the cutter…and for the first time he could recall, he had utterly no idea what to do.

*   *   *

"You're weak, and some actual food would probably do wonders for you, but your condition is nothing short of amazing, Atara. I'll want to monitor you for a couple days, of course, and you'll need to revise your normal exercise routines, work your way back up to where you were—you're down about nine kilos of muscle mass—but, otherwise, I don't see any…"

The sickbay lights picked up a reddish cast, as *Dauntless*'s battle stations lamps snapped on.

Travis lurched up, reaching out and grabbing onto the rails alongside the bed to catch herself, as a wave of dizziness almost overtook her.

"You can't move like that, Atara…not so quickly. Not yet. Don't make me sorry I took you out of the pod." He turned, looking back toward the main area of sickbay. There was considerable confusion, and multiple voices calling out. "Stay here… I'll go find out what's happening." Weldon had just started back to the main bay when one of the techs walked by. "Carlson, what's the alert?"

"It's the admiral's cutter, Doctor." The woman was clearly unnerved. "A wing of fighters has taken up position around it. They're demanding he surrender himself."

"What? That's not possible."

Travis sat up again, a bit more deliberately than the previous time.

"I need you to stay in bed, Atara."

"The admiral's in some kind of trouble, Stu…it's going to take more than you to keep me in this bed." She shifted, letting her legs slip off the edge, and paused for a few seconds, taking a breath to steady herself.

"Atara, please…"

"I'm fine, Doc…you said so yourself…and this looks like some kind of emergency." The truth was, Travis couldn't think of any reason garrison forces from Megara would come after Barron. It didn't make any sense at all. Even on the frontier, she could imagine various all sorts of issues…but on the capital?

She pushed herself off the edge of the bed…and her legs almost buckled as her feet hit the floor. She grabbed onto the rails and managed to keep herself up.

"Atara…"

"We're not going to discuss this anymore, Doc. I am still *Dauntless*'s commanding officer, or have I been relieved?"

"No, you weren't relieved, but…"

"Well, we're in some kind of trouble, that much is clear enough. So, are you going to help me? Or are you going to stand there acting like nursemaiding your patients is the only thing that matters in the galaxy?" She slowly let go of the railings, finding her balance—tentatively—and taking a small step.

Weldon stood where he was, looking conflicted. But Travis gave him one more hard stare, and he gave in. "Fine, Atara...I'll help you to the bridge...but you have to promise me after this crisis is over, you'll come back here. You need fluids, prophylactic antibiotics and antivirals...and you need more rest. A lot more."

"I've been resting for four months, Doc." But she had to admit, she did feel shaky. She looked back at him. "Fine, I promise. Once whatever is happening is resolved, I'll come back and let you poke and probe me all you want." She paused. "Now, will you help me, or do I have to crawl up to the bridge myself?"

Chapter Seventeen

Battleship Danais
Barbaricum System 2703 (Unknown System 20)
Year of Renewal 260 (316 AC)

The chamber was large, its ceiling very high, especially by the standards of space vessels. It was dimly lit by a series of small lamps. The walls were covered with large, curved screens, showing the dispositions of the fleet and of the enemy forces. The enemy ships, which had been fleeing for so long, had slowed and were now apparently offering battle.

There were five people in the room, each seated atop his or her own large pedestal chair, rising several meters above the spotless gray deck. They were clad in fine clothes of a silky material, in shades of gold and white…the uniforms of their service's high command.

The two men and three women were all Masters, the genetically superior beings that ruled over the Hegemony with unquestioned dominance. The ship and the fleet surrounding it were mostly crewed with Inferiors, predominantly the Red Kriegeri. They had been cultivated from the various worlds of the Hegemony, chosen for their genetic suitability for their role. The Inferiors chosen for fleet duty were among the most intelligent beings to be found in the Hegemony, outside of the caste of Masters itself. Among their ranks were even bloodlines once of Master class, which had fallen below minimum standards through careless breeding.

The Hegemony's system was rigid, and no doubt, to beings observing it from without, brutal…but it was unerringly fair in its own way. It was a pure genetic meritocracy. Leaders unquestioningly gave way when a superior genetic specimen turned up to take their post. Even the Highest, the supreme ruler of the entire Hegemony—and thus, by their doctrine, of all human habitation—held her position solely on the strength of her genetic rating. When a new Master came of age who had bested her in that regard, she would stand aside without rancor or resistance, as he whom she had displaced had done.

The society was one virtually without dispute or political rancor. The dedication to genetic excellence was held above all things, and no deviation from that standard was tolerated. Even Inferiors could see their children rise to Master status with careful programs of mate selection.

The Hegemony had risen up near to the center of mankind's previous, vast range of habitation, amid the ashes of the Cataclysm's worst horrors. In its early years, it had not yet achieved such comprehensive adherence to a single mode of thought. War had swept the systems it now occupied, all manner of groups struggling to seize the mantle of the dead empire. In the end it was genetics, the superiority of those who were to become the Masters, that had secured the peace…and eradicated all those who could not adapt. The founders of the Hegemony had built the new empire on a single creed, forged in the still-fresh memories of the Cataclysm. Never again.

The Rim-dwellers who had invaded the Hegemony were clearly inferior creatures…creatures of violence, dominated by the warlike drives that had destroyed the old empire. What little the Masters had been able to ascertain of their organizational structures suggested little or no adherence to genetic mandates for positions of power and authority. They were chaotic, wild, and for all their technology and power, they could not be allowed to spread their undisciplined ways and ideas across the galaxy. Their destruction—or at the very least, their absorption into the Hegemony as obedient Inferiors—was essential.

A beacon of light illuminated the man sitting on the far left, and he spoke. "The enemy fleet has slowed, and now seems to be offering battle. This is illogical. They have utilized their small attack craft with considerable skill to delay and damage our forces, but I do not believe they can defeat our fleet. They are either attempting some sort of trick, or there is some factor at play we have not yet discerned."

The light moved to the right, stopping on the woman one place from the end of the group. "I do not believe that they have chosen to fight at random...nor that they have any secret tactics. They have already utilized their one advantage, the small vessels. I see no logic in their having hidden another advantage so long, while allowing their small craft to be gradually eradicated. I believe that there is some reason they do not wish to continue with us following. It appears there are a minimum of two other warp tubes in the system, so they are not preparing to fight because they are trapped. Our mission was simply to follow, in case our assumption that they were trying to lead us away from their home system was incorrect. Perhaps it was, and we are now close to the enemy's home. They may be willing to face utter destruction here, rather than lead us to the others of their kind. We have seen some tendency toward selfless sacrifice in their conduct so far."

The beacon moved to the rightmost place, the occupant of which simply nodded, signaling her assent with the general consensus. Then the light focused on the central figure. This man was clad similarly to the others, though somewhat more elaborately. "I find your logic and deductions to be sound, and in agreement with my own. I am inclined to believe the scenario put forth by One Hundred-Sixty-Two, that we are, in fact, relatively close to the enemy's home systems."

The man paused a moment, silent, still. Then, he continued. "The second likelihood is that they wish to test us...for they have surely determined that we could have caught them earlier if we had wished."

The central figure paused again for a few seconds, the light remaining focused on him. Then he said, "Either options calls for us to attack, for there is no other way to force the enemy to reveal whether his intention is to fight to the death, or whether he is simply testing our resolve. If the enemy stands, we will have to determine if our interests are best served by eradicating the force we face…or pulling back and allowing some portion of it to survive."

The figure turned to the left, then to the right, looking at his companions. When he was done, he turned his head forward, staring straight ahead. "Let the orders be given. The fleet is to attack at once with full power. The battle line is to ignore the damage caused by the small craft and close on the enemy battleships without hesitation. It is only by destroying a large number of their major ships that we can determine whether they will stand and fight against all odds."

"So let it be," the others said, in nearly perfect unison.

*   *   *

"They're coming in, Commodore. You can see it in their formation. We should have launched already. You have to give us the order." Stockton's voice was loud in Eaton's headset. She could tell he was edgy, anxious…even more than usual. Eaton almost argued with him. But she didn't, and for one simple reason. Her strike force commander was right. The fighters were her biggest edge—likely her only one—and every minute she held them back only worsened the fleet's already dire position. Yet she found it difficult to issue the command. Once she gave that order, the fleet was committed. She would never be able to recover the squadrons in time and retreat…and she knew she could never leave them all behind and run.

Not that she could run anyway. She was fighting because she had no choice, because continuing on could only lead the enemy closer to the Confederation. Stellar geography had played the final joke on her, and stripped her of every choice save for suicidal combat.

If we're going to do this, we owe it to ourselves to hurt these bastards as much as we can. "You are authorized to launch all wings, Captain." She paused, sucking in a raspy breath. "Good luck, Raptor. Give them hell."

She listened to Stockton's acknowledgement without really hearing it. She tried to hope for the best, to retain some shred of optimism, but in her heart, she believed Jake Stockton and his pilots were launching their fighters for the last time. She'd analyzed and re-analyzed the enemy fleet, imagined countless tactics and battle plans…but her people were just outgunned. The enemy had more powerful weapons, longer ranges…and bigger and more ships. She could hurt them, perhaps badly… she was sure enough of that. But she couldn't win.

"Sonya…issue a fleet order. All ships are to increase reactor and battery output to one hundred ten percent. We're going to give these bastards everything we've got." She had made a concerted effort to speak formally to her sister on the bridge, ever since the younger Eaton had transferred from *Dauntless*. She'd used Sonya's rank when addressing her, and hid any emotion she felt looking across the few meters toward her sibling. Now she let that small bit of her iron discipline slide away. She believed they were both going to die in the hours to come…and she wouldn't deny either of them the last bit of closeness they would likely ever share.

"Yes, Admiral." Sonya's voice was crisp, sharp. Whatever fear she felt was clearly under firm control, and her determination to fight was utterly clear. Sara was proud of the woman and officer her sister had become, though she also felt a touch of sorrow that Sonya couldn't as easily repeat her own informality. Such things flowed far more easily down the chain of command than up.

Sara turned and looked around the bridge, wondering as she did what was truly going through the minds of her people. From the first moment she'd ordered her ships to set a course for unexplored space, they'd all known that their prospects were grim, that utter destruction was the likeliest end to their desperate flight. She also knew such things were easier to accept when they lay in the future, and far darker and more imposing when the moment was at last at hand. The crew looked normal, or close to it, focused on their stations, their duties. Still, she had a pretty good idea of the thoughts ripping through their minds… if only because they were in her own as well.

"All ships acknowledge, Admiral. They all report at battle stations and ready, power systems at one hundred ten percent." A short pause. "Six vessels report unable to comply fully due to battle damage. I've sent a list to your screen."

Sara glanced down, but she didn't really look. She knew the condition of every vessel in the fleet, and she was painfully aware of the six with reactor or power system damage.

She took a deep breath, watching as more and more tiny dots appeared in the display. Her squadrons, what was left of her exhausted and battered fighter corps, were moving out in front of the fleet, preparing to strike the enemy one more time.

But this time, they won't be fighting alone.

Chapter Eighteen

"Do what they say, Lieutenant." It went against Tyler Barron's very core to yield to an enemy. But right now he wasn't facing an enemy. He was in a shuttle high above the Confederation's capital, and the men and women threatening to fire on him were pilots serving the same navy he did. He didn't really have any options to fight or resist anyway…but he wasn't sure he would have used them, even if he did.

"Yes, sir." The pilot's voice was frail, shaky. Barron wondered how Stockton would have reacted if he'd been here, at the controls. Whatever his veteran fighter commander might have done, he realized the young pup of a pilot sitting next to him was well out of his depth.

"It's okay, son. Just follow their instructions and bring the ship into whatever bay they tell you to. I'm sure they'll let you go back as soon as I disembark."

Actually, Barron wasn't sure of anything at all. He was reacting, trying to defuse the situation…but he couldn't, for the life of him, imagine why he would be under arrest. He'd come back without most of his fleet, and he could see that provoking questions, even a board of inquiry in some instances…barring, of

133

course, the historic news he'd brought back. But four squadrons of fighters surrounding him like he was public enemy number one? It just didn't compute.

For an instant, he'd forgotten why he was even there at all. The Hegemony. He had the most vital and deadly piece of news, perhaps in all of Confederation history, and the people he'd come to warn were arresting him? He wondered if they would listen at all now to what he'd come to report, and a cold feeling went through him. He'd come all this way, left most of his people behind, to get the warning to the Senate. There wasn't time for…whatever this was. They had to listen to him, and they had to listen immediately.

He reached down to the comm. "This is Admiral Barron. I have instructed my pilot to follow all instructions. There will be no resistance." He was surprised at how difficult it was to say those words. He had to be careful now…if any kind of fight broke out, not only was his shuttle likely to be the first ship destroyed, but the confusion would wreak havoc on the delivery of the warning *Dauntless* had brought back to Megara.

Barron looked over at the pilot and nodded. Then he said, "I have news of extreme importance, a discovery made by the White Fleet that must be delivered to the Senate and the Admiralty at once. I request comm access to the current fleet commander, and to representatives of the Senate as soon as we land."

"I *am* the current fleet commander, Admiral…and you will see the Senate soon enough, I can assure you of that. But there can be no conditions to your surrender. You must land immediately…or action will be taken.

* * *

"No sign of him. Nor of his aide or his guards. Not even the transport he was riding." Bellingham was clearly frustrated, but there was something darker in his tone, and Peterson knew what it was. The major was starting to think that perhaps the charges against Striker were true, that the admiral had gone into hiding just ahead of the authorities.

Peterson understood that…it was what anyone might think. There had been no sign of violence, no evidence of any kind of struggle. The transport had been out on one of the busiest streets of Troyus City. He couldn't think of any explanation other than the apparent one. He didn't believe that, not for an instant, but he knew Striker well, and he was one of the most loyal—and stubborn—cusses in the Corps. If someone like Bellingham was starting to have doubts…

"We just haven't found the evidence that will lead to the truth yet, Hank. It's out there, I know it is. Van Striker is no more a criminal and a traitor than I am." He *did* believe that… but he also understood why his friend was less convinced. He was trying to think of something else reassuring to say when he saw Kate Britten walking into the room. Striker's aide looked haggard, exhausted, like she hadn't had any sleep in three days… which he suspected she hadn't.

"Colonel, may I speak with you for a moment?" She'd walked up right to Peterson, coming as close as she could without it looking strange. Her tone was hushed. Clearly, she didn't want anyone else to know what she was saying.

"Of course, Commander." He looked expectantly toward her.

"Not here, Colonel." She turned her head, looking quickly in both directions. "Let's go into the admiral's office."

Peterson nodded, and when she turned and walked down the hall toward Striker's door, he gestured for Bellingham to wait where he was.

Britten took another look around, and then she opened the door and slipped inside, closing it as soon as Peterson entered.

"What is it, Commander?" From what Peterson had seen of Britten in the past weeks, she was a no nonsense officer, and one who was utterly loyal to Striker.

"I think I've discovered something…it may not seem like much, but it's difficult to explain."

"Tell me, Commander. At this point, I'm looking for any scrap to go on."

"Well, Colonel…the day the admiral left, he went down to the front of the building to get his transport. That isn't normal procedure. Admiral Striker usually comes and goes from the subterranean level…for security reasons."

"That makes sense." The streets of Troyus City in midday weren't particularly dangerous, especially in the middle of the well-policed government district, but Striker was—or had been until the day before—the navy's top commander. A certain amount of caution made sense in his comings and goings.

"He used the front entrance because we had gotten a notification that the underground facilities would be closed for maintenance." She paused. "I didn't think anything of it at the time." Peterson could hear guilt in her tone, or at least self-admonishment. "After the admiral disappeared, I checked the notification more carefully. It *did* come from the operations office…and every other department I checked received it as well."

Peterson had felt a burst of hope that Britten had found a clue, but then it slipped away. "That was a good thought anyway, Comm…"

"That's not it, Colonel." Britten looked right at him. "I almost left it at that, but I couldn't find anything else…and I *knew* there had to be *something*. So I checked with the maintenance teams to find out what work had shut down the whole underground level…and it turns out there was no work done at all."

Peterson's eyes widened. "None?"

"None. I checked with the main maintenance office, and with each individual crew chief. Not only do none of them have any idea what work was done on the subterranean levels… every on duty maintenance technician is fully accounted for elsewhere." She paused. "Someone in the operations office issued that memorandum…but its purpose wasn't to keep the lower level clear for maintenance work. Something else was at play."

Peterson looked at Britten, and he realized he was nodding. Striker's aide was on to something, he was sure of it. He wasn't sure yet where to go from there, but he no longer had any doubts about one thing.

Van Striker hadn't run away from any bogus charges. He had been abducted.

*   *   *

"Scramble all squadrons…now!" Atara Travis stormed onto the bridge from the lift, if a woman hunched over, leaning on a powered cane as she hobbled forth could be described as "storming." The officers on the bridge turned and looked over at her, seemingly in utter shock. As far as any of them were concerned, she was down in sickbay in a coma, as she had been for months.

"Yes, everyone, I'm awake…I'm back. We'll have to save the welcome ceremonies for later, though. We've got a problem here, and it looks like a big one. The Admiral's in trouble, so let's do what we have to do to help him. I want those fighters in the tubes…right now."

There was still a pause, despite the urgency of her words. Finally, Cumberland looked over at her and cleared his throat. "Captain…I'm happy to see you." He wasn't stammering, exactly, but he was still clearly unnerved by Travis's sudden appearance. "I'm sorry…but, we don't have any fighters aboard. Admiral Barron ordered them all to remain behind with the fleet."

"With the fleet?" Travis suddenly realized she had missed months of activity, and she really had no idea what was happening. But she knew her friend was in trouble, and that he needed her. Nothing else was important now. She'd catch up on the rest later.

She shuffled over toward the command chair and let herself drop into it with clear relief. Her faculties had come back to her, mostly, but her body was lagging. She'd lost weight and muscle mass, and despite the medpod's application of electrical stimulation to her muscles and nervous system, she was weak and stiff. She put that out of her mind, and she looked over at the main display.

"Range to Prime Base?"

"Approximately one hundred four kilometers, Captain."

Cumberland had more or less adapted to her presence, but her question clearly surprised him.

"Activate primary batteries…full override procedures. I want those guns charged up as quickly as possible."

Cumberland paused…and then understanding flashed on his face. "Yes, Admiral." It was hard for Atara to tell from his tone whether he was excited…or terrified. Or, more likely, some combination of the two.

"Primaries charging, Captain."

Travis looked across the bridge toward the row of readouts that tracked the battleship's heavy weapons. The small bars were moving to the right, slowly, about a tenth of the way so far.

"Get me Prime Base on the comm, Commander."

"Yes, Captain." A moment later. "Admiral Whitten on your line."

She nodded and reached down to grab the headset. "Captain Travis here, sir," she said, after she pulled the unit over her head. "There must be some kind of mistake. That is Admiral Barron's cutter out there, sir. Those fighters…"

"There is no mistake, Captain. Admiral Barron is accused of being part of a treasonous conspiracy, along with Admiral Striker and many other officers. There is a Senatorial arrest warrant outstanding for him, and the fighter squadrons from this base are simply executing it. You are not to interfere, Captain… is that understood? *Dauntless* will stand down and await further instructions."

She heard the words. At least they entered her auditory canal and her brain processed the meaning…but they still didn't make sense. If she'd been told Barron had punched an officious fellow officer—someone like Whitten, for example—or that he'd refused to carry out some kind of outrageous order, she'd have believed it. Barron had always been a maverick thinly disguised as part of the establishment. But part of a treasonous conspiracy? She'd have bet her life that wasn't the case.

"Admiral, that's not possible. Admiral Barron is a war hero, commander of the White Fleet, a…"

"He is a traitor, Captain…and unless you want to give up

your own bars and join him in the stockade, I advise you to obey my orders immediately."

A flood of responses poured into her mind, most of them composed of the foulest curse words in her repertoire. Whitten was exactly the type of entitled, pompous fool she most detested. She held it all back, forced herself to stay respectful, to wait. To buy time…

Her eyes darted back toward the monitors tracking the primaries. Eighty percent charged. *I need more time, twenty seconds…*

"Admiral…"

"Captain, we are reading *Dauntless*'s energy buildup. You are to shut down all weapons and reduce reactor output to normal levels immediately…or you will be guilty of mutiny, and you will endanger every man and woman on *Dauntless*."

"Captain, Prime Base is charging up its port batteries." Cumberland was clearly unnerved, but he was holding himself together, barely.

Travis gasped for a breath, struggling to maintain her focus. The exhaustion was pulling at her, trying to drag her from the showdown she faced. She regretted not ordering Weldon to give her a dose of stims before she'd left sickbay…and then she wondered if she'd had a chance of him obeying that command. By her estimation, she'd barely gotten herself out of sickbay as it was.

"Admiral…"

"There will be no further discussion, Captain. You will obey my command at once, or you and your crew will face the consequences."

Travis turned her head slowly, flashing a glance toward some of the nearby workstations. The bridge was silent, and she had no doubt every member of the crew was well aware of the tension, the danger stalking them all. Were they defiant, ready to face whatever came…or about to rise up and remove the lunatic sitting in the command chair, leading them to treason?

She put the crew out of her mind—they would stand with her or not, there wasn't much she could do to influence that. She thought about Whitten, trying to gauge her adversary. She

didn't know him well, and from what she did know, he was a useless fop, another damned fool who'd been born into his privilege and had never earned a bit of it. She'd always hated pander-
ing to officers of his type, obeying their orders and feigning a
respect she could never truly feel. This miserable scrap of lucky
sperm wanted her to betray her best friend…and there was no
way she was going to do that. Not for him.

Not for anyone.

She checked the monitor. Ninety-two percent.

Prime Base was enormous, packed with as much weaponry
as a battle fleet. But Whitten was bluffing, and Travis knew it.
She had the jump on him. *Dauntless*'s guns would be ready to
fire before any of the base's weapons could be. A single battleship would normally have no chance against a base the size of
Prime…but *Dauntless* was already in orbit, barely one hundred
kilometers from the huge platform. She couldn't even imagine
the destructive force of *Dauntless*'s primaries at so close a range,
one unheard of in space combat. She was willing to bet one
direct hit would be enough to turn even that monstrous construction into a ball of expanding plasma.

There was no way *Dauntless*'s gunners were going to miss
something that big and immobile at one hundred kilometers.
She'd have bet her life on that, too.

In fact, she suspected she was about to do just that.

She took a deep breath, steeling herself to deliver a final ulti-
matum to the admiral. She wasn't going to yield, but she knew
the order she might have to give would kill thousands of fleet
personnel…and she still wasn't sure she could make herself do
that.

She looked over at the weapons readouts, just as the glowing bars moved across the final few millimeters, and the yellow
lights at the end illuminated.

The primaries were ready to fire.

Chapter Nineteen

"We've only got one clean run this time, so let's make it count. I want all squadrons' attacks synchronized. We're going to hit these bastards with seven hundred eight plasma torpedoes, all in a stretch of two minutes' time." Stockton wasn't even sure that level of synchronization was possible, even for his veteran pilots.

But he was going to find out.

His fighters were crammed together, at least in the terms applying to space combat. Actually, not one of his ships was less than ten kilometers from another. The concentration, and the number of warheads he intended to hurl at each of the chosen targets, was unprecedented. It was a formation that would have been impossible if his forces had faced enemy fighters... but that was the one advantage the White Fleet had in this fight. And "Raptor" Stockton was the man to make the most of it.

He checked off as the acknowledgements came in. He'd reordered the strike force, combining shattered squadrons to create units that were full strength, or nearly so...and then he'd organized his craft into fifteen makeshift wings, each tasked with attacking a single enemy battleship.

He hadn't targeted just any enemy ships, either...he'd picked

141

the fifteen biggest, the ones he knew had heavy railguns. He wasn't sure how many his people could take out in a single assault, or how many of the enemy's primary guns they could disable, but he had the targets in his mind.

Fifteen.

Every last stinking one of them.

He wasn't sure there were no other railguns in the Hegemony fleet. In fact, he suspected there almost certainly were. His audacious attack was the best way he could think of to knock out the maximum amount of enemy firepower. Taking out most of the enemy railguns wouldn't equalize the technology or firepower of the two sides. It wouldn't even give the White Fleet a fighting chance in the battle, but it would be the closest he could come to achieving that goal.

He'd taken his fourteen most experienced veterans, and he'd placed each in command of a wing. The fifteenth he commanded himself. That last force had been cobbled together from what remained of the old *Dauntless*'s strike force—Blue squadron, his first command, and the other units he'd led after Kyle Jamison's death…including his old friend and rival's Scarlet Eagles.

He'd had to add other squadrons to the mix as well. Far too few of the old *Dauntless*'s pilots had survived the ship's final battles…and yet Stockton could see them all in his mind—and his heart—men and women who'd fought at his side, and who had fallen, in so many battles he could hardly keep track of them all.

He'd made one other change, after his close call of some week's before. He'd appointed an official second in command, Olya Federov. She was the clear choice. Apart from kill rates and years of service, she was, in his mind, the best pilot and, more importantly, the most capable leader, he had. She hadn't had to lead the squadrons out during his brief incapacity, nothing more than routine patrols, but now that he considered it, he had no doubt she could have handled any crisis that had arisen, perhaps every bit as well as he could. He'd always walked a thin line balancing ego and skill. He was a talented and experienced pilot, but no amount of pure capability could have made him do the insane things he'd had to do. But he had to admit that Olya was up to the challenge of replacing him if it came to that.

He glanced at the scan, at the circles representing the ships of the fleet. The vagaries of transit point geography had played a vicious trick on the fleet, turning its heroic run across a vast gulf of empty space into a route back, almost directly toward the Confederation. The fleet couldn't go any farther, not without leading the enemy home. Not unless they wiped out the Hegemony forces on their tails.

Even at his craziest, Stockton knew that was impossible.

His eyes shifted to the cloud of tiny dots moving steadily away from the fleet, closer to the Hegemony ships lined up along the top of the screen. He looked over at the range display, checking the time until his forces would reach engagement range. Even before he saw the numbers, his gut had done the calculation for him…and hit the target almost exactly.

Sixteen minutes.

He checked the formations of his wings, snapping out a few navigational orders to shift the squadrons until they were exactly where he wanted them. When he was finished, he checked again.

Eight minutes thirty seconds.

He was ready. His people were ready, as they always were. But one thing was different this time. His desperate flight back to *Repulse*, his crash landing and narrow escape from death, had stripped him of the veneer of casual invincibility in which he'd cloaked himself since *Dauntless* had left the fleet.

Stockton was leading his ships into battle. And for the first time, he knew that he might—probably would—die.

* * *

"All ships, commence navigation plan Sigma." Sonya Eaton repeated her sister's orders, directing the ships of the fleet to activate their engines and move toward the approaching enemy ships. Concepts like "approaching" were somewhat relative, of course. The White Fleet was still moving toward the destination system at considerable velocity, and the enemy's approach was the result of its own higher speed gradually reducing the distance between the two forces. Eaton's orders would result in greater thrust applied to deceleration, reducing the fleet's velocity and increasing the relative rate of approach of the Hegemony forces.

The fleet had been running since the very instant *Dauntless* had left to return to the Confederation with its warning. But as far as Sara Eaton was concerned, the time for running was over. She couldn't flee anymore, not without leading the enemy closer to Confederation space. And that she would never do.

"All ships acknowledge, Admiral." Sonya Eaton turned and looked back at the admiral. The navy had always discouraged close relatives serving together, and certainly in a direct commander-subordinate situation, but the fleet had come well beyond any normal situation, and Tyler Barron himself had approved the younger Eaton's transfer from a position as his aide to the same role under her sister.

"Very well, Commander." Sara Eaton's voice was cold, hard. She was a veteran commander, one who had seen some of the worst fighting the Union War had produced. But there was something different now—something that had been present in all her earlier fights, no matter how desperate, that was gone now. Hope.

Eaton knew this would be the fleet's last battle. It had to be. There was nowhere to go. Her only escape route would be a betrayal of the entire Confederation. She knew the enemy would likely explore the systems beyond after the fleet was destroyed...but, with any luck, it would take them considerable time to find the correct path. Hopefully that time would be enough for Barron to rally the Confederation. To get ready to meet the coming danger.

"All battleships...I want primaries charged and ready to fire the instant we enter range." The Confederation primaries were deadly weapons, and they could badly damage even the advanced Hegemony ships. They were long-ranged weapons, but she knew her ships would have to pass through the fire of the enemy's railguns before they would be able to shoot...and not all of her vessels would make it through that deadly assault, not with their fragile primaries still online.

She could feel the thrust from *Repulse*'s engines, not the g-forces exactly—the ship's dampeners were fully adjusting for that—but she'd always been able to pick up the artificiality of the force offsets that hid the thrust pressures, mostly because they always made her just a little bit nauseous.

She'd ordered the fleet forward, moving up right on the heels of her fighter strike. She wanted to enter the range of the enemy's railguns the instant after Stockton's fighters had gone in… and knocked out as many as they could. She didn't want to give the Hegemony time to make any repairs, recover from any disorder. Her line would hit theirs right after the squadrons…and then they would fight.

They would fight until the end.

* * *

Stockton brought his fighter around, adjusting his angle of attack to match the target ship's thrust. He'd never seen anything he could characterize as fear or nervousness in the enemy, not until now. It was clear the giant battleship was trying to evade the incoming fighter assault, and the slight taste of weakness inflamed Stockton's inner predator.

"Stay with me," he snapped into the comm. He was set to the wing channel, and right now, his focus was on the seventy-three ships lined up behind his own. He commanded the entire strike force, but he'd given his orders, and he'd resolved to trust the fourteen men and women he had placed in charge of those unit, pilots with whom he'd fought countless battles. They deserved his trust, and he was going to give it to them.

"We're not letting them get away." Stockton knew that was easier said than done. The Hegemony ships had tremendous thrust capacities, not enough, perhaps, to escape from a perfectly-executed fighter attack…but damned close. There wasn't any room for carelessness or mistakes.

Stockton looked back at the screen, his eyes focusing on

the small numbers next to the glowing red circle. The enemy's thrust output and vector.

He tapped the controls again, adjusting his course slightly, and then he cranked his thrust up almost to full power. The enemy captain had performed well, his evasive maneuvers well planned and executed. Against most adversaries, he might very well have succeeded in moving his ship away from the incoming attack. But the Hegemony officer wasn't facing just any commander, and against Jake Stockton, his brilliant maneuver had been just a touch too late.

Stockton watched as his ship responded to his actions, almost flawlessly. The formation wiggled slightly, a few seconds' delay before his people adapted to his abrupt moves, and then it tightened again…no more than two minutes from launch.

The fighters were already well within conventional range, but Stockton wasn't leading a normal assault. Throughout the running fight from system to system, he'd led his people to ranges so close they were previously unheard of…and this attack would be no different.

"Hold those torpedoes, all of you. No one fires outside one thousand kilometers…and any of you who hold to under three hundred, I'll polish your boots when we get back."

Three hundred kilometers was a nearly impossible range for ships traveling at such high velocity, but there wasn't much chance of anybody making it back to the fleet anyway. He wasn't likely to do much polishing, however brilliantly his people performed.

He could hear the banter on the wing's channel, the boasts of pilots, the friendly taunts of just how each one wanted his boots done. Whatever the chances were that he'd have to pay up, Stockton had accomplished what he wanted. What he needed. His pilots were ready.

He turned his attention to the screen, and the ship looming up ahead of him. He wanted to check the other scans, see how his other fourteen wings were fairing…but that was a luxury he knew he couldn't afford. There was nothing he could do to help any of them now.

He brought his ship around, adjusting his vector slightly every few seconds to match the increasingly frantic evasive maneuvers of the Hegemony vessel. For all the dire grimness of the situation, a smile slipped onto his face as he watched his enemy become more and more desperate. As huge as the enemy ship was, he knew his wing had enough firepower to destroy it... as long as they all stayed focused and planted their bombs just the way they had planned.

He was close now, less than three thousand kilometers. He'd lost eight ships so far to the enemy's defensive fire. That was a light toll, especially for an attack at such intensely close range, but it hurt nevertheless. They all hurt.

He tried to imagine what an enemy combat space patrol would have done to seventy unescorted bombers closing to such range. It almost defied comprehension, and he suspected no more than a few of his people would have made it to the designated launch point.

Instead of the more than sixty that were with him as he closed the final distance. Two more of his vessels vanished from the screen—and he himself barely dodged an incoming shot—but he realized the wing had made it intact. It was time to launch.

He adjusted his targeting one last time, and he brought his ship in below five hundred kilometers. He almost fired, but after his challenge to his people, he knew he *had* to launch from below three hundred. He'd blurted out the figure almost without thinking about it, and now he wondered, if it was even possible. Or, at least, possible without slamming into the target right after the torpedo was launched.

He didn't have time to think about it for more than a fraction of a second. His eyes were dead on the target, his hands moving almost robotically. His shot would be a combination of mathematics, experience, focus...and gut feel. He felt his finger tightening. The resistance of the trigger gave way, and his ship shook with the release of the torpedo.

It took every bit of his veteran discipline to ignore the shot he'd just made, to focus instead on getting his ship the hell out of there. He pulled the controls hard, blasting every bit of thrust his fighter had to offer…and for some portion of that instant, he wasn't sure if he was going to make it.

Then he saw the blackness of open space ahead of him. He'd cleared the enemy battleship by seven hundred meters, and the sweat pouring down his back, and from his hairline onto his face, was a testament to just how close he'd come to turning himself into a deadly projectile.

He took a ragged breath, and he struggled to regain his composure, to push away the trembling that had taken his arms and legs. He'd survived by a fraction of a second. How much of a fraction, he didn't know.

He didn't want to know.

It seemed like an eternity before he was back in total control, though he knew in reality it was only a few seconds. Then he turned toward the targeting display, confirming what he'd somehow known already in his gut.

He'd planted the torpedo right into the center of the enemy ship. He'd launched at two hundred-twenty-nine kilometers. He looked again, double checking that astonishing range, almost certainly the closest ever for such an attack. Then he looked at the scanning display, concerned for an instant he had been *too* close, that the torpedo hadn't had time to convert to a plasma before it impacted. But the damage readings coming in removed any doubt.

Even as the realization sunk in that he'd scored a direct hit, he saw the rest of his ships coming in. They'd all followed him in to the insane range, or close to it, and another seven had fallen to enemy defensive fire at such short distances. But the rest began to launch.

Most of them fired at ranges from seven hundred to one thousand, but more than one followed Stockton's lead, clearly gunning for the boot polishing and the glory that would go along with it.

Stockton watched as he brought his ship around, counting off…and ultimately reaching six pairs of boots that would be waiting for him back on *Repulse*. He smiled, hoping against hope that he had the chance to clean those boots, and the pilots who own them the chance to wear them again.

He should have had seven pairs to polish...but the last attacking ship came in just a bit too fast, held on an instant too long. The pilot had clearly been out to beat Stockton's two hundred-twenty-nine kilometers...and he had done just that, closing to two hundred-eighteen.

But he'd paid dearly for those eleven kilometers, and he'd missed his pullout, slamming into the enemy ship at a velocity of better than eight hundred kilometers per second, and adding even more impact to his heroic assault.

Chapter Twenty

Cilian Globus sat quietly on his chair in the center of *Fortiter*'s command center. The battleship's bridge was a fairly cramped space by comparison to the seemingly immense volumes devoted to the bridges and control rooms of the Confederation's vessels. The Palatians considered themselves a warrior race, and their ships of war were spartan affairs, with as little mass as possible devoted to comfort and other frivolities.

Despite the generally cramped nature of the ship, Globus, as a Commander-Altum, the supreme leader of a battle fleet, had his own private retreat. An office of sorts, or perhaps a space better described as a private study. It was just off the bridge, in almost the same spot the Confeds put their—considerably larger—versions of the same thing. Globus wanted to be there, he longed for the quiet, the solitude…but he also knew his place was to be seen by his officers. They, too, were officers of the Alliance, each sworn to the same standards of duty and perseverance as he was, but they had all seen the Hegemony forces, and they were not fools. They understood the magnitude of the White Fleet's discovery…and the conflict it likely portended. Even for men and women sworn to Palatian standards, there was bound to be doubt. Even fear.

The struggle was likely to come upon the Confederation first, that power's misfortune in terms of interstellar geography. But Globus had no illusions of where the Alliance would stand if the Confeds were defeated, and he didn't think many of his officers did either.

Globus was a man of honor, and as far as he was concerned, he had promised Tyler Barron he would fight at his side in the coming struggle. If the Alliance failed to come to the Confederation's aid, Globus would resign his commissions and take his place at Barron's side as a volunteer...cleaning compartments of radioactive waste if that was the only way he could contribute. But Globus didn't think that would happen. Vian Tulus was the Alliance's Imperator, and a man who owed his very position to Confederation assistance. He considered Tyler Barron a blood brother.

The Alliance wasn't an autocracy, of course, and the decision to rally to the Confeds' aid wasn't Tulus's alone. Nevertheless, the Imperator carried great weight, and it would take a significant bloc of the greatest families to successfully oppose him. Globus didn't doubt the Alliance would side with its allies in the end. He was just concerned about how quickly that could happen.

The Alliance had fought a terrible civil war, one that had ravaged its fleet and its warrior classes...and the survivors had fought alongside the Confeds against the Union, losing yet more ships in the last battle against the Pulsar. The Palatians were devoted almost entirely to martial strength, but Globus knew the fleet was in as parlous a state as it had seen in half a century, and the massive efforts to rebuild were far from complete. Not many Palatians would argue to stay out of the coming war...but Globus was afraid more than a few would lobby to move slowly, to wait while new ships rolled off the assembly lines and fresh spacers graduated from the academies.

Globus feared the calls for delay for a number of reasons, not the least of which because it seemed a logical strategy. He had no evidence of Hegemony forces actually moving on the Confederation...for that matter, he barely had enough to prove the enemy existed at all. If Confederation worlds were ablaze, their systems falling to invasion, he didn't doubt his people would respond. But it would be difficult to argue against those who called for caution when the threat seemed ephemeral, or at least distant.

"Commander, I have...the Imperator on the line for you." The officer at the comm station was a veteran, one who had served with Globus for many years, but he was clearly unnerved. It was highly irregular for the Imperator to communicate with an approaching ship, and utterly unheard of for him to be on the initial transmission, speaking to a mere comm officer.

Globus was surprised as well...and then less so, as he thought about it. Vian Tulus had once been as steeped in old tradition as any Palatian officer, but his service alongside Tarkus Vennius, and Tyler Barron and the Confeds, had changed him significantly. He'd reluctantly taken the Imperator's scepter after Vennius's death, and when he'd done it, he'd vowed to rule by combining the best of the Palatian and Confederation cultures. The informality on display suggested he had stayed true to his promise.

"Your Supremacy...it is an honor to be addressed first by you." Globus wasn't sure exactly what else to say.

"Welcome home, Commander Globus. I am pleased to see you return...and yet somewhat surprised. You were not expected for quite some time."

"That is true, Your Supremacy. I return with news...vital news that I must deliver to you directly, as soon as possible."

"I suspected just that when the outer scanners confirmed *Fortiter* had transited. So, let us not waste any time. What have you returned to report?"

Globus hesitated. He wanted to tell Tulus, to share the burden of what he knew. But he didn't want to speak over an open comm line, not even an encrypted one. He wasn't sure there was a need for secrecy, and he didn't suspect news of a new enemy would cause any widespread panic, certainly not among Palatia's warrior-citizens. But he felt discretion was wise anyway.

"Your Supremacy, with all due respect, I would prefer to wait until I am in your presence to discuss the news I bring."

There was a short pause before Tulus answered...and when he did, it was clear from his tone he was concerned. "Of course, Commander. *Fortiter* is cleared for immediate approach, and a detachment of my guard will be waiting to bring you to me as soon as you land."

"Thank you, Your Supremacy."

Globus sat for an instant after hearing the click of the line closing. He'd thought of almost nothing for weeks except for reaching home and warning the Imperator.

Now, he realized, he still had no idea what he was going to say.

* * *

Globus walked down the aisle, his freshly-polished boots cracking loudly on the gleaming marble floor as he approached the Imperator. The main reception room was vast, an impressive piece of architecture Globus's Palatian pride would put up against anything he'd seen on his travels. But there was something missing, in terms of the magnitude of his recollections of past moments in the room.

Imperator Tulus had clearly done what he could to reduce the pointless pomp and frill of the Alliance court. Globus could tell that by the vastly smaller number of people present in the room...and the miniscule size of the guard detachment on duty. Aside from the two troopers leading him forward, there was a pair flanking Tulus's seat, and another two at the main entrance. Globus could remember when there would be fifty or more guards on duty when the Imperator was present...and that was *before* the civil war.

He suspected the general reduction in ceremony was partially behind the force reductions, but he also imagined Tulus was responding as much to that internecine conflict, sending out a message of trust to the officers and warriors accepted back after the civil war. Many of the defeated Reds had been executed, but only those who had refused to yield and swear allegiance to the new regime, then headed by Tarkus Vennius. The others had been welcomed back and absolved of their misdeeds, and, while that had caused some bitterness among warriors who'd fought on the Gray side, Globus himself had come to recognize the wisdom of Vennius's mercy. Most of the Reds had served innocently, in pursuit of what they had perceived at the time as the right and legal choice.

Vennius had been a far wiser ruler than anyone had expected from the grizzled warrior, but, tragically, he had not long survived his ascension, falling during the Krillian War less than two years later. It had been left to Tulus, a man who'd been shocked when Vennius's final testament specified him as the chosen successor—and even more so when the great families largely supported his elevation—to complete the healing process his esteemed predecessor had begun.

Globus stepped up to the end of the aisle, standing at rigid attention less than three meters from Tulus's seat. Then he bowed, remaining silent by custom until the Imperator spoke.

"Rise, Cilian Globus, honored commander…and come forward. Let us not waste time on idle ceremony. Walk with me to my chambers, old friend." Tulus got up, startling the guards around him until he gestured for them to remain in place. "Cilian is a man who has saved my life in battle. I will meet with him alone, without the need for guards. I would not dishonor him by suggesting I need protection in his presence." There was Palatian honor in his words, but past Imperators had rarely met alone and unguarded with anyone.

The warriors didn't look happy, but they obeyed the Imperator's commands and stood where they were, maintaining their rigid and respectful poses.

"Come, Cilian…" Tulus ignored the guards, and the quiet rustle of commentary among the gathered courtiers, and he reached out his hand to grasp Globus's. "Let us have a long talk, such as we have not had in some time."

Globus wasn't really surprised at Tulus's informality…though perhaps he found it a touch unexpected not to be. He'd known what Tulus had intended to do, the changes to procedure and ceremony and other reforms he'd planned to implement. Still, it was still startling to see the reality of it all in place so quickly. Globus suspected Tulus had used the disruption still remaining from the civil war to his advantage, pushing changes through far more quickly than would normally have been possible.

He followed Tulus to a room Globus had visited on many occasions, and one he remembered as being considerably more ornate than it was now. He recalled tapestries all along the now mostly clean gray walls, and several collections of captured standards and banners that had once lain on both sides of the entrance.

"Have a seat, Cilian." He had clearly noticed Globus's eyes darting around the room. "Yes, I removed much of the decoration. The battle trophies are now in the new War Museum, where they belong, and much of the other trappings are in storage, awaiting use elsewhere. I have not rejected our peoples' mementoes of victory, but I have continued Vennius's work of restoring the Imperator's office to what it was in the earliest days of the Alliance…a supreme military commander, not a monarch surrounded by gilded trappings." He paused a moment and smiled. "Nevertheless, I can assure you, old friend, that the chairs are as comfortable as ever." Tulus sat down himself, not behind the large wood desk, but on one of a pair of facing sofas sitting in front of a hearth with a roaring fire.

"I'm afraid my simplification efforts fell a bit short on the hearth, however. I find the warmth of seasoned West Hills hardwood soothes the pains of my war wounds, and the soft crackling relaxes me when little else serves to do so. It is a bit of softness in one who considers himself a warrior, I confess, but I like to imagine it is a fairly harmless one." He noticed that Globus was still standing. "Sit, my friend…please."

Globus sat on the facing sofa. He was glad to see a comrade of so many years, and he wished they could just sit and discuss old battles and catch up on family histories…but he had far grimmer business to discuss with the Imperator. And he still had no idea how to begin.

"Your Supremacy…I bring dark news, word of a new enemy.

A deadly and dangerous one."

Chapter Twenty-One

High Orbit
Planet Megara, Olyus III
Year 316 AC

"All squadrons, you are to break off from the cutter and return to base…*immediately.*" Atara Travis was fighting off grogginess, struggling to stay sharp as fatigue closed on her from all sides. She'd awakened from her coma less than an hour before—and emerged right into the middle of a crisis. She'd practically had to threaten to space Stu Weldon to get the doctor to let her out of sickbay…and she acknowledged to herself that "let" was a strong word for what he'd done. He had restrained himself from tackling her to keep her there. That was a bit more accurate.

She knew she shouldn't be on *Dauntless*'s bridge, for her own good, and also because there was no way she was up to handling a crisis like the one unfolding. However much she pushed herself, she wasn't in a condition to command the battleship. But Tyler was in trouble, and if anyone wanted her off the bridge, they'd better bring a platoon of armored Marines with them.

"Commander…" She turned toward Cumberland and stared with a withering intensity. "…lock all primaries on Prime Base." Her voice was cold, and her eyes shone with a frigid glow. She'd never commanded Cumberland directly before, though she

knew the officer fairly well. And he knew her. She wasn't sure
he'd obey her in the current situation…but she figured there was
a chance. "We've got to help the admiral," she added, figuring it
might push Cumberland over the edge.

"Yes, Captain," the officer said after a lengthy hesitation. He
paused again, for long enough that Travis thought he was going
to disobey her. But then he turned toward the comm unit and
said, "Gunnery station…lock onto Prime Base."

Travis wasn't sure the gunners would obey either. She was
struggling to keep her thoughts clear, but there was no haziness
about the fact that she was threatening to fire at a Confederation
base. Not any base, but the main fortress that protected the capital. It was an almost unimaginable situation, a standoff made
possible only because *Dauntless* had been allowed to approach in
order to dock. Her ship floated in the capital's orbit, the base
in her sights at a range so short, the very idea that her people
might miss was an absurdity. No enemy would ever get so close
to Megara, not without a titanic battle.

Prime Base had been designed as a major part of the capital's
defense system. It was heavily armored and armed to the teeth,
intended to take on an entire task force of battleships approaching Megara. But at *Dauntless*'s range, its hundreds of millions of
tons of steel would crumble into useless debris at a single shot,
melted and deformed chunks sliding down into the atmosphere.
Prime's crew of nearly twenty thousand would be killed, likely
to a man, almost instantly…and flaming debris would descend
all over the heavily populated planet, no doubt vastly increasing
the death toll.

Atara Travis would become the most notorious traitor in
Confederation history. She wasn't sure *she* could give the final
order, not even for Tyler Barron. The one thing she did know
was she could take the bluff to the very end…and see what
those on the other end of the comm were made of.

"Captain Travis, this is Admiral Whitten. I am expressly
ordering you to stand down, to deactivate your weapons, and to
allow the fighters currently deployed to complete their mission.
This is the last time I will issue this order, Captain. It you wish

to retain your rank and avoid a court martial, you will obey it to the letter."

Travis listened to the words, and though she could tell Whitten was trying to sound tough, she could sense the fear in his voice. She didn't know much about the new commander of Megara's defenses, but what she did know was far from impressive. She was taking a horrible chance, possible throwing her career down the drain, but her gut told her she could stare him down.

"Admiral…"

"Atara, you are to stand down at once. Deactivate the primaries and follow Admiral Whitten's orders."

The words came through the speakers on *Dauntless*'s bridge, and she recognized the voice instantly.

"Tyler…" She didn't know what to say. She wasn't sure firing on a friendly base was in her, but she was positive disobeying Barron *wasn't*. Still, the thought of allowing him to be taken prisoner over what *had* to be false charges…

"It's okay, Atara. I'll be fine." A pause, and then his voice was more emotional. "I can't tell you how glad I am to hear your voice, my old friend. I'm stunned, and I don't understand…but I'm happy. Welcome back."

"Enough. Captain Travis, you have your orders." It was Whitten again, a hint more courage in his voice now that Barron had voiced his willingness to yield.

Travis sat where she was, stunned, uncertain what to do. She realized there were tears streaming down her face, and she ached to talk to Barron in person, to hear his voice again, see him. She knew what she had to do. It was a relief in some ways…and agonizing pain in others.

She looked across the bridge, her eyes meeting Cumberland's. "Disarm all weapons, Commander. Reduce power output to normal levels."

"Yes, Captain." Travis had figured the order would come as a relief to her people, one that absolved them of the choice between mutiny and treason. But Cumberland's tone was somber, and every pair of eyes on the bridge was downcast. *Daunt-*

less's crew were devoted to their admiral, and she realized they were all feeling the same thing she was.

Travis just watched as Barron's cutter headed toward the station, disappearing into one of the landing bays. She was silent for a moment, and then she looked down at her screen, confirming the inter-ship comm lines were all closed.

She'd obeyed Barron's orders, allowed Whitten to take the admiral prisoner…but she was damned if she would leave it at that. She didn't know how long she'd have command of *Dauntless*…Whitten might relieve her immediately for what she'd almost done, or even because she was medically unfit for active duty. But she was on the bridge now, and the foppish admiral in charge of Prime Base would have his hands full with Barron.

She didn't intend to waste a moment.

"Commander…I want the entire research section at work. Access all Megara information nets. I want to know what's going on, why Admiral Barron was arrested."

"Yes, Captain." She could hear the energy in Cumberland's voice, and she knew immediately the aide was with her one hundred percent.

"All of you," she said, turning and looking around the bridge, waving her hand. "Any data you can find, however insignificant it may seem, get it to me immediately."

"Yes, Captain." Half a dozen versions of the acknowledgement came back at her, every one of them infused with a new energy. *Dauntless*'s crew might not have been ready to open fire on their Confederation comrades, but one thing was unmistakably clear.

They weren't willing to give up on their admiral either.

* * *

"I don't know what you expect to get from me, Lille, but it's never going to happen. So you might as well just shoot me in the head now and start another war." Van Striker sat on a hard chunk of concrete, all that was left of what looked like some kind of pillar or structural support long since replaced.

His body ached in a dozen places, though the only torture he'd received so far had been the incredibly invasive—and painful—search for tracking devices. He'd tried to tell them he had none, but they hadn't believed him, as, of course, he'd known they wouldn't.

His cuts and incisions had been bound up fairly well, with a degree of cleanliness that had surprised him. He'd expected rough treatment, and while he'd certainly gotten that, his captors appeared to want him alive, at least for a while longer. That meant they hoped to get something from him. For all the bluster of his words, he was deathly afraid that once they really started working on him, he would give them whatever they wanted. Striker considered himself a tough nut, but he wasn't arrogant enough to believe he couldn't be cracked. He realized his captors had come startlingly close to breaking him with the search for scanning devices.

If anyone could break him, it had to be Ricard Lille. The thought of what the Union assassin must have done to his victims over the years terrified Striker, a man who did not quickly feel fear.

"I don't want anything from you, Admiral. Not right now. I don't expect to need anything from you at all, save having you out of the way while…other things…are transpiring. Though perhaps sometime in the future we may discuss things like naval dispositions and production manifests. I don't anticipate renewed hostilities between our nations anytime soon, but preparedness is always worthwhile."

Striker almost responded, but then he held back his words. Lille's voice was almost pleasant, and Striker found that grated on him more than the direst threat and foulest invective would have. But it was the agent's reference to "other things" that truly twisted his gut.

"Other things?" he said, regretting it almost immediately.

"Yes, Admiral. There are some activities going on right now I believe you would find most intriguing, were I to share the details with you. But I think not. There's nothing you could do to stop any of it, of course, but I see no gain in being careless with details. You'll just have to be patient, Admiral. I assure you, it's worth the wait." Lille smiled. "I can promise you that I will tell you before…" Lille's voice stopped there. He didn't have to finish. Striker didn't know what was going on, but he knew his captors would never release him. Could never. If word got out that Sector Nine agents had kidnapped the Confederation naval commander, the outcry would be deafening. The people of the Confederation, war weary as they were, would demand immediate action. Whatever scheme Sector Nine was up to—and it couldn't be good—Striker couldn't imagine that the Union could be ready for war again any time soon.

So what are they doing now?

He tried to think of it, to figure out what could be happening, but he kept coming up with nothing.

Almost nothing. He suspected Gary Holsten's disappearance had something to do with it. He'd been sure the Senate had Holsten, that the secret deliberations had involved the Intelligence chief somehow…but now he wondered if Lille and his Sector Nine cronies had taken the intelligence chief as well.

The more he thought about it, the sicker he felt.

                              *   *   *

"I haven't been able to find out much, Andi…not beyond the news stories." Vig stood under a small stand of trees in one of Troyus City's many small parks. Fully a third of the ground area of the Confederation's capital city was dedicated to greenspace and recreational areas, a fact that sounded high-minded until one realized that the vast majority of those who lived in the breathtakingly expensive metropolis were government officials and highly-placed executives and financiers. Troyus City's beauty had more to do with those in charge creating a virtual paradise around themselves than for any civic responsibility or obligation to the Confederation's poor and middle classes.

"There has to be someone who knows something." Andi was frustrated. She'd come to Megara expecting to have trouble discovering anything…and she'd arrived to a tidal wave of newscasts announcing Holsten's conviction on a staggering list of criminal offenses. She'd had to hear it three times before it had sunk in, and she still struggled to understand it. There had been a mistake, almost certainly. Gary Holsten wasn't one who respected rules, perhaps even no more than she did. But he wasn't a thief or a conspirator who would steal billions of credits from the military budgets. She'd have bet her life on that.

Perhaps, she realized, she was doing just that. She'd upped the intensity of her search efforts, and she knew that could draw attention to her…attention that could catch the interest of dangerous people. But that wasn't going to stop her. Things like that never had.

Her first thought had been to find Admiral Striker, to see what he knew about Holsten. She'd been a little worried about talking her way past security at the Admiralty, but when she got there, she'd found her name on a list of people to admit at all times. She'd been excited to see Striker, both to find out the latest on Holsten, and because she missed the admiral and considered him one of her closest friends. But she didn't see end up seeing him at all. Instead, one of his aides, Commander Britten, came to see her along with a pair of Marine officers— none other than Jon Peterson and his second in command. And instead of telling her where Striker was, they had hoped she could tell them. That was how she'd found out that Striker, too, was missing…just a few hours before stories hit the news about the admiral's alleged involvement in Holsten's corruptions.

Listening to those broadcasts, watching politicians and news anchors demonize two of her closest friends, and two men she'd seen risk their lives for the Confederation countless times, infuriated her. Her goal to find and kill Ricard Lille burned as intently as ever, but to it she now added finding Striker and Holsten, and helping to defeat whatever plot was in effect against them.

She conferred with Britten and the Marines, told them what little she knew of Holsten's arrest on Dannith, and agreed they should all work together…as quietly and unobtrusively as possible. She'd realized already that Megara was not like Dannith, that strolling into bars and roughing up local miscreants wasn't likely to accomplish much in the capital except perhaps landing her in a cell somewhere. So she'd switched over to the other tool she had now, one she imagined would fit in perfectly among the political dealings and high finance of Troyus. Money.

Andi was a vastly wealthy woman, a fact that still seemed foreign to her and had suddenly come to mind when she was trying to think of how to proceed. The interstellar banking system didn't allow instant interplanetary transfer of funds, at least not the massive amounts she had in mind, but with a bit of effort, she had managed to build up a substantial war chest, which she used to bribe every sleazy information broker and political influence peddler she could find.

It had been an inefficient use of funds, certainly, and one she'd found frustrating, especially when Troyus City's level of law enforcement denied her the tactics she usually employed against those who cheated her. In the end, she simply wrote off the unproductive bribes as a cost of doing business and reminded herself even the few million credits she'd spread around the capital was just a small bit of her vast fortune. A treasure she'd fought for all her life and, to her own stunned surprise, the one she cared less and less about. She didn't long to return to her days of miserable poverty, but now she realized those had long been gone from her life…and were unlikely to return.

"It just can't be a coincidence that Lille is on Megara somewhere, so soon after Holsten was brought here." She was sitting in a room in her hotel suite, with Britten and Jon Peterson also at the table. They'd all agreed that whoever was behind what was happening almost certainly had some eyes in the Admiralty, so Andi had rented the largest suite at the Grand Hotel, and they'd turned it into their makeshift headquarters.

"No, Andi…I'm sure it's not a coincidence. That means this is more than just power politics in the Senate. The Union is somehow involved…and that means *trouble*." Britten shook her head as she spoke, and the frown on her face became even grimmer.

"That means war." Peterson's voice was gruff, his anger far

less concealed than Britten's. If the Union has been interfering in Senate politics, that's a blatant act of war. If they abducted… or worse…Admiral Striker or Gary…" He hesitated. "This time, we'll do what we should have done two years ago. We'll blast those bastards back into the Stone Age." It was a Marine's answer, and one Andi agreed with…except she knew the problems they faced went far deeper.

"I wish it was that simple, Jon, but if they've got some kind of influence in the Senate, then we are really…"

"Andi…you've got to see this. *Now.*" Andi hadn't heard Vig's voice so unsettled in a long time. Her oldest friend was standing on the doorway, looking at her with genuine shock in his expression.

She leapt up from the table, the instincts of years of adventure kicking in. She walked, more of a jog actually, into the next room, and the instant her eyes focused on the vid, she froze and her blood ran cold.

"To repeat," the newscaster said, "CFS *Dauntless* has returned from its mission, considerably sooner than expected and without most of the White Fleet. In a surprising development, Admiral Tyler Barron has been arrested and is being held on suspicion of involvement in the growing military procurement scandal. The names drawn into this growing investigation have included some of the most beloved and famous military figures in the Confederation, and the addition of Admiral Barron, the grandson of the legendary savior of the Second Union War, to this list is without a doubt the most startling of them all. Again, Tyler Barron, arrested and due to appear before the Senate to be charged in the growing scandal."

Andi just stood where she was, stunned, unable to focus her thoughts. *Tyler is back?*

Arrested?

It didn't seem possible.

She was sure Holsten and Striker were innocent…but there wasn't any doubt at all in her mind that Tyler was uninvolved in any illegal activity. He'd spend most of his days at the front, and the bulk of his free time with her. He'd never had much use for the vast Barron wealth, much less a drive to obtain more by betraying the spacers he loved. She'd been worried enough about what was happening before…now, she knew something truly dire was unfolding.

And Lille *had* to be deeply involved in it.

She felt the rage taking control of her. She had to help Tyler…she had to rescue him, before some kangaroo court put on a fraudulent trial and shipped him off to a penal planet.

Or worse.

"Colonel Peterson…you said you brought some of your Marines with you. How loyal are they? Will they do *anything* you order them to do?"

Chapter Twenty-Two

Bridge
CFS Repulse
Unknown System 20
Year 316 AC

"The battle line will open fire on my command." Sara Eaton was in her chair, leaning forward, her body tight and tense. It was something she hadn't been able to fight off, despite the fact that it only exacerbated the pain from her old war wounds. She'd fought many battles, and she'd escaped some by the slimmest of margins, but she'd never been as sure as she was now that she was fighting her final one. She was determined to make every shot count, to sell her life and those of her loyal spacers as dearly as possible.

"Yes, Admiral…all gunnery stations are standing by. All primary batteries fully charged and ready to fire."

The enemy fleet had already opened fire, their heavy railguns exceeding the range even of the Confederation's deadly primaries. Those Hegemony weapons had been deadly, and they had nearly crippled two of her battleships with their opening shots. Only two things kept the enemy from using their superior weapons to obliterate her line before she even got into range. First, the enemy weapons took longer to recharge even than Eaton's primaries, making their fire devastating, but slow.

And, second, Jake Stockton and his fighters had launched a withering attack against the enemy's largest ships, destroying eight of their fifteen targets outright, and leaving only two with functioning railguns. To those two survivors had been added another two vessels the fighters hadn't attacked, cutting the number of railgun-armed enemy ships to four, at least in the enemy's forward line.

That was a deadly force by any measure, and every shot they fired took a horrendous toll. But Eaton had pushed her ships forward with close to maximum thrust, reducing the number of attacks the enemy would get before her people could open up and return the fire. Even as she sat calmly in her chair, waiting for the line to enter range, she thought about the unimaginable destruction her ships would have endured without Stockton's heroic attack.

The fighters had paid dearly for the damage they had done, most of their losses coming as they closed beyond point blank range. They had attacked with a level of vicious aggression Eaton had rarely seen before…if ever. By the time the squadrons had completed their assault, they had lost no fewer than one hundred of their number…and then Stockton had rallied them and led them back in to do what damage they could with their lasers.

Eaton had almost ordered Stockton to call off the second attack, not to lose more of his people for the small amount of damage they could do without their heavy payloads. But she had nowhere else for them to go. Every mothership she had was about to enter combat range, and there was no way they could recover their squadrons when fighting against an enemy like the one they faced. She'd almost ordered a repeat of the supply shuttle operation that had refit the squadrons in the previous system, but she'd lost too many of the small ships, as well as the freighters that carried the fighters' fuel and weaponry. The White Fleet was rapidly reaching depletion. Whatever happened in the next hours, her ability to support fighter operations in any way was almost at an end. She might be able to mount one more all-out assault, assuming her battleships survived long enough to get the chance, but that was all.

She stared at the screen, her focus unbroken despite the thoughts of her pilots drifting through her mind. She watched as the icons on the display finally moved into range…but she held back.

She'd been counting since the enemy had last fired its railguns. She had no intention of waiting until they got another shot, and possibly knocked out more of her own batteries, but she was damned sure going to use every second she had to lessen the range for her opening shot. The first attack had to be as effective as possible, and she knew every thousand kilometers her ships traveled would increase the hit rate, and the number of enemy ships damaged and destroyed.

She was counting softly under her breath as she tried to decide just how closely she wanted to cut it. She figured she had twenty seconds for sure, maybe as many as forty. The gambler in her told her to wait, to push it to the brink…but she knew the odds didn't favor that option.

"All batteries…open fire." Her tone was calm, her voice soft, almost as though she was ordering some routine maintenance procedure instead of directing nearly eighty massive particle accelerators to fire as one.

She watched as the small yellow lines flashed across the display, depicting the various shots tearing out from her ships. *Repulse*'s own lights blinked as the giant weapons briefly sucked up virtually every watt the battleship's reactors could produce.

She waited as the AI processed the raw scanning data and determined how many shots had connected…and prepared estimates of the damage they had done.

Repulse had hit with three of its four primaries, every one of the beams slamming into a single Hegemony ship that had already been ravaged by Stockton's fighter squadrons. Eaton stared at the screen, waiting for the AI assessment to come through. She didn't have to wait long. The small circle floating in the main display expanded to three times its normal size… and then it winked out entirely.

The readings on the screen left no doubt what had happened. The enemy ship had been one of the railgun-armed vessels, and while the heavy weapons had been knocked out already, Eaton knew it still held the antimatter pods that powered the massive gun. One of the primaries had likely sliced open an antimatter storage facility, allowing the volatile material to mix with regular matter and annihilate in a spectacular explosion that utterly obliterated the ship.

Eaton felt a burst of excitement, like she had in so many in other battles, watching her spacers perform with their usual professionalism and courage. *Repulse*'s first shot had drawn blood, taken down a ship millions of tons larger than the Confederation's most immense battleship. It was a tremendous first volley, and as she checked the row of screens on the far wall, she could see her entire line had done well. No fewer than forty percent of the shots fired had been hits, an astonishingly good result at long range.

The Hegemony had fought against the fleet's fighters for several months now, but they were still inexperienced at close quarters combat against the Confederation's battleships. Eaton knew the enemy's tech was a cut above her fleet's…but they'd have to show her more than they had so far before she'd concede that same honor to their crews. Her people were the best spacers she'd ever seen, veterans, and deadly serious when facing an enemy. They might be overwhelmed and destroyed, but the Hegemony forces that defeated them would never forget the cost they paid for their "victory."

She grabbed the sides of her chair as *Repulse* shook. For an instant, she feared the flagship had been hit by one of the enemy railguns, but then she realized the jolt hadn't been hard enough…and a quick view of the screens showed that the enemy didn't have many of the big weapons still in action, not in their forward task force…and perhaps none at all. It seemed like the powerful guns were somewhat like the Confederation primaries in many ways, powerful but fragile.

Even as she looked over at the displays, she saw the countdown moving into single digits. *Repulse*'s primaries were still online…and as she saw the "one" replaced by a "zero," she knew they were ready to fire again. No more than a second or two later, the bridge lights darkened again, and her flagship cut loose with its deadly beams once more.

And scored another hit.

Then the ship rolled again, harder this time, and sparks flew from a series of conduits running down the far wall. The lights went out, and they stayed out this time for perhaps twenty seconds before power was partially restored.

Repulse paid for the hit it had just scored, taking one of its own.

She could see her bridge officers scrambling at their stations, trying to determine what was working and what wasn't. Eaton was already on the comm to Fritz. Of all the tools she had to prolong this fight, Anya Fritz was at the top of the list. *Dauntless*'s old chief engineer had long been a legend in the fleet, and her ability to get shattered systems back online was regarded as nothing short of magical. Things had gotten to the point where captains wrestled with each other to secure engineers who'd served alongside Fritz at some point in their careers, hoping some of what she clearly possessed had rubbed off on them.

From all Eaton had heard over the years, the consensus was that some of it generally had.

"It wasn't a railgun hit, Commodore. Just one of their heavy beams, but it caught us in a vulnerable spot. We've got some reactor damage—probably a thirty percent reduction in power output, at least for a while—but most of the rest of it is severed lines and the like. We've lost the primaries, and I don't think we're going to get them back in this fight, but otherwise, we'll keep her going."

Eaton was nodding as Fritz spoke, amazed at how she somehow knew so much about *Repulse*'s status just seconds after the hit. "All right, Captain…don't waste any more time talking to me. Do what you can."

Eaton heard the line click off, and she turned back toward the scanners. The screens had all gone down after the hit, but most of them had booted up again. *Repulse* didn't have her primaries anymore, but a quick glance at the display confirmed what Eaton had already known.

The secondaries were in range now.

The primaries were *Repulse*'s heaviest guns, but she only had four of them. There were eighteen secondaries lining each side of the battleship, and combined, they dished out as much damage as the great particle accelerators, even more. At least at close range.

"Engine room…I want another 2g thrust, now. We're going down their throats." She nodded as her sister acknowledged the order, and then a few seconds later, as she passed it on to the engine room.

She felt the increase in g-forces for a few seconds before most of it disappeared. The dampeners were still online, but they were clearly damaged, their response time and overall effectiveness degraded. But none of that mattered. Her people would endure the g-forces with no offsets if they had to. A small malfunction was nothing of consequence, not to her veterans.

A quick look at her screen told her two of the starboard secondaries had also been knocked out. That left sixteen ready to go. By any measure, that was a powerful broadside.

"Secondary batteries…commence fire."

*   *   *

"All right, all of you. This is why we're still out here. We've got damaged ships all around now. As long as they're still there, as long as their reactors are producing energy, they're a threat to the fleet. You all showed just how close in you could bring those Lightnings on your torpedo runs…and now you're going to do it again. Our lasers won't do much to the undamaged hulls of those things, but if you can plant a shot through one of the breaches…well, now we're talking. Those are hard shots, we all know that, damned hard. So, let's not waste time talking about it. Let's just get it done. Because, Goddammit, we're going in again." Stockton slapped his hand down on the comm controls, shutting down the channel. He didn't want his people chattering now, sending him acknowledgements or getting each other

whipped up for battle. If they weren't there now, if the devastating attack they'd delivered moments before didn't have them
pumped up to the edge of madness already, nothing would.
Now, he wanted them focused, no thoughts in their mind except
delivering death to those who had chased them through a dozen
systems, who had killed so many of their comrades. Those who
were still killing their friends, and tearing apart the motherships
that were their only way home.

He brought his own fighter around. Isolated groups of ships
were moving in already, benefiting from their positions closer to
potential targets. Every fighter was connected to the fleet data-
net, and for all the Hegemony's technology, they didn't appear
to have anything jamming communications. That meant every
one of his fighters had the full data on damage assessments, the
complete information the fleet possessed on just where those
hulking battleships had been most hurt by the plasma torpedoes
and the fleet's primaries.

Stockton was the type of commander who preferred to lead
in an attack, but now he held back, watching as the closer fighters zoomed up on the target vessels. He stared at the screen,
matching up clusters of fighters with damaged enemy ships, trying to direct his people to where they had the best chance of
hurting Hegemony vessels.

He watched his first group, nine fighters, led by a veteran
squadron commander. The ships streaked across his screen,
closing rapidly on the target battleship. The Hegemony vessel
was shooting at the approaching fleet, but Stockton could see its
rate of fire was well under fifty percent, and from its movement,
he guessed its engines were at less than half of normal capacity
as well. It was still a danger to the fleet, a considerable one, but
it was also a cripple of sorts, and its hull was covered with deep
gashes.

The fighters flew directly toward the ship, dodging the few
point defense turrets still firing. Stockton could see immediately that the pilots were disregarding evasive maneuvers, driving
straight toward the target. It was a bold move, even reckless,
but one that would make precise targeting easier. The defensive

fire was far lighter than it had been when the first attack went in, a function, he suspected, of both damage and attention to the capital ships the vessel now faced. Still, one of his fighters winked off the screen. He reached out, ready to increase power to his scanners, to see if the pilot had managed to eject…but then he decided he didn't want to know. His gut told him he wouldn't like the answer, and he preferred to keep a sliver of hope alive, even if it was only ignorance supporting it.

His eyes went back to watching the other eight birds zooming in, slipping under one thousand kilometers. Stockton was impressed at the mettle of his pilots, at their seeming disregard for danger. He suspected most of them knew they had little chance of ever making it home, and he imagined grim acceptance of that fact made reckless courage easier. Regardless, he didn't want to take away from the valor his people had shown… were showing.

The first two ships went in, closing to perhaps six hundred kilometers before opening fire. The lasers were powerful enough when fired at another fighter, but Stockton's scanners confirmed both shots had impacted on the vessel's intact armored hull… without any apparent damage.

He knew what they were trying to do was almost impossible…but he was sure about the "almost" since he himself had done it before. A ten-kilometer long battleship was a difficult enough target across the distances in space combat, but a hundred meter gash in the hull was almost microscopic by comparison. Still, it was the only way his people were going to do any more damage, so it was their objective. One quick look at the Confederation battle line, already at close range and still moving in, told him there would be no landings and refits, not in this battle. Not unless the enemy broke off.

Not likely…

Another three fighters finished their runs, none of them hitting one of the deep cuts in the hull. Stockton felt his stomach clench, his hopes start to dwindle, as he imagined all of his squadrons going in and getting the same results. Solid hits, but not the pinpoint shots they needed.

He tapped his controls, nudging his ship forward. *He wouldn't miss…he was sure of that.* But as he moved, blasting toward the ship currently under attack, he saw the next fighter score a hit.

A direct hit.

His scanners confirmed it…the pilot had landed the laser blast right into a deep hole on the ship's surface. A few seconds later, a huge plume of energy erupted out of the breach, tearing at the hull, widening the opening. New explosions followed and great blasts poured out into space.

Stockton felt a burst of excitement. The hit had done serious damage, and preliminary scans suggested another three turrets had been knocked out. But the battleship was still there, and it was still firing.

Then another fighter scored a hit. Stockton didn't know if the pilot had managed to target the original opening, or if the shot had slipped through where the gash had widened to more than twice its original size. He didn't care. The explosions were even heavier this time, and the ship rocked hard, its thrust slipping down almost to zero, and half its remaining guns going silent.

His people had that ship under control. They'd almost brought it down, like a pack of deadly predators stalking much larger prey. They didn't need him.

He looked around, his eyes finding another target, the next closest Hegemony battleship, damaged and limping along.

He felt his feral instincts running wild, and an evil smile slipped onto his face as he brought his ship around to pursue.

Chapter Twenty-Three

Senate Hall
Troyus City, Planet Megara, Olyus III
Year 316 AC

"It is with a regret I can barely express, Admiral Barron, that I read these charges, and formally begin your trial before this august body. Never in all my years in the Confederation Senate did I expect to stand before you, or any member of your famous family, and detail evidence of corruption so vile, greed so unrestrained, it falls little short of treason. I cannot find the words to state the emptiness I feel as I face the duty I simply cannot ignore." Ferrell stood in front of the assembled Senate, somberly clad in a dark suit, looking to all as though uttering the words came close to breaking his heart.

Tyler Barron sat quietly, calmly, watching the contemptible fool feign regret while inside he no doubt felt thrilled to be at the very center of the Confederation's affairs. Barron hadn't known much about Ferrell before he was arrested, and he hadn't had access to any significant information since, but he had been able to discover that the man had spent almost two decades as an almost nameless member of the Senate. In the past he'd no doubt been approached only when some bloc or another needed his vote, but otherwise treated with the disregard that had always attended his irrelevant home world. That, clearly, had changed.

"The past month has been a grim one for the Confederation, as what began as a scandal surrounding the actions of a single man has expanded to include well over one hundred of our highest-placed military officers and government officials. I know many of you wish not to be here to witness the travesties that the defendant and his cohorts have inflicted on a loyal and adoring population…but, my fellow Senators, it is our duty to see that justice is done, against the mighty and privileged no less than the common citizen."

Barron had tried to remain controlled, to hold his temper in check and not make the problem worse…but listening to Ferrell was testing his mettle in that regard. The man was a disgusting worm, and, perhaps worse, almost certainly caught up in the true criminality clearly taking place on Megara. Barron was concerned about his own situation, of course, but his worries went far beyond his personal position. Something disastrous was in play, and half the capable leaders in the military had been implicated in what he could only assume was some kind of massive fraud. To make matters worse, he'd been denied access to anyone…counsel, other officers, government officials. He'd come back to Megara to report on the Hegemony and the threat they represented…and no one he could reach would even listen.

He'd had one bit of good news since reaching the capital. Atara. She was out of her coma, and somehow up and around, at least enough to have taken command of *Dauntless*. After all the months of watching her lay motionless in the medpod, he couldn't quite make sense of such a rapid return to duty…until he started to remember Atara, and her unstoppable determination. Doc Weldon probably hadn't cleared her for duty, Barron realized. She'd just ignored him and marched up to the bridge herself.

Probably when she heard I was being arrested…

It was the one thing that had brought a smile to his lips since his arrest.

He still remembered their exchange on the comm, the cold menace in her voice, despite the weakness and fatigue that were there just as clearly. He didn't know if she would have fired on Prime Base, or if *Dauntless*'s gunners would even have obeyed such an order…probably not on either count. But he'd decided he couldn't take the chance. Such a course of action would only have made Atara and *Dauntless*'s crew outlaws—not to mention killing thousands of their comrades, most of whom Barron couldn't imagine were truly involved in whatever was going on.

He'd planned to get word back to her as soon as he was able to retain a counselor…but then he'd been denied even that basic liberty, his rights rescinded by a Senatorial Order he knew was illegal. But one that was enforced nevertheless.

He'd spent every hour he wasn't in the Senate chambers in a nine square meter room, a sequestered cell far from any visitors, or even other prisoners. In the cutter, yielding to Whitten's demand for surrender, he'd imagined he would be able to clear things up rather quickly, that there had been some kind of misunderstanding. Now he realized he had been set up, along with a whole list of other vital Confederation officers and officials. Something bad was happening…very bad, even without the reality that a deadly enemy was likely preparing to attack. He could barely control his restlessness, as he sat and listened to the pointless political prattle.

The worst thing was, he had no idea what to do about any of it.

*　*　*

"Captain Lafarge? May I have a word?" The man was well-dressed, handsome, looking in every way like some privileged Troyus City dandy. Everything Andi detested. She was about to tell him to disappear when he added, "I believe you know a friend of mine…Gary Holsten."

She felt her insides tense. She didn't know if the man was one of Holsten's people…or if he was trying to set her up somehow. Things had gone completely insane on Megara, and ever since she'd found out Barron was back—and also a prisoner—she'd struggled to concentrate, to try and figure out what to do. She wanted to help Tyler. She *had* to help him. Whatever the current state of their relationship, she'd admitted to herself long ago that she loved him. She wasn't going to let him end up framed for something he didn't do and sent to some prison out on the Far Rim. And as much as her focus had shifted to Barron's predicament, she was still determined to track down Lille, perhaps even more now, as she was sure the Sector Nine agent was behind the misfortune that had come upon Barron and Holsten. And probably the missing Van Striker as well.

"Gary Holsten is a criminal. He was tried by the Senate and found guilty." She felt guilty even saying the words, but she hadn't decided what the stranger was truly after, and she wasn't taking any chances.

"Yes, he was, Captain. For crimes he did not commit, something you know well." The man paused. "Gary told me you have a lovely home on Tellurus. He particularly liked the painting over the fireplace in the main reception room."

The words sliced right through her. Holsten *had* noticed the painting, and he'd commented on it. It was possible an enemy might be aware of that, but she wasn't sure how. She'd been leaning against trusting the man, but now, with a single sentence, he'd pulled her back.

"What do you want from me?" She was still cautious, but she'd made the decision to go along and see where things led. She and her cohorts had been struggling to find a way to help their friends…and she had to admit, for all the money she'd spread around, for all the efforts her Marine allies and Striker's aide had put in, they had made almost no progress.

"I work with Gary…I have for a long time." The man paused, and he looked all around the room before continuing. The bar was nearly empty, just two or three tables still occupied, all on the far end of the open space. "I am going to help him… and I would like you and your friends to help me." Another pause. "My name is Ethan Zacker. I've known Gary since we were children."

"I'd like to help him as well, Mr. Zacker…but I'm not sure what we can do. The Senate trial was conducted in secret, and he has been denied any right of appeal. I'm not sure who can clear up this mess."

"Only one man, in all likelihood, Captain. Gary himself."

"That's all well and good, Mr. Zacker...but Gary is in custody, and no one can get near him."

"That's true...but I have my sources, Captain...and I happen to know when he will be taken to the spaceport and placed on a secret transport to prison. Once he gets there, he will be lost, perhaps forever...but on the way to the spaceport..."

"You're suggesting we break him out?" She felt another wave of tension. Someone trying to entrap her might very well suggest the same thing, trying to get her to agree...and then arresting her on the spot.

But he knew about the painting...

"Yes, Captain...that's exactly what I am suggesting. I have, unfortunately been cut off from most of my resources. The Senate has appointed an interim director to run Confederation Intelligence until a permanent replacement is selected... and she is political creature, no ally of Gary's. If I draw on agency resources for this, at least overtly, we'll almost certainly be caught. I already know when he will be moved, and where."

"So, what do you need? Money?"

"I have secret accounts I believe I can still access to fund operations...what I don't have is personnel. I'm hoping you'll speak with your Marine friends. I believe I can smuggle Gary off-planet, if you can provide the strength to rescue him from the armed convoy."

"You want me to convince Confederation Marines to attack an armed Senate prisoner convoy?" Andi looked around the room. "Are you crazy?" But what was truly crazy was what she was thinking...and how much she liked the plan.

"Gary has access to vast amounts of information. If we can get him out, he can do more than any of us to find out what's truly going on. It's a risk...but if we can bring the truth out, there's a good chance everyone involved can get a pardon."

Andi scowled. She didn't believe that for a second. If she knew anything about government bodies, it was that they never admitted mistakes...or forgave those who stood up to them. If she agreed to help Zacker, she would be taking a terrible risk.

She could end up on a prison planet herself, spending the rest of her life mining rare minerals until the radiation exposure killed her. She was still thinking about that when the words blurted out of her mouth.

"I'll help you…and I'll try to convince the Marines to help. But we have to get Tyler Barron out as well."

Zacker looked back at her, a troubled look slipping on to his face. "Captain…I sympathize with Admiral Barron's situation, and I would like to help, I truly would, but…"

"There's no negotiation. You had the sources to find out where Gary would be…you can do the same thing with Tyler." She paused, staring at him intently. "I'm bringing a whole company of Marines to the table, plus the fastest free trader within a dozen systems of here, one with a still-valid priority certificate. You can find out where one more prisoner is being held."

The agent sat for a few seconds, silent, unmoving. Finally, he sighed softly and said, "I'll try, Captain. I'll reach out to every contact I can trust now…but I can't guarantee I'll succeed."

"I'm confident you'll succeed…and what do you say we drop the Captain-Mr. Zacker nonsense. If we can plot something like this, I think it calls for first names, don't you, Ethan?"

He nodded. "Yes, Andi, I do."

"Good…and as I was saying, your best effort is fine, because that's all you're getting from me. Anybody who tells you they're sure they can get a hundred Marines to do something like this is full of shit."

*   *   *

"Yes, I believe I can assist in that effort." Atara Travis sat on the floor, leaning against cargo shuttle's cold metal wall. It wasn't the ideal place for a meeting, not in most respects. But it was useful in terms of privacy…and Atara didn't want anyone knowing she was even having a meeting, and especially not with whom she was speaking.

"I knew you were the one I had to reach." Andi Lafarge sat right next to Travis, so close they were whispering, their words barely audible past a few centimeters.

The shuttle was locked, the AI instructed to allow no one to enter until Atara authorized it, but she also knew the sensitivity of what they were discussing…and as much as she trusted her people, there were over a thousand spacers on *Dauntless*. It was just too easy to slip a spy or informant into a group that large. Everyone on the ship had been part of the White Fleet, away from home for months, but she had no idea what was happening on Megara, or how long it had been underway.

"I was surprised to hear from you, Andi…and relieved." In truth, she'd been stunned. As far as she'd known, Andi Lafarge had retired to a mansion on Tellurus to enjoy the fruits of her success. Megara was perhaps the last place she'd expected to encounter her friend. "I was trying to come up with a plan to help Tyler…and to be honest, I wasn't having much success."

"No more surprised than I was to find *Dauntless* here…not to mention all that seems to be going on. I really can't give you much insight on what's behind all these charges. I don't know if this is just some insane mistake of some kind…or if the Confederation is teetering on the brink of civil war, but one thing I do know is, we can't leave Tyler down there. I saw what happened to Gary Holsten. The Senate will conduct a show trial, but Tyler won't have counsel, or a chance to review the evidence. He *will* be convicted, and then he'll be sent to some prison world…and we'll never see him again."

Atara knew, perhaps more than anyone other than the two of them, how Andi felt about Barron…and the reverse. Now, listening to the tone of her friend's voice, she realized that hadn't diminished at all in the nearly two years since they'd seen each other.

"We're not going to let that happen." Atara's words were firm, but she knew she didn't have the goods to back them up, not yet. She'd spent the two days after Barron's arrest nervously awaiting her own relief from command, and possibly even her arrest. She hadn't disobeyed Whitten's orders in the end, nor opened fire on any Confederation installation, but she'd been sure she'd gone too far. She wondered if she owed her continued status as *Dauntless*'s commander to the sheer magnitude of the things going on. Had Whitten just overlooked her out of carelessness? If he'd checked her out at all, he'd have known she was very unlikely to sit and do nothing while Barron was railroaded and condemned to life on a penal asteroid.

."No…we're not."

Atara could hear the resolve in Andi's voice. She'd been shocked—and thrilled—when Lafarge's message had gotten through to *Dauntless*, a communique to her disguised as a social call to an old friend. She'd almost ignored it, as she had all incoming mail that hadn't come on official channels, but she'd happened to glance at it and see who had sent it.

"You have a plan?"

"I do…but I need help."

"You know I'll do whatever you need." That was true, to an extent. *Atara would* do *anything*…but she was far from sure what she could get the crew to do. They were loyal to her, and they loved Tyler, but asking them to commit what could be considered treason was a shaky prospect at best.

"I'm working with one of Gary Holsten's people…and a pair of Marine officers and their company."

Atara listened, and she couldn't help but feel the desperation of their situation. The two of them, hiding in a supply shuttle that had come to *Dauntless* with a load of fresh foodstuffs for the crew—and one stowaway—discussing taking on the Confederation Senate with a hundred Marines and a handful of other conspirators.

"They wanted my help to rescue Gary…and I agreed. But I had my own price. That they also help break Tyler out."

Atara was shocked for a moment, but then it passed and she smiled instead. The idea was dangerous, reckless…but after a second's thought, she'd decided she wasn't at all surprised to hear it come out of Andi's mouth. No one had ever accused the ex-smuggler of a lack of audacity.

"What can I do?"

Andi hesitated. "I'm afraid participating will put you at terrible risk, Atara…you and all of your people."

Atara wasn't sure every spacer on *Dauntless* would appreciate her making a decision like this for them, but Tyler Barron had led them all, and saved most of their lives at one time or another. She wasn't going to give up on him…and she didn't think most of the crew would either.

"Go on."

"We're going to intercept the convoy taking Gary Holsten to the spaceport. He's been convicted already, and he's being shipped out early in the morning in two days."

Atara smiled again. "I'm not even going to ask how you know that."

Andi just grinned. "Holsten will be out in the open…and we'll have the element of surprise. But Tyler is still on trial. He'll be in his cell when Gary is moved. If we don't break him out then, at the same time we get Holsten…we'll never have another chance."

Atara nodded, an instinctive agreement with what Andi had said. If Holsten was rescued from captivity, the security level around Barron and the other prisoners, already intense, would become almost unimaginable. Whatever chance there was of getting to him would be lost.

"Do you have the location where he's being held?" Atara suspected it was somewhere on the Senate campus, but a successful rescue operation would need far more specific coordinates than that.

"I will."

Atara looked at Andi with a quizzical expression on her face.

"It was part of the deal I made. The Marines would help free Gary…and the Confederation Intelligence people would find out exactly where Tyler is."

"Do you trust your contact?" Atara looked doubtful.

"I didn't have any choice. It's the only chance we have to get to Tyler."

Atara's dubious look slipped away, and she nodded again. "I don't like it, but you're right. There *is* no other option." A short pause. "So, you'll need some kind of diversion when you're ready to strike. That's what you need me for?"

"Yes…With *Dauntless* in orbit, you can probably jam communications in the capital, at least for a short time."

Atara stared back blankly for a few seconds. She knew Andi was direct, and practiced a sort of controlled recklessness, but the idea of a Confederation battleship jamming communications in the capital was insane. Brilliant. "Yes…I think we can manage that." Atara wished that Anya Fritz was still onboard, but she'd been left behind along with the rest of the White Fleet. Still, she had enough engineering muscle aboard to pull off what Andi needed…and even one or two engineers she trusted enough to bring into the plan. "What else?"

"I'm not sure what else you can do, Atara…" She hesitated, uncomfortably. "…except, of course…we'll need to get off Megara, and out of the Olyus system, until we can clear things up. I think I can get them to orbit in *Pegasus*…but we'd never make it out of the system. But *Dauntless*…there's not a ship here that's a match for her."

Atara had been thinking the same thing. She could think of a million reasons to refuse. They'd be on the run, fugitives, until—unless—they could clear things up. She'd be making that choice for a thousand loyal spacers, men and women with friends, families, careers. Amid all of that, a single word came to her lips.

"Yes."

She looked at Andi, her eyes burning with intensity. "You get *Pegasus* back to *Dauntless*…and I'll get us out of the system." Atara could see the relief, and the gratitude in Andi's expression. "You have a company of Marines…that's what, about a hundred?"

Andi nodded. "A bit more."

"That's not enough for two operations like this."

"It's all I've got."

"I've got Marines on *Dauntless*, too." Atara didn't know how she felt about asking her Marines to assault the Senate campus… and she had no idea which ones were most likely to go along with it. But she was sure just who would know. She reached for the small comm unit on her belt and pulled it to her lips.

"Bryan…it's Captain Travis. I'd like to see you…immediately, if possible."

"Of course, Captain. Your office?"

"No, General, I'd like you to come to…shuttle bay alpha. And I'd like you to come alone." She paused. "Please don't tell anyone where you are going."

"Yes, Captain. I'll be there at once." Atara knew the Marine had to be surprised, but his voice didn't give any indication of it.

Andi looked at Atara and said, "How are you going to get your Marines down to the surface without setting off a firestorm?"

Atara smiled and turned her head, looking across the shuttle's cargo bay. "The same way we got you up here. I assume you made some arrangement to get aboard this shuttle…I'd wager you can manage to make a similar one to slip a few Marines off on the ground, once it returns."

Chapter Twenty-Four

Bridge
CFS Repulse
Unknown System 20
Year 316 AC

"All batteries…redirect fire to target beta." Sara Eaton was in her chair, her body angled to the side, as her eyes darted between the bank of status screens on the outer wall and the 3D display in the center of the bridge. Her whole body ached from the relentless tension, and sweat had plastered her uniform to her back. The battle had raged for more than eight hours, and while ultimate victory was as untenable a goal as it had been at the start, her spacers had performed beyond even her greatest hopes. The Hegemony fleet might very well obliterate her force, but they certainly wouldn't bring home any reports that their victory had been an easy one.

"Yes, Commodore." Sonya Eaton was at her station, looking no less disheveled than her sister, or any of the bridge crew. But she was as focused on her duty, as resistant to the effects of fatigue and fear as her older sibling. "All guns locked on target beta."

Sara glanced at the symbol in the display, the Hegemony battleship *Repulse* and two of her sister-ships had been battering. The idea of letting up on a wounded enemy before it was finished went against every instinct in her battle-hardened body, but she and Jake Stockton had somehow developed a new tactic, one that came about organically between the two of them.

Stockton was bringing his fighters in against the badly wounded Hegemony ships, recklessly closing to insane ranges to target the hull breaches and weak spots in the battered vessels. Eaton had been stunned by the amount of damage the squadrons had managed to inflict with only their lasers remaining in their arsenals.

The cost had been high, of course, the knife-fighting range vastly increasing the hit rate of the enemy's defensive fire, just as it allowed the fighters to target with such pinpoint accuracy. Losses had been increased further by Stockton's efforts to conserve fuel in order to keep his fighters in action as long as possible. He'd kept velocities down to a minimum, reducing the need for massive amounts of fuel-guzzling thrust, but also making his birds easier targets for the enemy defensive batteries.

Sara had stopped counting casualties among the squadrons when the number reached two hundred. It had increased probably by another hundred since then, but despite the lack of any kind of relief provided by not knowing, she hadn't checked again.

She could hear the distant whining of *Repulse*'s broadside. About half the battleship's guns were still in operation. The fleet had suffered terrible losses, and many of the ships remaining in the line were near-cripples, some with just one or two secondary batteries still in operation. But her people had known the reality of their situation for months now, and they fought on with all the tenacity and courage she could have hoped to see.

She peered across the display, and she saw another of her battleships pounding away at a critically-damaged enemy vessel. She understood…but she also knew the fighters could finish off that wounded ship…and there was a whole line of fresh Hegemony vessels still advancing, outnumbering her remaining forces by a greater ratio than they had at the start of the fight.

"Commander…order *Northland* to break off from its current target and engage the nearest intact enemy vessel." A pause.

"The squadrons will deal with the ship they're facing now."

"Yes, Commodore." Sonya repeated the order.

Even as she finished, Sara said, "All ships are ordered to break off from severely damaged opponents. We've got to hurt as many of those ships as we can…and the fighters can swarm the cripples."

"Yes, Commodore. At once." Sara could hear her sister's agreement in her tone. Sonya had surprised her older sibling with the bloodthirsty edge she displayed in battle. She'd always been the quiet one, the passive one.

Years of watching friends die can harden anyone…

She listened as the order was repeated…and as, one by one, acknowledgements came in. Sara doubted anything she did would make a difference in the final outcome of the battle… but if her people could hurt the enemy enough, just maybe they could discourage them from attacking the Confederation.

*   *   *

"Keep those tubes clear. Send another few 'bots in there if you have to, but I want those things open." Anya Fritz spoke calmly, her voice showing none of the stress of the moment. She was in *Repulse*'s engineering section, near reactor number three. She'd been from one end of the massive ship to the other during the battle, and she'd continue racing around until the Hegemony forces overwhelmed the fleet and finished her off, along with the rest of the battleship's crew.

Technically, Fritz wasn't part of *Repulse*'s complement, no more than she'd been part of *Dauntless*'s. Hers was a fleet-wide command, and she was in charge of all engineering operations, not any individual vessel's. But that was mostly an honorific, at least in the middle of a battle like the one going on. Comm jamming, distances between ships, and the inability to closely examine damage on the other vessels, all combined to make the idea of a fleet-wide damage control commander somewhat useless in the middle of a fight. For all practical purposes, she was now *Repulse*'s chief engineer, as she had been on the old *Daunt-*

less for so many years.

She stumbled as the ship rolled to the side, reaching out and grabbing onto one of the metal bars extending from the wall to steady herself. *Repulse* had been hit again, and while she didn't have any data on it yet, she'd become adept over the years at monitoring things by feel. It was a solid hit, but she was pretty sure it hadn't caused any major damage. The severity of a hit depended on a lot of things—range, angle of impact, the location on the ship struck. A beam could slice through a ship's guts, tearing into its reactors or main power lines…or it could expend itself boring through heavy armor and vast, empty cargo holds. The difference between a critical hit and one that was ineffective could be less than one percent variation on the impact angle.

"We've got it, Captain. I just deployed two more of the 'bots," Walt Billings replied. "We've got all but four of them deployed now, so if we need to deal with another major hit, we're probably going to have to pull some off of something else." Billings had served under Fritz on the old *Dauntless*. Her first impression of the officer had been that he was something of a clown, a man of some intelligence, who would likely never excel—and certainly wouldn't make it long term as part of her team—but she'd had to admit, he'd surprised her, and he'd become one of her few true errors of judgment. By the time she was bumped up to the fleet's top engineer, Billings had taken her place on *Dauntless*, with her blessing. Nevertheless, when *Dauntless* set out for home, Billings had volunteered to stay with the fleet, as Fritz had, and he'd transferred to *Repulse* to take over for the flagship's wounded chief engineer.

"It's a damned certainty we're going to get hit again, Commander…so go ahead now and figure where you can spare some 'bots…and a few of your engineers, too." She'd stepped back from doing things like that herself, even though she had a pretty fair idea where they could best spare resources to divert to the next crisis. She knew Billings would reach the same conclusions she would, and she'd decided to let him do just that. If he resented her stepping into his role, pushing him back into the effective number two slot, he hadn't shown it. But Fritz didn't see any reason to run roughshod over the officer, especially since he'd long ago won her respect.

She'd mellowed somewhat with age, softened her hard and aggressive style…a bit.

"I'm on it, Captain." Billings snapped off a salute, a much sharper one than he'd managed in his younger days, and he turned and walked across the deck toward a ladder leading to one of the catwalks snaking across the engineering section.

She turned to walk back to the main console, to check on the status of a half dozen damage control parties at work in different areas of the ship when *Repulse* jerked forward again, hard. Showers of sparks descended all across the engineering deck as one system after another shorted out. It had been a bad hit, she knew that immediately, but she wasn't sure just how bad yet. The main lighting was still active in engineering, and that was a good sign. Her mind raced, eyes darting around, processing the damage she could easily see. She narrowed it down to two likely scenarios, one she could deal with fairly quickly, even getting *Repulse* back into the fight in a few minutes.

And one that was far, far worse.

* * *

"Raptor…the flagship's comm is down."

Stockton jerked his head toward the comm unit, an instinctive reaction that served no real purpose. He'd been focused on selecting targets, directing the disordered clusters of fighters that had once been his splendidly-organized wings toward the places they could do the most good. He'd mostly ignored the comm chatter going back and forth, but this was Olya Federov, and he took everything Lynx had to say deadly seriously.

He flipped a series of switches, trying to raise *Repulse*. Nothing. Lynx was right…the flagship was off the air.

That can't be good…

He turned toward his scanner, changing the setting from the enemy ships nearby to *Repulse*. It didn't take more than a few seconds to confirm that the flagship had taken some kind of damage. Stockton's first guess was it was bad.

And there were two enemy ships heading toward her…one of which had fired the deadly shot…

His hand jerked back onto the controls, firing up his thrusters and angling his vector back toward *Repulse* as he spoke into the comm unit. "All fighters within fifty thousand kilometers of my position…lock on and follow me. We've got two enemy ships moving in on the flagship, and the commodore needs our help."

He pulled back hard, firing the engines at close to maximum thrust. He knew he'd have a better chance to organize a meaningful strike if he waited, organized the ships that would be following him in…but there just wasn't time. He was barely going to make it as it was.

Getting there was going to burn up most of the fuel he had left. If he got there in time to save *Repulse*, he and his pilots were going to have to manage some kind of landing under combat conditions. If they didn't save the flagship, they'd all be screwed…out of fuel and flying off into deep space, without any real hope of rescue.

He glanced down at his screen, watching as fifty or more of his ships began to change vectors, no more than half of them within the range he'd specified. He was far from sure most of them could make it before the enemy finished off *Repulse*, but he let them come anyway. The fleet had fought hard and inflicted more damage on the enemy than he'd dared to hope, but it was still as hopeless as it had been at the start. And things were getting close to the end. Even without the mad dash back toward *Repulse*, his squadrons didn't have much time left.

Might as well end on a glorious note…

His eyes narrowed, focusing on his target, the nearest of the two enemy ships. Both vessels were damaged, but they weren't outright crippled like most of the ones Stockton had sent his people after. He wasn't even sure laser attacks from his birds could do enough damage to take them down, no matter how well targeted and executed. But he had to try.

He was staring at the screen when the lead ship fired again…

another hit. This one wasn't critical, he was almost sure of that as he watched the data coming in, but getting blasted again and again wasn't going to help whatever damage control efforts were underway on *Repulse*.

He pulled the throttle the rest of the way back, his face twisted as the g-forces slammed into him. He'd get there with even less fuel than he'd expected…but he'd get there maybe a minute faster.

From what he could see, that minute could make all the difference.

Hang on, Commodore…we're coming.
We're coming…

Chapter Twenty-Five

"If our information is correct, the convoy should be here in the next few minutes." Andi spoke softly into her comm unit, crouched down below a large transformer box along the side of the deserted service artery. Troyus City had been built from reclaimed swampland as the Confederation's capital eighty years before, and no effort was spared to maintain its grandeur and beauty. But a large city—and Troyus's population exceeded ten million—required massive amounts of freight and maintenance, everything from delivery trucks to refuse collection. Unlike cities that were centuries old, or even millennia, those who built Troyus had planned for all of this. There was a maze of service roads and passageways underground, and a network running on the surface between the blocks of buildings, hidden from the view of those on the public streets and in the many parks.

"We're all set, Andi." Jon Peterson's voice was steady—mostly—but she thought she could hear something else there. It wasn't weakness or fear, not in the veteran Marine colonel. Hesitation? She didn't have a doubt Peterson was one hundred percent onboard with the plan, but she didn't kid herself how difficult it had to be for the career Marine to launch an attack on other Confederation troops. They could call it a rescue all they

194

wanted…it was also an attack.

That was tough to handle, even if all their people were armed with stun guns and non-lethal ordnance. They had deadly weapons, too, in case they were needed.

Andi, Vig, and the rest of her people waiting along a similar road, one leading out to the main network and to the spaceport. They were keeping an eye out for any problems on the route to the spaceport. It was the fastest way to take a prisoner to a waiting spaceship, and every bit of information Ethan Zacker had been able to obtain—from his shockingly wide net of intelligence sources—confirmed that Holsten would be brought this way…at this very time.

It had taken several hours to get her people in place. She'd brought them in a few at a time, working with Colonel Peterson to select their positions. If the convoy guards saw anything, smelled anything, suspected anything…the desperate rescue was doomed to failure. As it was, she was counting on the jamming Atara Travis was ready to provide to prevent the guards from calling for help. She'd didn't have a doubt that the entire operation to bring Holsten to the spaceport was heavily monitored, that even with every safeguard she had in place, her people would have no more than a few minutes before an alert was sounded and half the military forces in Troyus City surrounded them all. Hell, *Dauntless* activating its jammers at full power would put the whole city into an uproar. She could just hope that the confusion lasted long enough for her to get the job done.

She didn't like the idea of dying under any circumstances, but for all her past years on the fringe of outlawry, she found the idea of being executed as a traitor to be a very unpleasant end.

Then don't screw up…you can do this…

She told herself that, and she tried to believe it, but she wasn't sure. It had all sounded better on the drawing board, but now, crouched down in the damp predawn air, it seemed nearly impossible.

She reached down and pulled up the assault rifle she'd set down against the wall behind her. It was a real gun, but it was loaded with ammunition designed for dispersing mobs. By all accounts, the shots were painful, but they were unlikely to kill anyone.

Her hand slipped down to the ammo strap looped over her shoulder. She had half a dozen cartridges there, three more filled with the non-lethal slugs…and three loaded with deadly, armor-piercing rounds. She didn't want to kill any Confederation personnel, and she was prepared to do anything she could to prevent that from happening. But if the guards were too heavily armored for the stun rounds to affect, or if something else went wrong…well, she'd have to make a decision then, and she and the Marines were ready for whatever that might be.

I don't even know if these Marines would obey an order to switch to lethal ordnance…assuming I could give it.

She was still thinking about the situation, wrestling with her concerns, when she heard something. The sounds of vehicles approaching. She took a deep breath and tried to steady herself. Even as she did, her thoughts wandered, to a different group of Marines, waiting at another location. She felt she should have been there, too…no, she *knew* she should have. But Bryan Rogan had convinced her to go with the team rescuing Gary Holsten. Every man and woman in Rogan's hand-picked group was a combat veteran of five years or more. The force was small, but it was tightly organized, and however good she thought she was, she'd realized she would be a disordering factor. It was Rogan's final point that had gotten to her…any slipup could cause the mission to fail, or even get Barron killed.

The words had struck at her deeply, and she thought about just how crazy the whole mission was to begin with, and how difficult it was going to be for Rogan's people to get into the Senate's holding facility and get out with Barron. None of that changed her determination to proceed, but she could feel the tension, the fear, in a way she hadn't before…another gift from Ricard Lille.

Another reason to kill the bastard…as soon as I'm done here.

"All right, Jon…we've definitely got multiple vehicles coming, and at this hour I have to believe it's what we're waiting for."

"We're ready, Andi. Good luck to you."

"Good luck to you, too."

Her hands tightened around the rifle, and her legs tensed up, ready to spring forward.

Ready to do what had to be done.

Then her scanner went crazy, the neatly displayed dots representing the Marines and the small ovals standing in for the approaching transports vanishing in a storm of static.

Dauntless had begun jamming.

It was time.

* * *

Rogan reached out, his fingers slipping under the guard's helmet, jerking upward—and trying to hold back, to keep himself from breaking the man's neck as he slipped the stun rod in and shoved it against the exposed flesh of the soldier's neck. Rogan had been a Marine for a long time, but this was his first actual operation where the rules of engagement called for only non-lethal force. He agreed with Andi's instructions…the Senate was wrong to imprison the admiral, they were all sure of that. But the guards, or most of them were simply following orders. They were comrades of a sort, and while his Marines might look at them as less capable warriors, even as useless Senate lapdogs, the idea of actually killing any of them was horrifying.

The man let out a short yell, but only for a second or less. Then his body went limp, and he slipped to the ground, Rogan supporting him as he fell, trying both to minimize any injuries… and any noise.

Even as he was straightening up, Marines were racing past him, moving swiftly and quietly down the corridor. Andi's ally from Confederation Intelligence had managed, somehow, to obtain plans of the secret facility, and so far they seemed to be accurate. His Marines had gone over the plan several times, but there had been no way to do any practice runs. They'd almost been caught sneaking out of the shuttle that brought them down from *Dauntless*…and they'd just managed to get into hiding without triggering some kind of alarm. Once they were stashed in the building Zacker had provided as a temporary hideout, Rogan had ordered his people to stay in place, not to so much as peer out a window. They'd brought water with them, and rations...everything they needed before the op began.

Now, they were inside the secure facility. Rogan didn't know how far they would get without some kind of alarm reaching the guards. His people had left a dozen troopers behind, all of them stunned or otherwise incapacitated, but as soon as any of them were found, things would get crazy. *Dauntless*'s jamming was helping, at least it was causing a distraction, but at the cost of Rogan's own comm and scanning.

He raced down the corridor, following the Marines that had jumped ahead of him. They knew what had to be done, and every one of them had his complete confidence. But he knew a hundred things could happen, anything from an unexpected sentry going by, to some kind of lockdown procedure that functioned even with the jamming.

The corridor was long, and the lighting was fairly dim. There was no place to hide or take cover, and he reminded himself that any guards who opened up on his people wouldn't be firing stun rounds. He was authorized to use deadly force as a last resort, but he didn't know what it would take for him to order his people to kill other Confederation soldiers.

Then he heard the sounds of firing up ahead...barely. His people had full silencing gear on their weapons, but then he heard three loud cracks. Someone firing back...with live rounds.

He rushed forward, trying to get to the head of the column. The firing slowed almost immediately, and as he reached the front of the formation, he could see a pair of prison guards down, one of them apparently unconscious, the other propped up against the far wall, looking up as four Marines pointed their assault rifles at him. Rogan walked up as one of his people, a sergeant, pulled out a small baton and leaned down, tapping the guard.

The man convulsed from the stun rod's charge, and he dropped completely to the ground, unconscious now, like his comrade.

"All right, let's move. Someone *had* to have heard those shots." He pulled out the small tablet from his pouch and stared at it. His scans were all blacked, but he had the map stored in the unit's memory. Barron's cell was just down the corridor, perhaps another six or eight meters.

Assuming the intel he had was correct, of course, something his career had told him always to take with a healthy dose of skepticism.

He jogged down the corridor, a bit less cautious than he might have liked under most circumstances. But time was the enemy now…a fact that was confirmed a few seconds later, when he heard an alarm going off in the distance.

"We're out of time," he snapped, stopping in front of the door that his map told him led to the cell. He couldn't waste time trying to get into the lock or hack the system. "Blow this thing open," he said, waving to a pair of Marines carrying explosive kits.

He turned and looked both ways down the corridor. His Marines were spread out along both sides of the hall, covering the approaches to the cell. *Dauntless*'s jamming was powerful, and he knew it had likely interfered with at least some of the surveillance systems. But it was a damned certainty now that someone in the facility knew something was happening, if not exactly what. And that meant more guards would be coming.

"We're ready, sir." The Marines had affixed their explosives to the locking mechanism of the door. It was a small device, just enough to obliterate the lock and hopefully allow the Marines to force the door open.

"Do it." Rogan stepped back himself, even as the other Marines did. A moment later, the charge detonated, blowing a hole in the wall about twenty-five centimeters in diameter. "Get it open…now."

Rogan watched as three Marines moved forward, leaning against the door, forcing it open. At first it didn't move at all, but then it started to shift slowly. Rogan's stomach was twisted in knots. He was still wrestling with the fact that what he was doing was more or less treason, and he knew the chances of his people getting out, much less of the entire enterprise ending well, were small. Even worse, he imagined the door open and his eyes fixed on an empty cell, that his people had thrown their lives away not to save their beloved leader…but for nothing at all.

Even as he started to think again about that worst prospect, that all he'd done, convinced his Marines to do, had been a waste…he peered into the cell and saw a single figure standing there, tall and proud, despite his circumstances. He wore some type of prison uniform in place of his usual naval garb, but it only took Rogan an instant to recognize the brown hair, long for a naval officer, and the piercing gray-blue eyes.

Tyler Barron.

"Admiral…we're here to get you out. We've got to *move*." Rogan had a million things he might have said, but there was no time to waste, and the no-nonsense Marine part of him was in charge now.

"Bryan, what is the meaning of this? Do you realize how much trouble you all are in?"

"Yes, sir…but we're in it already, so come with us. Please."

Barron stood for a few seconds, clearly trying to decide what to do. He'd been framed, unjustly accused—there wasn't a man or woman standing in the corridor who thought anything other than that. But it was clear Barron didn't want to risk the lives of his people.

"Sir, we've got to get you out of here. Remember why we came back, what's coming. We've got to get you someplace safe, so you can get the word out…somehow." Rogan had known Barron for years, and he'd expected his commander, and his friend, to resist endangering his subordinates. But even Barron's selfless honor couldn't overrule the threat the Hegemony posed to the Confederation.

Barron paused for just another second. Then he nodded and stepped forward, out into the corridor…just as all hell broke loose.

Chapter Twenty-Six

Bridge
CFS Repulse
Unknown System 20
Year 316 AC

"Captain Fritz…" Eaton knew badgering Fritz wasn't going to accomplish anything, but there was nothing else she could do except sit quietly and watch her ship die around her. "…we're running out of time."

Repulse's bridge was a mess, littered with loose cables and jagged bits of debris. The lights were mostly on, though some systems were running solely on backup power. The air was acrid, the scent of burned machinery and smoke burning her lungs with every labored breath. The last hit had been a bad one, damned bad, and Sara Eaton's great flagship was in trouble.

"I know, Commodore. We're on it…doing everything we can." Fritz sounded distracted, which was the surest sign of just how serious the damage was. The engineer was clearly busy, probably with half a dozen things at once, as she answered the commodore's call.

Eaton sighed softly, trying to keep it to herself, with limited success. The damage was repairable. It was just a question of how long it would take, and if *Repulse* would survive that long in her current state. Eaton only knew that because Fritz had already told her, right after the engineer had restored some of the internal comm systems. The comm to the launch bays was still out, as it was to most of the decks with crew quarters. But she had her link to engineering restored, and to gunnery as well, and those were the most important ones now.

At least for whatever time we've got left…

"I know you are, Captain…I just wanted to say, if it comes down to taking a risk, even a wild one…if we don't get partial power restoration quickly, none of it's going to matter anyway."

Fritz had restored some scanner input as well, enough for Eaton to see the two ships about to finish off her flagship. Tactically, she understood it was vital for her to know what was out there…but if she wasn't going to get a chance to even fight back, she wasn't sure she wouldn't have preferred the blindness.

"Understood, Commodore…and we're going to be taking some chances for sure." A brief pause. "Make sure everybody's in their harnesses up there." Eaton caught the edge in Fritz's voice, and her gut told her they were all in for a rough ride.

Eaton heard the click signaling that Fritz had closed the line. Technically, Fritz was the junior officer and should have waited until Eaton had dismissed her, but Sara didn't care about that. Fritz, perhaps more than anyone else on *Repulse*, would determine how much longer they all lived. The engineer didn't have time to waste on rank etiquette, and no one had less of a problem with that than Eaton.

She reached out and grabbed the arms of her chair as *Repulse* shook yet again, taking another hit from the incoming Hegemony battleships. Her vessel was tough, but she was painfully aware it couldn't take much more of the pounding. Luck had been with her for the last few shots. They'd been solid hits, but— save for the one—all in non-vital areas. If one more shot struck the ship in its guts…that would be the end.

Eaton wanted to believe her ship—her whole fleet—had more fight in it, but she wasn't sure it did…and she suspected it didn't matter, either. Did it really make a difference if they survived an hour longer? They'd still all be dead, and taking out one or two more ships wasn't going to stop the Hegemony.

C'mon, Anya…I know what you did on Dauntless *so often. We'd all counted you out…and somehow, you did what had to be done. Do that for* Repulse, *work your magic one more time…*

* * *

Stockton looked again at the figures on his fuel gauge, watching the numbers drop every time his eyes darted back. But he was almost back to *Repulse*, close enough to attack the two enemy ships that were killing Commodore Eaton's flagship.

Repulse had absorbed shot after shot, each one noted with a tightening of Stockton's innards. All the while he had been racing back, he'd expected to see the hit that finished the massive battleship. But, even crippled and unable to respond, she'd stood and took everything the enemy could send her way. She'd held long enough for Stockton's fighters to arrive.

He wasn't sure his people could save *Repulse*, even though they'd made it back in time. The two enemy ships had their own damage, but they were still in reasonable condition, and normal strafing runs weren't likely to have a massive effect. He was staring at the updated scanner readouts, looking for weak spots to attack, but so far, he'd come up with little for his efforts. There were hull breaches, but they were mostly small. That didn't mean there weren't sensitive spots, damaged locations where hits could penetrate and cause critical damage. But it did mean it was going to be hard to hit such precise and rare targets.

Damned hard.

He nudged the controls, bringing his sleek fighter around toward the nearer of the two ships. The closer one was the most damaged, and the one his squadrons could most likely hurt. He looked down at his readouts again. It was also the only one he was sure his people could reach with enough remaining fuel to execute a solid attack run.

He knew this last assault would leave him virtually dead in space, and he was sure his pilots did as well. But they'd launched into the battle knowing the reality of the situation, and, like him, they were all veterans who'd faced death before. In their own ways, they were each ready for it every time they went down the tubes and back into the fight. If the end *had* to come, he was also certain it would come easier to them if it achieved something, like saving *Repulse.*

He could see the target getting larger on his scanners. The ship was heavily engaged with *Repulse,* and it was immediately apparent that the focus on the Confederation battleship degraded the effectiveness of the enemy's point defense turrets. They were still firing, but not all of them, and not as accurately. Stockton didn't know if it was a limitation of their information systems or power transmission, or simply the Hegemony's lack of anti-fighter doctrine. He didn't care. Anything that took the heat off as his people came in was welcome to him.

His eyes moved over his screens, scouring the enemy ship for weak spots. The vessel had taken a number of hits. Some of them had been glancing blows, leaving partially-melted and refrozen gouges across the hull…nothing his fighters could exploit with any real effectiveness. But there were two solid hits, both of which had left twenty meter or larger breaches. The cuts looked deep as well, giving him hope they exposed some vital systems.

Hitting a twenty meter wide target while coming in at attack speed wasn't going to be easy, not even for ace pilots. He thought about giving his people a final pep talk, but he decided that was pointless. Those that had followed him were committed…and they knew what to do. And actions spoke far louder than words. He would show them, not tell them. He would hit one of those holes in the hull, no matter what it took…and demonstrate to his pilots they weren't impossible targets after all.

He adjusted his vector, choosing an angle of assault that would give him the best possible shot. Success would be measured by fractions of a second, and coming in the right way might give him an extra tenth of a second. That could be the difference between a hit and a near miss.

He checked his guns, making sure they were fully charged. He wasn't sure how many shots his reactor could power. He'd turned off the safeguards that diverted all energy from weapons to engines when fuel levels dropped below three percent of capacity. He hadn't come all this way to have engine power for an extra fifteen minutes. He'd come to blast that damned enemy ship, and to do that, he needed energy for his lasers, even if that left him helpless after the attack run.

Next, he cut down his thrust and evasive maneuvers to minimal levels in a bid to save enough power to ensure he could finish his assault. It made him a better target for the enemy, but the defensive fire was still weak, and the steadier course would help his own targeting as much as that of anyone shooting at him.

He flipped the arming switch, activating the already-charged laser turrets. His guns were ready to fire.

The range was close now, and even the spotty enemy fire was beginning to feel dangerous. A few laser blasts came within five hundred meters or so of his ship. Not near enough to cause any damage, but close enough to make him feel a coldness in his spine.

His eyes flicked down, checking on the growing formation behind him. Almost one hundred fighters had formed up, following his lead. Many of them were close now, tucked in right behind him, and the rest were rapidly approaching. That meant some had burned even more fuel than he had. They'd all make it through their runs—he hoped they would—but he'd have people running out of juice almost immediately after. Without enemy fighters out there to pick them off, they wouldn't be in any danger at first. But their emergency life support wouldn't last forever, and he doubted any of them expected *Repulse* and the other Confederation ships to survive much longer, even if they saved the flagship from immediate destruction. The best his stranded people could hope for was to live long enough to watch their comrades on the big ships fight to the end…and then slowly suffocate or freeze to death.

The range meter dropped below ten thousand kilometers, pulling Stockton's attention from his morose thoughts to the attack at hand. If this was going to be his final fight, the last thing he was going to do was miss. He checked and rechecked his targeting, made minor changes to the gun sighting. He knew his attack angle to a thousandth of a degree, and he'd imagined the run a hundred times in his mind, over and over again as he came closer.

His hand tightened around the throttle, his finger over the firing stud. Eight thousand kilometers.

He stared straight ahead, began taking deep, regular breaths. He needed everything his AI could give him…and all he could dredge up from his gut, too. He could feel his heart pounding, the sweat pooling on his shoulders, dripping down his back under his flight suit.

Thoughts intruded of the people who were important to him—those gone, like Kyle Jamison, and those still here, like Stara…waiting on *Repulse* to see if he would save her, or at least buy her a few more moments…

He pushed it all out of his mind. It was time for Raptor Stockton's last attack.

*   *   *

"Twenty seconds, Commodore. I'm restarting the reactor, and then I'm going to feed the energy through the lines to the batteries, at a far faster rate than regs allow. It will either work… or it will fail catastrophically, and we'll be blown to atoms." A short pause. "The bright side is, if the worst happens, I doubt we'll even have time to know it didn't work."

Eaton's hands tightened on her chair. Fritz hadn't given much warning—or time for her to cancel the operation—but she *had* told the engineer to take some risks. Apparently Fritz had taken her words to heart.

"Good luck, Anya." There was nothing else to say, really. Just a few more seconds…and if they were all still there, chances were the guns would be up almost immediately.

We'll be back in the fight.

Eaton glanced around the bridge. She'd had Fritz on her headset, and none of her bridge crew knew what was about to happen. There was nothing to be gained by telling them.

Besides, there really wasn't time.

A few seconds later, the lights on the bridge—and every instrument she could see—went dark. She could feel the ship vibrating, and then it shook violently, lurching to the side, throwing most of her people hard into their harnesses. She could hear yells that told her there were broken bones and other injuries on *Repulse*'s bridge. It took her a few more seconds, and the return of the lights and instrumentation, to realize that her ship was still there.

And that means…

"Commodore…gunnery reports starboard batteries are online, with power flowing to all active guns."

"They are to open fire as soon as they're fully-charged." She looked up at the restored screen. Stockton's fighters were moving in on one of the enemy ships. She wasn't sure what they could do with nothing but lasers…but that was "Raptor" Stockton out there, and he had almost a hundred ships coming in with him. The odds didn't seem all that encouraging, but she figured Stockton was as good a bet as any she was likely to see.

"All batteries are to lock on target beta, Commander…and they are to continue at their maximum rate of fire until ordered to stop."

"Yes, Commodore."

Eaton felt a burst of hope, one she knew had little to do with reality. Even if Stockton managed to take out one enemy ship, and her gunners the other one, they'd only buy a brief respite. The enemy fleet still had enough ships to finish her entire force in almost any conceivable scenario. But she was only thinking moments ahead now…and she would consider defeating the two enemy ships to be a victory. Even if it turned out to be the last her people would ever see.

She could hear the distant humming as the batteries opening fire. She watched the screen impatiently, her hands balled up into fists, waiting to see if her people managed to score any hits.

* * *

Under one thousand kilometers.

Stockton was close…but he was going to get closer still. He had the targeting system locked on the small gash in the enemy ship's hull, and his eyes were focused there as well. He tried to let himself relax, to allow his instincts to participate as well as his intellect and his ship's hardware. A lifetime in a Lightning's cockpit had utterly convinced Stockton that such unmeasurable things were integral components of a pilot's skill.

He'd stopped checking his fuel status and the positions of his squadrons. There was nothing he could do about any of that now, anyway. All he could do was make sure none of what he'd done had been in vain.

He was gripping the controls even more tightly, his fingers white from the intensity of his handhold. He was breathing deeply, holding the air for an instant before exhaling hard. His breathing was becoming almost rhythmic as he closed to the fire point. He'd decided to come in *close*…less than two hundred meters. He wasn't sure he could pull out in time after, but he'd prefer to crash into the enemy ship rather than gasp for his last miserable breath in a frigid cockpit after he'd watched *Repulse* vanish in a thermonuclear explosion.

The one thought troubling him was that his people would follow his lead…and if he couldn't pull out in time, he doubted any of them could. It was strange. He could decide for himself he'd just as soon die immediately, but he couldn't extend the same to his pilots. His urge was to keep them alive for as long as possible, fighting wildly for every additional moment.

He was down to the last few seconds now…and his eyes caught something on the scanner. Lights, flashes. *Repulse* was firing?

He wasn't sure, but he didn't have time now to look more closely. With one herculean effort, he pushed the thoughts into the back of his mind, along with all those that threatened to distract him…and he focused on the enemy ship in front of him. That was all that existed…his fighter, and the behemoth it was approaching.

His finger tightened, the action driven by instinct, and he heard the familiar sound of his lasers firing. He'd deviated slightly from the AI's recommendations, and he felt a wave of doubt…and then elation, as he watched the display, and realized his shot had hit its target.

He'd placed the laser blast dead center, all of its energy slipping inside the enemy ship to hit the far softer targets of inner decks and systems. The laser hadn't even touched the edges of the roughly circular twenty-meter gash. With any luck, the blast would wreak havoc.

His hand had moved backward immediately after he fired, pouring every bit of power into his engines, struggling with all his exhausted ship had to give to escape the collision that appeared so imminent. For an instant, he thought he was done, that his ship was going to hit the enemy vessel.

Then he saw open space in front of him, and he realized he was past the Hegemony vessel.

He'd made it.

He almost looked at the nav screen, to check how close he'd come. But then his hand moved to the controls and he flipped a row of switches, taking the data off the screen. He didn't want to know. His gut told him the number would be in mere meters, and the less he thought about that, the better.

He knew his fighters were coming in now, but before he looked to see how they were doing, his eyes moved to the longer-range display. *Repulse had* fired. And her broadside had been deadly, almost every gun hitting the enemy in a single volley. The Hegemony ship had been caught by surprise by *Repulse*'s return to the fight, and its evasive maneuvers were sloppy, inadequate.

Stockton laughed derisively. *I guess Hegemony computer systems aren't programmed to account for Anya Fritz…*

He felt a rush of excitement at the flagship's return to the battle, and it only rose up as he watched his fighters begin to come in. Their shots impacted all around the gash in the enemy hull, an opening that had nearly doubled in size as internal explosions had roared up from Stockton's deadly shot. Great geysers of instantly-freezing gas and liquid had blown out into space, tearing into the metal of the battleship's armored skin and giving his attacking fighters a target more than twice the size it had been seconds before.

Another shot went through, and right after, a third. He watched as his fighters continued to come in, one at a time, delivering their laser pulses at an ever-enlarging weak spot. Another shot hit, and then another, and the Hegemony ship began to shake as explosions began to wrack her from bow to stern.

Stockton winced as one of his fighters came in too close, too fast, and crashed hard into the enemy vessel. He mourned for the lost pilot, but the impact caused massive damage all along the vessel's stern, and he watched as the engines flared out, leaving the vessel stuck on its current course and velocity. The ship was a cripple now, at least until its own damage control could restore some level of function. Even if his people couldn't finish it off, *Repulse*'s gunners could target the vessel's predictable course and blast the thing apart in minutes.

Stockton felt another wave of excitement as the flagship fired yet again at the second enemy vessel…and, seconds later, the battleship was blown to plasma.

It was one against one now…and Stockton's people were still coming in, savaging the remaining enemy ship.

His elation was interrupted by alarm bells, his system warning him of critical fuel levels. He had to land, and he had to do it quickly. There was no platform in range, save the Confederation flagship.

Landing on *Repulse* under combat conditions wouldn't be easy…and getting back out into the fight would be even harder. But that was just what Stockton was going to do.

His people—some of them—might even get the chance to land as well. Assuming *Repulse* had any functional bays left when they got there.

Chapter Twenty-Seven

Service Road A212
Troyus City, Planet Megara, Olyus III
Year 316 AC

"Here they come…gun teams ready. And remember, these are Confederation soldiers, not Foudre Rouge. We're shooting to disable the vehicles, not blow them to hell."

Andi listened as Jon Peterson snapped out orders to his Marines. *Dauntless*'s jamming had knocked out the Marines' scanners as well as their comm, and Peterson had picked up the approaching vehicles with a pair of far more primitive devices. His ears. Andi knew that, because she'd ID the transports the same way.

The only question that had been eating at her was, what would the convoy do now that their communications and scanners were out? Would they race forward, trying to reach the spaceport as soon as possible—as Andi and her people were hoping—or would they turn and head back to the prison? Peterson had a detachment waiting in case the trucks did turn around, but it was smaller and less well-positioned. But the transports hadn't turned around. They were coming.

Her stomach was tight, waiting to see how Peterson's people did with the rocket launchers she'd provided. The Marines hadn't been able to bring any of their own heavy weapons, not on a trip posted as recreational leave, and it was next to impossible to buy anything larger than a pistol on Megara…but Andi still had her secret cache in *Pegasus*, and—courtesy of Admiral Striker's dispensation—her ship was excused from any inspections on docking or landing. So when Peterson had expressed concern about having enough firepower to take on armored transports, she'd come to the rescue.

She listened as Peterson's Marines acknowledged, their voices grim. She'd become close to the Marines on Dannith, the ones Peterson had assigned to guard her against Ricard Lille. She'd known then, just from the way they conducted themselves, that they were combat veterans…but on the way to Megara, she'd had time to do a bit more research. Peterson's division was one of the most prestigious and decorated in the Corp, and their list of battle honors stretched so far she'd had to scroll to a second page to read them all. The officer himself would almost certainly have received his promotion to general some years before, if he hadn't been as prone as he was to recklessly speaking his mind. But, lack of political astuteness aside, everything she'd read indicated Peterson was one of the three or four best combat officers in the entire Corps.

If she had to be on the capital planet ready to attack Confederation personnel, she suspected she couldn't be in better company. Still, she wondered what this would do to the Marines, especially if some of the guards were killed. They'd spent their entire adult lives fighting under the Confederation banner, and after what was about to happen, she was certain some people would always look upon them as traitors. What she didn't know was how the men and women standing around her now would react to that.

She squeezed her hands around the assault rifle. The cartridge in place was loaded with heavy stun projectiles. With some luck—*a lot of luck*—they just might get through the operation without having to kill anyone. Just maybe, they could disable the guards, rescue Gary Holsten, and be gone before anyone recovered enough to resist. But Andi didn't believe in things working out that well…mostly because they never did.

She looked down at the sling thrown over her shoulder, and

the three cartridges loaded with armor-piercing slugs. Normally body armor was a protection in battle, but in this case, it could be a death sentence for the guards in the convoy. If they were too well protected to take out with non-lethal ordnance, Peterson and his Marines—and Andi—would have no choice but to use the deadly ordnance.

She was still thinking about the situation, and its likely consequences, when things began to happen quickly.

She saw the lead transport come around the corner and head down the straight length of road where Peterson's people were deployed. She held her breath for an instant. The jamming should have knocked out the scanners on the transports, and she was pretty sure all the Marines were well-hidden from view… but things often found a way to go wrong. Those first few seconds stretched out, passing with agonizing slowness.

Then she saw the second transport, and finally the third. They didn't stop, didn't even pause. There was no sign they were aware of any danger. There was a guard on top of each of them, manning an autocannon, but as her eyes focused on the one in the lead vehicle, she could see he was inattentive. Hell, from where she was, he looked half-asleep.

Prison guards and Senate Lictors aren't Marines…you know that…

Still, it seemed like more good fortune than she'd dared to expect.

She watched as Peterson raised his arm…and then dropped it quickly. The signal for the rocket crews to fire.

Andi held her breath. They had the advantage of surprise, and they had planned things as well as time allowed. But this was no desolate battlefield out in the Periphery. They were just outside the center of Troyus City, and even without communications, it wouldn't take long for authorities of some kind to respond to gunfire, not to mention explosions. Peterson's Marines could do this, she was sure of it. But there was no room for error.

None.

She heard the sounds of the launchers firing, and almost

simultaneously, the six snipers opening fire, taking out the three
gunners on top of the vehicles. She saw the first two guards
lurch backwards as two of the heavy stun bullets hit each of
them. The targets had helmets and breastplates, but the marks-
men had all hit them in the neck and face. Andi knew those
hits had been painful, and probably injurious, too. But a few
broken teeth, or even a shattered jaw, was better than being shot
to pieces by assault rifle fire.

The three gunners were motionless as the rockets slammed
low into their transports. The team had fired at a sharp angle,
tearing the wheels off all down the one side of the lead vehicle
but hopefully not killing the occupants. The transport skidded
to a stop, the momentum shaking the disabled gunner, who
dropped to the ground, hitting with a sickening thud.

He's probably still alive…

Andi wrenched her thoughts away from such worries, quickly
confirming that all three gunners were down…and all of the
transports were disabled.

The attack had not been a quiet one, despite every effort to
shield as much noise as possible. The lack of communications
should slow any response…but she had no idea how long *Dauntless*'s jamming would be able to suppress the comm system. The
big battleship had the element of surprise, but now she would
have to deal with other Confederation vessels responding, and
meanwhile, the crews on the ground would eventually power
through the jamming.

Andi figured they had three minutes. Maybe four.

She jumped into the street, the line of Marines doing the
same. The transports were all at a complete stop, two of them
leaning over at an angle. Her eyes darted around, looking for
the hatches, anyplace that would swing open for emerging occupants. She was sweaty, edgy. Her weapon might be armed with
non-lethal ammunition, but she knew damned well that wasn't
the case for the guards in the transports.

Normally the attackers would be working off their scanner
units as well, the electronic surveillance assets delivering them
far better intel than their own eyes in the predawn light. But

they had none of that.

As she closed the distance to the center vehicle—the one she'd guessed held Holsten—she expected someone to emerge, to start firing at her and her Marine comrades. But then she reached the vehicle, and checked the hatches along the side she was on. Both were locked shut.

They decided to stay inside and wait for help. That could be the smart play...

She looked around, imagining every sound she heard, however faint, was a virtual army descending on them. It had been less than a minute, and she knew no response could be there yet. Still, when it did arrive, it would probably be armored troops, and that meant the non-lethal part of the operation would be at an end. Getting caught or killed were obviously the worst outcomes she'd considered...but next in line was being faced with a single way out, to open up and gun down dozens of Confederation troopers. She'd do it if she had to, at least she'd told herself she would...but the feeling in her gut told her it was far better to avoid the test on that.

"All right, Sergeant, let's move it. Get these hatches open now."

Andi heard Hank Bellingham yelling at the Marines. The major had given up all efforts at being quiet, a reasonable choice since three huge explosions had just echoed through the waning night. Anyone who hadn't been alerted by the rockets wasn't going to be by one Marine officer's voice, no matter how hard and loud it was.

Two Marines raced up to each of the hatches. There was nothing non-lethal about the charges they carried...though, hopefully, they would simply blow apart the doors, and not anyone standing behind them. Andi watched for a few seconds as the teams began to put the devices in place, and then she turned, watching and listening for any signs of approaching intervention.

So far so good.

"Andi, step back." Bellingham's voice shook Andi from her inspections. The charges were ready to go. The Marines had been faster than she'd expected, another reminder of just how hardened Peterson's unit was.

She jerked herself away from the transport and around to its rear, still watching for anyone approaching. She crouched forward, shielding her head, even as she heard the explosions, and felt the heat…and a painful shower of debris hitting her back.

She lurched forward, letting out a partially restrained shout of pain, and jumped up. She straightened out as she did, her hands sliding over her body, confirming to herself she wasn't badly hurt. Then she spun around, weapon still in hand, and came back around the side of the transport…just in time to hear a crack and see one of the Marines fall backwards, his face a bloody mess.

She couldn't recognize who it was, not from what was left of his face, but she was pretty damned sure he was dead. That wasn't a surprise…she'd allowed herself to hope for a bloodless victory, but she hadn't really expected one.

The Marines were returning fire, pouring a withering burst of stun slugs into the vehicles. Andi cringed, realizing that Holsten was probably in the transport, too, but she knew very well that if they didn't disable all the guards, *now*, none of them were getting away—Holsten included.

She walked to the back of the transport and looked inside. There were four guards, all disabled. Three appeared to be unconscious, the fourth lying doubled over, wincing in pain as he clutched his clearly broken arm. An instant later, one of the Marines leaned into the vehicle and hit the man with a stun rod. The hapless guard convulsed and collapsed into a motionless heap.

Andi winced, but she also knew she would have done the same thing. A wounded, even a dying, man could easily kill a dozen enemies. If veterans learned one thing, it was not to take chances they could avoid.

She moved toward the hatch, but the Marines were climbing in before she got there. She glanced quickly forward and backward, confirming the same thing was going on at the other transports. She didn't take time to check her chronometer, but she estimated they were two minutes in now. Still safe, probably, but they didn't have long before some kind of intervention became a real possibility. And they still had to get to the spaceport…and get the hell off Megara.

Her head jerked around as she heard another burst of rifle fire, from behind, near the rear vehicle. The dawn light was increasing slightly, but it was still mostly dark, and she couldn't see what was going on. She thought she saw at least one Marine fall, but even as she was squinting, trying to get a better view, she heard a familiar voice from inside the transport closest to her.

"What the hell is going on here, Sergeant?" It was Gary Holsten, talking to the Marine closest to him. He'd been sitting along the far edge of the vehicle's compartment, his arms shackled and locked onto a heavy metal bar.

She could see the Marine freeze, uncertain how to respond. Andi knew the situation was above his pay grade, and she took pity on him. "We're here to rescue your sorry ass," she said, stepping up with one foot and hoisting herself halfway into the transport. "So, say 'thank you,' and then follow us. Because it's a damned good bet that trouble's on the way."

"Andi…" Holsten looked stunned to see her, and she got a strange sense satisfaction from that. She couldn't recall ever seeing the spy even slightly befuddled any time before. "What…"

"Later. We've *really* got to go." She gestured toward one of the Marines, who popped out the cartridge with stun ordnance and popped in the armor piercing rounds. He aimed the gun at the chain, as far from Holsten as he could, and he fired one well-placed round, shattering several links and freeing the prisoner.

"Come on," Andi said again, grabbing Holsten's shoulder and pulling him forward. "We've got to get the hell out of here."

*   *   *

Barron stepped out into the corridor, and he looked at Rogan. He was concerned—about his situation, about what the Marine general and his people had gotten themselves into… and about the prospects of actually getting out of the prison, escaping to somewhere that would be even temporarily safe for a group that would-be outlaws, even traitors. At least until—unless—they could clear things up somehow.

He was emotional about the loyalty his people had shown as well, their willingness to come for him despite all the concerns he was sure they understood as well as he did. He was about to say something to them when the sounds of boots stomping against the sheet metal of the floor got his attention.

An instant later, fire erupted...from one end of the corridor, and an instant later, from the other. His instincts took over, combat reflexes pushing him back into the cell, reaching out and grabbing one of the Marines nearby and pulling him into cover as well, even as the man stumbled and began to fall.

Barron swung around instinctively as gunfire out in the corridor increased in intensity. He reached out, his combat reflexes in full control now, grabbing Bryan Rogan by the collar and pulling him into the cell as well. He reached out and grabbed another of the Marines next, even as three more dove in by themselves. But that left more of them out in the corridor, a lot more...and Barron saw two of them drop to the ground, even as their comrades were returning the fire.

"General, what is the meaning of this? Do you know what you've done?" Barron's mind was racing, trying to decide what could have caused his normally methodical and "by the book" ground commander to go rogue and come barging into the Senate's own compound with a pack of armed Marines.

"Sir, it was Captain Lafarge's idea...and Colonel Peterson's. Captain Travis went along with the plan, as well. She even..."

"Captain Lafarge? She's on Megara?" Barron's mind reeled. He'd struggled for months to keep his sometimes lover out of his mind since he'd returned to prepare the Confederation to face invasion by the Hegemony. An effort that had gone stunningly poorly. But now it all flooded back—affection, longing... and a cold sense of dread at what she'd clearly involved herself in.

"Yes, sir. She's with Colonel Peterson. They're rescuing Mr. Holsten."

Barron was a combat veteran, and a very intelligent man, with a mind that adjusted quickly even to rapidly changing situations. But his thoughts were swimming now, confusion hovering in his head like a dense fog. It was insane, his crew and a few allies taking on the Confederation forces on Megara. It was hopeless, irrational…and the more he thought about it, the less surprised he was.

"Sir…there's something going on, some kind of conspiracy. Admiral Striker is missing, and there's an arrest warrant out on him. Several hundred officers have been arrested as well. We had to get you out of here, so we can deal with what his happening…and with the Hegemony."

Barron fought to clear his head. He pushed the Hegemony aside for the moment, along with almost everything else that wasn't tactically useful at the moment. He couldn't quite force out the thought of Andi being so close.

Another pair of Marines slipped inside the cell, carrying a wounded comrade. Barron looked around, and he realized one thing. His would-be rescuers were trapped. He saw that they had non-lethal arms, and he understood why they'd come that way. He found the prospect of killing Confederation comrades as repellant as they did. But he quickly realized they had no chance of getting out firing stun ordnance, not with the guards coming at them from two sides firing real ammunition. And if they didn't escape, if he didn't get some chance to get out the warning about what was coming, Hegemony fleets would arrive and cut through an almost defenseless Confederation.

"Did you bring standard ammunition, Bryan?" Barron's voice suddenly went cold, as frigid as space itself.

"Yes, sir, but…"

"There are no 'buts,' General. Either we get out of here and find a way to get the word out…or hundreds, maybe thousands, of Hegemony warships will cut through the Confederation without resistance, possibly killing billions." He paused, trying to ignore the nauseous feeling in his stomach. "We're not getting out of here unless we fight…with everything we've got."

Barron could see the realization in Rogan's face, and the pain as well. But the Marine turned and yelled, loud enough for all his people to hear. "Switch to standard ammunition…we've got to fight our way out of here."

Barron watched, and he wondered if the Marines would obey. He guessed they would. Rogan's people worshipped him, and men and women under fire tended to react with whatever means got them through the fight. They might agonize with guilt afterward, but they would do what they had to do to survive.

"Marines…this is Admiral Barron. I'm with you. We have to get out of here. We have to spread the word about the Hegemony." He'd thrown in with Rogan, added his influence to the general's. If the Marines obeyed, if they killed dozens of Confederation troops—and Barron had no doubt now that they would—it was on him as much as Rogan or Travis or anyone else.

More on him. They were all there to rescue him.

He could see the Marines in the cell moving quickly, grabbing clips from their ammunition belts, and slamming them into place…and a few seconds later, he could hear the familiar sounds of assault rifle fire in the corridor.

Rogan's Marines were good…the best. That meant Confederation guards, who had nothing to do with any conspiracies or plots, would soon be dying.

Barron knew what happened in the prison would haunt him forever. But there was no time for such concerns, not now. He reached out toward Rogan. "Give me your sidearm, General."

Rogan hesitated for an instant. Barron half expected the Marine to try to convince him to stay back, but he didn't do it. There would be no safe place during this escape, nowhere to hide. Rogan took one hand off his assault rifle and grabbed the pistol at his side, spinning it in his hand and giving it to Barron.

Barron nodded his thanks, and he took a deep breath.

Then he exchanged glances with Rogan…and both men plunged out into the corridor.

Chapter Twenty-Eight

Eaton couldn't hold her smile back as the bridge erupted in cheers. *Repulse* had put every weapon it could bring to bear into its broadside, and it had pounded away at the targeted enemy ship. The Confederation flagship had overcome the enemy's technological edge, and, perhaps by nothing more than sheer guts and determination, won the deadly exchange.

Eaton doubted her ship could have done it without Jake Stockton and his fighters. *Repulse* had been fighting two enemies, and that was more, even, than her veterans could have overcome alone. But the fighters had come at the second enemy ship with a terrible abandon, driving in so close, no less than six of them had failed to pull up in time, slamming into the Hegemony vessel at high velocity. She ached for the losses suffered, though she couldn't banish the realization that the suicidal collisions had inflicted more damage than their comrades had done with their targeted laser attacks.

Eaton wasn't happy with herself for the excitement she'd felt watching the enemy ship being torn apart as fighters—her people—missed their escape trajectories, but she'd lost count of the casualties the fleet had suffered so far. Six more was a small price to pay to save *Repulse* and the survivors of its thousand-strong crew. She hated that kind of calculus, but she was too logical to ignore it.

Not that it mattered much. *Repulse* and the fighters had bested the two ships that had closed to destroy her, but her survival prospects past the next few moments hadn't improved. The battle had expanded in breadth, the two formations breaking up as the struggle continued. Clusters of ships were now spread across a quintillion cubic kilometers, a dozen or more localized combats combining to make up the overall engagement. For all the distance, and the time it added to the battle's resolution, it was as apparent to her as ever that her people, for all their heroism, were in a hopeless fight.

"Commodore, Captain Stockton requests permission to land his squadrons." Sonya turned and stared across the bridge, a troubled look on her face. Sara understood immediately. *Repulse* would soon return to conducting wild evasive maneuvers, as more enemy ships moved toward it. The landing bays were a calamitous wreck, strewn with debris and even localized fires still being fought by her damage control crews. Successful landings would be difficult at best, and maybe close to impossible. And any ships that really lost it on the way in could slam into *Repulse* at high speed, damaging the battleship worse than a direct hit from the enemy would.

But Stockton and his people had saved *Repulse*, too, as much as Anya Fritz and the gunners had. She knew they had to be just about out of fuel.

"Permission granted." A pause. "Have them start with gamma bay…and get as many in there as possible." *Repulse*'s number three bay was in the best shape, though that designation was purely a relative term.

"Yes, Commodore."

Sara looked over at the main display. There were another two battleships heading directly for *Repulse*. She knew, with a cold certainty, that there was no way her battered ship could defeat two more. She wondered what good she was doing for Stockton

and his people. She doubted her shattered bays would be able
to refit and relaunch any of the fighters before the enemy ships
engaged. And that new duel would almost certainly be *Repulse's*
last.

She wondered for a moment if Stockton wouldn't rather die
in his fighter than in the battleship when it was finally overwhelmed…but then she realized that he—and she—had to fight
to the end. Stockton and his pilots needed whatever miniscule
chance they had to refit their fighters and get back into the fight.
Eaton couldn't deny them that.

"I want bay crews on full alert, Sonya. Launch control is to
supervise every landing. We're going to get those pilots back on
board, whatever it takes."

"Yes, Commodore."

Sara knew she had the fleet's best flight control officer in
Stara Sinclair.

She also knew Stara was sitting down there, amid a pile of
debris that had once been her control room…facing an almost
impossible task.

* * *

"All right Yellows…let's move it. *Repulse's* gamma bay is
open, and they're waiting for you. Stay on the line with launch
control, and do every damned thing the launch officer tells you."
Stockton knew just who would be on that line, and he knew
how good she was, too. Stara would get his people in, if anyone
could.

His own ship had already passed by *Repulse*, and now he was
burning most of what remained of his fuel to bring his ship to
a stop and then ease it back toward the flagship. He knew he
couldn't stay out that much longer, and that *Repulse* was heading
into another close quarters fight, one that would make landing
even more difficult. But Stockton was in command, and he took
that seriously. He wouldn't land, not until all his people had.
And he was far from sure the damaged *Repulse* could take in so
many fighters.

He listened as the Yellows acknowledged, and he watched as they formed up for a final approach. He had seven members of the squadron still with him, and that was the most of any single unit. He'd lost track of the other Yellows, and he wasn't sure if these seven were all that remained, or if the others had just gotten separated. But he did remember many of Yellow Squadron's exploits, even from before the war, when they'd been commanded by a rival of his, Tillis "Ice" Krill.

Krill had been an enormously skilled pilot, one Stockton knew the Confederation forces could have sorely used in the war against the Union. But, Krill had died fighting against the Alliance battleship *Invictus*, in the desperate duel *Dauntless* had fought with that famous Palatian vessel, a victory that had paved the way for the Confederation to ultimately turn an enemy into an ally.

Krill and Stockton had been considered somewhat of equals back then, and as he watched the Yellows begin their difficult landing runs, he thought of how their paths had diverged. Krill had been one of the first of his close comrades to die in combat, falling to an Alliance ace who could as easily have bested Stockton. Jake had avenged his rival, and then he'd gone on to become the most celebrated ace in the Confederation service… but he'd never shaken the guilt for surviving when Krill died, or the doubt as to which of them would have become the best had they both survived that day.

He was tense as he watched the first fighters approaching *Repulse*. He was worried that they would crash, that more of them would die trying to land…and he was also afraid one of them would not just lose the approach, but crash hard into the bay. That would, at the least, close the ship to more landings, and it would very likely cause considerable damage to the already wounded vessel.

But the Yellows performed well. Stockton ordered up the next group, and the one after that, one squadron at a time coming in with whatever fragments of its strength had joined the attack.

Not all of them made it. At least six crashed, though they

had all managed to control things enough to minimize the damage caused to *Repulse*. Stockton heard enough chatter on the comm to realize that two of the pilots had been killed.

He counted as each ship landed, visualizing *Repulse*'s flight decks, trying to imagine just how many ships Stara and the deck crews could cram in. Then he heard her voice on the comm, and he had his answer...an amazing sixty-four.

"Gamma bay is full up...I need all remaining ships to come into alpha bay." Stara's voice was tense, and from her tone, Stockton had an idea just what shape *Repulse*'s beta bay was in, one she confirmed herself an instant later. "Beta bay is in rough shape, so you're all going to have to bring your A game. Come in slow and easy, and be ready to maneuver with your positioning jets, because there's a lot of debris down there."

Stockton smiled as he heard her voice. He knew she was likely unsurprised that he'd put himself last, but he was also sure some part of her was cursing him for it. She'd never ask him to go against his sense of duty, he knew that. He wasn't an easy person to love...and he also knew he had caused her a lot of pain over the years. For that, he was immensely sorry.

He tapped his positioning thrusters, angling his now-stationary ship back toward *Repulse*. He wasn't sure he was going to make it, that his fuel would last. But he wasn't sure it wouldn't, either. He put the odds right at fifty-fifty, a cold reality he tried to soften by thinking about how many times his chances had been worse.

He tapped the thrust, and his ship lurched forward, accelerating slowly. He was anxious to get back, and he could see that the queue outside *Repulse* had diminished significantly. There were less than fifteen ships still waiting—and what looked like six that had run out of fuel and were drifting. Stockton knew those pilots were as good as dead, though he would do anything possible to rescue them, however futile his efforts might be.

Repulse had engaged the approaching enemy ships, and the flagship had increased its evasive maneuvering. He watched as five ships in a row failed to land successfully, two of them pulling up at the last second and running out of fuel as they sailed off into the depths of space, and the other three crashing, the last one fatally, and with enough velocity to slam hard into the bay, shutting it down.

Stockton was approaching *Repulse* now, and he linked up with the four other pilots still floating outside the battleship. He waited, quietly, feeling as though an eternity had passed as he waited for Stara's voice to return, when it had actually been less than a minute. Finally, he spoke himself.

"Stara…this is Jake. We're going to have to come into beta bay, so give us the go ahead and get the bay doors open.

"Jake…" He could hear from the tone of her voice how bad it was. "Beta bay is in shambles. The door is jammed shut, with a huge gash in the middle. The whole deck is in vacuum conditions, and power is out. There's no way you can land there." He could hear the tears she was fighting back. She had access to his ship's monitors. She knew he had maybe five minutes of fuel left.

And she knew just as well as he did that none of the pilots stranded in dead ships were going to be rescued.

He paused for a few seconds, coming close to giving up, to yielding to the inevitable end that seemed to be on him. None of the other battleships were close enough for his people to reach with the fuel they had left. There was nothing to do except stay where he was…and wait for death.

Except for one thing. "Raptor" Stockton didn't give up. Not ever.

"Listen to me, Stara…get some battery-powered lights down in the bay. We've got to see where we're going, especially since I suspect the whole place is covered in wreckage."

"Jake, there's just no way. We're trying to clear out some of the ships crammed into gamma bay and get it open again. Maybe…"

"There's no time, Stara." He was surprised by the strength and confidence in his own voice. He knew perfectly well, if Stara was telling him beta bay was a no go, it had to be in really bad shape. "Just do what I say…please. Get me some lighting down there. Somehow."

He waited, once again for a few seconds that seemed like an eternity. Then her voice was back, and stronger. His strength was contagious. He'd made her believe he could do it, at least for the moment. That was all he needed.

"We're sending down portable lights, Jake. It's going to take ten minutes."

"I've only got five."

"Jake, there's no access, no lifts working anywhere near the bay…"

"And in six minutes, I'll be out of fuel…and as good as dead. So will the others out here with me."

"All right, Jake…we'll get it done. Somehow." Another pause. "Just give me as much of that five minutes as you can."

"You know I'll give you everything I've got, Stara, my love."

* * *

"The analysis is complete. The AI has determined a 98.3765 percent chance that the enemy stopped here because there is something that they do not want to expose, almost certainly a course leading to their home worlds. I have cross-checked this with astrographic surveys, and determined a similar likelihood that the transit points orbiting this system's inner star lead to destinations near the Rim. Considering the enemy's actions, I believe we have virtual certain evidence to support the conclusion."

The man spoke calmly, coolly, though in the system around the vessel he currently occupied, a fierce battle was underway. The barbarians had fought with far greater skill and capability than any of the Masters present had expected. Indeed, their losses would greatly exceed even the most pessimistic projections. Nevertheless, the enemy could be obliterated…if they were willing to sacrifice enough of their own ships to achieve that.

"I agree with your conclusions, Ninety-Six." Genetic ranking was considered a more formal mode of address among the Masters. While Inferiors would always address a Master by his ranking, among themselves, they often used their given names—Raketh, in the case of Ninety-Six. However, Raketh was the commander of the fleet, and the highest-ranking Master present. That alone, notwithstanding the fight taking place, justified the use of more formal address. "There is therefore a question we must consider. In our pursuit of the barbarians, we have held back our thrust levels. However, we are capable of engaging sufficient thrust to exceed theirs. We can, therefore, disengage and proceed forward along our projection of the enemy's original course, to discover clues as to the location of their home worlds. That is our primary mission. We need not waste time on the tedious job of hunting down and destroying the remnants of this single fleet. They are already worn down close to tactical worthlessness."

Ninety-Six breathed deeply, centering his thoughts, considering One Hundred Sixty-Three's proposal. He was in command, and he was above his comrades, as they were above almost all humans who existed. On the fleet, his was the final word on any matter, as was the responsibility for all that transpired. It ran counter to his tactical sense to allow a wounded and cornered enemy to survive…and yet, he knew it was possible the enemy had been able to get some kind of warning back to their home worlds. He couldn't imagine any group of humans capable of mounting a meaningful defense against the massed strength of the Hegemony, but his view of strategy clearly opposed his tactical view. The sooner he could discover the route to the enemy's home, the less prepared they would be for the coming onslaught.

He sat quietly, analyzing every option, considering advantages and disadvantages. In the end, he reached a decision. He was not entirely comfortable with it…the situation defied an easy choice. But he was certain it was the best option to pursue.

"The fleet will break off at once and set a course toward the inner primary. We will then divide our forces and proceed through all transit points discovered." He paused for a moment, turning his head and looking out over his comrades. "We will find the enemy's home worlds…and then we can begin the final subjugation of these Inferiors."

Chapter Twenty-Nine

"You're insane, all of you…you know that, right? Do you realize what you've done?" Holsten had been more or less silent during the frantic race to the spaceport, but now he unloaded on his rescuers. "I'd have had trouble getting you out of this when I was in my office, in full command of Confederation Intelligence…but now, I'm a fugitive, too. I appreciate the loyalty, but I didn't want you all to become renegades…" Andi suspected "traitors" was the first word that came to Holsten's mind, but he'd held it back. "…to break me out."

"You don't know what's happening, Gary," she said, beating Jon Peterson to a response. "Hundreds of officers have been cashiered and charged with criminal corruption. Tyler has been arrested, and Van Striker has been charged, too, though he's still missing. This isn't just some political vendetta against you. It's far more, some kind of wide-ranging plot."

"Van is missing?" A second later, with even more surprise in his voice, "Tyler is back? The White Fleet has returned?"

"No, not the fleet…just Tyler on *Dauntless*, with a few other ships."

"Why did he return? And without the fleet? That's not like him. What would get Tyler Barron to leave his command behind?"

"I don't know, Gary." Andi's voice was strained. She was worried about Barron, worried sick, and talking about him was only making it worse. Her team had gotten to the vehicles they'd hidden and made it to the spaceport…far more easily, she realized now, than she'd expected. And Vig and the others had *Pegasus* ready to go. Not for the first time, Andi was grateful that she'd had her old ship streamlined for atmospheric operations. It had been expensive, certainly by her standards at the time, when she'd had a dozen other uses for the money. But the ability to slip into an atmosphere and escape a pursuer who couldn't follow had been extremely helpful at times.

Still, there was no sign of Bryan Rogan and his Marines. No sign of Tyler.

She looked across the large paved surface around her ship. Troyus's spaceport had extensive modern terminals, with docking tubes and other conveniences, but *Pegasus* was out in the port's hinterlands, along the edge where low-budget tramp freighters and other dated vessels landed. She could have afforded the docking fee anywhere in the spaceport, of course, but her place out among the transient craft brought with it a considerable increase in privacy.

She stared off in the distance, her frustration and fear growing with every moment Barron and the Marines didn't appear.

She turned back toward her ship. Her crew was already aboard…as were the bodies of the two Marines killed in the operation. Holsten stood next to the ramp, looking pensive now, clearly concerned about everything he'd just heard. Andi wanted to take Peterson and his people back to *Dauntless*, too, but there was just no way *Pegasus* could manage Bryan Rogan's Marines *and* Peterson's. And the colonel's Marines had a far better chance of blending in than *Dauntless*'s.

Peterson had told her half a dozen times not to worry. He was confident his people wouldn't be traced to what had happened, that they could simply finish their leaves and depart back to Dannith to rejoin their units…or come up with reasons to remain on the capital. Andi didn't completely believe him, though she'd also decided she wouldn't bet against the grizzled Marine keeping his people safe somehow. Taking the bodies was the best way she could help. Peterson might avoid unwanted attention, but if two of his Marines were found dead at the scene…not even the stubborn old colonel could explain his way out of that one.

There was room in her ship—just—for *Dauntless*'s contingent of Marines. It would be crowded, and damned uncomfortable, but they'd manage. At least for the ride to orbit.

Assuming Bryan even makes it back.

Or Tyler…

She knew it hadn't been *that* long, but to her it seemed hours had passed. Despite her best efforts, she was beginning to lose hope. Time wasn't an ally, and *Pegasus* had to lift off—soon. She couldn't imagine giving that order without Tyler aboard…and, yet, she knew she might very well have to.

She stared off across the flat expanse of the spaceport, her vision obscured by the tears she was struggling to hold back.

Come on, Tyler…come on…

Please…

* * *

"*Dauntless*, this is patrol cruiser *Stafford*. You are emitting energy frequencies that are jamming ground-based communications in Troyus City. Is this some kind of malfunction? You must stop at once, even if it is necessary to shut down all but emergency power." The signal was weak, the reception heavy with static. The jamming effort was concentrated on ground targets, but it was wreaking havoc on orbital communications and scans near the ship as well.

Atara Travis listened to the words coming from her comm. She'd almost switched it to her headset, so only she could hear what was happening. But her people weren't stupid. They knew what was going on, and she figured being secretive was likely to do more harm than good. She was counting on the crew following her orders…regardless of the fact that those commands looked very much like treason right now.

She glanced across the bridge toward Cumberland, taking her read on the officer as she did. Tyler had chosen him after Sonya Eaton had transferred to *Repulse*, and Tyler Barron had a very good sixth sense when it came to choosing officers.

If Tyler trusted him, I will.

"Commander, advise *Stafford* that we are experiencing a major information systems malfunction. We will be shutting down the main AI, and that should terminate the jamming." It was the lamest piece of garbage she'd ever tried to pass off on anyone, but it was all she had. *Stafford* wasn't a threat to *Dauntless* in a fight, but Atara didn't want to be forced to blast the patrol ship either.

Or to find out if her gunners would even fire at the vessel…

She'd managed to subtly alter *Dauntless*'s orbit to keep the ship out of the firing arc of Prime Base. Unlike the patrol ship, the vast orbital station was certainly a danger to her ship. In fact, she imagined the fortress could blast *Dauntless* to plasma in an astonishingly short time. Nevertheless, even without Prime's guns targeting the battleship, there was no spot in Megara orbit where multiple defensive facilities weren't in range.

It would take some time for the situation to escalate to actual firing. She didn't know exactly how high up an order would have to come from to authorize attacking a Confederation ship, but she had a pretty fair guess that blasting *Stafford* would accelerate the whole process considerably.

She watched Cumberland, keeping her eyes on the officer as he sat there and looked back at her for a few seconds. She stared, enduring the agony of the pause, waiting to see if he would do as she'd commanded. Then he turned and relayed her answer, cleaning up the wording a bit. He spoke slowly, clearly…and surprisingly convincingly. He was with her.

His words still didn't sound all that believable to her, but she had to admit that Cumberland's version was better than hers had been.

She sat for a few more seconds, waiting for an answer that would give her an idea of just how long she had. Her eyes shifted instinctively toward her screen. She wanted to see *Pegasus* on the display, but, of course, *Dauntless*'s jamming blocked her own scanners as well. She knew she was close enough to do the same to the orbital forts. The platforms had been designed to face an attacking enemy approaching from space, not a ship that had been allowed into close orbit, and the jamming would exacerbate the sub-optimal firing arcs of the fortresses in range. She thought about moving the ship, adjusting the orbital course to throw off anyone targeting her…but she couldn't do that either. Without scanners, *Pegasus* wouldn't be able to find *Dauntless* unless the battleship was in the exact spot she was supposed to occupy.

"*Dauntless*…you are instructed to cut all power immediately, and then to release your system to control by Orbital Command."

Atara sighed. Whoever was in command on *Stafford* didn't seem to be a fool. She'd been hoping to buy enough time for *Pegasus* to get back from Troyus City, but she didn't think she could stall for long enough.

Then an idea came into her head. Maybe she could cripple *Stafford* without inflicting casualties…or too many casualties. That would trigger a response from the orbital forces, of course, but again…not too many officers would open fire on a Confederation battleship without orders from much higher up, and certainly not the famous *Dauntless*, even if she was only the successor to the celebrated vessel.

The problem was arming the weapons. Even with the jamming effects, if she maxed out *Dauntless*'s reactors, it would be detected. And then someone would have to respond.

She turned toward Cumberland. "Commander…engineering is to increase the output of reactor one…incrementally, one percent at a time." She didn't need all of *Dauntless*'s power, not to disable a patrol ship. At this range, one good shot from a secondary battery would accomplish that with the right targeting… and her gunners were the best in the fleet.

"Yes, Captain." She guessed from Cumberland's tone that he suspected what she intended, and if he didn't agree, he didn't oppose it. She listened as he repeated the orders, and then she leaned back in her chair, looking out over the bridge, wondering just what was going through the minds of her officers.

What would be going through your mind? They all have families, loved ones, lives, careers…and following you now could cost them all of that.

But she knew they were loyal, as well…to her, and even more to Admiral Barron. Every one of them knew just what was coming, what an unopposed Hegemony invasion would mean to those families and loved ones.

She decided she would bet on her people, that they could understand what was happening, that they would refuse to believe Tyler Barron was a criminal.

That they would do whatever they had to do to ensure the Confederation was ready for the war that was coming…even if that action was one they'd previously considered unthinkable.

*   *   *

Barron winced. He'd taken a slug in his arm, and while the wound wasn't critical, it hurt like a sonofabitch. The Marines had fought their way out of the wing of the building where his cell had been located, and now they were heading toward the underground level. Rogan's people had brought transports with them, but the whole area was on alert now, and even without active comm systems to coordinate the search efforts, it was hard to imagine the vehicles hadn't been found.

Barron's answer to that problem had been a simple one. If they didn't have their own transports, they'd have to steal some. And his gut told him the best place for that would be on the subterranean parking levels.

As soon as his rescuers had truly started fighting back, they'd cut through the opposing guards in just a few minutes, gunning down half of them and sending the others off in ignominious flight. That had been a welcome surprise, for as long as he managed to hold back the thoughts that he was responsible for the deaths of several dozen Confederation troopers. He told himself it was necessary, that billions would die if the Confederation wasn't ready to defend itself against a Hegemony invasion. That was all true, but he also found it cold comfort, all the more because his prison garb was stained now with the blood of the dead. In its own way, that got to him more than anything else.

He pushed aside the angst he felt, struggling to turn it into more determination. The great cost of his escape made it even more vital that he succeeded. If he failed, those men and women—and those of Rogan's Marines who'd died as well—would have been sacrificed for nothing, and everyone he cared about...Andi, Atara, Rogan, would all be destroyed, arrested on charges of treason and imprisoned for the rest of their lives. Or worse. And the Hegemony would...

He raced toward the stairs, following the emergency exit signs. The lifts would be faster, but he couldn't be sure what tracking ability his pursuers retained...and getting trapped in an elevator shut down from a distant control center was not an end to the escape he was willing to risk.

He ran down the stairs, almost recklessly, his arm hurting even more as his heart rate increased. He knew some of the Marines were carrying wounded, that he had to be pushing them to their limits...but he'd rather that than see them captured or wiped out by pursuing guards.

He reached the bottom of the long set of stairs and came to a sealed hatch. The building was on lockdown, but that wasn't going to stop him. He turned and shot a glance at Rogan, and then he stepped back as the Marine general ordered two of his people to blast the door open. It was a heavy, thick metal hatch, too strong for gunfire to obliterate, so the Marines affixed a pair of charges to the thing. After everyone had stepped back, they blew it apart, the explosion considerably stronger than what was needed.

The door was gone, nothing remaining but scattered shards of metal...and beyond, Barron could see his instincts had been correct. It was a massive garage, three-quarters filled with all sorts of vehicles.

He turned around, looking at Bryan and the rest of the Marines gathered up behind him.

"Do we have anyone here who remembers a misspent youth boosting transports before the Corps got you?"

Chapter Thirty

8 Kilometers from CFS Repulse
Unknown System 20
Year 316 AC

"All of you…follow me, and stay on *tight*. I'm not going to bullshit any of you. This is the toughest landing any of us have ever tried. But the alternative is sitting out here in powered down fighters, waiting to die." He felt a wave of guilt at the words. He was on the open comm, and he knew he had people listening who were already in just the situation he'd described. He ached for them, and later he would mourn for their loss, and blame himself. But he couldn't do anything for them now…and he *could* save the four ships still with him.

Maybe.

"Jake…you've got lighting in place in the bay." Stara's voice, followed by a pause. "It's not very bright, but it's the best we could do in four minutes." She hesitated again. "Be careful…" Then, a few seconds later, and still on the open comm: "I love you." He knew her words were genuine, but the fact that she'd said them only told him she wasn't sure he would make it.

Which made them even, since he wasn't sure he'd make it either.

Jake's relationship with Stara was no secret, despite his early efforts to keep it that way, but he was an intensely private person about his feelings. It was a part of him with which he'd always maintained a shaky relationship. He wanted to respond, to tell her the same thing. But he couldn't do it. Not then.

And he knew she knew that.

"All right, focus! Stay sharp every second. Do exactly what I do, and none of you mess it up. Trust me, you don't want to deal with me if you screw up, not now."

He brought his ship around, adjusting the angle toward what was left of *Repulse*'s beta bay doors. Stara hadn't been kidding. What should have been a giant metal hatch, or prior to a landing, a large, open, rectangle, was a jumble of sharp and twisted metal…with a jagged hole in the middle wide enough to accommodate a fighter. Just.

Doubt flooded into his mind, a sudden certainty that what he was trying to do was impossible. Thoughts like that were generally alien to Stockton, but his eyes focused on the opening. It was a rough circle, with two knife-like shards of the door protruding into the center of the open area. He'd have to slip between them, and there wasn't much room to spare. He was worried enough about himself, but he could feel despair gathering in his mind for the pilots following him.

They were all veterans, like most of his people. Few of the rookies who'd come with the White Fleet had survived the struggles of the past months, and the ones who had could no longer be called raw. They'd earned their status alongside the rest of the elite warriors. Still, the landing they all had to make would be one of the most difficult maneuvers any of them had ever attempted, and the chances of all five of them making it in were…well, he didn't want to think too hard about that.

He tapped his thrusters again, slowing his already crawling ship a bit more. There wasn't much time. *Repulse* was in a fight of its own, and he was well aware that the needs of the battleship outweighed those of a few pilots trying to land. If Eaton had to change position, or blast the engines at 10g, she would do it…and none of his people had the reflexes to react or the fuel to follow.

He was close now, no more than ten kilometers, and he could

see the hulking ship with his naked eyes. She was battered… there were half dozen scars on her hull where enemy weapons had sliced into her.

Where her spacers had died…

She was gyrating wildly, too, evasive maneuvers designed to confuse enemy targeting. *Repulse* wasn't changing her basic vector or her velocity, she was just blasting her thrusters for seemingly random periods and at unpredictable angles. Stockton knew enough about such maneuvers to realize they were a complicated mix of insanely complex AI-driven calculations, combined with a good portion of utter randomness. It was far from simple to jerk a ship around, making it difficult for enemy gunners to lock on while ultimately maintaining a steady course and speed. Stockton had done the same thing countless times in his fighter, but he knew the complexities increased exponentially with a ship the size of *Repulse*.

He reached down toward his comm unit, activating the link to *Repulse*'s AI. The enemy's jamming cut the effective range of such a connection, but there was no way he could land without it. He was a good pilot, but no human being could match the evasive maneuvers of the battleship without assistance from the AI.

He breathed a sigh of relief when he saw the small blue light indicating the link was in place. Then his eyes moved back up to the cockpit's forward visor, with *Repulse*'s great bulk now completely covering the field of view.

He had an even better view of the flagship's damage now, not just the fresh wounds from the current fight, but the hasty patch jobs from the battles of the past months. Stockton was no stranger to war—in fact he'd become disturbingly accepting of it as the norm in his life—but he rarely got such a close-up view.

He was less than a kilometer away. He couldn't recall ever approaching a landing so slowly. He just hadn't had the fuel to accelerate and then decelerate again, and he knew the only way he was going to thread the needle and get into the bay was *slowly*.

He was lined up with the opening now…and it was even

worse than he'd expected. He'd have to bring his ship in at a slight angle to match the shape of the hole.

He tapped the controls again, slowing down even more. He was crawling toward the bay, the shattered doors completely covering his field of view as he approached. He could see the ripples on the metal now, places where it had melted and instantly refrozen, and beyond was a barely visible glow—the portable lighting, everything *Repulse*'s teams could get in place in time.

And all he'd have to see by as he landed.

His eyes were focused, his concentration complete. He shut everything out of his mind but the gash in the bay doors. He relaxed as much as he could and allowed his intuition, his experience, to play its part.

He took a deep breath. He was meters away now, and even as he exhaled and let his hands move slowly over the controls, his fighter slipped through the opening.

He was inside the bay!

The lights were positioned along one end of the cavernous compartment, casting a light that dimmed quickly as it reached the center of the great open space. Stockton wished he had better conditions, but he suspected the effort required to get even the units that were there into place had been astonishing. He knew dozens of crewmembers had worked to get him back aboard—him and the four pilots following him. And they had done it in the middle of a desperate battle, one that called for everything *Repulse*'s people had to give.

His head was unmoving, trying to make out the deck in the shadowy illumination. He could see dark spots all around, chunks of debris covering virtually every meter of the deck. He had to find someplace to put his ship down, but there was nothing.

No...wait...

His eyes caught a small section of deck that looked open. It was large enough for all five ships...barely. He reached out and flipped a switch to activate his beacon, directing his pilots to follow him.

He tapped the positioning thrusters, bringing his ship toward the flat area and lowering it slightly. It was fine work, as precise and delicate as anything he'd ever done in his fighter. There was no room for error...none. And he swore to himself that he would make none.

His hands were covered in sweat. His whole body was, and it took all he had to hold himself steady, to move slowly, steadily toward the spot he'd chosen. He was coming in on the extreme end of the open space, leaving as much room as possible for the other pilots.

Assuming they get past the doors...

He was on target, everything under control. He had made it. He was going to land without...

Suddenly, *Repulse* shook hard. The flagship had taken a hit, Stockton realized immediately, just as he was bringing his ship down toward the deck.

From his perspective, the deck and walls of the bay jerked wildly. He felt a coldness everywhere in his body, a panic he somehow managed to keep under control, even as his hands moved on the controls, seemingly on their own. It was pure reflex, raw instinct...and it saved his life.

His fighter slammed down on the deck, hard...but not too hard. It took him a few seconds to realize he had made it, and another few before he understood that he'd managed to come down without causing substantial damage to the bay...or blocking the space he'd picked out for the four ships following him in.

He sat where he was. The bay was in vacuum, and he couldn't leave the ship until the flight crew came to get him with a vac suit. He could hear hissing all around him as his ship lost the last of its air through the small rents the hard landing had torn into its battered hull...but he flipped on the emergency system, and the small escape cocoon, the capsule that would have kept him alive in space for some hours if he'd ditched, enveloped him. *Repulse* couldn't launch rescue ships, but Stockton didn't have doubt the deck crews would get to him quickly in the middle of the bay.

Repulse shook again, even harder than the last time. Yet

another hit.

They'll get to me, all of us…as long as Repulse is still here.

* * *

"What's going on?" Sara Eaton had intended the words as a silent thought, but they came out of her mouth anyway. The scanners all showed the same thing. The enemy fleet was disengaging and pulling away from what remained of her fleet at massive acceleration rates. It looked very much like a retreat, save for two facts. First, the enemy had no reason to break off. They were on the verge of total victory.

And second, they weren't moving back the way they had come. They were flying past her ships, heading toward the inner primary.

She felt relief…for a few seconds. *Repulse* had been outmatched, bracketed by another two enemy battleships and under an intense barrage, one she knew her vessel couldn't long survive. And the rest of the fleet was in no less dire a situation. Her people had fought hard, even brilliantly, and she was deeply proud of them all…but the end had been near. Then the enemy just broke off, ceased their relentless attacks and blasted away at better than 80g.

The relief faded quickly, driven off by a cold realization. There was only one explanation for the enemy's action. They had concluded that the fleet had stopped and offered battle for the very reason it had. Because the transit points ahead led not into the depths of unexplored space, but back to the very home worlds the fleet had fled into the darkness to protect.

Eaton's body went tense, the last vestiges of the satisfaction she'd felt when Stockton and all four of his comrades had successfully landed gone in an instant. As Eaton considered the implications of the enemy's actions further, she realized she didn't know how to respond.

None of her ships could match the enemy's acceleration. A fighter strike might have a chance of reaching the enemy ships before they got too far out of range, but only if she launched one now. And most of her fighters were still out in space, their fuel and energy reserves almost exhausted. The only fighters in launch bays were the ones that had just landed on *Repulse*, and they were utterly depleted as well, not to mention crammed into half-functional bays. It would be hours before her people could get even a few squadrons launched, if they could at all, and that would be far too late.

She took a deep breath, trying to resist the despair threatening to take her. The spacers of her fleet had fought hard, and many had died…and now, it looked like all of that had been for nothing. The enemy would transit through the points orbiting the primary, and then they would be close—dangerously close—to finding the Confederation. Worse, perhaps, the chance of discovering meaningful clues to direct them the rest of the wa, would be very high. A lone smuggler's ship or some kind of survey vessel exploring the closest in-systems of the Badlands was all it would take to lead the enemy to Dannith or to one of the other frontier worlds.

Then darkness would descend on the Confederation.

Eaton drew her strength from a single hope, that Tyler Barron had used the short time she'd bought him well, that he'd rallied the fleet, begun the process of recommissioning warships from the reserves, put the whole Confederation on high alert.

Because if he hadn't…the future would be a grim one.

Chapter Thirty-One

"Andi…we have to go. We're out of time." Vig Merrick's voice was soft, filled with the pain he felt at his friend's misery. Andi knew that Vig understood, perhaps more than anyone, just how important Tyler Barron was to her…and he knew what it would do to her to launch *Pegasus* without him, to leave him behind, to almost certain recapture. Or worse.

She turned toward him, her face wet from the sobbing she'd hidden from the others. "If we leave him here, he doesn't have a chance. They'll recapture him, add an escape attempt to his charges…if they don't just take the opportunity to get rid of him. 'Shot while trying to escape' is one of the oldest tricks in the book." Andi knew very well that something was going on in the Confederation's capital, something dark and dangerous… and she had to believe whoever had instigated Barron's arrest would be just as glad to be rid of the famous officer for good. "If I leave him, I could be killing him."

Vig just looked back at her, silent for a moment. Then he said, "I've got the ship ready to go, Andi…but it can't be long before the spaceport goes on alert and we're stuck down here. I think we can get to orbit without an assist from ground-based systems, but if they want to ground us, you know they can do it easily enough." He paused.

She knew he wanted to urge her to take off again, but he didn't say anything. She looked back across the spaceport. Vig was right. They were almost out of time, if they weren't already. As hard as it was for her to imagine, she knew Barron could be dead already, killed in a botched rescue attempt. The thought cut through her like a dull blade, but she'd always been a realist…and she knew if Barron himself could speak to her then, he would have told her to go.

She sighed softly. "Okay, Vig, go back and get the launch system ready." She looked back across the spaceport, hoping against hope to see something, for some kind of miracle. But there was nothing.

Vig nodded, and he turned and raced up the ramp, into *Pegasus*. The others were all aboard already. Only Andi had remained, looking out in the distance through her tears. She turned around and followed her first officer. She paused at the top of the ramp, turning back and taking one last look before her hand moved toward the controls…and pressed the button to close up her ship.

There was no more time to cling to hope. They had to go.

*   *   *

Barron bounced around in the transport, slamming hard into the wall as the vehicle raced along the road leading to the spaceport. It was past dawn now, and the light was coming up over the horizon, stripping the convoy of stolen vehicles of what remained of the cover of night.

Barron hadn't been surprised when no fewer than four of Rogan's Marines had answered his call, confessing to some level of knowledge of stealing transports. The Marines recruited from some of the poorest and toughest worlds in the Confederation, and more than a few of its recruits joined up to escape lives of poverty and crime. Or the reach of local law enforcement.

His makeshift gang of thieves had managed to grab three large transports from the garage and get them started. Barron knew they all had antitheft systems, but he was hoping the jamming would shut them down and give his people a headstart before they were pursued. Or, at least, pursued by another set of enforcement personnel besides the units from the prison that were undoubtedly searching for them even now.

And the spaceport isn't exactly the hardest destination to figure out for when chasing an escaped prisoner...

"What kind of ship do we have waiting? One of *Dauntless*'s big shuttles?" Barron was trying to keep his mind out of the abyss, but he couldn't see how a shuttle was going to escape when there would almost certainly be some kind of pursuit before they reached orbit. The small vessels were good for transporting personnel and supplies, but no one would call one of them fast or maneuverable.

"No, sir..." Rogan sounded hesitant to answer, and he paused for a few seconds before continuing. "*Pegasus* is waiting for us, Admiral." Another few seconds of silence. "Assuming we get there in time."

Barron was both excited and horrified. He was anxious to see Andi, more than he'd even imagined in the almost two years since he'd last seen her...but he hated the idea of her being involved in any of what was going on, putting herself at such grave risk. She'd finally achieved what she'd pursued her whole life, and the idea of her losing it all and ending up on some penal colony was too much for him to imagine.

The transport shook hard again as the driver—not one of the Marines with experience stealing vehicles, but another who'd confessed to a shady past—pushed it to the limit. Once Barron had asked about experience stealing vehicles, the floodgates had opened...and Corporal Sandor Donovan had admitted to serving as the getaway driver for one of the infamous local gangs on the rugged world of Toranol. His candor had landed him in the driver's seat of the largest of the transports, and given him the task of getting Barron to the spaceport.

"We're almost there, sir...but I think we picked up a tail." The Marine's voice was rough, raspy. He sounded almost as though he had reverted back to his days as a gang member.

Barron looked down at the small display screen. The scanners were still more or less useless, but he switched to the rear camera. There they were. Four or five heavy transports, lightly armored…and definitely military. He'd just begun to wonder if they were armed when he saw a small turret on top of the lead vehicle. A few seconds later, his eyes caught a flash of light, and he heard an explosion off to the side.

"Faster, Donovan." Barron said the words without knowing if it was even possible. He'd been banged all around in the transport's main cabin as the Marine drove just like Barron imagined a getaway driver would. But now they needed even more speed. And evasive maneuvers, too. If that gun scored a hit, the chase would be over. Even if they all survived the inevitable impact from a crash, their pursuers would be on them before they could even think of climbing out and running.

Or fighting back.

The transport's power plant whined loudly as Donovan called for more energy, squeezing every extra kph he could get. Barron reached down and grabbed his rifle, just as Rogan did the same. He doubted they would have much chance to fight their way out, but it was instinct as much as anything else.

"We're at the spaceport, sir." Donovan's voice was surprisingly calm, considering the Marine was driving the transport to a near overload and dodging incoming fire while he was doing it.

Barron felt a small burst of hope that they were almost there…until he realized he was leading the pursuers right to *Pegasus*.

To Andi.

*   *   *

"All right…everybody, make sure you're buckled in. It's likely to be a rough ride before we get there." Andi was morose, as depressed as she had ever been. She was driving herself forward by pure stubbornness, by a sense of duty to Holsten, and by the hope, however fleeting, that the intelligence chief—ex intelligence chief—could somehow deal with whatever was happening…and maybe even save Tyler.

If he's even still alive…

She reached down, putting her fingers against the engine activation switch.

But before she pushed it, she turned one last time to look at the screen, at the feed from Pegasus's exterior security cameras. Then she froze.

There were three vehicles racing across the spaceport's tarmac, heading straight for her ship. She felt herself filled with surprise, and then a new hope. It was Tyler. It had to be.

Her joy lasted only a few seconds, until she saw an explosion next to the lead transport. Chunks of blasted concrete flew through the air…and a second later, she saw the vehicles following Barron's. Six of them, all armored vehicles, firing from top-mounted guns.

And, no doubt, full of armed soldiers…

"Vig, take the controls." She snapped off the command to her friend as she unhooked her harness and raced off the bridge, climbing up the small ladder to the cockpit surrounding the controls for *Pegasus*'s main turret. Her ship wasn't heavily armed, not by the standards of war vessels—and Megara's atmosphere would quickly attenuate what strength the laser bolts did have. But such thoughts generally centered on spaceships and other large targets. At less than one thousand meters, *Pegasus*'s guns would obliterate a transport, even an armored military one— atmosphere or no.

She slid into the chair, pulling on the headset and goggles and running her hand across the control panel, flipping on the row of switches. She reached out and grabbed the controls, moving her arms to position the gun. The scanners were still down, but the goggles gave her a view in any direction, assembled from data fed in from the external cameras.

She brought the sights toward the lead transport, the one firing at Barron's convoy. She didn't like the idea of frying a truckload full of Confederation troops, but she'd be damned if she'd let them kill Tyler…or take him back to prison. She aimed and fired once, a warning shot less than three meters in front of the transport.

But the vehicle kept coming, racing across the open space, as Barron's transports slowed to a stop in front of *Pegasus*.

The slow-moving—soon to be still—trucks were sitting ducks. She didn't have a choice. She had to show Barron's pursuers she meant business.

That she would kill to stop them.

She aimed her second shot, bringing the sights in line with the front of the first vehicle. She hesitated, for a second at most, one last blast of guilt...and then she pressed the firing stud.

The laser flared out in a blinding flash, the normally invisible pulse lit by the dust and early morning fog, even in the brightening dawn sky. She couldn't see it very well from inside her ship, but she knew what it looked like. She was staring right at her target when the laser ripped through the forward armor. Perhaps five seconds later, the transport skidded to the side and flipped over, leaving a trail of flames behind it.

She brought the gun around, locking on the second vehicle, all the while hoping the fate of the lead transport would send the others into retreat. For a few seconds, the trucks still moved forward, and her finger tightened again. But then they skidded to a near stop and turned around, fleeing from *Pegasus* in considerable disorder.

Andi sighed, her relief almost palpable. It was overlaid by guilt for what she'd done already, and she wondered how many she'd killed. But she was deeply grateful she hadn't had to add to that toll.

She stayed where she was for a few seconds more, until she was sure the vehicles were in wholesale retreat. Then she jumped up and slid down the ladder, racing toward the cargo bay and shouting for Vig to open the rear doors again.

She hadn't seen Tyler yet, and she had no way to be sure he was in one of those transports, that he'd gotten out alive. But, somehow, she knew he was, with a certainty she couldn't explain.

She knew the trip to orbit would be difficult and dangerous, that she might be reunited with Tyler only for both of them to die in moments. But she didn't think about that, not for an instant. All she wanted was to get him on board, to see him again, to confirm her belief that he was still alive.

* * *

Barron leapt out of the vehicle, turning as soon as he hit the pavement and shouting for the Marines to hurry. They'd come a long way, and *Pegasus*'s laser had pushed back their pursuers, but he knew there would be reinforcements arriving any second. Probably heavier vehicles with stronger armament… guns powerful enough to threaten *Pegasus* herself. He felt nearly unrestrained joy at the sight of Andi's ship, and dread as well at her presence, but he knew he didn't have time for any of that.

He didn't have time for anything.

"Let's go…move it!" he bellowed with his harshest command tone, waving his arms as he yelled. Even as he stood there, he heard the sounds of boots on metal, the Marines streaming up *Pegasus*'s ramp and into the vessel's cargo bay.

"Admiral, you have to go!" It was Bryan Rogan, standing right next to him, his hand reaching out, grabbing Barron's arm. "You have to board, sir."

"Not until everyone is aboard. You all came to get me, and I'll be damned if we're leaving anyone behind." He knew it was foolish, at least in terms of overall danger assessment. The Hegemony was coming, and it brought the threat of death on a mass scale with it. He *had* to get away. He had to find a way to get the word out, to prepare the Confederation for what was coming. But none of that moved him…not until the last of the Marines had raced aboard, and he and Rogan stood alone, looking out over the tarmac at another column of assault vehicles racing into the spaceport.

He turned and grabbed onto Rogan's arm, even as the Marine was holding onto him, and the two men raced up the ramp, onto *Pegasus*…and a chance of escape.

Chapter Thirty-Two

Grimaldi Base
Krakus System
Year 316 AC

"Sir…we have a ship emerging from the Wrangor transit point. It's not on any schedule." The officer's voice carried only the slightest hint of concern. A military installation as important as Grimaldi Base never ignored any possible risk, but a single ship emerging from a transit point that led deeper into the Confederation, and away from any enemy, was unlikely to be a danger. Still, regulations were clear on the standard procedure.

"Order Force Beta to intercept. Send out a communique. Instruct the vessel to identify itself and power down to await inspection." Admiral Clint Winters sat in the center of the base's enormous control room. He'd inherited the command when Admiral Striker had returned to Megara after the war to assume his position as supreme naval commander. The sector Grimaldi guarded, which had seen so much fighting, had become quiet. So quiet, even, that Winters had found it almost nerve-wracking after six years of bloody war.

Grimaldi was enormous, the greatest construct in the Confederation, and by extension, the entire Rim…rivaled only by Megara's massive Prime Base. The Confederation and the Union had faced each other as enemies for nearly a century, fighting

four all-out wars and engaging in more than a few skirmishes
and border disputes between those formal conflicts. Grimaldi
was the nerve center of operations on the hostile border.

But that great headquarters was silent now, the huge fleets
that had once surrounded it mostly gone, their ships decom-
missioned or sent to peacetime stations throughout the Confederation. The fighting had ceased—as had the dying, much to
Winters's relief—and he was left with nothing more important
to do than argue with supply officers who shorted his logistics
requests, and to deal with the occasional foul-up in communications and manifests. With the continuing peace, it looked
as though things would stay that way for a long while. By all
accounts, the Union was in dire shape, in no condition to lash
out at the Confederation again. Not for some time.

"Yes, sir." The communications officer relayed the orders,
and a moment later he turned back toward Winters and advised
the admiral that the force commander had acknowledged.

The admiral looked at the display, watching as a small symbol
appeared right next to the transit point. It wasn't the first unexpected ship that had come to Grimaldi, though such incidents
were far from common occurrences. Operations and proto-
cols around the base had relaxed somewhat with the coming
of peace, but they remained the tightest in the Confederation,
mostly because everyone involved understood the strategic
importance of the base and system.

And they all knew Winters would tolerate only so much
before the admiral, who was widely referred to as "the Sledgehammer" would come down hard on those responsible for any
shirking of duty or sloppiness in operations.

Winters watched as the ships of Force Beta moved to intercept the newly arrived vessel…just in case. He looked at the
display, thinking that "Force Beta" was a bit too grand a name
for a light cruiser and two patrol ships. But the naval forces
stationed at Grimaldi were a fraction of what had been there
during the war, and the three battleships assigned to duty there
were docked, in a partially inactive status.

He glanced back at his screen as scanner data began to flood in. Force Beta was more than enough to handle the new arrival in the unlikely event it had come to cause trouble. The ship was small, even tinier than the patrol ships in Beta.

What little worry Winters had diminished even further when the readings of the ship's beacon came in. She was a Confederation light corvette, barely larger than a scoutship. Then, the name appeared on his screen.

Travers.

Winters had assumed the ship was carrying some officer or dignitary, perhaps even a Senator looking to get press by touring the great base…now that it was completely safe. It wouldn't be the first time a communique with the scheduling of a trip like that had gone awry.

But something about the ship's name troubled him.

He was about to ask his AI to look it up when it came to him.

Travers had been assigned to the White Fleet.

Winters's edginess returned, because he had no idea how or why the vessel was at Grimaldi when it should have been dozens of jumps away, with Tyler Barron and the exploration fleet.

"Confirm ID, Commander." Winters's tone was more serious than it had been before.

"Beacon confirmed, Admiral. The vessel is identifying itself as *Travers.*" A short pause. "Mass readings and basic shape and size all match the warbook entries for the vessel, sir."

Winters nodded. "Advise Force Beta to…"

The admiral was interrupted by the sound of the comm system. A second later, the officer said, "Incoming message, Admiral." A moment later: "Sir, it's in Code Sigma-9…designated for your ears only."

Winters was really on edge now. Sigma-9 was a wartime code, and any message using it now was unlikely to contain good news. He stood up, an abrupt move driven partially by the stress building up inside him. "I'll take it in my office, Commander."

He walked across the control room toward the small hallway that led to his private office, the very room from which Van Striker had directed the latter stages of the war. His pace was normal at first, but as he moved out of sight of the control room staff, it quickened. Something was wrong, he was almost sure of that. And the sooner he knew what it was, the better.

He slipped inside the office and sat behind the desk, tapping the comm unit as he did. "On my line, Commander." He was alone in the room, but he scooped up the headset anyway and pulled it on.

"Yes, sir. Coming through now."

Winters sat at his desk, motionless, listening to the message, and his tension grew with every word. The vessel was indeed *Travers*, and it *had* set out the previous year with the White Fleet. The recorded message sent to Winters was from none other than Tyler Barron himself.

Barron's words were grim, and as he listened, Winters' confusion about the presence of the patrol ship turned slowly to clarity. *Travers* had returned, with a small number of other vessels, including *Dauntless*. They had come to warn the Confederation of the White Fleet's discovery…not a cache of old tech or detailed histories of the old empire, but instead other survivors of the Cataclysm—likely billions of them—spread across an interstellar polity that was, by all indications, truly vast in scope.

A nation called the Hegemony, and led by an elite utterly convinced of their own genetic superiority, and their natural right to rule over all others. A new enemy, more advanced and far more dangerous than the Union or any of the other Rim nations.

Winters might have found the whole thing difficult to believe, had it not been Barron himself on the message. He knew the famous admiral well, and the two had fought together during much of the war. He took Tyler Barron's word as indisputable truth.

He sat for a long while after the message finished, trying to truly understand what he'd been told, and the implications of it all. The war had ended two years before, and for all he tried to maintain a constant sense of readiness, no one had expected any chance of new hostilities, not for a decade or more. The Union was, by all accounts, in a desperate state. With the Alliance an ally, there was no other power on the Rim strong enough to threaten the Confederation. And, until a few moments earlier, Winters had been sure all the humans left alive in the galaxy were on the Rim.

He had to act…immediately. That meant he had to tell his people what was happening. Barron had advised that the enemy was likely to hit Dannith first if and when they reached Confederation space, and he'd requested that Winters do whatever he could to support the defense of the frontier world.

Now, he looked down at his desk and wondered just what he *could* do. He did have ships stationed at Grimaldi, a reasonable fleet by peacetime patrol standards…but not what he'd want to lead against a new enemy so deadly they could send Tyler Barron racing back to the Confederation to shout out the warning.

But there was no choice. The once imposing fleet that had won the war was scattered all across the Confederation. Grimaldi had the single largest concentration of military strength, but it would take months to gather a true battle fleet. With any luck, there would be time…but Barron had been clear that he had no idea how long it would be before enemy forces struck.

Winters leaned back and sighed. He was tired…he'd been about to go off duty when *Travers* transited into the system. But rest was nowhere on the horizon for him, not now. First, he had to send out his own alerts to every major naval base in the Confederation. Barron had said he was en route to Megara to warn Admiral Striker and the Senate. Winters didn't know what other messages Barron had been able to send, and he wasn't going to take any chances.

He reached down to the comm unit, setting it to his aide's comm line. "Liane, I need you in my office…immediately." He'd just sent his aide off duty, no more than an hour before. He felt bad about calling her back, but this was the first real emergency any of them had faced since the end of the war.

"On my way, Admiral." She was clearly trying to hide the grogginess in her voice, and she came close to success, but not quite close enough. At least not to escape Winters's fine perception.

"Very well, Commander…and I'm sorry to wake you, but it's important." He closed the line, relieving her of the need to deny that he'd disturbed her sleep.

He looked down at his desk, trying to decide where to start. He had communiques to send, orders to issue…a fleet to organize. He'd already decided he would assemble the strongest fleet he could from the ships posted to the station. And he would lead it to Dannith himself, setting up the best defense he could until reinforcements arrived.

He was focused, hard edged, grim…and shaken. Deeply.

The reality of what he'd been told was still setting in, and as it did, the darkness enveloping him became denser. Barron had sounded almost unnerved in his message. And anything that could shake up Tyler Barron was enough to make Winters's stomach do flops.

Chapter Thirty-Three

CFS Dauntless
High Orbit
Troyus City, Planet Megara, Olyus III
Year 316 AC

"Fire!" Atara put everything she had into holding her voice steady, banishing the fear, the regret, the trepidation from her tone as she uttered the single word. Ordering *Dauntless* to fire on a fellow Confederation ship was the hardest thing she'd ever had to do, and despite the intense effort she'd put into targeting the shot where it would have the smallest impact on *Stafford*'s crew—while still crippling the smaller vessel—she'd barely managed to actually issue the command.

Now she would see if her people obeyed it.

She listened as Cumberland repeated the command. At least the tactical officer was with her. That was a good sign…either it was an indication that the crew would indeed trust her enough to side with her on this, or at the very least, a sign that she wouldn't have to face the resulting mutiny alone.

She pushed aside the failed gallows humor and looked straight ahead, trying not to let herself look around to gauge the expressions of the faces all around her, the cold stares she could almost *feel* burning into her back. Her people didn't need to see her looking uncertain, not now.

She waited as the seconds passed. *Dauntless*'s gunnery teams were the fleet's best, and their response times were normally almost undetectable. Now, as she counted five seconds, and then six, she felt her hopes fading away. They weren't going to obey. She felt a flush of anger, but it quickly faded. She wasn't even sure they *should* obey, or that she would in their shoes.

Then she heard something, or she thought she did. *Dauntless*'s great broadsides were usually clearly audible on the bridge, the combined force of so many guns firing reaching the control center in the form of a high-pitched whine. But with a single gun...she wasn't sure if she'd heard the shot, or if she'd just imagined it.

Not until the display updated...and the damage assessment flowed onto her workstation screen. *Dauntless*'s gun had fired, and it had hit...just where she'd plotted. *Stafford*'s engines had been targeted, and as she watched, she saw the vessel's power output dropping. She'd been hesitant to totally destroy the ship's thrust capability, but the vessel was in high enough orbit to offset degradation with just its small positioning jets. If she'd targeted any farther forward, the hit would have impacted more of *Stafford*'s crew. She would have killed more Confederation comrades than necessary. As it was, she hoped she'd avoided inflicting any serious casualties, though she suspected that was mostly wishful thinking.

She'd delayed taking action for as long as she could, but she'd pushed things as far as they would go. She'd cut the jamming as planned, and almost immediately picked up *Pegasus* coming up from the surface. Andi's ship had just lifted off, which meant they were behind schedule. And she'd delayed *Stafford* with words as long as she could.

"Commander, get me a line to *Pegasus*, now!"

"Yes, Captain...done."

"Andi...this is Atara. You've got to give it everything that ship of yours has...because the shit is about to hit it good up here."

With the jamming down, she could only imagine the communications flying back and forth, the confusion, the desperate calls to superior officers, asking what to do.

Requesting permission to fire on *Dauntless*.

"Sorry we're late...couldn't be helped. I'm pouring everything she's got into the engines now. Give us six minutes."

Atara knew that was fast, and she couldn't imagine what Andi was doing to her ship to reach high orbit so quickly. But she wasn't sure she could hold *Dauntless* in place that long... not without things escalating, without having to fire on more Confederation ships.

And if the orbital fortresses with arcs on *Dauntless* opened up...

"Commander, I want scanners at full power. And launch a spread of drones. If anything's heading toward us, or if those forts are powering up their weapons grids, I want to know."

"Yes, Captain."

Atara was falling into her old routines from years of almost non-stop battle. But it was different this time. All she wanted was time for *Pegasus* to reach orbit and dock, and then to get the hell away from Megara without having to fight anyone else.

She knew they'd all have to come back eventually, that they couldn't abandon the Confederation's capital to whatever was happening there. But they needed time, to regroup...and to rally as much of the fleet as possible.

Atara was analytical. She tended to look forward, tearing things apart, figuring where they might go. But she tried to push that aside now, to ignore the impulses...because they told her something she didn't want to see, didn't even want to imagine. She'd fought in the Alliance Civil War, seen the Palatians killing each other, brother against brother, father against son. And now she feared she would see the same thing far closer to home.

The Confederation looked very much like it was sliding into its own civil war...and right when the Hegemony was likely searching for a route to the Rim and massing its fleets for invasion. It would be a catastrophe of epic proportions, and it *had* to be averted, whatever it took.

Getting Tyler and Gary Holsten on board was the first step. They were both massively influential, each in his own way—

Holsten quietly, along backchannels, and Barron as the grandson of the Confederation's greatest hero, and a celebrated warrior in his own right. It would be far harder for whoever was behind the plot clearly underway to discredit Barron while he was out, able to speak for himself and defend against the clearly bogus accusations instead of held in a cell and kept silent.

That meant holding where she was—for five minutes now—whatever came at her.

Whatever she had to do.

* * *

"Oh my God…" Andi stared at the screen, stunned at what she saw. *Dauntless* was drifting along in orbit, surrounded by smaller ships…all of them firing at the battleship. As far as she could see, the battleship wasn't shooting back. She understood Travis's reluctance to open fire on Confederation vessels, but even a heavily armored ship like *Dauntless* could only endure so much fire. It was a break that nothing larger than small patrol vessels had arrived yet. The small guns of the escorts had a hard time penetrating *Dauntless*'s defenses, even at the short range of the orbital combat. But there was a cruiser approaching, too, and while no match for the great capital ship, its guns were a lot heavier than those of the smaller escorts. Even as Andi watched, she saw one of its turrets open fire and score a hit… and there was no doubt that one inflicted damage.

"There's no way we're going to make it through that, Andi." It was Vig, sitting at his station next to hers. "Even one of those small patrol ships would blast us to atoms."

"There's nowhere else to go, Vig…unless you want to surrender. It's straight through the maelstrom, or nowhere at all." She knew she was talking big, but she was also aware that Vig was right. *Pegasus* didn't have one chance in a hundred of reaching *Dauntless*, not with those warships out there.

"You mind if I help?"

Andi recognized the voice, and her head spun around. She hadn't seen Tyler in nearly two years, and when he'd arrived with the others she'd just lowered the ramp before heading back to the bridge, ready to blast off the second they were all aboard. She wanted to jump out of her chair, run to him, throw her arms around him.

Tell him how much she missed him.

But she was a warrior in her own way, just as he was. And her ship needed her now, her crew. Her passengers, including Tyler Barron.

"What do you suggest, Admiral?" It was nothing like the first words she'd imagined having with him, but business had first position in her thoughts now. And right now, business was getting the hell out of the mess they were in.

The targeting systems on those ships are configured for longer-ranged engagements. I know how they work." He paused, just for a second. "If you don't mind me taking the helm, I think I can work up an evasion plan good enough to get us to *Dauntless*...hopefully without taking any hits."

Andi felt a few seconds of reflexive resentment. *Pegasus* was, after all, her ship, and the suggestion that anyone could fly her better than she could poked at a raw nerve. But it quickly passed. What Tyler said made sense...and beyond that, he was probably the person she trusted most in all of the universe. She jumped out of her seat and looked back toward him, gesturing with her arms toward the chair. "By all means, Admiral. The helm is yours."

Barron nodded, and he raced over, leaping into her chair. He pulled the movable workstation around, positioning the nav panel in front of him, and began working at the controls.

Andi watched nervously. She knew Barron was a gifted capital ship pilot, and probably the best ship commander she'd ever known...if not the best that had ever lived. But he'd never flown *Pegasus*, and his experience had been with much larger vessels. Her controls were different in a number of ways from those of a Confederation warship.

She could see him struggling for a moment, and then getting the hang of it. The ship jerked hard to port, and then about ten seconds later, to starboard. After that, the changes began to happen more quickly, every two seconds, or even faster.

Andi looked at the display, confirmed her suspicions. Several of the patrol ships were firing at *Pegasus* now. Their lasers were like candles to *Dauntless*, but one solid hit would probably disable *Pegasus* completely. But none of their shots hit. None even came close.

Barron handled her ship flawlessly, maneuvering as though he knew exactly where the attacking ships would fire. Which, in a way, he did.

She reached out and grabbed onto the handhold around the perimeter of the bridge, hanging on as her ship began shaking wildly. Barron hadn't let off on the forward thrust at all, save for the diversions to alter the ship's course enough to avoid attacks. As she watched, she also realized he'd brought *Pegasus* around on a course that put *Dauntless* between her and most of the attacking ships.

"*Dauntless*…this is *Pegasus*. We're coming in fast. I'm going to break hard and clamp onto the hull. I'll signal when we're on tightly, and then blast the hell out of orbit and make a run for it."

"Admiral?" Andi was looking at Barron when he heard the voice, and she saw the emotion in his expression. She remembered what Atara had told her, how she'd been in a coma for months, and only recovered after Barron had left the ship.

"Atara…my God, I'm glad to hear your voice."

"And I'm glad to hear yours, Ty…but I suggest we leave all that for later. The hits from these ships are starting to smart, and I'd really like to get out of here without having to blow them to bits. And when those fortresses open up, we've got real problems."

"Roger that, Atara. We're coming in hot. I'm going break hard and slip right into the cradle. Less than two minutes."

"I'll hold you to that, sir. Two minutes."

Andi gripped harder onto the rails. Two minutes to docking meant one *hell* of a ride in.

She trusted Tyler to get it done, to bring them all safely to *Dauntless*.

She just wasn't sure she trusted her stomach to make it though his wild maneuvers. Her gut was usually iron, but then again, she'd never seen anyone fly a spaceship quite the way Barron was right then.

Chapter Thirty-Four

"We're picking up massive energy trails, Commodore. There's no question, the enemy came through this system."

Sonya's words cut through her sister like a knife. The Z-21 system was on a direct course toward the Confederation, and the fact that Hegemony forces had been there, and were already gone, was about as bad a piece of news as she could have expected.

She'd reorganized her battered and dispersed fleet after the Hegemony fleet disengaged. They'd raced forward toward the very transit points to which her ships had been headed before they discovered they were on a line to the Confederation and not out into unexplored space as they had all expected.

Her first instinct was immediate pursuit, to stay as close to the faster Hegemony ships as she could, but cold reality demanded a different set of priorities. Most of her ships had suffered considerable damage, and very few of them were in a condition to deploy maximum thrust, or anything close to it. In the end, the fleet had waited almost eighteen hours before beginning pursuit, and even that repair period had allowed no more than two thirds of her ships to achieve something remotely close to maximum acceleration. She'd left the others behind, in a stretched-out trail of vessels limping along at whatever thrust levels they could manage. For the most part, they were clustered together, forming small groups for mutual protection. Most of them would make it back, if they weren't intercepted and destroyed by some enemy force. But what they would return to was a guess she didn't even try to attempt.

The Hegemony had also left its stragglers behind, though in their case a far more brutal calculus was at work. The enemy had to know she would follow them, that the ships left behind would be overtaken and attacked by massively larger forces. She left her people behind in the sincere hope they would make it back to the Confederation. The Hegemony commander or commanders—she had no idea at all how their hierarchy worked—had cast their cripples aside to be chased down and destroyed.

Eaton had ordered her ships to hunt down and obliterate those Hegemony stragglers with a grim satisfaction she found somewhat disturbing in terms of her view of herself. There was animosity in all war, of course, but she was surprised at just how quickly she'd developed a searing hatred for the Hegemony and its forces…and she knew the war to come would reach a level of brutality beyond even the worst of the Union-Confederation struggles.

The turn of events, the disastrous accident that had likely put the enemy on a course toward the Confederation, had one bright spot. There was a chance now, maybe a good chance, that the fleet would make it back home to stand with their comrades in the coming deadly, savage conflict.

Eaton sat quietly, and her thoughts were far different from her usual reasoned rationality. She wanted to kill Hegemony spacers. She wanted to destroy the new enemy utterly and without mercy. They were a blot on humanity, and the restraint she usually felt and exercised was gone now.

Completely gone.

* * *

Stockton sat on the cot in his quarters, slouched forward, his head in his hands. He'd pulled off the nearly impossible landing, and all four of the pilots following him in managed to do the same, hanging close to his tail, emulating everything he had done on the way in. It was a miracle, or as close to one as he'd ever seen, but now, sitting in the quiet, with no combat imminent, he had time to think.

And that was a dangerous thing.

Stockton always tried to keep busy. He carried too many ghosts around with him, too much sorrow and loss to endure endless quiet hours. There were friends who, even now, he still expected to see walking through the door one day. One of those was Kyle "Thunder" Jamison, who had been Stockton's commander for most of his career. He'd been more than a friend—even…a brother. Stockton had been moments short of saving his friend that fateful day, even seconds. Every time he thought about that day, his mind went to what he could have done differently, just a little bit better…and he felt it pulling at the fraying bonds of his sanity.

And Jovi Grachus…she had killed Jamison, and Stockton had nursed a burning hatred for the Alliance pilot, even after the Palatians became Confederation allies. Then, in a perverse twist of fate, he'd worked through his anger toward Grachus and learned to accept the new ally…just in time to see her die in battle. In place of the satisfaction he'd expected to feel at Grachus's loss, there was only more sorrow and mourning.

The door slid open, pulling him from the increasingly morose train of thoughts. Stara walked in. They had each had their own quarters on *Dauntless*, though they'd spent most of their down time together in his. When they'd both transferred suddenly to *Repulse*, no one had even bothered with the window dressing of giving them separate cabins. Things were tight with so many spacers moving onto the fleet's new flagship, and there was no space for quarters that would be left largely unused.

He'd been wild as a young pilot, and he'd enjoyed gambling with the others, bragging about his exploits, and generally living up to the legendary image of the ace pilot. Now, he realized he had become a grim creature, focused on duty not just because of dedication, but also because there was so little else left of him.

"The strike force is in far better shape than we could have hoped, Jake. Better than ninety percent of the fighters are ready for action or close to it. As soon as we get enough of the bays back in full operation, you'll be ready to launch most of your force, if need be." Stara Sinclair had slipped into the room, unnoticed by a Stockton deeply immersed in his brooding.

He looked up and managed a smile for her. He appreciated her, in so many ways. She was beautiful— to his eyes, at least— but she was also smart…and she had a kind of good sense he found to be very rare in people. She didn't come in with point-less phrases, telling him to "cheer up," or something equally nonsensical. She understood, as he did, that such things were not just idiotic, they were also insulting. They implied the things causing his depressed mood weren't important, a kind of thinly disguised, "I'm sorry you lost so many of your pilots and that all of your good friends are gone, but give us a smile!" Stara was far more sophisticated in her approach, and while he generally saw through it, he appreciated the effort and intellect behind it.

"That's good news." He noted she didn't mention that sev-enteen of his people had died trying to land in barely-functional bays…or that more than three hundred had failed to return at all from the last, seemingly endless battle. Including thirty-four pilots who'd suffocated or frozen in disabled fighters or escape pods, simply because none of the fleet's ships had been able to launch rescue boats in time.

Less than half the pilots that had been with the fleet when *Dauntless* left were still in service, and the fact that about eighty of those had survived and were in the fleet's sickbays didn't go very far to mitigating the severity of the losses. Neither did the fact that he'd pulled the last of the crated fighters from the fleet's supply ships and drafted everyone he could find with flight experience to fill in some of the holes in his order of battle. He shivered at the thought of the losses a bunch of shuttle pilots and flight school washouts would endure when he had to lead them against a Hegemony fleet.

Stara plopped down on the bed and sat silently for a moment, leaning slightly toward him so her head was resting on his shoulder.

Stockton could hear her breathing, and he could feel the tension in her body. He pushed back his grief and his dark thoughts, and he tried to rally himself to be there for her, as she had always been for him. She endured the losses as he did, and the fact that she did it sitting in flight control only meant she had a better view of the carnage, and generally more contact with those who died. She had lost friends, as he had—in many cases, the same people—and he reminded himself he had no exclusive ownership over pain and loss in war.

"We've got to get as much of the strike force ready as we can, Stara." He wanted to talk to her about anything but fighters and squadrons and the inevitable next battle. But he couldn't. There would be more fighting ahead, that was a virtual certainty, and the less he prepared, the more of his people would die.

There was more to his choice of subject than that, though, and it nagged at him. He was afraid he was losing the ability to talk to her about other things. Their personal relationship had always existed alongside their professional combat roles…and he was realizing it had always been subordinate. For all their time together, all the nights they'd spent next to each other in the dark, the vast majority of their time had been spent discussing fighter tactics and the business of the squadrons. He wondered, when it was all over—if it was ever over—what would actually remain for them. He loved her, he didn't doubt that, and he knew she loved him. But what would they be like together in peace? Would they be happy? Or would they drift apart when the duties and responsibilities that kept them close were no more? Would the pain they shared—so much pain—doom any chance they had of happiness?

He pushed those thoughts aside, as he usually did when they tried to find their way back into his mind. He had other things to think about, to do…first and foremost, trying to make sure that he lived long enough to face such problems with Stara. The

Hegemony was a huge obstacle in the way of that goal.

He thought about the battles he knew lay ahead. He had almost no idea of the size of the Hegemony's forces, or how quickly they could be mobilized…or for that matter, whether the Confederation would face the challenge alone, or if the other nations on the Rim would see the danger and come to its aid.

He only knew two things for sure. First, that fighters would be a huge part of the struggle to come, the one real advantage the Confederation had against an enemy that was otherwise technologically superior.

Second…that advantage would be fleeting. He didn't think for an instant that the Masters would allow the situation to continue for long. He didn't know if that meant Hegemony fighters would appear, or simply that the enemy's defensive doctrines would improve, but he was certain that six months later, or a year, the squadrons would face greater danger from the enemy.

That meant the squadrons had to make their strikes count, exploit their advantage to the greatest extent possible.

Before they lost it.

* * *

"We can go faster, Admiral, but the cost will be more ships dropping out of the formation. I've got repair crews working on all vessels, and I'm monitoring their progress hourly. But it's just going to take time. The fleet suffered considerable damage, and we need to get weapons systems back online, too."

Eaton listened to Fritz's report, agreeing with every word but still growing more frustrated. Under the best circumstances, the enemy would leave her fleet behind, but her vessels were staggering along at just over half their normal maximum acceleration. She was tempted to order all ships to push forward at their best thrust levels, but there wasn't much point in catching the enemy without the strength to put up a fight. Tyler Barron had already brought home the news of what was coming, she was sure of that. She needed to get the White Fleet back, somehow, combat ready and prepared to renew the fight.

"I understand you're doing all that can be done. But we have to get back before the Hegemony ships locate the route home. We're out of time. I need you to work your magic. Take some chances if you have to, cut some corners, whatever you have to do. But get this fleet moving faster." She knew she was being unfair, that the fleet would be even farther back if it hadn't had Anya Fritz directing repair efforts. Eaton couldn't even imagine keeping track of work on so many ships at the same time, which Fritz appeared to be doing with remarkable effectiveness.

But she also knew they *had* to get back. Now.

"Yes, Commodore. I will take another look at everything and try to come up with some ways to speed up the work." She paused. "Meanwhile, there's something you should consider. Every ship is in a different condition, so the time to get the fleet up to maximum thrust is however long it takes to repair the most heavily damaged ship. Leaving vessels behind is the clearest way to cut the time. You're going to have to decide the minimum number of ships you will take forward, and how many you'll leave behind. Because, in the end, that's the choice."

"Very well, Captain Fritz. You do what you can, and I'll consider my answer to that question." She cut the line.

Fritz was right. She'd been thinking about it for hours now, and she was no closer to an answer. The entire fleet had been hopelessly outmatched against the Hegemony forces. She'd only be weaker if she led barely half of the remaining ships forward.

But the enemy was probably scattered now as well, sending detachments through every transit point, searching for a route to the Confederation. The faster she could move her forces, the more chance she had of picking off small enemy forces, cutting off branches on the exploration tree.

She shook her head. Everything felt like desperation, choices between one bad decision and a worse one. She'd never been as uncertain as she felt now. She had no idea the smallest number of ships she would lead forward, and no clear sense how to reach a final decision.

She just knew that number was more than what she had ready now.

Chapter Thirty-Five

ITN Headquarters
Troyus City, Planet Megara, Olyus III
Year 316 AC

"Admiral Whitten is here."

Marieles was sitting at her desk, staring at the screen, still trying to comprehend the unmitigated disaster that had just occurred. So many months of effort, culminating in success far beyond the wildest imaginings she'd allowed herself at the start…and half of it lost, in a matter of hours.

She'd expected setbacks, of course, but for both Holsten and Barron to escape…that was dire. They were probably two of the three most dangerous opponents to her plans. Admiral Striker was the other, and the fact that she'd just confirmed he was still secure in his hidden cell was the sole bright spot in an otherwise horrifying morning.

"Send him in." She'd summoned Whitten…no, she'd asked him to come. She reminded herself not to let anger and frustration drive her to cause more damage. She'd spent a long time winning the admiral's trust—and affection. But Whitten was a proud sort, and not the kind to be successfully manipulated by anger or imperious commands.

And he had no idea how deeply involved she was in everything that had happened, in the corruption and machinations that had pulled him from obscurity to a hair's breadth from command of the entire navy. Or even higher, if her plans reached total success.

"Desiree…I just took a shuttle down from Prime Base." He paused. "It's terrible. There's chaos and confusion everywhere." He was clearly unnerved, a state of affairs that didn't bode well for his ability to hold up his end of things. She didn't need that much from him, but he had to inspire confidence to the panicked Senators, or things would come quickly to a halt.

"I know. I just heard." A lie, of course. She suspected she'd known something was happening before he did.

Before he let Dauntless *get away.*

"They opened fire on Confederation ships. They're traitors…but no one else will act fast enough. Tyler Barron is very popular, especially in the navy, and Gary Holsten is…"

"All of that's true, Alex." She still called him by his middle name, a tactic she felt had worked well in developing the sense of a true relationship between them. And she was well aware what Gary Holsten was capable of…which was why Whitten's inability to stop *Dauntless* before it blasted out of orbit was such a disaster. "The Confederation needs a strong hand now. It needs you…in total command of the navy." She paused.

He puffed up. "Do you think that's possible?"

She'd chosen Whitten because she'd bet she could control him, but she hadn't realized quite how weak he truly was. It wasn't going to be easy battling Tyler Barron with someone like Torrance Whitten.

"Yes, I think it is possible. What choice does the Senate have now? There is an active insurrection in progress…and the longer Tyler Barron is out there, the worse it's going to get." She paused. She'd played him most often by putting the ideas in his head and allowing him to feel that they were his, but there was no time now for such subtleties. "I have several contacts in the Senate, Alex…I'm confident I can help you gain the assignment that should have been yours anyway. We have to move quickly…so you have the resources to truly hunt down Tyler Barron, and anyone following him."

"You're right, Desiree, of course. I will request a hearing

before the full Senate at..."

"I took the liberty of arranging that for you already... through one of my Senator contacts." She paused. "I'm sure you can imagine that in my career as a lobbyist, I have developed working relationships with a number of politicians." She left out any mention of the billions of credits in bribes. And all the blackmail. The less he knew about all that, the better. She had to remind herself Whitten was a pompous fool, but not a traitor. If he knew her purpose was to destabilize the Confederation, she would lose him in an instant.

Whitten looked surprised, and for an instant concerned.

"Don't worry, Alex...I just reminded a few key Senators how fortunate they are to have you available to take charge and see that the navy gets through this very troubled time."

The doubtful look vanished, almost as quickly as it had appeared. Marieles held back her smile, but she still felt amusement at how easily egotism led to gullibility. "So, when is this hearing?"

"In two hours...just enough time for you to issue orders for the ships of the Megara garrison to pursue *Dauntless* and its companion vessels...and change into your dress uniform."

She looked up at him and smiled. "I hope you don't mind my help, Alex...with such a desperate situation, I just thought there was so much you had to deal with. And I do know my way around the Senate, after all. There's no harm in me being your lobbyist for a few hours, is there?"

"No, of course not," he said after a brief pause. "You're right. I should send forces after *Dauntless* myself, to track where they go if not to attack immediately."

No, you should have sent them hours ago, you fool.

"By all means...perhaps you should issue those orders now. I can offer you access to the network's main comm center." *Because you're not getting out of my sight without getting some ships on Tyler Barron's tail.* "Then you can go and change...and get to the Senate before the hearing begins." She knew she couldn't go with him. It would seem suspicious, and for all the influence she exerted in the body, the vast majority of Senators still had no idea who she was. Ferrell knew what to do, and while she didn't really trust his ability any more than she did Whitten's, the whole thing was pretty straightforward. The Senators were nothing if not pompous, and the audacity of anyone defying them—and breaking into their own complex to free prisoners—was almost certain to have them all screaming and crying for action.

"Of course, Desiree…you're right. Are you sure the communication is no problem? It will save me time not to have to go back to the Admiralty."

"It is absolutely no problem." She lowered her voice. "Have I ever refused you anything?" She reached out and ran her hand over his arm, just for a few seconds. "Now," she said, taking hold of the arm she'd just rubbed, "let's get you to the comm center and on a line to Prime Base."

* * *

"I didn't believe it when I heard your voice on the comm, not at first." Barron sat in his office, not behind the desk, but in one of the two chairs in front, looking at Atara Travis, who occupied the other. "You were in that medpod for so long. For a while, Doc thought we were going to lose you, but I told him you were too damned stubborn to die."

Atara smiled. "Doc almost went apoplectic when I told him I was going to the bridge.. I'll admit, my brain *was* still a little fuzzy, but my thoughts were clear enough to know that you being arrested *had* to be some kind of mistake. Or worse." A pause. "Turns out it was worse."

She took a deep breath. It felt right to be back on duty, and to have Barron there. Which was good, because everything else felt wrong. *Dauntless* was blasting across the Olyus system, running away from the Confederation's capital, now a renegade vessel carrying fugitives fleeing from the Senate. That was bad enough…and yet, remarkably, it wasn't the worst part of their current situation. The Confederation was also under threat of invasion, from an enemy virtually no one else believed existed.

"You're right about that…it is worse." Barron's voice was

solemn, matching the obvious grimness of his mood. It was clear he was glad to be out of prison, and thrilled she had emerged from her long coma, but Atara knew he was troubled by the fact that his rescue had put his people into terrible jeopardy. She had no doubts about what she'd done, and she knew she would do it again if she had to…but she also carried guilt for all of it. For involving her officers and spacers…and for the unknown number of Confederation personnel who'd been killed in the operation.

"I don't know what's behind events on Megara, Ty…but we've *got* to do something about it. The Confederation is probably outmatched by the Hegemony anyway…if they find us while we're unprepared…worse, while we're divided and fighting with each other…" She didn't continue. She knew she didn't have to. Barron understood, perhaps even better than she did.

He exhaled hard and shook his head. "I wasn't in a good state coming back from the Badlands, Atara, I can tell you that much. It was…hard…to leave the others behind, to run home like a scared puppy." He paused, but before she could reassure him that he'd done the right thing, he continued, "I never imagined anything like this, that I would come to find Megara itself embroiled in some kind of conspiracy. I'm just not sure what to do next."

The AI interrupted their conversation. "Captain Lafarge is at the door, Admiral."

Barron looked up with a start. "Let her in," he responded immediately.

The door slid open, and Andi walked in.

"Well, Admiral…I think I'll get back to the bridge and check on…"

"You don't have to leave on my account, Atara." Andi managed a brief smile at Barron, and then she looked over at *Dauntless*'s captain. "Though, I appreciate the thought." No one was more aware of Andi's relationship with Barron than Atara Travis…and she was perhaps the only person on *Dauntless* who knew that Lafarge hadn't even entered her assigned quarters since *Pegasus* had docked with the battleship. She was glad.

Barron needed whatever comfort he could get right now, and so, she suspected, did Andi. Atara was sure there would be little enough joy in the coming weeks, and she wished her two friends all they could muster in the interim.

Coming weeks? More likely the coming years.

She stood up. "That's okay, Andi…I've got to check on things on the bridge anyway." She and Barron could continue to catch up later. She turned toward the door, just as the comm unit buzzed.

"Yes?" Barron said into the small unit on his desk.

"Sir, we're picking up scanner contacts. Multiple vessels. We can't be sure, but it looks like they might have followed us through the transit point from Olyus."

Atara froze at the door, standing stone still. It was no surprise, not really—or it shouldn't have been—but when no ships pursued *Dauntless* immediately, she'd let herself hope they'd slipped away. That the chaos on and around Megara had made it impossible for the authorities to send ships after the fleeing battleship and its three companion vessels.

"We'll be right there, Commander." Barron turned and stood up, his eyes meeting with Atara's. "I'm sorry, Andi, but I've got to…"

"I know. Go and take care of things. I'll go check and make sure my people are all settled in…especially if it looks like we're going to have to make a run for it."

* * *

"We've got them on scanners, Captain. They're 1.876 billion kilometers ahead of us, and from their course, they appear to be heading toward the Zinar transit point."

"Very well, Lieutenant." Captain Davis Heaton sat on *Titania's* bridge, looking every bit the calm, "by the books" ship commander he considered himself. Inside, he was considerably less certain than he appeared to be. Whatever else he was, calm wasn't a part of it. Heaton had always been a member of the Whitten camp, a group of officers loosely aligned with one of the navy's great families. There were other officers in similar positions with the Barrons, the Prescotts…all the clans who'd shaped the Confederation navy throughout its existence. It was all informal, of course, and whatever rivalries existed between senior officers, navy pride and duty had always come first. Heaton was loyal to Torrance Whitten…but the idea of chasing Tyler Barron made him a little sick to his stomach. He knew all that had happened over the past several days, but he still had a hard time imagining Tyler Barron as a criminal…and even more seeing the illustrious admiral as a traitor.

Still, his orders were his orders, and he was bound to carry them out, especially since more than informal loyalty to the Whittens was involved. The Senate had given Torrance Whitten supreme command of the navy, along with strict orders to hunt down Tyler Barron, Gary Holsten, and anyone who aided them in their escape. He hated the whole situation, wished that someone else had been given the orders he had. But he would do his duty.

Even if that meant firing at the navy's greatest hero.

Former hero, he reminded himself.

He leaned forward and looked toward his tactical officer. He'd delayed long enough, seeking solace in his inability to catch *Dauntless*, and the resulting lack of a need to engage his former comrades. But he wasn't an officer who could deliberately fail… and it was clear that *Dauntless*'s engines had taken minor damage in the combat around Megara. It was a slight reduction in thrust, almost unnoticeable. But it was enough. *Titania* was *Dauntless*'s twin, a vessel of the same class…and that meant even a few percent decline in the pursued ship's thrust offered the edge he needed.

"Advise engineering I want every fraction of a g they can give me, Commander." He paused, again pushing back the urge to simply let Barron and his people escape. "We've got a job to do, and the sooner we get it done, the sooner we can go home."

"Yes, Commander." The tactical officer sounded uncertain, and Heaton could tell the commander shared his doubts, even his pain, at the prospective battle. But there was determination there as well, as their was in Heaton. He wouldn't like hunting Barron down, engaging *Dauntless*…destroying the ship and its renowned crew. It would sicken him, and he might never purge himself of the regret and self-flagellation for having been the one who killed Tyler Barron.

But he had his orders.

And he would follow them, wherever that led him.

Chapter Thirty-Six

Battleship Danais
Outskirts of Ventica System
2,300,000,000 Billion Kilometers from Planet Dannith
Year of Renewal 260 (316 AC)

"There can be little doubt we have crossed the border of the polity that calls itself the Confederation. The crew of the small vessel we captured proved to be extremely helpful in plotting the final jumps necessary to reach this system." Raketh paused for a moment, then he added, "If all of the people of this Confederation are as susceptible to aggressive interrogation as those five, we will have little trouble gaining the intelligence we require for a speedy completion of our pacification campaign."

The four others present all nodded, silently agreeing with the fleet's supreme commander. Raketh, otherwise known as Ninety-Six, was the most genetically superior human among all those crewing the fleet. There were many thousands of officers and crew aboard the vessels, of course, though most of them were mere Kriegeri. There were other Masters, as well, apart from the five of the command council. One-hundred-six in all, commanders and sub-commanders of capital ships and various specialists.

The Master, the only one in the advance fleet ranked in the top one hundred of the Hegemony, was the absolute commander on the scene. The others, even his four comrades in the command chamber, were there to advise and consult. But Raketh's was the final word on all matters.

"We were prepared to destroy the enemy fleet utterly in our prior engagement, having determined the likelihood that they would lead us to their home worlds had declined to insignificance. It is clear now that such a decision would have been in error, that either the enemy was indeed en route to their home worlds, or that an accident of transit point geometry unexpectedly returned them to such a course. I am inclined to believe the latter, though that is speculation."

Raketh paused for a moment, looking briefly at each of his comrades. "We must now make another decision…how to approach the enemy's worlds. In the longer term, of course, this decision will be made by Number One and the Supreme Council. However, I do not believe that their orders for this war will be extermination. These humans, though obviously inferior, have displayed considerable abilities, clearly significantly above those of most of our raw Kriegeri stock. Their warships, while technologically inferior to our own, are not of inconsiderable power, and their small one-man vessels have challenged our defensive capabilities with surprising effectiveness. I believe the Council's instructions will mirror my own inclination, which is to conquer but not destroy. There is much to gain by absorbing these humans into the Hegemony…once they are put into their place in the natural order, of course."

"I agree, Ninety-Six. The Hegemony must continue to grow, or it will stagnate. These…people…represent a substantial human population previously unknown to us. Save for the Others, it is the only such pool of fresh genetic specimens we know of amid the ruins of the Great Death. It would be wasteful to simply annihilate them." The man next to Raketh spoke calmly, as though debating whether a piece of fruit was spoiled or still edible rather than the deaths of billions of humans.

"I agree as well, in principal. Yet, I have doubts, too." The woman on Raketh's other side spoke now. Her designation was One Hundred Twenty-Four, and her name was Lialla. Her ranking made her the second in command of the fleet. "For one, our land forces in the fleet are somewhat limited, and quite possibly not sufficient for a full planetary assault. We are still too far out for detailed scans and population estimates, however the energy readings are sufficient to suggest a planetary population possibly measured in the hundreds of millions. We have some records of the enemy ground forces from Keltath. The natives there, admittedly among the most primitive of the Defekts in the Hegemony, apparently even believed they were a force sent by the Masters. I agree that this enemy is inferior, but they are likely to prove considerably more difficult to defeat than the scattered and deteriorated populations we have so often faced. To commence a ground assault and be defeated would only inspire pointless confidence in our enemy, and significantly increase the difficultly of subjugating them."

Raketh nodded respectfully. "Your words are wise, Lialla, and your rationale is unassailable. Yet, while I believe this war will be fought to conquer and not obliterate, the populated planet in this system is but one of what must be many. We can, therefore, employ harsher measures here. Our Kriegeri strike units may be fewer in number than we might hope for…but with sufficient orbital bombardment, I believe they have a reasonable chance to successfully execute the assault. Our losses may be higher than we would normally consider optimal, but Kriegeri are, after all, replaceable. Our primary goal here is to obtain data on the enemy polity and its reach, and whatever other intelligence may assist in planning the ultimate war effort. I believe we can successfully complete this objective even in the event that civilian losses exceed ninety percent. Even ninety-five."

He remained silent, allowing his colleagues to disagree, or to offer alternative suggestions…but the room was silent.

"Very well," Raketh said at last, "it is decided. The attack will commence at once. We will destroy the enemy space forces and their orbital defenses. When that is complete, we will evaluate their ground defenses, and implement sufficient orbital bombardment to degrade their military formations and render those on the planet…pliable…to our control."

He allowed another pause, but there were no comments, only silent nods from the man and three women present.

"We are all agreed. Let the attack begin."

* * *

Clint Winters reached down and grabbed the part of his harness that had slipped from his grasp, and he pulled it up, sliding it into place with a sharp click. His ships were formed up around Dannith, within support range of the planet's defensive array. Normally he'd offer battle much farther out, to protect the planet from possible enemy bombardment. But it was clear his force was heavily outnumbered, and he needed every bit of force he could bring to bear. Even with the orbital forts in the mix, he was vastly outnumbered and outgunned. The fleet that had emerged into the system was one of the largest forces Winters had ever seen, and from Tyler Barron's warning, he knew they were advanced.

"I want everyone ready, harnesses on, emergency life support in place." *Because we're going to have one hell of a fight here.* He managed to keep that last part from escaping his lips. It would serve no purpose, and he was sure his people already understood just how dire the situation had become.

"Very well, Admiral." The tactical officer was scared. It didn't take a lot of study to realize that. *Hell, they're all scared... I'm scared.* But they'll do their duty.

Winters had only arrived three days earlier, an amount of time that had allowed for limited study of the situation. He'd known a bit about Dannith, but when he began to think about tactics and how to defend the system, he realized how insignificant his knowledge store truly was. He'd been a front line officer his whole career, spending years patrolling the Union border before the last war. He'd fought all along the Union frontier, and he'd led one of the task forces in the final, fateful battle in the Bottleneck, when *Dauntless* had destroyed the enemy's pulsar weapon, but Dannith was nowhere on the list of systems in which he expected to serve. It was a border world, but along a frontier long considered empty.

Now, someone had gone further, and discovered there was more out there than haunted, dead planets…a previously unknown threat, one that was now approaching Winters's fleet.

He'd sized things up pretty quickly after arriving. The planetary administrator was a reprehensible coward, and Tyler Barron had left a small detachment of Marines to throw together some kind of meaningful planetary ground defense program. The handful of troopers had done that with remarkable success, whipping the undertrained and lackluster planetary levies into a remote semblance of a fighting force.

Dannith's orbital defenses were considerable, if a bit out of date and behind on maintenance. Winters had even convinced himself to feel a bit optimistic about his prospects.

Until he got his first look at the enemy fleet.

He could feel what little remained of his hope fading away as his eyes moved across the display, watching as the enemy ships advanced steadily across the system.

Their largest battleships were the most massive vessels he'd ever seen, just as Barron had warned. And, thanks to Barron's notes, he knew all about their enormous railguns, heavy weapons with ranges considerably in excess of Confederation primaries.

Winters looked down at the screen on his workstation. He had the order of battle displayed. He'd taken all three of the battleships that had been deployed at Grimaldi, but that was still only three. He knew his battle line was miniscule for the fight that was coming, another reason he'd kept his vessels tucked in tight near the planet, and linked his defense grids with Dannith's network of forts. He didn't really think he had much of a chance no matter what he did…but his mind was racing, trying to think of anything else he could do.

Barron's report had mentioned one other factor. The enemy did not appear to utilize fighters, and while they had considerable point defense capability, it was designed predominantly for missile interception. Winters had taken Barron's words to heart, and right before his fleet departed, he'd transferred two squadrons of Grimaldi's fighters to each of his battleships. That meant their bays were crammed full, and that their flight crews would be stretched to the max during the battle. But it also meant he had ninety extra fighters, plus the two hundred ten already on the three battleships…and close to four hundred in Dannith's fortresses.

Nine hundred fighters constituted a massive force. They were by far the strongest weapon he had against the enemy, even if the Dannith squadrons were low-tier reserve formations.

They will become veterans now…or they will die.

Chapter Thirty-Seven

"This is not good, Desiree." Ricard Lille sat across from Mariele's desk, a reproving look on his face. The events of the last two days had been unproductive, she was the first to admit that…but she'd handled it all well, she thought, and, with a bit of luck, she might even turn it all to her advantage. Even with Barron's and Holsten's escapes, she'd truly managed to destabilize the Confederation, and the ripple effects of what she'd done would spread out across its systems. There would be an economic crisis, at the very least…and maybe even something resembling civil war. Whatever happened, the Confederation would be in no condition to threaten the Union, and that would buy them time. Time to rebuild, to prepare for the next fight.

She looked back across the table, trying to maintain a neutral expression. In truth, she was pissed off. She was sick of Lille's attitude, his arrogance…and she was tired of being afraid of him. She might have even risked an attempt at getting rid of him, if he weren't so damned tight with Gaston Villieneuve.

"I'll admit, I would prefer not to have Admiral Barron and Mr. Holsten free…but their escapes were actually useful in one sense. The whole affair has created a sense of crisis and urgency in the Senate that may, in fact, accelerate and expand the level of disruption we are ultimately able to inflict."

"That's true, Desiree...unless Tyler Barron rallies the fleet and comes back here with ten divisions of Marines to hunt down every member of your carefully planned cabal. And that doesn't take into account what resources Gary Holsten will be able to reach...on Megara, and elsewhere." A short pause. "I have tangled with both of them before, Desiree, and I can tell you without a doubt, they are not to be underestimated."

Because they both got the best of you...

She managed to keep the thought to herself, though she was barely holding back her anger. Tyler Barron had utterly wrecked Lille's earlier plan to seize control of the Alliance through a puppet ruler, and now she bristled at his assumption that she couldn't handle what he'd been unable to.

"I understand they are both very dangerous, Ricard...but this situation is different." She hesitated, reminding herself she needed Lille on her side. "I not only have all the resources I have put into place over so many months...I have you. In the Alliance, you were virtually alone, without significant financial resources. It was a desperate time for the Union, and you were given an almost impossible goal. We have advantages now that you did not have then."

She detested what she saw as obsequiousness, but, as always, she did what she thought would get her where she wanted to be.

"I appreciate your efforts to appear respectful, Desiree, but I am immune to such efforts. You have done well here, I don't argue that. And you're right, you do have advantages here I did not have on Palatia. That does not change the fact that you are underestimating the threat Tyler Barron and Gary Holsten represent." He sat quietly for a few seconds before continuing. "Nevertheless, there is little point in continuing to discuss the matter. You have dispatched Admiral Whitten and all the force he could muster to pursue—and hopefully destroy—*Dauntless*. I will admit, it might have been preferable to have Tyler Barron as a prisoner...but I believe the risk in attempting to recapture the escapees is simply too great. Your...advice...to Whitten was clear, was it not? To attack *Dauntless* and its companion ships as quickly as possible…and to destroy them at all costs?"

"Yes, Ricard. I was very clear. Still…"

Lille looked at her for a few seconds. "Still?"

Marieles was angry with herself for saying too much. She was worried about Whitten facing Barron, but it wasn't something she particularly wanted to share with Lille. "I was just going to say that Barron is a very capable commander, and I reminded Torrance not to underestimate him." She wasn't sure Lille bought that, but his face remained impassive.

"So, we have one other matter to discuss. Admiral Striker. He's in a secure location, but, of course, there is always risk in holding a hostage. My people checked him for a tracker, and they are almost certain he has no means of signaling for help—a conclusion supported by the fact that he has received no assistance. Still, my feeling is, it's safer to eliminate him now. We can dispose of the remains, and everyone will simply believe he has gone into hiding or changed identities to escape from his crimes. I believe that will be useful to your operation."

Marieles was silent. Her first inclination had been to agree, but, something held her back. She didn't know what purpose Striker could serve, but she'd lost Holsten and Barron, and she liked the idea of hanging on to the one prisoner of note that remained.

"I think you should wait, Ricard. I understand the effort involved in keeping Striker hidden and under guard, but it seems to me, we should try to gain whatever information we can from him." She knew the imperatives of the Union's spying operations were different in peacetime. During the war, Striker would have been a prisoner almost beyond value, one with an almost indescribable knowledge of Confederation military and logistic information. Now, there was less he could reveal that Sector Nine couldn't derive from other sources.

Lille glanced back at her, his expression doubtful at first. He looked like he was going to disregard her suggestion…and she didn't doubt that anything she said to Lille was just that, no more than a request. She didn't let the position Villieneuve had given her on the Megara op go to her head, not where Ricard

Lille was concerned. The assassin took orders from one person, and only one. And Gaston Villieneuve was lightyears away, back on Montmirail.

But Lille didn't refuse. He sat quietly for a few more seconds, and then he said, "Perhaps you're right. There is no pressing need for tactical information, but Striker is—or was—the navy's senior admiral. I'm afraid my inclinations run to cleaning up loose ends, but in this case, some aggressive interrogation is in order before we eliminate the admiral."

Marieles caught Lille's expression in the glow of the ceiling light fixture…and she had to suppress a shiver. She wasn't hesitant to employ harsh tactics in pursuit of her goals, but she had an idea of what Lille meant by "aggressive interrogation," and she felt a little squeamishness in her stomach.

The assassin was the coldest fish she'd ever met, and the thought of what he would do to a hostage shook even her stone cold resolve.

* * *

Van Striker was lying on his back, looking up at the dark gray concrete of the ceiling. The bench, the closest thing he had to a bed or a chair, was cold and damp, and best guess, made from the same material as the rest of his surroundings. He was in some kind of cellar, he'd guessed…and from the lack of any apparent rescue attempt, he had also surmised it was a well-hidden one. There wasn't a doubt in his mind that his people were frantically looking for him, even as he lay there helplessly. He was the supreme commander of the Confederation navy, and he knew the loyalty many officers felt toward him. He imagined Troyus City had been turned upside down to find him.

He shifted his body to the side, wincing as the soreness that had become his normal state of being morphed into significant pain for a few seconds. He hadn't been tortured, not in the sense of being abused while under questioning, but the search for scanning devices hidden in his body had been the most painful thing he'd ever experienced. The lack of any kind of anesthetic was a message from his captors, he suspected, one designed to encourage good behavior…and to give a glimpse at what punishments were possible if he made trouble.

The wounds from the pseudo-medical process had healed considerably, and the pain was far less than it had been…but that didn't mean it didn't still hurt…or that the poor conditions in the cell hadn't added half a dozen infections to his discomfort.

Striker had remained defiant, even as he lay in the cell, writhing in agony from the deep incisions his captors had made in a dozen places. He'd expected his people to find him days ago— not that he had a clear sense of how many days had passed. Even without a homing unit, he'd expected the Marines to come bashing through the door at any moment…and he'd steeled himself to resist anything his adversaries did to him until that time.

Only no one had come. He'd endured the pain and embraced the slow recovery that lessened that agony a bit each day. But, for all the pain and discomfort, the passage of time had worn him down the most. It wasn't just being held prisoner…it was the fact that he knew something was happening on Megara, something bad. Being held back, unable to intervene, was the purest form of torture for him. Worse, his kidnapping was very likely involved with whatever plots were underway, a suspicion he'd elevated to virtual certainty when no sign of rescue appeared.

That meant Ricard Lille was involved, a fact that escalated whatever was happening from some kind of local politicking to a full-fledged Union plot, and quite possibly a dire risk to the whole Confederation.

He'd expected to be interrogated, an expectation of impending brutality that had him huddled over on his slab, struggling to control the shivering, both from fear and from the damp cold of his cell. But so far he'd been left to himself, visited only by guards who brought his meager rations and emptied the waste bucket his captors had thoughtfully provided. And, once, by a medical technician who'd administered a powerful antibiotic when one of his infections seemed to threaten becoming serious. Apparently, Lille was fine with inflicting all manner of pain and misery, but not with Striker dying on him. Not yet.

He'd found some spark of encouragement in that, an urge to stand firm, to resist…and even to try to escape. But it had quickly faded, and in the grim darkness that remained, he lost some of the respect he'd always had for himself. The brutality his captors had inflicted on him had done more than cut at his flesh and draw out his screams of pain. It had broken a part of what he'd been, what he'd believed of himself. And in that realization, he saw the true pain they had inflicted on him, the ache deep inside he knew would never be gone.

Chapter Thirty-Eight

Dauntless jerked hard, and Barron lurched to the side in his chair, slamming into his harness hard enough that he lost his breath. *Dauntless* had been on the run for hours, partly because the forces in pursuit outnumbered and outgunned Barron's ship, and partly because he was desperately trying to avoid firing on another Confederation vessel.

The rescue missions had not been accomplished without the spilling of Confederation blood, nor had *Dauntless*'s escape from Megara orbit, but Barron was determined to do whatever he could to see it stopped at that. He would do what he had to do, of course. Nothing was as important as making sure the Confederation was ready for a Hegemony attack…though he had no idea how he was going to manage that. It seemed almost unattainable, and right now, he'd count just making it through the transit point before the pursuing ships caught him as a success.

Atara was next to him, at the captain's station, even though he'd been more or less commanding *Dauntless* from the admiral's chair since he'd returned. The two had tried to show themselves together as often as possible, setting an example of unity and

292

camaraderie to a crew he knew had to be at the very least confused by the situation.

The crew's obedience in the face of orders that seemed blatantly illegal, even as they watched other Confederation ships pursuing *Dauntless*, was a testament to their deep loyalty and trust for both their captain and their admiral. Many of those aboard had served with Barron and Travis since before the war…and they all knew about the Hegemony, too. They understood what was coming, and they knew whatever was happening on Megara, it could only hurt the Confederation's chances of defending itself.

"Captain…see if engineering can coax any more thrust from the engines." Barron wasn't hopeful as he issued the order. *Dauntless* was one of the newest and strongest ships in the fleet, but the race back to the Confederation and to Megara—and then the hurried escape from the capital—had been hard on the ship's systems. Her engines were in good condition, but not in perfect condition…leaving the pack of cruisers, and the brand new battleship following her with an edge in thrust capacity.

The cruisers had the clear speed edge, but their weapons were shorter-ranged. Barron knew they would catch *Dauntless* eventually, but he was pretty sure he could get through the point up ahead before they did. If he couldn't, if he had no choice, he could blast them to scrap before they got close enough to attack. The battleship was his concern. The big ship was back a little farther, but *Titania* mounted quad primaries, just as *Dauntless* did, and the deadly particle accelerators had a long enough range that they just might get off a shot or two before Barron's vessel could escape, especially since the pursuer seemed to be managing thrust almost one percent higher than *Dauntless*'s.

His tactical sense was screaming at him, telling him to alter *Dauntless*'s facing, to bring his own primaries to bear. He'd put the battleship's gunners up against any in the Confederation, even without the half dozen veterans who'd remained behind with the White Fleet. He could win a long-ranged duel against another ship of the class…he was sure of it, though the addition of the cruisers to the mix was problematical. As was the fact that such a course would mean killing another thousand Confederation spacers. He wasn't ready to cover his hands in that much blood from men and women who'd fought at his side against the Union just two years before…and killing so many spacers would make it almost impossible to rally the navy against the approaching Hegemony threat.

"Admiral, Commander Glaven says he will try, but he is not hopeful."

Barron turned toward *Dauntless*'s captain and just nodded. He hadn't expected anything different. Anya Fritz *might* have come up with something, some kind of bizarre feat of engineering that seemed impossible to everyone else. Glaven was a top notch engineer, experienced and well-respected. But he wasn't Anya Fritz.

Who might be dead as far as Barron knew.

Likely was dead, he thought, before pushing the thought out of his mind.

Barron stared at the display, his eyes darting from the transit point to *Dauntless*, and then to the battleship chasing him. His ship wasn't going to make it, not unless the captain of the pursuing vessel was careless and sloppy. *Titania* would get off a shot for sure, maybe even two…and every vestige of his battle experience told Barron he wanted to shoot first, to inflict the first damage, not take it.

But the ghostly faces of all those Confederation spacers stared at him from the edges of his mind.

Damn…

He didn't know what to do. He wasn't sure if he could even bring himself to fire first. He knew they would most likely fire at him, that waiting would only put *Dauntless* at a disadvantage… but, still, he didn't give the order. He waited, his eyes fixed on the point, his mind willing his ship to reach it, to transit to the next system…to get through before the pursuing ship could open fire.

For what that would be worth. It was just one system farther. He knew he'd never escape again, that the battle he'd avoided here would almost certainly take place there.

He looked at the large-scale display detailing the Confederation's network of transit points. He'd tried to head out for Dannith or Grimaldi, but his pursuers had gotten there first, boxing *Dauntless* in. It forced him to turn away from any kind of union with major forces stationed at Grimaldi, or at Dannith, where the White Fleet would most likely return…if any of it did.

Dauntless had raced across much of the Confederation, her course further constrained by the approaching interception forces. Finally, she'd blazed a trail across a large section of the Iron Belt, and then back out toward the Far Rim. Barron knew that area well—the naval base at Archellia, and beyond, the route to the Alliance. There were advantages to going there… he was a legend on Archellia, the planet's greatest hero, and it was a place where he knew he had a good chance of rallying the local forces to his cause.

And he would have access to the Alliance as well, a chance to communicate with his allies there…to request help, if necessary, to fight his own people. He'd provided that very same assistance once to Tarkus Vennius and his Gray Palatians, and he had no doubt that Imperator Tullus would side with his old ally.

Still, for all the advantages of Archellia, there was one huge negative. The system was distant, both from the heart of the Confederation and from the threatened border along the Badlands. Barron had come home to prepare to face the Hegemony, and now he was on the run, fleeing to a remote planet, far from the deadly threat he had no doubt was coming.

"Four minutes to transit, Admiral." Atara Travis's voice sounded calm, professional…to everyone on the bridge save Tyler Barron. He could hear the tension his friend was hiding so well from the others, and he knew she was as aware as he was that the pursuing battleship would open fire any second.

"Increase evasive maneuvers to level three." Barron had held back on the most aggressive evasion plans, because they would also slow *Dauntless* down. But if he didn't give *Titania*'s gunners a challenge…

"Engaging level three maneuvers now. Transit time now…" There was a short pause, barely noticeable. "Four minute forty seconds."

Barron took a deep breath, even as he saw the bright flash in the display. For an instant, he wondered if *Titania*'s weapons had scored a hit, but then he realized *Dauntless* hadn't shaken or vibrated, nor had she shown any signs of damage…and no alarms had gone off. An instant later, the scanners confirmed it.

A clean miss.

Barron felt a rush of excitement, but he knew *Titania* would get a second shot…and maybe a third.

He sat, struggling with the feeling of helplessness, knowing there was nothing he could do. Even returning fire would require him to divert energy to charge up *Dauntless*'s primaries.

He could see *Titania* slipping back slightly, and he knew the battleship had cut her thrust to recharge her own guns. That would help, but not enough. The two ships were traveling at high velocities, and a minute or two of extra thrust wasn't going to get *Dauntless* out of range before *Titania* fired again.

Even if *Dauntless* made it through the transit point with no damage, he didn't see how he would get his ship across the Delphi system and to the next point. All he was playing for now was time, a small delay before he'd have to surrender…or fight it out with Confederation vessels. In any other circumstance, he suspected he might surrender rather than spilling friendly blood. But yielding now sold out all those who'd put themselves on the line to rescue him. Atara and Bryan Rogan—and all of *Dauntless*'s crew—would pay a grievous price if he surrendered.

Worse, he would lose any chance of spreading the word about the Hegemony. Confederation officers and citizens would no longer listen to what he had to say. There would be no one to take heed of his warning and prepare for the holocaust he feared was even now coming for them all.

No, he would have to fight, no matter what it did to him to kill so many comrades. But he still wanted the extra time. He wasn't sure what he expected another day or two to accomplish, but he kept the hope alive that something would happen, that he would find some way to get the warning to those who would listen, before the unthinkable happened.

His eyes caught another flash, *Titania*'s second shot. It was considerably closer than the first, but still a miss. He checked the distance to the transit point, the time until *Dauntless* would wink out of existence into the Santorus system through the strange alternate space that lay between the points. It was a sanctuary of sorts now, a few seconds of escape from the grim reality of normal space.

And then, into Delphi...and a chance to alter *Dauntless*'s vector. Barron figured the chances of it buying enough time were about one in ten.

He watched as his destination grew on the main screen, as the distance from his ship to the alien blackness of the point's core loomed ever closer. They were there...only seconds more before *Dauntless* entered the point. Barron took another deep breath, one he intended to hold until he saw the Delphi system all around him.

Then *Dauntless* spun wildly around, flipping end over end. Barron could hear the distant explosions far off toward the battleship's aft. His ship had taken a hit, he knew that immediately, and from the feel of it, a bad one. He only had a few seconds to think about it before he felt the strange floating sensation, the vaguely sickening feeling of alien space...and then, a few seconds later, stillness, as *Dauntless* returned to normal space, her scanners and instruments still recovering from the transit.

Barron let out his breath, and even as he did, he could feel the sensation of free fall...and he realized, *Dauntless*'s engines weren't blasting.

At all.

* * *

Davis Heaton watched as the damage assessment reports streamed in. It was good news. *Titania*'s primaries had scored a hit on *Dauntless*—by all indications, a serious one. The commander of the force sent to stop the renegade battleship was excited at his gunners' success, all the more because Barron's evasive maneuvers had been extremely effective...but there was something else, too, regret at firing on another Confederation vessel.

Heaton's family had been aligned with the Whittens for three generations, and he'd been brought up to continue that tradition, a career choice that had hindered him as Torrance Whitten had failed to achieve the command levels expected of him. Until just a few weeks earlier, when Whitten himself had been named commander in chief of the navy…and had entrusted Heaton with the command of *Titania*, along with a mission presented as crucial, to track and apprehend Tyler Barron on *Dauntless*.

If he was unable to take the renegade officer prisoner, his orders were explicitly clear. He was to destroy *Dauntless*.

The words seemed almost unreal. Heaton hadn't been a Barron loyalist, at least not in the sense of looking to members of that family for patronage and career support. But he'd looked up to Tyler Barron as a hero with as much genuine feeling as any naval officer, or, for that matter, any Confederation citizen. Barron was one of the fleet's greatest heroes, and *Dauntless* its most famous vessel, even if the current bearer of that designation was a replacement. To a career Confederation officer, chasing Tyler Barron was a nightmare become real.

He'd read the reports on Barron, seen much of the evidence that had been released. It all looked damning, he had to admit that much, but still, part of him simply couldn't believe it. He'd tried to convince himself it was true, to accept the reality, however distasteful, but every time he considered it again, something held him back from full acceptance.

Why hasn't Dauntless turned and fought us? If they're all traitors, they'd do anything to make good their escape.

He'd expected the fleeing battleship to turn and give battle for hours now, days. His force outgunned Barron's battleship, but the admiral had a reputation for taking on forces far larger than those he commanded…and somehow clawing out a win in the end. *Titania* led a small task force, but she was the only battleship, and *Dauntless* was her twin. Criminal or not, the Tyler Barron he knew of would never let a few cruisers and escorts hold him back from an otherwise straight up fight.

Unless he doesn't want to fire on Confederation vessels…

Heaton knew troops had been killed in Barron and of Gary Holsten's escapes, but it certainly seemed that the fleeing admiral was trying not to engage any Confederation ships if he could help it. And that didn't match up with the idea of Barron as a criminal and a traitor.

"*Dauntless* is transiting, Admiral."

Heaton turned, flashing his eyes toward the tactical station. If the readings were correct, *Dauntless*'s engines were completely down. Barron was escaping now only because his course had been a direct one to the transit point…and his velocity would take him through before *Titania*'s main guns could recharge and fire again.

"Deactivate primary batteries. All power to the engines." It was a command decision, and the correct one. He could continue charging his guns, but that would be ignoring reality. *Dauntless* would be lightyears away by the time the weapons were ready to fire…and *Titania* and her companion ships needed to adjust their vectors to match up with *Dauntless*'s insertion angle and follow Barron's ship through the point. As it was, *Dauntless* would have an hour's jump on his ships. If he wasted time and energy, that would only increase.

As much as he hated the idea of fighting—even destroying— Tyler Barron and *Dauntless*, he intended to see it done in the next system. The chase had gone on long enough, and if *Dauntless*'s engines were really offline, it would over soon enough.

It was time to finish things.

No matter how sick it made him.

Chapter Thirty-Nine

Battleship Danais
Ventica System
1.5 Million Kilometers from Planet Dannith
Year of Renewal 260 (316 AC)

"Honored Master, our scanners have detected large numbers of the enemy's small attack ships on a course toward the fleet. Preliminary estimates suggest in excess of nine hundred units inbound." The man had entered the room and prostrated himself before Raketh, speaking only when the Master gestured for him to do so.

"That is not unexpected, though we might have hoped for a smaller number of the troublesome craft." Raketh would never condescend to discuss his thoughts with an Inferior, but in truth, he was concerned about what the fighters meant for the battles to come. The enemy's invasion fleet had possessed a similar number and, if Raketh's assessment of the size and scope of habitation on the Rim proved accurate, the world his forces were attacking was only a frontier planet. Even if it was a regional capital, there was little doubt larger and more powerful worlds lay beyond. How many of the attack craft would a major industrial planet possess? The enemy's primary capital? Or their military headquarters?

The man kneeling before Raketh was a Red Kriegeri, one of

the highest ranking of the Hegemony's Inferiors. Indeed, he was so close to Master rank himself that several generations of careful breeding might result in his descendants achieving the coveted status one day. But in the presence of the commanding Masters of the fleet, he was little more than a slave.

"Go," Raketh said, his voice cold and unemotional. "Issue a fleet command. All ships are to plot a maximum speed course toward the enemy planet…and execute at once." The fleet couldn't simply accelerate all the way to the target world. If it did, it would simply fly past at high velocity, without enough time to engage the enemy ships or orbital defenses, much less land an invasion force. But he was wary of the approaching small craft, and well aware that they were capable of attacking repeatedly if they had time. He wanted to limit the window when the attack ships could engage before his own fleet was in range of their launch platforms.

"As you command, Master." The man remained bowed low for a few seconds, a show of respect to the Masters present. Then he rose and walked out of the room to execute Raketh's orders.

"We must again endure the assaults of the enemy's small craft." There was frustration in Raketh's tone, an emotion he could express now that there were no Inferiors present. For though he had been raised from birth in the Hegemony's culture of assured superiority, he still understood the danger represented by the small craft. He knew how badly they had hurt his ships, and how frequently they had disordered and halted his fleet.

The fleet could face hundreds, that was certain. The forces of the Hegemony, once massed and directed forward into enemy space, could endure such attacks by thousands. But he had no idea how many there were, and as he considered that, he realized how little he truly knew of the enemy. That was not a concern worthy of a Hegemony commander, and certainly not of a first century Master…at least not according to all he'd been taught. But there was something there, something new. He didn't doubt a Hegemony victory in the coming war…the thought of outright defeat was inconceivable to him. But for the first time, he wondered just what the cost would be, how difficult a fight it would take to subdue the Rim dwellers.

* * *

"You must issue the orders, Administrator Cantor…and you have to address the planetary population as well. Admiral Winters's fleet has taken position in support of the orbital defenses, but we must prepare in the event he is defeated. If the enemy lands ground forces, it will be vital that we are prepared to resist strongly during the first hours…and turn them back at their beachheads. To have any chance at all, we will need not only the defense forces, but the militia as well. It will take every citizen of Dannith to hold the planet." Captain Blanth was beyond frustrated with Cantor. The Administrator, as far as he could see, was utterly useless. No, worse, he was an impediment. The Marine remembered Admiral Barron's final comment, his authorization to shoot Cantor if he had to. He hadn't taken that seriously when Barron said it, and he was pretty sure such a thing exceeded the admiral's authority, but still, it had crossed his mind more than once since, if not entirely sincerely.

Cantor looked back at the Marine, his eyes bloodshot, his expression one of despair. He'd harassed Blanth relentlessly, trying to come up with some way he could escape from the planet that had foolishly elected him as its leader. But the Marine had clear orders from Admiral Barron, and despite the limitations of his miniscule force, he'd kept the politician under constant surveillance. He suspected his actions had violated a dozen laws, both local and Confederation, but he didn't care. As far as he was concerned, Tyler Barron's orders were as good as the word of God, and the fact that General Rogan had repeated them solidified Blanth's resolve into pure, unyielding steel.

"Administrator?" Blanth was ready to have the politician dragged down to the broadcast center if need be, but there was no way the man elected as Dannith's leader was going to sit in his office and whimper as the planet faced the greatest threat it ever had. Not on his watch.

When Cantor still remained where he was, Blanth leaned forward and put his hand on the man's shoulder…quite a bit more gently than he'd intended at first. "There is no time. You must issue the final mobilization orders now, and then you *have* to go to the comm center and speak to the people…you have to tell them what's happening before rumors run wild and panic sets in." Blanth had a good idea that panic was coming no matter what he did, if it wasn't already spreading.

He'd despaired of finding a way to defend the planet when Barron had first given him the assignment, but then he'd made a miraculous discovery. There was an entire Marine division on Dannith, and not just any unit, but a hardcore veteran formation. The division's commander and XO were gone, apparently on some kind of leave. It seemed strange to Blanth that the commander and the second in command would be gone at the same time, but he put it out of his mind. He was just excited to find thousands of veteran Marines available to help defend Dannith, though the presence of the unit made his own situation more complex. Barron had put him in charge of the local defenses, an order of dubious legality, perhaps, but one Blanth intended to obey. But the Marine division had half a dozen officers who outranked him, and thirty or more his equal. He'd had to tread carefully when integrating them into the defensive plans, framing his directives as requests and dropping Barron's name often. So far, none of the division's senior officers had refused or disagreed. With any luck, that would continue.

"Now, Administrator." His tone was harsher, and he pulled Cantor out of his chair and led him over to a large workstation against the far wall. "Issue the orders, now." Blanth wondered if the "and don't force me to put my gun in your mouth" that resounded in his head was apparent in his tone.

Cantor leaned forward, activating the station with his thumbprint.

"Awaiting your command, Administrator." The AI's voice was familiar, its cadence much like that of the familiar units on *Dauntless*.

Cantor took a deep and ragged breath. "Defense Order One, effective immediately," he said, with rather more certainty than Blanth had expected. "All defense units are to mobilize at once. All members of the militia are to report to their units immediately."

Blanth was impressed. Against all odds, Cantor had done well. He looked at the still clearly terrified politician and grinned. "We'll make a leader out of you yet, Administrator."

* * *

"All wings, stay tight, keep your focus on your assigned targets...and let's hit these bastards hard." Alicia Covington sat in her cockpit, a place that had become intimately familiar over seven years of war against the Union. She was a Survivor, the unofficial term the fighter corps had attached to those who'd been serving when the war broke out...and were still there at its end. It was a depressingly small group, even when expanded to include those still alive but too badly injured to remain on duty.

Covington was the commander of Base Grimaldi's entire fighter strike force, and Admiral Winters had called on her to accompany his fleet to Dannith. Until Winters had shared Tyler Barron's communique with her, she hadn't realized just how desperate of a fight they faced. Dannith's orbital forts had a large number of squadrons, but they were second tier units, garrison forces of the type assigned to worlds not on a threatened frontier. At least those thought not to be. *Clearly, that's changed.*

Covington had led some crack units during the war, and she'd reached the highest tier of pilots, those ranked just below Jake Stockton, and until his tragic injury, Dirk Timmons. She'd been fortunate enough to have a considerable number of experienced pilots under her at Grimaldi. Even with peace, and with the clearly disordered state of affairs in the Union, the fortress was the Confederation's highest defensive priority.

But Dannith was another matter entirely. Its orbital platforms were considerably larger than she'd expected, and she knew the base there had always been fairly busy trying to suppress and deal with smuggling and unauthorized activity in the Badlands. But fighters were little use in such activities, and no one had expected an enemy to appear from the depths of dead space.

Covington checked her display and adjusted her course. She hadn't assigned herself to a wing command, preferring to remain free and able to go wherever she was needed. The enemy fleet was impressive, and some of its ships were the most massive she'd ever seen. Barron's notes had strongly emphasized the need to hit the largest ships as quickly as possible, as they possessed powerful railguns capable of crippling even the largest Confederation vessels in one or two shots. As she looked at the mass readings, and saw the immensity of the vessels on her screen, she wondered how her mostly green pilots were going to manage.

She saw energy readings spike, and her scanner reported the enemy ships in the front of their line had opened fire. The small point defense batteries weren't much of a danger, not at the current range of her squadrons, but she knew they would become steadily more deadly as the distance decreased…and her gut told her she was going to lose many of her rookie pilots. Skillful execution of evasive maneuvers was something that came more from experience than training. And that meant two-thirds of her people were going to have one hell of a hard time.

"Wings one, two, and three…prepare for attack runs." The three wing commanders acknowledged, and Covington watched as her lead squadrons moved forward. She had significant forces closing on the targeted enemy ships, but she had a nagging feeling it wasn't going to be enough. She'd never battled enemy battleships that didn't have their own fighters, and her mind was racing, trying to develop tactics on the fly. She needed something…and she needed it now.

She flipped her comm unit to a direct line to the lead wing commanders. "Listen up, you three," she said, still trying to think of exactly what she wanted to say. "We've got to hit these ships hard. We don't know anything about them, but Tyler Barron said they were tough…and we know Admiral Barron isn't easily shaken by anything. We don't have tactics for fighting without having to worry about enemy fighters, and from the size of these ships, we've got to hit them as hard as we can." She paused. "We don't know how effective their point defense batteries will be in close…but we need to come in anyway, down to shorter ranges than normal. Much shorter. We need to pump up our hit ratios, because it looks to me like these bastards can soak up some serious damage before we take them down."

"Roger that, Commander. Agreed."

The other officers replied with similar responses.

Covington was still calculating, trying to guess at how cutting the range would increase hit rates…and how badly her rookie formations would get hurt penetrating so deeply into the enemy's fire area.

"Come in as close as you can…we need as many hits as we can get. This is no fight in deep space. There are millions of Confederation citizens on Dannith, right behind us, and Admiral Winters only has three battleships to face the attackers once we're done."

Her commanders replied again, and she could hear confidence in their tones, and aggression. That wasn't a surprise. Her first three wings contained most of her veterans, many of the pilots from the battleships, and the extra units Winters had drawn from Grimaldi's forces. She was hoping the experienced pilots would set an example for their green comrades. She didn't expect miracles, but anything she could do to help make her rookies ready before they went in was worth it.

Because they needed something, and without it, she dreaded watching the garrison pilots trying to take on those battleships.

Chapter Forty

"Still no response, Admiral." Atara spoke calmly, softly, but Barron knew her better than anyone, and he, perhaps alone among all those present, could hear the stress in her voice. "We're still pretty far out for high certainty on scanner readings, but it looks like their reactors are at full power."

Barron nodded briefly, then looked back down at the small screen on his own workstation. He had the warbook files up, the database of all known vessels, both Confederation and foreign. The ships coming at *Dauntless* were Confeds, for sure… but he hadn't been able to get reliable IDs yet. One thing was certain. They were coming from a totally different direction than Titania and the other vessels that had chased *Dauntless* into the Delphi system. That meant Barron and his people had hostiles coming from two vectors, and that they were now hopelessly outnumbered.

He looked back up at the main display. No sign yet of *Titania*, nor any of her escorts. But it wouldn't be long, mostly likely just a matter of minutes, before the vessels that had pursued *Dauntless* across a dozen systems emerged to continue their

307

relentless hunt. And joined up with the new task force now showing ominously on his scanners.

It would be different this time, though…with or without the intervention of the new flotilla coming from the Haustus transit point. *Dauntless*'s engines were completely offline. The ship was traveling at a considerable velocity, but without the ability to accelerate, Barron knew he could never escape from *Titania*. And without changing the current vector, *Dauntless* couldn't reach one of the other transit points, either, or try to evade an approaching attacker.

"Status report from Commander Glaven?" Barron knew he was treating Atara like his first officer and not *Dauntless*'s actual captain…but it was clear she didn't object. He'd tried to get her to go to sickbay a couple times since they'd fled the Olyus system, just to get checked out, but she'd remained stubborn, and Barron hadn't been able to bring himself to make it an order. No matter how exhausted she looked, or how recently she'd been in a deep coma. They'd both taken small breaks, left the bridge when *Dauntless* hadn't been in any immediate danger, but Barron hadn't gotten more than six hours of sleep since he'd been rescued, and he'd have been willing to bet Atara hadn't gotten any more.

She didn't respond, she just tapped at her comm, and then snapped a request for an update once she had a line to engineering. Then she listened to Glaven's response, and she looked back across at Barron. "Commander Glaven reports he will be attempting an engine restart in approximately thirty minutes, sir. He believes he can regain sixty percent thrust at that time… perhaps as much as seventy."

Barron nodded, and then he took a deep breath. If Glaven was successful, it would vastly improve *Dauntless*'s tactical situation, giving the battleship plenty of power for evasive maneuvers. But anything less than one hundred percent thrust rendered any attempt to escape futile. *Titania* would close to range again, this time long before *Dauntless* could escape through the next point.

And if the new force was also hostile, as he was virtually

certain it was, it would also catch *Dauntless* and engage, possibly even before *Titania* did.

Barron looked at the local stellar display, a map of all transit points in the current system and all those within two jumps. Haustus had four points, leading both Rimward and back toward Megara…which meant the new ships could simply be passing through, headed inward from some frontier system with no idea of what had happened on Megara. Or they could be coming from the capital, another force sent to hunt down *Dauntless*. Barron had hoped, at first, that the vessels were just on a normal deployment…but their failure to respond to his repeated communications didn't bode well.

Barron had struggled to avoid combat with friendly forces—those that should have been friendly—but he realized now, with a sickening feeling, he'd gone as far as he could without fighting. He might have surrendered, even at the cost of sacrificing himself, of yielding to whatever plot was at work back on Megara… if it hadn't been for the Hegemony.

He had to escape the pursuit, remain free and able to rally the Confederation's forces. Somehow. He didn't know what he could do, how he could accomplish what seemed like an insurmountable goal, but he knew he had to try. Even if he had to kill fellow Confederation spacers to do it. The prospect of the Hegemony striking a totally unprepared Confederation was simply too terrible to contemplate. Billions could die…the entire Rim could be reduced to virtual slavery. Or even extinction.

He didn't have a choice. Not anymore.

"Captain…put me on ship-wide comm."

"Yes, sir." She reached out, her hands flying over the controls. "On your comm, Admiral."

He took a breath, pausing for a second before he began. "Officers and spacers of *Dauntless*, this is Admiral Barron. I cannot explain what is happening, what machinations are behind my arrest on Megara, except to say that I have never engaged in anything remotely like that of which I was accused. I can offer no proof, save my word, which I hope you will accept. We have served together before, many of you for years and through more desperate battles than we can easily recount. I ask all of you to stand with me now...even though we face a fight we would do almost anything to avoid."

He stopped, glancing over at Atara, drawing some strength from the look of absolute loyalty in her haggard and exhausted face. "We face two task forces. The one approaching now has not answered our communications attempts, and while we cannot yet be sure they are hostile, it seems likely that they will prove to be so. And the forces we faced in the Santorus system will almost certainly transit imminently. We cannot hope to prevail against both of these forces, not if they are able to join together and fight us as one." Another pause, as Barron mustered all the strength he could to say what he knew he had to say. "Therefore, as soon as the engines are back online, *Dauntless* will move directly toward the force already in the system. We will engage and...defeat...these ships..." He'd almost said "destroy," but he'd stopped himself at the last second. He wasn't sure if it was because he was worried about how his people would react...or if he had convinced, or fooled, himself that he could disable his pursuers and leave most of the crews alive. "...and then we will turn to face the forces following us from Santorus."

Barron held his voice steady, mustering all his command experience to push back against the doubts, to give his spacers what they needed. But he knew just what they all faced, and he realized a battle against either force would be a difficult one. The chances of defeating both were vanishingly small, especially since *Dauntless* was already damaged, and she was without her fighter squadrons.

"I understand how difficult it will be for all of you to engage in battle against Confederation comrades, to fight with the fire you have always shown in combat. I cannot offer anything that will make this any less painful, save to remind each of you that the Hegemony is coming. You have all seen this new enemy, the power of their ships and technology. You know we have no higher duty than to prepare the Confederation to face what is coming. If we must fight our comrades, spill the blood of fellow Confederation spacers...then that is what we will do. Our

Black Dawn   311

only alternative is to stand by and do nothing, as cataclysmic
war comes, and millions, perhaps billions, die in the onslaught."

He turned toward Atara and nodded, signaling for her to
cut the line. Barron's people had followed him in many battles,
and he was hopeful, if not confident, that they would stand with
him again.

He sat silently for a few minutes, trying to center himself, to
prepare for what was coming. Then he found out exactly what
was coming at his vessel.

"Admiral...we're picking up the beacons on those ships.
They're all from the Megara garrison, sir."

Atara didn't elaborate. She didn't have to. Barron knew
exactly what that meant. More ships sent to hunt him down,
just as he'd suspected.

More he had to destroy if he was going to have any chance
at all to prepare the Confederation for a Hegemony invasion.

He had to hit those ships and take them out. Quickly.
Before...

"Admiral...we're picking up energy readings from the Santorus transit point. We've got ships coming in."

Barron felt his insides tighten. His ship was alone, soon to
be bracketed between hostile forces. He *had* to destroy the ships
on his scanners, and he had to do it quickly...before *Titania* and
her escorts caught him between two enemies.

That was just what they were now, these old comrades. Enemies...however uncomfortable that made him, however much
the guilt of what he was about to do would go with him to the
grave, he understood that those spacers would be trying to kill
his.

"Commander...set a course toward the forces already in
the system. I want maximum available thrust the instant Commander Glaven gets the engines back online."

*   *   *

"Scanners confirm, Captain. *Dauntless* appears to be accelerating toward the unidentified force. Readings indicate signifi-

cant thrust levels in excess of fifty percent."

"Very well, Commander." Heaton leaned back, trying to
ease the disappointment he felt at the report. *Dauntless*'s engines
had been dead when the ship entered the transit point...or at
least it had appeared that way. He'd tried to hold his excitement in check as he brought his ships around to pursue, but
the prospect of engaging Barron's battleship with her engines
down had inflated his hopes nevertheless...not just of victory,
but of the chance to disable *Dauntless* and not have to destroy
her. A chance to take Barron prisoner, instead of killing him
and a thousand of his crew.

That prospect now seemed to be lost. While *Dauntless* might
have less than its full thrust, it was still clear the battleship had
enough power to fight. He didn't fool himself that Tyler Barron, or any of his veterans, would yield, not while their vessel
was still battle-worthy...if they would under any circumstances.

His eyes moved to the other force, the one *Dauntless* was
heading toward. He expected help in pursuing Barron, and the
presumed entry point of those ships into the system could indicate a route from Megara...or half a dozen other things. Heaton was just a ship captain, and until days before, the largest
vessel he'd commanded was a cruiser. He wasn't privy to naval
dispositions across the Confederation, and he had no idea what
those ships were, if they were from the Megara home forces or
not...and he wouldn't until he got close enough to pick up their
beacons.

Or until they opened fire on *Dauntless*...or the reverse.

He could see Barron's ship moving in, heading almost
directly toward the other ships. If *Dauntless* wasn't attacking,
it damned sure looked like she was. He could see the waiting
ships reacting, too, accelerating forward and engaging in evasive
maneuvers. He had rough mass totals now. There were six
ships facing *Dauntless*, but none had the mass of a battleship.
Dauntless would outrange them, and there wasn't a doubt in Heaton's mind, Tyler Barron would use his primaries like a virtuoso
playing a violin. The cruisers would move to their own range as
quickly as possible, but *Dauntless*'s guns would take their toll first.

But Barron wasn't going to escape. Not with fleets coming at him from two sides. Heaton knew the gifted admiral would try to finish off the cruisers first, before he could get his own ships into range. He also knew Barron just might pull it off...but not without taking damage. And Heaton had no intention of leaving *Dauntless* unmolested while his ships moved into range. He'd been concerned at first about *Dauntless*'s legendary fighter squadrons, but Barron hadn't launched so much as a single ship over the entire time Heaton had been in pursuit. He'd come to believe *Dauntless* didn't have her fighters aboard.

But Titania had hers.

His squadrons were made up mostly of rookies, no match for *Dauntless*'s veterans. But if Barron truly didn't have his fighters or his pilots...

"Commander, bring us to red alert. Scramble all fighter squadrons and prepare to launch. All fighters are to move toward *Dauntless* at maximum speed and engage at once."

Chapter Forty-One

Steven Blanth stood on a grassy hill, a pleasant spot in the highlands that he knew would turn into a slice of hell if enemy forces landed. There was no doubt in Blanth's mind the invaders would come right at Dannith's capital. Port Royal City and its surroundings contained most of the planet's industry and close to two-thirds of its population. If the capital fell, there would be little chance to hold the planet save, perhaps, for some sporadic resistance from the wilderness areas.

Blanth wore his body armor, and he carried his full complement of weapons, too. He knew he'd get warning from orbit before any enemy forces could land—giving him plenty of time to don his battle gear—but he needed his people at peak readiness, and he'd decided to set the example himself. The Marines of Peterson's division were deployed in their assigned places, every unit at full battle readiness, as he was himself. But the motley assortment of garrison units and part-time militia were restless, disordered and shaken in far too many cases by paralyzing fear. He suspected they would firm up a bit if the enemy did begin to initiate landings…it was a strange reality of battle that, especially for inexperienced soldiers, the waiting could be far more difficult to endure than the actual fighting, when survival

314

instincts took over.

And the cold reality that they were fighting for spouses and children and friends and family would set in, creating a form of courage where there had been none before.

Blanth was a veteran, and his discipline was in charge of his actions. Still, he couldn't help but think about the strange set of circumstances that had put him where he was, taken a company commander and placed him in command of the defense force of an entire planet. Dannith's military had its own officers, of course, including a fair number of generals, but they were mostly political appointees with no combat experience. Blanth benefited from the effect of Tyler Barron's immense reputation, and, though not without some tension and negotiation, he'd managed to get the Dannith force commanders to do just what he wanted.

Fear is a great motivator, even stronger than arrogance, at least in the shadow of death…

Blanth had done all he could, labored tirelessly, worn the hat of a diplomat as well as that of a teacher, in addition to his own as a combat Marine. He'd done all Barron had entrusted him to do, and he believed the admiral would have been pleased with him.

But he suspected it wasn't enough. That was part analysis and part feeling…along with a not inconsiderable recollection of Barron's tone when he'd given the Marine his orders. Tyler Barron had been afraid…and nothing scared the hell out of Steve Blanth more than that.

*　*　*

"Nice shooting, third wing!" Covington brought her fighter around, following the course taken by her second wing. She was angling for an approach at the battered battleship the forty-eight attacking fighters had left behind, but now, her eyes were on her scanner. She watched as the damage reports streamed in from the vessel third wing had assaulted…and then as the massive ship vanished in a cataclysmic blast of raw energy and hard radiation.

The four squadrons in the victorious wing had closed to the shortest ranges of any of her formations, a few of their vessels coming in under a thousand kilometers before they'd launched their plasma torpedoes…and the wing as a whole had scored an astonishing hit rate, almost forty percent, as torpedo after torpedo slammed into the massive ship.

It was clear to Covington that the enemy had never faced a weapon like the plasma torpedoes. Their defensive batteries seemed designed to intercept missiles or some other kind of physical weapon, and they worked fairly well against fighters. But the plasma torpedoes converted to pure energy on their way to the target, and while the enemy seemed to have more than enough thrust to conduct effective evasive maneuvers, they seemed dumbfounded as to how to avoid the deadly torpedoes.

She knew that wouldn't last. If the Confederation did indeed face a long and deadly war with—whoever these people were—the enemy would quickly adapt, and fighter hit rates would plummet. Casualties would escalate, too, though the effort to close to such short ranges had already jacked up the number of fighters hit. Her three wings had devastated their targets, but altogether, the one hundred forty-four fighters had lost eighteen of their number. Some of those had managed to eject, but no matter how she tried to imagine the battle proceeding, she couldn't come up with a scenario allowing rescue boats to arrive in time to save any of them.

She checked her own range, and her eyes froze on the display, watching as she slipped under two thousand kilometers. Her torpedo was armed and ready, and she could launch at any time. She was far below what had been long been considered point-blank range, but without enemy fighters to worry about, she was pushing it to the limit. She didn't just want to hit the enemy ship…she wanted to deliver her missile right into its weakest spot, and area of its hull scarred with great gashes and riddled by secondary explosions. If she could put the torpedo right where she planned, she just might manage to repeat third wing's feat, and push the battered enemy ship over the edge.

She knew she shouldn't be risking herself so recklessly. She was the strike force commander, and hundreds of pilots were looking to her for leadership. But she knew Admiral Winters needed everything the fighters could give, and she also wanted to set an example for the rookie wings even then moving toward their targets. She intended to come in closer…much closer.

The range dipped down to fifteen hundred, and it continued to drop. The defensive fire was heavy now, both because she was so close, and because she was the only ship attacking. The thought that every defensive battery remaining on the battleship was targeting her Lightning struck her suddenly, and she could feel the sweat all over. She had a reputation as a disciplined pilot, but in the barely controlled fighter corps, that was most definitely a relative term.

Her ship was bouncing around wildly as she put all she had into evasive maneuvers. The enemy would almost certainly get better at targeting, she realized, but now, as dangerous as the laser blasts all around her were, she was confident she could avoid them.

Reasonably confident.

Her range had dropped below one thousand kilometers. She had never been so close to any enemy ship, and the defensive fire was all around now, so thick it felt almost like she could reach out and touch a passing beam. She'd imagined going even closer, but now she realized she was pushing too hard, and in an instant, she pressed the firing stud, sending her torpedo off toward its target. The warhead triggered the reaction that converted its entire mass to plasma almost instantly, an automatic function at such a short range…and seconds later, it slammed hard into the enemy ship.

But Covington wasn't watching when it did. As soon as she'd fired, her eyes had darted up…and she'd seen the massive ship growing rapidly in front of her. Her course had been right toward the battleship, and now she pulled back on the throttle, pulling her tiny craft up and over the giant ship ahead. A quick check of her instruments showed her she had cleared the enemy by over one hundred kilometers, a hair's breadth by the standards of space battle, but not as close a call as she'd imagined at first.

She took a few deep breaths, struggling to restore the calm she was known for…and then she checked the scanner logs. She'd hit the enemy, there was no question of that. But had she planted the torpedo right where she'd needed to?

She could see the damage assessments coming in, more internal explosions, energy levels dropping until the battleship's thrusters cut out entirely. The ship was crippled, or close to it… but as she watched and waited, she could feel her excitement fading away. She'd hurt the already wounded ship, badly enough to take it out of the battle. But she felt only disappointment when the vessel didn't lose containment, when no massive thermonuclear blast lit up on her scanners.

It shouldn't matter. Tactically, she'd likely attained as much as total destruction would have, but Covington as far as she was concerned, the Confederation was at war again, and this time, not against a neighbor like the Union, but against an enemy from far away. An enemy who had crossed a vast void to bring war and death to a peaceful nation.

The rage she'd felt during the Union War was back, hotter and stronger than ever. She wanted to defeat this new enemy, certainly, but now she realized she wanted more.

She wanted to kill them. Every last one of them who came to the Confederation.

Who invaded her home.

* * *

"Your people did a remarkable job, Commander. All fighters are to return to base at once." Clint Winters paused, then he added, "Redirect all squadrons to the orbital stations, Commander." Winters knew his squadrons had done well, better than he'd dared to hope. He also knew it hadn't been enough to save his battleships. He'd never faced the Hegemony in battle, but he had an idea what to expect from Barron's notes…and his meager three capital ships weren't going to get the job done, even supported by cruisers, escorts, and Dannith's orbital platforms. The forts were large—not by the standards of Grimaldi, of course, but Dannith's position as a frontier world had gained it added funding for expanded defenses over the years. The planet had the tonnage in orbit, and the stations were well-armed, but the crews were raw, untested in combat, and Winters doubted they could make up for the immense superiority of the enemy forces.

He knew his only chance was to inflict as much damage as possible, to see if the enemy would break off if their losses were too high. He wasn't optimistic about that either. Barron had suggested the enemy was highly tolerant of casualties.

"We're on the way, Admiral. Unless…" Covington's voice sounded tentative, and Winters knew exactly what his strike force commander was going to say, even before the words came from her mouth. "…we launch strafing runs with lasers."

"Negative, Commander. Your people would be killed for no gain." Winters had considered the very same thing, and as difficult an order as it would have been to give, he might have done it…if his pilots were all veterans. But the vast majority of them were green garrison pilots, and while they had performed well enough with their torpedo runs—despite suffering fairly heavy losses—he couldn't imagine any of them were up to precision laser attacks. Anything except the most perfectly-place shots would be ineffectual against the enemy's massive capital ships. He knew he faced a desperate fight, and he figured his squadrons might get one more strike in if he could hold the enemy back from the orbital platforms long enough. He didn't think they would all get back out, but there was a good chance some of them would…and he knew Covington would preference the veteran formations.

"Yes, Admiral. Directing all units toward the fortresses now, sir."

Winters cut the line, and then he stared across the bridge toward his primary aide. "Commander…the fleet will engage thrusters. Twenty percent power to the engines, and full evasive maneuvers once we close to five hundred thousand kilometers."

"Yes, Admiral."

Winters had intended to stay where he was, engage the enemy forces alongside the orbital forts...but now he had reconsidered. The fighters were his best weapon, and the more time he could give them to land and refit, the more damage they could inflict. He wasn't going to make a mad charge at the enemy, but maybe he could delay them for a short time.

"All ships report ready for thrust, Admiral."

"Engage," Winters said grimly. "I want primaries armed and charged before we enter firing range." Winters knew the enemy would fire first, at least any of those approaching ships that still had working railguns. Barron had been quite clear that the fearsome weapons outranged even Confederation primaries...and that they were harder hitting, too. But the fighters had concentrated on the largest enemy ships, and there was no question in his mind they had knocked out some of the powerful guns.

He adjusted himself slightly as he felt the thrust engaging. *Constitution* was one of the Confederation's newest class of battleships, and her dampening systems were state of the art. The crushing pressure Winters remembered so well from his earlier days was gone, replaced with a vague sense of discomfort as the offsetting force synced up with the engine output. It was actually relatively comfortable, even at full thrust...at least until aggressive evasive maneuvers began, and the system fell to playing catchup to the constant, rapidly cycling vector changes.

"All ships report battle ready, Admiral. All battleships acknowledge primaries online and armed."

"Very well, Commander." Winters leaned back in his chair, taking a breath as he watched *Constitution*'s velocity increase on the main screen and the range to the enemy decline. It was down to four hundred fifty thousand kilometers, and still dropping.

His eyes darted to the side, to the edge of the display showing Covington's squadrons. They were on their way toward the platforms, coming in rapidly. He guessed she'd be landing fighters in fifteen minutes, and that the entire strike force would be aboard the orbital bases in less than an hour.

Winters was far from sure he could hold the enemy back for

an hour, especially if the approaching ships were determined to reach the platforms as quickly as possible, and ignore the damage his small fleet could inflict.

The enemy was decelerating as they approached the planet. The battle would be fought at low velocities, as the attackers slowed to engage the planet. There would be little maneuver, and few opportunities for elegant tactics. Planetary assaults and defenses tended to be slugging matches, toe to toe exchanges with brutal losses on both sides. Winters knew he couldn't change that. He'd settle for getting some of Covington's fighters back out to make one more strike at the enemy as they engaged the fortresses and whatever was left of his ships. He didn't know if he had any chance at all, but that wasn't going to stop him from throwing everything he had at the enemy.

"Range, four hundred thousand kilometers." His aide's voice was loud, clear, the announcement intended for all present on the bridge.

Winters took a deep breath. He could fire his primaries at just under two hundred thousand kilometers. That was long range, and the hit rate wouldn't be good...but he intended to open up as quickly as possible. His ships would be taking incoming fire, too, even before that mark, and he wanted to get whatever he could from his main guns before he lost them.

He inhaled deeply, watching as the range counted down steadily. After two years of peace, what seemed now like the merest respite, he was back at war.

Back at what he did best.

Chapter Forty-Two

"Fire!" Barron felt the rush of adrenaline he usually did as *Dauntless* let loose with its devastating primaries…and seconds later the scanners showed a direct hit. But his elation quickly dissipated as his battle instincts faded away, replaced by the renewed realization that he was firing on Confederation ships.

By the time the damage assessments began to flow in, he was as morose as he was satisfied. Two of the primaries had taken one of the approaching cruisers directly amidships, and while he was still waiting for the AI's final estimates, he had a good idea just how badly that shot had hurt the smaller vessel. The cruiser was crippled or close to it, and it was a virtual certainty he had just killed Confederation spacers.

Worse, he had fired first. Part of him had wanted to wait for the oncoming ships to shoot, to eradicate any possible doubt that they had come to attack *Dauntless*. Then he could have been certain his people were only defending themselves. But that hadn't been an option. Range was his greatest advantage over the force he'd turned to face, and if he'd given it up, whatever chance he had in the fight would be gone. If he didn't knock out

322

two or three of the approaching cruisers before they could move into their own range and open fire, he wouldn't get through the fight in any condition to face *Titania* and her escorts.

Not that he had much chance of defeating both forces coming at him no matter what he did.

He'd tried to raise the incoming ships several times, almost begging whoever was in command to answer…and expressly stating that if he didn't get a response he would assume they were hostile and open fire. He'd given them every warning, and he didn't have any serious doubts they were closing to attack, but it had still been one of the most difficult commands he'd ever issued…and he suspected no less so for his gunners to obey.

The assessments came streaming in, confirming his suspicions. The cruiser had a massive, gaping wound in its hull, and a geyser of gaseous material was pouring out from the inside, spewing into space and instantly freezing into long, spear-like shards. The ship's energy levels had dropped well below half of normal, and there were signs of secondary explosions. The cruiser was out of the fight, and there was little doubt the casualties among her crew were severe.

Dauntless's primaries were already recharging. Barron figured he'd get two more shots off before the cruisers closed to their own range. *Maybe*, three.

He was fortunate to even have the option to face the ships coming at him separately. *Dauntless* had barely evaded becoming a sitting duck, cruising through space on a fixed course, with no thrust at all. That would have allowed the pursuing vessels to join up and launch a devastating combined assault. He knew he had Dave Glaven to thank for that, and if the engineer wasn't the equal of Anya Fritz—and who was?—he had surely earned his keep on this mission. Barron had fully eighty-two percent of *Dauntless*'s normal thrust capacity, more than he'd dared hope for just an hour earlier.

Even as he completed his thought, the big guns fired again. Another hit, though only with one of the four beams this time. Barron's instincts again leapt into action guessing at the damage level. Bad, he suspected, but his best guess was, the ship was still in the fight, at least to some extent.

He felt the instinctive urge, for about the hundredth time, to launch fighters, to send one of his squadrons to take advantage of the cruisers' lack of their own small craft, only to recall once again, with growing frustration, that *Dauntless* didn't have any. He'd grown accustomed to having the best fighter wing in the navy at his disposal, and now that he was without Stockton and his pack of veterans, he realized just how much he'd relied on them in his many battles.

He turned toward Atara, feeling as though he should issue some kind of order. But there was nothing to do…nothing save wait to see what his gunners could do with one more shot, or perhaps two, before *Dauntless* faced incoming fire.

The familiar whine told him the primaries had fired again, and a few seconds later the scanners confirmed yet another hit. He'd just turned to the display to wait for damage assessments, when that became unnecessary. All four of *Dauntless*'s primaries had hit one of the cruisers. The stricken ship hovered in space for a few seconds…and then it disappeared in the fury of nuclear fusion.

One less ship to fight, one step closer to extricating his people from the trap they were in.

And a good three hundred Confederation spacers dead…

No, he thought to himself, dragging up a detail from the depths of his mind. The exact complement of a *Springfield*-class medium cruiser was *three hundred forty-two*.

And not a chance a single one had survived.

Barron felt nauseous, and he clamped down on his emotions, held back the bile rising up his throat. There was no time for any of that now. He had to get his ship out of the Delphi system. He had to get somewhere he could begin to rally forces to face the Hegemony. He had to save the Confederation.

Even if he had to kill thousands of Confederation spacers to do it.

Because if he didn't the Hegemony would kill millions.

* * *

Heaton sat in his command chair in the center of *Titania*'s bridge, watching as *Dauntless* tore into the cruisers she was facing. He'd known Tyler Barron's reputation, and he was as aware as any Confederation officer was of the admiral's long list of accomplishments and victories. But watching it happening and knowing his own ships would soon have to engage the renegade admiral, was something else entirely.

"*Capella* has fallen out of formation, Captain." A pause. "That makes four of our six ships out of action."

Heaton nodded, but his only audible acknowledgement was a deep grunt. The tactical officer was only doing his job reporting on the loss of another one of the vessels fighting *Dauntless*, but he wondered—unjustly, he knew—if the fool thought he'd forgotten how to count. He knew damned well there were only two ships left, and that both of them were damaged. For all his force outnumbered the fugitive vessel, he had to admit—to himself, at least—he was scared shitless to go up against Barron and his people.

There had been one advantage to watching *Dauntless* chop up the force of cruisers so thoroughly, though. Heaton had been fighting the sense that it was wrong to be chasing the great hero, that something was clearly amiss in the orders that put him up against his own comrades. But watching Tyler Barron cut down those ships and kill so many Confederation spacers, just to save himself from prosecution, had gone a long way to purge him of his earlier hesitation. He wasn't exactly thirsting for Barron's blood, not yet, but he knew he had to stop the fugitive, and stop him now…before more of his comrades died.

Still no fighters…

He couldn't understand why *Dauntless* hadn't launched her squadrons. At first, he'd guessed Barron was holding back his deadly veterans until he really needed them. Then he'd wondered if the great admiral faced dissension among the fighter corps, if his pilots had been unwilling to follow the rest of *Dauntless*'s crew in fighting their comrades. But that didn't seem quite right either. Heaton would have guessed the wild pilots would have been the first to rally to Barron's side.

He still didn't understand it, and while he'd been thinking for some time that Barron didn't have his squadrons aboard, he couldn't shake the thought that the brilliant admiral was planning some kind of trap.

Heaton had wanted to equip most of his small craft as bombers, but he'd held back, allowed his caution to prevail. Only a single squadron was equipped with the deadly plasma torpedoes, and all his other ships were fitted out as interceptors, ready to deal with any surprise launch from *Dauntless*. Heaton knew that Jake Stockton had shipped out with the White Fleet, and if that crazy son of a bitch came tearing out of *Dauntless*'s bays with his borderline insane pilots behind him, *Titania*'s squadrons needed to be ready.

He was still looking at the display when *Dauntless*'s broadside opened up on one of the remaining cruisers. The battleship had switched from her longer-ranged primaries to her more numerous secondary batteries, and seven of the shots hit the target. Heaton knew what the battleship's guns would do to the more lightly armored cruiser, and as the reports came in, he just nodded somberly. *Cranston* wasn't a complete wreck, but she was close. That meant *Dauntless* was down to one opposing ship.

Heaton had hoped his fighters would engage Barron's ship before the cruisers were defeated, but now all he could hope for was for them to arrive at the tail end of the fight. If *Dauntless* had any fighters, he had to believe Barron would launch them any second.

If not, his strike force would hit in less than ten minutes, and they would come in against a vessel with no fighter screen.

If that was the case, they might not take out *Dauntless*, but they would almost certainly damage the battleship…and set the stage for *Titania* and her escorts to finish the deadly pursuit in Delphi.

* * *

"Commander Glaven is to divert all possible damage control assets to the defensive array." Barron was tense, sweating, his eyes darting from one screen to another as he monitored the attacks coming in from all angles.

"Yes, sir." Atara's voice was sharp, and in the immediacy of her response he saw that she had been thinking the same thing.

His people had almost finished off the cruisers. He'd left three of them burned out ruins, combat ineffective, but hopefully with life support for whatever portion of their crews had survived the battle. One ship was still engaged, but she'd lost two-thirds of her guns and most of her thrust. She was barely managing to keep what weapons she still had in range and arc of *Dauntless*, and, as much as Barron always worried about any combatant facing him, the vessel had been reduced more to a nuisance than a serious threat.

Now there were fighters coming in, and from the looks of the formation, it was *Titania*'s entire strike force. For a brief, terrible instant, Barron had imagined an entire wing of bombers, but as the ships came close enough for detailed scans, he realized with considerable relief that he was facing only a single squadron equipped with torpedoes. A smile almost pushed its way through the grimness that had taken hold of him, a nod to the power of Jake Stockton and *Dauntless*'s crack pilots…and their ability to affect an attacker's decisions even when they were hundreds of light-years away.

A squadron of unopposed bombers was enough of a threat, but seventy torpedo-armed ships would likely have been the end of *Dauntless*.

Dauntless had a considerable defensive array for use against attacking fighters, over sixty small turrets positioned all along the massive ship's bulk. But fighters were difficult targets for fixed guns, and he knew his people weren't going to get them all.

His mind raced. *Titania*…what did he know about that brand-new battleship? She'd come off the lines more a year after the end of the war, after he'd left with the White Fleet.

She'd almost been canceled when she was half-completed, and she owed her existence to the influence wielded by the Senators from the Iron Belt world from which she had come. The immediate post-war period had seen somewhat of a feeding frenzy over what remained from vastly reduced appropriations budgets. As was usually the case, the final decisions were based more on the political standing of a world's representatives than any real strategic consideration of what the navy did or did not need.

Barron didn't have hard data on the battleship's crew or its fighter squadrons, but he was willing to bet they were mostly green. Stockton's people could probably have cut them down like a farmer scything hay…but there was no gain in sinking into what ifs. Barron didn't have any fighters, and that meant his gunnery crews were all that stood between *Dauntless* and a barrage of deadly plasma torpedoes.

"Admiral, Commander Glaven reports he has already deployed two dozen bots and six engineers to the defensive array. He advises, if he diverts any more resources, he cannot guarantee to have the primaries back online by the time *Titania* is in range."

Shit.

Barron had always believed in prioritizing the immediate problem over one that followed, but he couldn't risk *Dauntless* having to endure *Titania*'s long-range bombardment with no ability to return fire. The primaries had been knocked out by a fluke hit from one of the cruisers, and while the damage wasn't critical, the repair process was tedious and work-intensive.

"Very well, Captain. He is to maintain his current organization." Most of *Dauntless*'s defensive guns were operational anyway. It would be useful to have the eight that were damaged back in the firing line, but it wasn't worth giving up on the primaries.

Assuming the big guns make it through the fighter attack without taking more damage…

The logic of his usual "deal with the immediate problem first" creed was only too evident in that last thought. But he stayed firm. There was no point worrying about new damage to the main guns if they never got back online to begin with.

"Gunnery control reports all stations ready. The enemy will enter range in…forty-five seconds."

"Very well, Captain. All gunners are to fire at will, and to maintain at maximum speed until ordered to halt."

"Yes, sir."

"They are to target bombers only. I'm not too worried about those interceptors and their lasers, but I want as many of those torpedo-armed ships gone as possible."

"Yes, Admiral."

Barron sat still, quiet…and he watched as the wave of fighters moved steadily closer on the display. The seconds passed, slowly, agonizingly, and he could feel every heartbeat, even every droplet of sweat breaking loose along the base of his neck and streaming down his back. He knew it had been less than a minute, but he'd have sworn it had been hours.

And then the defensive batteries opened fire.

Chapter Forty-Three

"All primaries, open fire as soon as we enter range." Clint Winters sat motionless, his face grim, looking as though it had been carved from stone. He was fortunate that *Constitution* still had operational main guns to fire, though he wasn't sure how much good they would do in the overall scheme of things, firing into an enemy fleet that vastly outnumbered his meager force. *Discovery*'s primaries were offline, if such terminology could be used to describe a system that had been so badly chopped to pieces, the only chance of saving the battleship's spinally mounted weapon was a full refit in a prime spacedock.

Still, he was grateful that one of his companion battleships still remained in the line, even if her primary guns offline. The enemy railguns had battered *Discovery*, but they hadn't put her down yet. He couldn't say the same for *Triumph*. The newest of his three battleships had also been the least fortunate. The vessel had been the first hit by the enemy railguns, and that initial assault had been followed by two more. The last one had torn off a huge section of the ship's bow and rendered the vessel dead in space.

Until yet another shot had struck her amidships...and split the unlucky ship in half. Winters had watched in undisguised

330

horror as *Triumph*'s structural spine snapped and her sections
drifted apart, two massive chunks of metal, now devoid of any
survivors save for two lifeboats his scanners had detected.

He'd lost ships before, and he was familiar with the pain,
and yet he was unsettled in a different way. The war against
the Union had seen its share of brutal carnage, but this was
something entirely different. He'd believed Barron's warnings
about the enemy's heavy guns, but being told something—and
actually *seeing* it—were two different things. The railguns were
enormously powerful, and a deadly threat to any battle line, be
it his tiny one of three battleships...or that of the combined
Confederation fleet formed up for matter.

There was one solace—the enemy appeared to have only
three ships with the heavy weapons still functioning. Barron
had said the systems were fragile, even more so than the Confederation primaries. It seemed he was right.

Winters knew that Alicia Covington and her people had
saved his small fleet—and the orbital bases around Dannith as
well—from immediate and utter destruction. He didn't know
how many of the enemy ships had the railguns, but he guessed
that Covington's squadrons had taken out a dozen vessels armed
with the deadly weapons. If those ships had closed to range
with their heavy weapons all intact, he doubted any of his own
would have survived long enough to have gotten off a shot.
The fixed fortresses would almost certainly have been gutted.

He watched as the distance to the enemy ticked down on
the display...and slipped under the maximum range of the primaries. He felt an impulse to repeat his earlier attack order, but
before he could get the words out, he heard the guns firing.

The range was long, and scoring even a single hit was far
from a certain proposition. If he'd had all three battleships still
fully functional, he'd have had ten shots. But *Triumph*'s four
guns were gone along with the whole of that unfortunate ship,
and *Discovery*'s two were just so much scrap metal.

That left *Constitution*'s four...and as he stared straight ahead,
he saw the report. All had missed their targets.

Damn!

He felt a flush of anger, but it was more at the situation than at his people. He'd written the section of "the book" on weapons targeting, and he knew the stats better than anyone. His guns had had less than a ten percent chance of scoring a hit at such extreme range…but he'd still hoped to get lucky with at least one of the beams. He'd ordered his gunners to ignore all other enemy ships save those with demonstrated active railgun capacity, and a single hit with one of his primaries could be just enough to knock out another of the deadly weapons.

He glanced up at the screen. One minute forty seconds to recharge.

Too long.

He'd been tracking the enemy's rate of fire, and he guessed he had a minute, maybe less, before the next railgun attack. *Constitution* had been fortunate so far, mostly at the expense of her companion vessels, but any commander worth his salt would be coming after the only untouched battleship next. *Constitution* might not attract *every* shot that was coming, but he didn't have a doubt that most of them would be heading his way.

"I want all scanners on those enemy battleships, Commander. There's a power surge before they fire their railguns, and it should give us a good two or three seconds warning."

"Yes, Admiral."

Winters was leaning forward, his workstation pulled around from its stowed position on the side to directly in front of his chair. He was hunched over, his hands over the controls. It was unorthodox for a ship commander to take the helm directly, and even more so for the fleet's admiral to do it. But Clint Winters had come up through the ranks as a capital ship pilot, and one of the best…and if *Constitution* didn't evade the railgun shots he knew were coming its way, the fleet would be down to a half-shattered battleship and a bunch of hopelessly outgunned escorts.

"Yes, Admiral. The AI is monitoring the readings."

Winters nodded. *Constitution*'s primary artificial intelligence would pick up any energy spikes far more quickly than human eyes could…but he wasn't trusting the evasive maneuvers to the computer, not entirely. He was going to add his own experience and instinct to the mix, and maybe—just maybe—give his people another chance to blast those railguns before they fired yet again.

"Energy spike detected, Admiral." The AI's voice was loud and clear all across *Constitution*'s bridge, and Winters was already reacting. He upped the engine power levels and blasted hard, the thrust vector almost directly forward. *Almost.* He slipped in a mild angle in both the X-Y and Y-Z axes, just enough to add unpredictability to the maneuver. *Constitution* would slip just far enough from the enemy's targeting plot to allow the deadly chunk of super-heavy metal to zip by his ship instead of crashing into it.

The railguns launched their projectiles at astonishing speeds, far beyond any hyper-velocity weapons the Confederation had ever possessed or faced, but they were still slow compared to speed of light-based systems like lasers. It took perhaps three or four seconds for the projectiles to cover the hundred eighty thousand kilometers from the Hegemony ships to *Constitution*. That wasn't long, but Winters was ready. The first three chunks of high-density metal zipped by as he altered the ship's vector yet again. One came within a hundred meters of the ship, but all of them missed, and seconds later, another three followed.

Clint Winters let out a loud exhale, one far more audible than he'd intended, and he let his body slouch back into his chair. It would be two and half or three minutes before the enemy's heavy guns were ready to fire again...and a glance at the countdown display told him he just *might* get off two shots with his primaries by then.

Two more shots. Two more chances to take out one of those railguns, before *Constitution* stared once more into the face of looming destruction.

*   *   *

"Yes!" Alicia Covington stood along the wall in the main launch bay for Station Number Two, otherwise known as Fortress Bennett.

No doubt named after some local politician even more adept at graft and malfeasance than the average one…

Her eyes were glued to the small display screen on the wall, currently showing the space around *Constitution* and the enemy ships rapidly approaching Admiral Winters's flagship…and Covington's mother ship.

Covington had spent the last half hour racing all around the bay, shouting, cajoling, encouraging, threatening, and once or twice, even begging…anything she could think of to speed up the process of refitting her squadrons. *Constitution* and the rest of the fleet were hopelessly outgunned, as good as dead if she didn't get another fighter strike launched. She might have managed to get some interceptors back out by now, but all her ships were fitted for bombing runs. Loading the cumbersome plasma torpedo units took a lot more time than just topping off a fuel tank and relaunching.

She'd felt every second passing, almost cutting at her as each slid by into the next. But *Constitution* had just scored a major hit on the lead enemy ship. Three of the battleship's primaries had struck the target, and from the looks of things, the hits had been well-located. Confederation primaries didn't hit as hard as the enemy heavies did, but they were deadly weapons nevertheless. Covington dared to hope that Winters had managed to knock out the devastating guns on one of the three remaining railgun-armed vessels he faced.

She stood where she was for a few more seconds, savoring the joy of the hit. Then she turned back and stared out over the bay, looking for the highest-ranking flight crew member she could terrorize. She had to get her ships back out at the enemy. She'd sent her pilots to grab some food, even an hour's sleep, but she hadn't left the bay herself. She'd wolfed down a sandwich one of her squadron leaders had brought her, but that was as much as she'd had time for.

"Lieutenant Foster," she shouted, waving toward one of the crew commanders working on her ships, "I want six of these squadrons ready to launch in twenty minutes, max. Do you understand me?" She moved away from the wall, walking swiftly out toward the center of the bay, before the officer could pretend not to hear her and slip way. "Lieutenant…"

*   *   *

"Outstanding, Captain Holcott. Really good work." Blanth stood next to the line of heavy guns, each of them almost completely buried under piles of fresh dirt and hastily constructed barricades. The hyper-velocity cannons were the heaviest ordnance Peterson's division possessed, and Blanth had been shocked when he'd learned the massive weapons had been landed along with the Marines themselves. He couldn't imagine what use Colonel Peterson could have had for the guns on a Confederation world. They were purely weapons of war, designed to target and destroy enemy ground armor and air assault units. Whatever had urged the renowned officer to disembark the guns—most likely an overdeveloped sense of preparedness—it looked an awful lot like prescience right then.

"Your authorization to organize the locals into work details was a big help, Captain." Holcott stood less than a meter away, looking every bit the veteran Marine Blanth himself was. The two men were of the same rank—indeed, Holcott might very well have had seniority…Blanth had purposely avoided checking such things. He was Tyler Barron's representative, in a manner of speaking, and that had proven to be enough to make him the de facto—if informal and enormously uncomfortable— commander of Dannith's defenses.

And the "authorization" to—"impress" was a more accurate description than "organize"—locals had almost certainly been wildly illegal, despite the administrator's signature next to his own. It was an addition he'd obtained almost at gunpoint. Blanth was fairly sure Holcott knew that as well as he did, but simply chose to ignore it, as he'd chosen to take orders from an officer who didn't outrank him.

"Yes, I figured we could use help digging in, getting ready… but I was shocked to find that we had these guns available.

They'll be useful if the enemy lands armor, but I bet we can even shoot down landers with these, especially if we get some AI-assisted targeting."

"They can definitely shoot down landers. We used them on Oldoran II, and we took out a good twenty percent of the Union landing craft, solely with these batteries. Took the bastards by surprise too, 'cause they knew damned well that shit-farming planet didn't have a ground battery of its own hot enough to cook dinner over."

Blanth smiled, but only for a second. He wished he had time to sit with Holcott and trade war stories, but the task Tyler Barron had given him—and that everyone around him seemed to go along with—didn't leave him time for sleeping or eating, much less indulging in bragging contests with his comrades. The battle in space was still going on, but even with Blanth's meager knowledge about naval combat, he was pretty sure Winters's forces, even including the forts, didn't stand a chance. One way or another, he expected a ground assault.

Unless the enemy just decides to nuke the hell out of the planet from orbit.

That would be extremely unpleasant, of course, but even then, his entrenchments and fortifications would give some of the armored Marines on the surface a chance to survive. It was notoriously difficult to completely exterminate a population from orbit. Possible, certainly, but the destructive force required was enormous.

"You've done a good job, Steve. You've handled the defense set up as well as Colonel Peterson would have, I'd say." Holcott's tone had changed, subtly but noticeably nevertheless. "I know you're in a tough position." It was the first time the other Marine had even hinted at a recognition that Blanth wasn't some kind of general in uncontested command of the defense operation. "Tyler Barron chooses his people well."

"Thank you, Vince. I've done everything I could think of. Now, we'll just have to wait…and see if it was enough."

He took a deep breath. From what he knew of the strengths of the attackers and defenders in the space around Dannith, he suspected he wouldn't have to wait long.

Chapter Forty-Four

Dauntless shook hard, the impact of the superheated plasma torpedo melting through the armored hull and into the internal systems beyond. Barron was already hunched over his comm unit, checking with Commander Glaven for a damage report. He'd hoped until about twenty seconds before impact that his guns could pick off the incoming warhead, but then the torpedo had converted to pure plasma, and the chance to shoot it down was gone.

Next, he'd tried evasive maneuvers, but for a group he'd pegged as a bunch of rookies, the attacking fighter's pilots not only showed considerable courage and determination, they also executed an almost perfect attack pattern. *Dauntless*'s gunners had shot down more than half of the approaching ships, but six had gotten through to launch their weapons. The turrets had taken out one of the torpedoes before the rest converted, leaving five heading for *Dauntless*, and Barron's evasive skill the sole remaining defense.

That skill had proven capable of evading four of the five weapons, but in the final pass, he'd had to deal with three com-

338

ing in at once from different vectors. With a nod to the unexpected skill of his attackers, he lurched the ship hard, giving the crew a hearty shakeup, and slipping past two of the three torpedoes.

It had proven impossible to evade the final one.

He'd felt the impact, and as soon as he did, he knew it had caused damage. Considerable damage. It had taken out a couple of his starboard secondary batteries, he was sure of that. And, in this instance, "take out" meant destroy utterly. The plasma was millions of degrees hot, and anything material it struck—armor, hull, laser turrets—vaporized in an instant. The lost guns couldn't be fixed because they were gone, nothing left of them but refrozen chunks of metal.

He knew he'd lost the primaries, too, even though Glaven hadn't reported that yet. Barron didn't know the new *Dauntless* with the completeness and intimacy with which he'd known his beloved old vessel, but he'd served aboard both ships in enough battles to understand the fragility of the complex power transmission system required to operate the main guns. He was sure the weapons themselves were still intact, just as he was also confident they were incapable of firing. He didn't know if Glaven would be able to get them back online before *Titania* came into range—he wanted to guess fifty-fifty, but his gut told him it was more likely a depressing seventy-thirty against—and there was nothing he could do about it. He had other things to do. His ship still faced swarms of interceptors, and even though the individual lasers mounted on the fighters were of limited power, he needed his defense grid up and running.

And he needed to know, primaries or not, that *Dauntless* would be ready when *Titania* came into range.

"It's not as bad as you probably think, sir. The power lines are cut in several sections, and we've lost a couple secondaries and four or five of the point defense turrets, but we've still got engine power at seventy percent plus, and all three reactors are in decent shape."

Barron almost asked what "decent" meant, in terms of how much power his engineer could give him. But it didn't matter, not unless he got the primaries back. The big guns were a huge energy suck, and he'd need everything the reactors could give him to charge them up while also executing some level of thrust or firing even the small defensive guns. Without the big guns, he could manage everything else with considerably less energy flow.

"Primaries?" Barron had to ask, even though he knew the answer.

"Down, Admiral. I think we can get them back, but it's going to take some time. There must be a hundred spots where lines and conduits are cut."

"Before *Titania* is in range?" It was the important question, the only one that mattered. If Glaven couldn't get the main guns back online by then, there was no point in working on them at all. The damage *Dauntless* would take fighting the other battleship, whether that fight was a victory or a loss, would almost certainly disable the main guns again.

A pause. Then: "I don't know, sir. 'Maybe' is the best I can give you now."

Barron hated vague reports, but he knew this one was simply the truth. It was a gamble. Deploy scarce resources to the primaries…and take a chance on getting any gain from it. Or give up on the big guns, and use the available engineers and 'bots elsewhere.

Barron considered the conservative approach, forgetting about the primaries and making sure the rest of his ship was in the best possible condition…but he'd always been somewhat of a gambler at heart, and his confidence in his people, and in their ability to accomplish difficult—if not almost impossible—tasks was all consuming.

"Get me the primaries," he said, with a certainty in his tone that did not match what he was feeling.

"Yes, sir. We're on it now." The engineer sounded edgy, nervous…clearly not sure he could do what the admiral had ordered.

Barron cut the line, returning his attention to the bridge… and for all the respect he'd developed for Glaven, wishing fervently that he could have Anya Fritz there, even for the next hour.

* * *

"Cut thrust to twenty percent. Full power to the primaries."
Heaton's voice was cold, emotionless, a state it was taking considerable energy to maintain. He hid his disappointment at the
fact that his strike force had hit *Dauntless* with only a single torpedo. He had known all along how good Barron and his people
were, but he'd still sat in mesmerized shock at the way the renegade admiral had maneuvered his ship, dodging four of the five
torpedoes that had gotten past the uncanny marksmanship of
Dauntless's defensive gunners.

Still, even the lone hit had most likely caused significant damage. At this point in the battle, *Dauntless had* to be damaged, and
possibly badly, and Heaton was betting that *Titania* was the only
participant in the coming duel with functional primaries. It was
an advantage, a big one, but he still had to score the hits against
a crew with extraordinary expertise at dodging incoming attacks.

His strike force had requested permission to make strafing
runs at *Dauntless* after the bombers had gone in, but he'd ordered
them back instead. The chance of the interceptors doing significant damage to Barron's ship with their lasers was miniscule,
and Heaton preferred to bring them back aboard before he
engaged *Dauntless* in the final struggle. He wasn't sure he'd have
a chance to launch them again, but he was damned sure going to
have them all outfitted as bombers in case he did. That would
give the strike force more than enough power to eradicate Barron's troublesome ship, and Heaton was finally convinced that
Dauntless was, in fact, without her vaunted fighter squadrons. He
regretted his earlier caution in sending out most of his fighters
outfitted as interceptors. It had been a lost opportunity.

"Thrust down to twenty percent, Captain. Primary batteries
charging."

"Very well." Heaton leaned back and sat quietly, waiting.
Dauntless was already damaged, which gave him an edge in the
coming fight….but he also knew Barron was better than he was,

and the admiral's veteran crew was the best the Confederation had. If he could score a couple hits with his primaries against an adversary whose long-ranged guns were offline, he was sure he could win the fight.

As the final struggle loomed so close, his unease returned. He'd allowed his rage to drive him, to override the uncertainty he'd felt at battling a former colleague. It had become considerably easier as he watched *Dauntless* gunning down the Confederation cruisers. But now, he realized that he was about to fight—to kill—a man whose exploits he'd followed with thrilled excitement for years.

He knew his duty, and he would see it done. And, whatever his recollections of Barron and his battles, the famous admiral was wrong here. Even if his prosecution had been a mistake, if he'd been unfairly targeted, he should have remained on Megara and fought to clear his name...not spilled Confederation blood to escape.

Heaton's eyes narrowed, focusing on the gauge tracking the progress of arming the primaries. He'd never commanded a capital ship before, and though he was a combat veteran, he was in unfamiliar territory now, facing off against a man who was unquestionably the Confederation's greatest battleship commander.

He'd analyzed the scanner reports, considered them from every perspective. The torpedo hit had knocked out *Dauntless*'s primaries, he was betting on that. He knew Barron would have his damage control teams working feverishly to get the weapons back online, but work like that took time, even for a crew like *Dauntless*'s.

He shifted in his chair, edgy, uncomfortable...and, if he was honest with himself, scared. He knew what he had to do, and he was going to see it done, whatever it took, but now he began to feel out of his depth, and the idea of Confederation ships firing on each other, Confederation crews killing each other, made him sick to his stomach.

His eyes moved to the display. The primaries were fully charged...and in another fifteen seconds, *Titania* would be in range of its target.

"Gunnery crews…prepare to fire."

The tactical officer repeated his command, and an instant later turned back toward him. "All crews report weapons operational and ready, sir."

Heaton took a deep breath and then exhaled hard. He struggled to center himself, to focus on what he was about to do, what had to be done.

"Fire," he said, knowing he hadn't kept all the tension from his tone.

He heard *Titania*'s main guns fire, and he turned toward the display, waiting for damage assessments. He felt anticipation at what the scanners would report, what his people had done…but only for a fleeting instant.

Then his ship pitched roughly, sending his body forward against his harness. He could hear the shouts on the bridge, and he knew instantly some of his officers were injured. He froze, only for a few seconds, and then he realized what had happened. His hopes were dashed. *Dauntless*'s primaries weren't down after all…and they had just hit *Titania*.

He wasn't sure yet what damage his ship had taken, or what the glancing hit his guns had scored had done to *Dauntless*.

But he knew one thing. *Dauntless* was still dangerous.

* * *

"Direct hit, Admiral. Two of the beams…and a solid location, just aft of their reactors." Atara's voice had lost much of the hesitancy Barron knew she'd felt about battling Confederation comrades. It was natural, and he knew it, the main reason why civil wars happened so often in history, and why they were always such bitter engagements. National loyalties and higher ideals tended to get stripped away in the heat of battle, and all that remained were the people standing at your side…and those shooting at you.

Barron had felt it, too, but he'd tried to fight it off, to cling to the doubts and pain and misery. The day he could shoot down

his Confederation brethren and feel nothing but satisfaction…
that was a moment he dreaded above all things.

"Very well," he said, his voice subdued. "All guns are to fire
at will as soon as recharged." He could embrace the misery of
what he was doing, but that didn't change the fact that he had to
do it. Every time he felt himself faltering, he imagined the huge
Hegemony battleships and their massive railguns. He thought
about Confederation worlds burning, its citizens butchered…
or shoved into the Hegemony's structured breeding programs
as Inferiors, forced into compelled mating pairs and roles based
solely on their genetic ratings. That waking nightmare fed him
strength, and pushed back his doubts. "Advise Commander
Glaven we need those guns ready to go as soon as possible." He
paused for an instant. "Seconds count," he added. "Anything
he can do to speed up power transmission will help."

"Yes, sir."

Barron looked around the bridge. *Titania* had fired her primaries too, but his evasive maneuvers had taken *Dauntless* almost
entirely out of the arc of the deadly beams, and *Dauntless* had
suffered only a partial hit of no significant consequence.

The whole exchange had been based on surprise. *Titania*'s
captain had assumed *Dauntless*'s primaries were down, as Barron
thought he might, and he'd failed to engage in sufficient evasion.
Barron had been ready, his main guns fully charged, and power
temporarily diverted to the engines for a wild, random pattern
designed to confound enemy targeting.

It had worked almost perfectly, but it was over now. Barron didn't know what *Titania*'s commander would do next, but
he was sure the officer wouldn't repeat his mistake. He would
adjust his targeting solutions, do all he could to offset *Dauntless*'s
evasion…and he would make sure his own ship was a much
harder target next time. Barron had gotten the first shot, the
edge he knew he needed. But he wasn't sure it was enough. At
best, he'd equalized things, inflicted enough damage on *Titania*
to match what *Dauntless* had already suffered. But the battleship
opposing him was backed by half a dozen smaller vessels, two
cruisers and four escorts. The supporting craft didn't have the

firepower of the battleships, but they still represented considerable weight on the scale against him.

He allowed himself to hope his people could prevail in the
fight that had seemed so unwinnable. But it was all he'd had in
what seemed like a long while, and he felt it pouring energy into
him. If he could escape, maybe he could figure out what was
happening on Megara, and he could get the word out to the fleet
that a new and deadly enemy was coming.

He turned toward the display, checking on the progress of
recharging. The guns were almost there, almost ready to fire
again.

But so are Titania's. He'd hoped to knock out the opposing
ship's big guns, but a quick analysis of hit locations and damage
assessments told him the weapons had likely survived.

He turned toward the display, staring at *Dauntless*'s position.
He'd just moved his hand to his board to make changes to the
evasion plan when his eyes caught something.

He felt the hope, so newly sparked, drain from his body like
water from a holed bucket.

"Admiral, scanners are picking up…"

He heard Atara's voice, but he didn't need the report. He was
staring right at the display, at the space around the Corinth transit point…and the fifteen or more icons that had just appeared.
New ships were transiting into the system.

For a brief moment, hope flashed through his mind that
perhaps it was a routine freight convoy, or something equally
innocuous. But Corinth was on a direct route to Megara, and
that could mean only one thing.

Those ships had come after him…yet another task force
sent to engage his ship, and to capture him.

But he could feel the doubt growing. It was becoming clear
that whoever was behind events on Megara didn't want to capture him, or Gary Holsten. Not anymore.

They just wanted him dead.

Chapter Forty-Five

"Let's go. All squadrons, full thrusters. We've got to hit those enemy ships, and we've got to do it now!" Alicia Covington felt the stress in her gut, like a rock, weighing her down, making her nauseous. It wasn't just the fact that she was leading a mere six squadrons against the entire enemy fleet, nor that her birds had launched with fuel tanks less than two-thirds full. No, it was the fact that she'd just looked at her scanners…at the condition of Admiral Winters's fleet.

Fleet had been a grandiose term when the ships had left Grimaldi, but now, one of Winters's battleships and a third of his escorts were completely gone…and *Discovery* wasn't far from being an outright cripple. The battered ship only had two or three guns left operational, and from the vessel's apparent rate of fire, it seemed to Covington that she was having trouble powering even that modest broadside.

Constitution was still in the battle line, but she didn't know how. Winters's flagship had been pounded relentlessly, and yet somehow had managed to remain combat effective. Winters had managed to knock out all the enemy railguns save one…but that final weapon had at last scored a hit, tearing down the port side of the flagship and destroying ten of its secondary guns.

346

She had smiled as she watched Winters do exactly what she knew he would…bring the ship around, and its starboard weapons to bear, replacing the destroyed port broadside and continuing the fight.

The admiral had been forced to fall back, though, to keep the smaller enemy support vessels out of range. There were just too many of them, and if he allowed them to swarm *Constitution* and the other surviving Confederation ships, the fight would be over in an instant. Considerations about the planet had become secondary. Dannith would face certain attack and possible invasion when Winters's ships were destroyed, whether or not the shattered fleet made a last stand alongside the forts.

The firepower of those platforms would bolster the defenders' strength considerably…but she also knew they wouldn't last long. They had modest positional thrusters that could be used in an evasive role, but in the end, they were mostly static platforms. Their batteries outranged the enemy weapons, save of course for the railguns, but once the attacking fleet closed enough, the incoming firepower would be overwhelming.

Covington was determined to lead her people in before that happened, to hit the enemy when they were being blasted by the forts…and before they had a chance to finish off *Constitution*.

She'd reorganized the entire strike force, leaving behind officers she trusted to lead out additional wings as soon as the base crews could get them ready. She'd get another six squadrons into the fight, she was pretty sure about that, but whatever happened after that had more to do with how long the fortresses held out than anything else. She'd done all she could, and there was nothing left to do but hope for the best.

And hit the enemy like a piledriver.

"We're going in close this time." She knew what her words must have sounded like to her pilots. The fighters had shredded all doctrine and every principle of their training in the last attack, driving their ships to previously unimagined ranges. But she intended to take it farther this time, and she was going to go in first, to show them just what she planned.

She ignored the responses. It was all the usual fighter pilot stuff, a seemingly endless display of bravado and confidence run amok. But this time she could hear the difference. There was a hesitation, an uncertainty that hadn't been there after the initial launch hours earlier. It wasn't fear. Even closing to dangerous ranges, her pilots were safer than they'd be against an enemy protected by swarms of interceptors. It was the realization that they were fighting a hopeless battle. No matter how well they performed, how many enemy ships they blasted, they couldn't really make a difference.

Whatever they did, whatever tactical plans Admiral Winters might conceive, none of it would be enough. Dannith would be invaded…or blasted from orbit.

Millions of people were going to die. Confederation citizens, men and women who'd depended on the fleet to protect them.

And the Confederation would have a new war…one Covington suddenly realized it might very well lose.

It was too much to take, the thought that the entire Union war had been fought—and won—for nothing. Defeat had come anyway, from the depths of a darkness they had all long believed to be empty.

She tried to control her emotions, direct her uncertainty—and her fear—into rage, and focus it on the enemy before her. The fleet might lose the battle. The Confederation might lose the war.

But her squadrons were going to show these bastards just what veteran pilots could do with their Lightnings.

"All squadrons…pump up reactors to one hundred ten percent. All power to the engines."

* * *

Winters watched as a large Hegemony task force moved toward Dannith's orbital fortresses. There was a line of what had to be battleships in the front, every one of them larger than *Constitution*. He imagined such a force could have shredded the platforms in a matter of minutes with their deadly railguns…

save for the fact that between Covington's fighters and his own shattered battle line, the enemy now appeared to have a single ship with the huge weapons still operational. Even that last ship's rate of fire had slowed considerably, though whether that was caused by damage or some other, unknown factor, he could only guess.

The fortresses had opened fire with their own primaries. But the forts were old and poorly maintained. Dannith's frontier had long been considered a safe one, at least from more than criminal traffic and rogue tech hunters. For decades, Confederation funds for upgrades had gone to other worlds, those on threatened borders…or with powerful political representatives able to direct the flow of funds back home. Being neither of these, Dannith's defenses had been neglected for decades.

Still, even with just a few primaries, the bases bristled with massive laser cannons, weapons two or three times the size of *Constitution*'s secondaries. They opened fire at ranges scarcely lower than those of the particle accelerators, and while their strength was highly attenuated at such distances, the string of forts carried a *lot* of them.

As fixed platforms, the forts had an advantage in power generation and the mass of weaponry, even over a technologically superior enemy like the Hegemony. Winters imagined that the enemy was taken aback by the amount of force directed at the attacking ships, though he wasn't sure if that was cold logic or just what he wanted to believe. Still, he could see the fire taking its toll, a pair of primaries slamming into one Hegemon battleship, ripping into its innards. The stricken vessel lost ninety percent of its apparent thrust, and Winters couldn't help but think of the hellish conditions that had to be ravaging the insides of the ship. He wasn't proud of the satisfaction he felt, imaging enemy spacers dying horribly…but he'd seen too many of his own people killed in the past few hours, and many of them just as terribly. Regardless of how he thought he should feel, in truth, he welcomed the lust for vengeance. He knew from past experience that it was a source of strength while the battle still raged. From the looks of things, there might be no after-battle wave of guilt and recrimination as he'd experienced so many times before…because it wasn't looking like any of his people were going to make it to the end of this fight.

The platforms blasted away with their guns, almost without any return fire…but only for a few minutes. They'd done considerable damage to the advancing vessels, and destroyed several outright, but then the attackers entered range and opened fire.

The sole remaining railgun fired first, and against the almost immobile stations, it was like shooting fish in a barrel. Winters watched as the projectile zipped across the display, right toward one of the largest of the platforms. Over a thousand tons of super-dense metal were moving toward the fortress at close to seven percent of light speed. The shot was going to take the fortress dead-center, and his usually quick mind grasped at wisps of nothingness as he tried to calculate the almost unimaginable amount of kinetic energy involved.

His brain did offer one detail, a scrap of knowledge he'd hardly been aware he knew. *Four thousand six hundred forty.* The complement of the orbital station.

The number of men and women who were killed as he watched the railgun projectile slam into the platform's hull… and more or less vaporize the whole thing.

Winters gasped, caught by surprise despite the fact that on some level he'd known just what would happen when weapons as powerful as the Hegemony railguns opened up on the stations. *Constitution*'s bridge was silent for half a minute, everyone present staring in stunned silence at the carnage.

Then the rest of the enemy force opened up on the forts, a massive barrage tearing into Dannith's defensive grid. The forts fired back with desperate intensity, and they did well—better than Winters had expected, knowing the relative inexperience of their crews. One fort in particular fought the enemy wildly, firing with uncanny accuracy, taking down no fewer than four of the attacking ships before a combined Hegemony barrage tore it into half a dozen sections. The pieces of the platform slipped from orbit, beginning a final journey toward the atmosphere. Chunks of the platform would land all over the planet, Winters didn't have a doubt…and if they hit populated areas, the casualties would rise well beyond the numbers of the already-dead crew.

He watched somberly, his own salute to the heroes who'd fought so well, but when his eyes returned to the main display, he was forced to accept a bitter truth.

Dannith's defensive array was in ruins.

There were a few forts still fighting, though most of them were damaged. They'd taken their toll on the attackers, destroying and crippling so many ships, they just might have beaten back the assault…save for the fact that a second wave was coming on. It was smaller than the first, but it was still beyond anything the last few battered forts could face.

Winters wanted to do more to support the platforms, but he had nothing. His fleet had been small when he'd arrived, and now he was down to the tattered remains. He didn't have a single ship that wasn't damaged, and many of them were in critical condition. He felt the call of duty, screaming out to him to defend Dannith, to keep the enemy from landing on a Confederation world.

But there was just no way.

"Admiral…" The tactical officer's voice was hesitant.

"Yes, Commander?"

"The battle around the planet is lost." A pause. "But we can pull back, regroup in the dust clouds just beyond the planetary orbit." Winters could hear the hesitancy in the man's voice, even a hint of shame at what the officer no doubt considered cowardly advice. But Winters knew his officer was right. Tactically right. Once the last of the fortresses had been pounded to dust, his ships would be the only Confederation force remaining in the system. He could do nothing by remaining where he was, save, possibly, destroying a very few enemy ships before his people were wiped out. Such a sacrifice would have no effect whatsoever on a potential ground assault.

He couldn't imagine what would change if he pulled back, but it made more sense than it did to throw the last of his forces away for nothing.

"You're right, Commander," he said, trying to sound as encouraging as he could. The tactical officer had remained focused on duty better than he had, and Winters was a man who could admit when he was wrong. He'd have continued the hopeless fight, led his people to meaningless deaths. Pulling back offered a chance to delay that final eventuality...and he'd take few more hours if that was all he could get. "All ships...set a course for the dust clouds...320.109.078." He paused. "All ships at their own maximum thrust."

He didn't know if the enemy would follow. His gut told him no, that they would focus on gaining control of Dannith's orbital space and launching a ground assault. His fleet was virtually combat ineffective, and there was no way to sneak back. If he led his people back toward Dannith, the enemy would have plenty of time to react.

They'll probably be content staying in place and bombarding the planet to oblivion...

Winters had considered that the enemy might choose genocide over conquest...but there was still nothing he could do to stop it. And his gut told him any invader new to Confederation space—even to the whole Rim—would want intel. That meant prisoners...and intact records on the ground.

He had no knowledge at all about the enemy's ground combat capabilities, but he guessed that the Marines—and various planetary forces and militias—waiting down there were in for one hell of a fight.

He sent up a silent battle prayer for those down on Dannith's surface, sitting in bunkers and trenches, waiting for the battle in space to be over...and for theirs to begin.

Their wait was almost over.

"Commander...all fleet units, execute withdrawal order. Now."

Chapter Forty-Six

"We're picking up multiple contacts now, Captain. Moving in from high orbit and approaching the upper atmosphere."

Blanth was sitting along the wall of the command bunker, leaning back against the cold concrete behind the rugged bench. Sitting felt unnatural, as tense as he was, but he'd been standing for the last hour, and his back and neck were aching from being hunched forward under the low roof of the fortification. He'd had the shelters and defensive positions built as quickly as possible, requisitioning virtually every construction crew and piece of equipment on the planet—through another series of illegal orders—to do it. His hastily-organized effort had been more successful than he'd dared to hope, but not without cutting a few corners, one of which was making ceilings high enough to accommodate his well-above-average height of nearly two meters.

"Have you confirmed they're landers?" *Stupid question...what else would they be?* Blanth and his people had hunkered down for the past six hours while the enemy blasted Dannith's surface. At first, he'd thought the enemy was just going to glass the

353

planet. That might leave a few survivors, some of his people in their deep entrenchments, and maybe one or two percent of the population...but for all practical purposes, Dannith would cease to exist. Then he'd realized the bombardments were far more targeted, mostly ignoring inhabited areas of the cities and concentrating on military positions and anything that even looked like something of tactical significance. There had been some attacks on civilian areas, enough to keep the people passive and hiding terrified in their homes, but it had quickly become apparent the attackers weren't trying to wipe out the population, only to soften up the defenders.

They had done quite a good job at that. Blanth was still trying to get over his surprise at the quality of the enemy's targeting. They had rooted out a large percentage of his positions, and hit them *hard*. He had no idea how many Marines had been killed in the last few hours, or how many of the local troops he'd so carefully organized and prepared...but he knew it was a lot. His defenses were badly battered, even before a single enemy soldier had landed.

"Impossible to tell, sir. We've lost contact with all orbital assets..." Blanth knew that was because the enemy had destroyed them all. He doubted there was anything larger than a chunk of melted and refrozen metal floating around up there from what had once been the planet's defensive array and satellite network. "...but what else could they be?" It was a logical conclusion, and it made sense to Blanth, even if it did lack the rigor of a typical military report.

Blanth was about to reply when the officer added, "Captain...one thing we're picking up is..." The man paused. "Sir, these things are *big*. They outmass our own landers by five or ten times."

Blanth sat quietly, but inside he felt his stomach clench. The earlier report had specified over a hundred incoming craft...and if all of them were that big, he was facing one *hell* of a lot of enemy troops.

Or something else huge.
What could those things be carrying?

"Very well, Lieutenant. Relay this report to all other command stations still on the air." That was a minority of those he'd started with, though he was still clinging to hope that the "missing" commands had just lost their comm feeds, and that at least some of their personnel were still in the field, combat ready. He wasn't sure where the line between realism and desperation stood, and he wasn't sure he wanted to know. Not just then.

"All right…let's see what Peterson's people can do with those big guns." Blanth had nurtured high hopes for the heavy artillery the Marine division had brought with them, but the bombardment had been particularly hard on those positions. He'd had the guns dug in and fortified as heavily as possible, which was why he had any of them left at all. But he'd still lost more than half, and veteran Marines or no, he couldn't imagine the crews of the remaining guns had avoided some level of casualties or simply morale decline. It was hard to endure a pounding like that the one the enemy had just unleashed, and Blanth didn't think anything less of Marines who were shaken up by it.

"Yes, sir…sending out orders to fire now."

Blanth exhaled hard and leaned backwards, hitting his head against the rough concrete as he did. It was the third time he'd done it, and he swore bitterly at the pain. He was distracted, trying to focus on so many things he was becoming completely unfocused. He'd been in battle before, but he'd never been responsible for more than one hundred twenty Marines. Now he had thousands looking to him, as well as the vast numbers of the planetary defense forces. It was too much, and for all he had rigidly obeyed Barron's orders to take charge, he could feel it tearing him apart. He hadn't even considered yet, save for a passing analysis of his declining military power, how many men and women under his command were dead already. There would be time for that if he survived the fight…an end result that seemed less likely than ever.

"Send runners to all batteries as well, Lieutenant." He needed every gun he could get…and he couldn't risk a functional gun crew remaining idle because they didn't receive the order to fire on their blasted comm units.

"Yes, Captain. I'll see to it now, sir."

Blanth just nodded, realizing in some hazy way how useless a gesture that was on an audio line. He opened his mouth to make some kind of verbal acknowledgement, but he realized he'd already closed the line. He shook his head and set the unit down on the bench next to him, standing up—careful this time not to hit the ceiling—and moving toward the small hatch that led out, and up to the surface. If the enemy was coming, it was time for his people to come out of their holes and get ready to fight.

He'd just reached the opening when he heard muffled cracking sounds in the distance.

The batteries had opened fire.

* * *

Luther Holcott ran up the steep hill, gasping for breath as he did. The full set of battle armor was a heavy load, and he'd been up and down the hillsides around his position a dozen times in the last hour.

It was midday…and goddamned hot.

"Keep those guns firing. I want shots going off as quickly as you can reload." He was shouting, but the hoarseness of his voice was reducing the volume that reached his Marines. That was too bad, because he was pissed, and he wanted them to know it. "You're leaving too much time between rounds."

"The guns are *hot*, sir." The respondent was a non-com, a sergeant with the misfortune to be closest to the raging captain. "If we fire any faster, we're going to start losing some of them."

"And what do you think the enemy coming down here is going to do? Let us keep them? The useful life of these guns is measured in minutes, and we either get something out of that time or we don't. Now, stop wasting my damned time and get these things firing faster." Hoarse or not, he was sure every Marines within twenty meters had heard *that*.

"Yes, Captain."

Holcott turned and looked for his aide. The Marine was just

a few meters away, but the captain felt a flush of anger neverthe-less. The aide must have felt it, because before Holcott could growl out an order, the junior lieutenant had almost jumped across the small space and was standing right next to him.

"Lieutenant, where's that tabl…" The words stopped as he realized the Marine was there, holding out the very object he was requesting. Quarrel was a good aide, one who probably deserved more praise and fewer angry words…but he was a Marine, too, and as far as Holcott was concerned, if he couldn't take whatever an angry captain dished out, he had no place in the Corps.

Holcott grabbed the tablet and checked the hit assessment reports. They were of limited value—none at all, he might have said in an especially angry moment—but they were the best avail-able on a planet virtually stripped of its communications assets. His batteries had taken down six of the enemy ships. As much as his pessimism was rising, Holcott knew it was likely there had been additional hits scored by other artillery units cut off from what remained of the data net. That wasn't a bad result—and it became an even better one, as he heard one of the nearby crews let out a series of primal howls that could only mean another kill had been added to the roster—but it wasn't enough. The ships coming in were huge, and it looked like eighty or more of them were going to hit ground.

With the disorder and casualties from the orbital bombard-ments, the beachheads were going to be met with only scattered counterattacks from the defenders, and not the kind of coordi-nated, large assaults that could defeat the invaders before they could fully organize their own formations.

Holcott shook his head, a way of letting out some of his frustration, and then he turned quickly as yet another of his crews, this one right next to his position, let out a series of wild yells.

This time, he added his own worn voice to the mix. His people weren't going to take enough of those ships out…but every hit helped nevertheless.

* * *

Blanth ran along the blackened dirt of the ridge, waving his arms to one group of Marines and then another. A dozen enemy landers had come down near his position, and he'd rushed out to organize the counterattack himself. If he could pin the enemy down, drive them back onto their landers and keep them from breaking out and moving against his scattered defenses, maybe, just maybe, his people could hold.

Along this ridge, at least. He knew the same dance was being played out in multiple places, but all he could do for those was hope the commanders on the scene were aggressive—and lucky.

"Move out," he shouted into the comm unit hanging in front of his mouth. He wasn't sure how many of his people were getting the signal. The enemy didn't seem to rely heavily on communications jamming—a break, and maybe the only one he'd get—but the bombardment and the residual radiation were both playing havoc on his comm capabilities. He wasn't sure why the enemy wasn't jamming the entire planet, whether they'd decided the effects on their own communications outweighed the benefits, or if, for whatever reason, their combat doctrine simply differed from that of the Rim nations.

Still, even with minimal jamming, there were widespread comm outages, and the over-air frequencies were as affected by the aftereffects of the bombardment, especially in the areas where the enemy had deployed nuclear weapons.

The Hegemony forces had stopped far short of a planet-killing nuclear holocaust, but they had committed a hundred moderately sized fusion bombs to the toughest sections of Blanth's defensive perimeter. Some of his deepest installations had still survived, even in the most heavily bombed areas, but the combat power of the units positioned there had been severely degraded by the radiation and the utter devastation on the surface all around them. His own command post had escaped such focused attention from the enemy—pure luck, he knew—and his bunker, and the units deployed there, were still in decent shape.

Which was a good thing, since the position seemed to be close to one of the enemy landing areas.

"Let's go…we hit them, and we hit them hard. Let's send these bastards back where they came from." He gripped his rifle tightly, and he ran toward the enemy landers, his head jerking from one side to the other, checking to see how many Marines he had with him.

About two hundred. Not bad, considering some of his people were almost certainly still digging out from buried bunkers. He was surprised to see about forty of the locals as well, mostly the planetary regulars, but a few of the militia as well. The vast numbers of the garrison and part-time soldiers were still dug in, clinging to their fortifications and foxholes and frozen by fear, but his training had gotten through to some of them. He was angry with the others, but it was controlled, muted. He was scared himself, and he didn't expect some Dannith local "soldier" or militiaman to rush out and charge what almost certainly would be an army of real professionals.

Confederation Marines, on the other hand, he trusted, and he expected them to charge into the mouth of hell without question if they were ordered to do so. He'd never seen that particular situation arise, but he could remember a few from the war years that came close.

War years? We're back at war now. The politicians might not have made it official yet, but when whatever's in those ships comes out, we'll be trying like hell to kill each other. That's war, whatever label a bunch of Senators put on it…

He was moving forward in a zigzag pattern, doing all he could to make up for the fact that he was basically running across an open plain. He didn't know if the landers themselves were armed. Confederation craft went both ways, some mounting a few support weapons and others unarmed. It didn't look like any of the ships had opened fire, at least as far as his limited scanning ability could detect, but he wasn't ready to bet his life on that.

He could see the ships now…and they were *big*. He tried to guess how many soldiers one could hold. He wasn't sure how accurate his numbers were, but he was damned sure that once the troopers aboard the closest one all managed to get out and deploy, they'd outnumber his own forces. And there were six other ships close enough to hit his people within minutes.

He picked up the pace. His only chance was to get his Marines close enough to pin down the enemy as they tried to evac. He didn't have much time. He could see the ramps coming down already, and the occupants would be racing out any second.

But his people were in firing range now.

"Open up…everybody. Keep that area hosed down with fire," he yelled into the comm unit. Then he did the one thing he suspected would get the message to any of his people who didn't receive the order. He pulled his rifle around and opened fire himself.

He stared with three-shot bursts. There were no visible targets yet, and he didn't want to waste ammunition he suspected he'd need later. He expected to see enemy troops coming out any second, but there was still nothing there, save the shots from his rapidly advancing line, slugs slamming into the metal of the landing ship and ricocheting all around.

A nervous feeling settled on him as the seconds passed. There were still no enemy soldiers visible, nor any fire from the landers. He'd expected to feel excitement about that, hope that his people could get into position and pin the enemy in their ships. But, instead, there was something ominous about it all. The enemy's technology was top grade, and their actions in the space battle had been efficient and well-planned. Why would their landing forces be any different?

He had almost reached the nearest ship, coming up directly behind. He could see the ramp, and the darkness of the inside of the craft. It was still…no, there was something there. Movement.

He tightened his grip on the rifle, and his eyes darted back and forth, looking for anything he could use for cover. The lack of enemy activity had lured him in, and now he was close.

Too close. There was no cover.

He was about to fall back, perhaps twenty meters, where there was a gully that offered some protection, when he heard a loud crash…and then he saw something coming down the ramp.

Something *huge*.

Blanth stayed where he was, frozen by shock, even after his brain had sent signal after signal to his legs to *run*. His eyes were fixed on the giant rear hatch of the lander, which had dropped down to the ground as a ramp of sorts. Rolling down that ramp was a vehicle. It looked like a tank, except it was bigger than any tank he'd ever seen. The thing was five meters broad, and from what he could see, more than ten deep, and it was bristling with weapons.

It rolled down the ramp and onto the torn ground, its giant treads sinking down more than half a meter through the mud… but that didn't stop it. It didn't even slow the thing.

It moved steadily forward, clanking loudly as it did…and through his mesmerized shock, Blanth heard other sounds. High pitched whines, loud cracks…and then, suddenly, he realized the thing was firing. Rockets blasted out of launchers, whipping across the battlefield at what had to be hypersonic speeds. Other guns fired a combination of solid projectiles and searing energy weapons.

A cold feeling took Blanth's insides. The thing was a massive war machine, the likes of which he'd never seen before. Just the sight of it was enough to terrify even the most hardened Marine, but that wasn't what shook Blanth the most.

No, what really got to him was the sudden realization that the thing wasn't just moving.

It was moving right toward *him*.

Chapter Forty-Seven

"I need all the power you can give me...whatever the risk." Barron was on the comm, speaking to Glaven. He had to finish the fight with *Titania*, to somehow win that combat before the ships coming in from Corinth could close. There were voices in his mind, ominous thoughts that it didn't matter. Even if he destroyed the battleship and its escorts, he had no chance at all of escaping the task force blasting toward *Dauntless* from across the system. Those ships were still fairly distant, but they'd come close enough for detailed scans, and the two lead ships were both battleships. Barron had tactics, tricks of war up his sleeve. He *might* be able to best *Titania*'s force. But *Dauntless* would be battered after that fight, and even fresh and with his absent squadrons in their bays and ready, he doubted he could survive the final assault heading his way. The two battleships had ten squadrons between them, one hundred fifty fighters...and *Titania* had almost certainly advised whoever was in command that *Dauntless* had no interceptors at all. That meant his ship would most likely face an attack by ten bomber squadrons.

Dauntless would never even engage the second set of

approaching vessels. The bomber strikes would obliterate his ship…and there was nothing he could do about it. It was almost a mathematical certainty.

"I can try to open the fuel lines, shoot for ninety percent on the reactors, but it's risky, sir. We can't know where we've got weakened feeds, and if the wrong one gives way…"

"Do it." Barron knew he owed his engineer more than a two-word reply. But he didn't see any advantage in adding, "because we're all as good as dead anyway."

He turned toward Atara's station. "As soon as those fuel lines open up, push it to the max. Those ships coming from Corinth are going to launch their bombers any minute, and we've got to be done with *Titania* before those ships get to us." *And finish us off…*

"Yes, Admiral. I'm on it."

Barron glanced over at his longtime number two—and his friend. He felt guilty for once again subverting her role as *Dauntless*'s commander, but if this was to be their last fight, something seemed strangely right about it, one final repeat of the teamwork that had earned them such success over the past years. At least, it seemed that way to him. For all her loyalty, he wondered if Atara harbored any resentments. Their missions together had been astonishingly successful, but she'd been in his shadow throughout. The Barron name had long focused the attention on him, despite his constant attempts to recognize the contributions of Atara and his crew.

"Increasing power to primaries now."

Barron watched as the meter showed the energy feeding into the main guns. Titania would be recharging her own weapons, and the race to fire first was a vital one. There was no guarantee the next hit would knock out the other ship's primaries, but both vessels had taken damage, and Barron knew *Dauntless*'s weapons were hanging on by a thread.

Whoever was in command of *Titania* was cautious, and likely inexperienced as well. Barron had seen it in half a dozen things, including the tentative move of launching most of his fighter strike as interceptors. That had cost his attacker a chance to finish *Dauntless* then and there, and, while such thoughts made him uncomfortable, he suspected his reputation had gotten to his adversary as well.

That was an edge.

"Advise the gunnery I want those weapons firing the instant they're powered up." He knew it was an unnecessary order, that his crack gun crews would perform as they always had…and, if he rushed them too much for them to properly target, that second or two shaved off the clock would be expensive indeed.

"Yes, Admiral."

He looked forward, his eyes fixed on the display. The lighted bar reached the end of the meter and changed from yellow to green.

The guns were ready.

*   *   *

Heaton sat on *Titania*'s bridge, trying to keep the contents of his stomach from rising back up. His ship was locked in a desperate duel with *Dauntless*, the two vessels trading shots with their deadly primaries. Heaton's force had the edge in numbers, but none of his escorts were in range yet. For the moment, the battle was primary versus primary, and the winner was likely to be the next ship to score a hit.

Heaton had let Barron's reputation get to him, psych him out. He was still kicking himself for not sending in more bombers. An extra squadron or two would have overwhelmed *Dauntless*'s defenses and crippled the battleship…if they didn't destroy it outright. A chance to end the battle, to defeat Tyler Barron, thrown away by his fear of his adversary.

He wasn't going to let that happen again. *Titania* was damaged, but not as badly as *Dauntless*. He had the edge, even in the one-on-one matchup, and he wasn't going to let it slip away. His gunners weren't a match for Barron's and he knew he couldn't maneuver his ship through its evasive patterns with the grace his opponent did…but all he needed was one hit. He wasn't an expert on battleship combat, but he knew how fragile the primary beams were…and his scanners had given him a fairly detailed reading on *Dauntless*'s condition.

He flipped on his comm unit, calling up the gunnery station. "We'll be powered up in thirty seconds," he said into the microphone suspended in front of his mouth, not addressing anyone in particular. "We need a hit…whatever it takes." He wondered what good his words could do, if they would encourage his people, or rattle them. He wasn't even sure whether he'd said what he had because he thought it would help, or because he was so tense himself.

The seconds counted down with an agonizing slowness he could barely endure. He took a deep breath as the readout dropped below ten seconds…and then five.

Then *Titania* shook hard, rolling around to the starboard, as alarm bells went off all around him. Barron had somehow managed to fire first, that was obvious, as was the fact that his gunners had scored a direct hit.

Heaton was pulling up damage control as he watched the timer drop down to zero. But then, nothing happened. He waited a few more seconds, and then he called up engineering and confirmed what he already knew.

Titania had lost her primaries.

His ship was sitting in space, too far out to open up with her secondaries, and in range of *Dauntless*'s still functional guns. Barron's ship would to continue to pound away, with her shots unanswered. Heaton's first impulse was to withdraw, to pull back and try to get out of range. But he was a Confederation officer, and he had his orders. He was to stop *Dauntless*, and capture or kill Tyler Barron…and no risk to himself or to his ship or crew changed that fact.

If he wasn't going back, he had to go forward. He had to get into secondary range…before Barron gutted his ship with *Dauntless*'s primaries.

"Forward, Commander…full thrust. All secondary batteries stand by to open fire."

* * *

"Another hit!" There was genuine excitement in Atara's voice, if only for a few seconds. Barron could tell that for that short, fleeting time, she'd forgotten they were firing at a Confederation ship, and that they were being run down by a force they had no hope of defeating. In that instant, there was only *Dauntless*, and its incomparable crew…and the fifth straight hit they had scored against *Titania*.

The battleship, a friendly vessel now turned enemy, had been trying to close with *Dauntless*, to bring the battle into secondary range. It made sense…it was just what Barron would have done. But it had failed.

Barron had ordered all spare power to the engines, decelerating as hard as he could, prolonging the time until *Titania* could close. And he'd continued the forced powering of the primaries, cutting twenty seconds between shots.

He stared at the screen on his workstation, analyzing the hit assessment data streaming in. *Titania* wasn't out of the fight yet, but Barron knew he could finish her off. The battleship had already lost most of her thrust, and it would be three more minutes until she entered secondary range. And even when she did, she'd already lost half her guns, and *Dauntless* had most of her broadside remaining.

Barron could see the escort ships moving forward, racing to the aid of the wounded battleship. Their combined fire was a danger, even to a battleship like *Dauntless*, but Barron's ship's guns would tear the smaller craft to scrap before they could close and inflict much damage. Everything relied on knocking *Titania* out, and as yet another blast of the primaries hit the stricken ship, Barron knew he was close.

The prize to be won was modest, perhaps another forty minutes of life before the bomber waves the two newly-arrived battleships had launched reached his victorious but wounded vessel. In one perspective, it didn't make sense to kill comrades when there was so little hope of survival. But giving up simply wasn't in Tyler Barron's makeup. He would fight until the end, until the last hit closed his eyes for good.

"Admiral…scanners indicate *Titania*'s power levels have dropped to near zero. No sign of any thrust." Atara stared across the small space between their stations. "I think they're dead in space, sir."

Barron felt the feral instinct he knew all successful combat commanders possessed, the call to finish off a wounded adversary. But he pushed it aside. He would destroy *Titania*, kill however many of its thousand strong crew were still alive…but only if he had to. It would gain him nothing now, and for all that his blood was up, he restrained himself.

"Primaries…cease fire. Those are still fellow Confederation spacers out there." He paused. "Let's get the defensive turrets armed and ready. We've got bombers coming in." He knew there wasn't a chance of defeating the massive wave of ships inbound…or even surviving the assault.

But he'd be damned if he wasn't going to give it all he had. If his people had to die, they would die fighting.

Chapter Forty-Eight

Blackstone Heights
Outside Port Royal City
Planet Dannith, Ventica III
Year 316 AC

"Fall back…now!" Blanth's order was loud, a primal scream shouted into the comm unit—and to anyone close enough to hear directly. The words tore at his throat as he put everything he had into them.

He was running now, freed from the momentary shock that had left him standing dumbfounded in front of the hellish war machine that had rolled out of the lander. He understood now why the ships were so big…nothing smaller could have carried such a monstrous vehicle, and even as he fled from its grasp, knowing he owed his life almost entirely to luck. The enemy tank—he used familiar terminology in his thoughts, though he realized such a label was woefully inadequate—had unleashed an astonishing amount of firepower, and the fact that none of it had come his way, despite his presence right in front of the thing, had been the purest act of providence.

Many of his Marines hadn't been as fortunate. He had no accurate count of casualties, but there were a dozen of the immense tanks out now, all of them firing and turning his counterattack into a hellish retreat. There were enemy soldiers, too, tight columns pouring out of the ships, right behind the great tanks. Blanth's plan had been valid, one that would have been well-suited to resist the planetary assaults he'd seen, but he had nothing—nothing at all—to stop those tanks.

His mind raced. The Dannith forces certainly didn't have anything that would be useful. Peterson's Marines might, especially since the colonel seemed to be the cautious type who didn't like to bring his people anywhere without a full complement of equipment. The heavy artillery pieces could probably damage the tanks, but Blanth knew a lot of those guns had been taken out by the bombardment…and the others were dug in. Deeply. It would take a long time to get them out, and to move enough transport capacity to carry them.

He wasn't even sure he *had* much transport left. He'd requisitioned everything he could find on Dannith when he was preparing the defenses—another series of legal gray area orders—but he suspected much of it, perhaps most of it, had been destroyed in the orbital strikes. Tracking down what remained, and organizing it to move heavy weapons while under attack by those…things…wasn't going to be easy.

More likely impossible.

He was getting ahead of himself. First, he had to get his people back into cover…before he didn't have any of them left. A quick glance around the plain showed entire groups had been wiped out, and most of those remaining had gone prone. The Marines were firing at the tanks, but their assault rifles weren't doing anything to the armored monsters. A few of his people had popped off rifle-mounted grenades, but those, too, had been too weak to cause any damage to the approaching vehicles.

He cursed himself for not issuing the hyper-velocity rocket launchers. He'd decided the weapons were too heavy and cumbersome, that they would weigh down his people and keep them from launching the lightning strikes on the landers that he'd envisioned. Now that his original plan was in ruins, his mind raced, thinking about where the launchers were stored, and the best way to get them into the hands of some of his units.

"Go," he shouted. "All of you…retreat. Get back to the

bunkers, or any cover you can find." He pushed himself even harder, and his jogging pace morphed into a full-fledged run that felt a little too much like a rout. His luck held, though, at least as far as enemy targeting. The tanks were all firing, their array of weapons sweeping the field. But fortune stayed with him, and he could see the entrance to the command bunker up ahead. He felt a few seconds of tentative relief…and then he realized the fortifications weren't going to do all that much to protect his people, not against the heavy weapons the tanks seemed to possess. His first thought had been to get his survivors back underground, but now he realized that would only be a death trap. He had to get them completely off the ridge, and someplace that could offer an impediment to the tanks. There he could set up a rally point, and cobble together whatever he could of the capital area defenses.

The enemy had completely hoodwinked him. He'd seen landings before, but the forces involved were always light. He couldn't imagine the logistics of transporting such massive war machines, and the power of the landing craft that brought them down to the surface. The fleet had faced a deadly enemy, one more powerful and advanced than its own forces…and now he realized it would be the same thing on the ground.

He needed his own heavy forces, and air combat ability as well, but he didn't have any of it. Not on Dannith.

He was nauseous, and he skimmed along the verge of panic. He was in over his head, and he wanted nothing more than for a superior officer to step up, to relegate him to his place and take command. But there was nothing…and he knew if he didn't hold it together, whatever slim chance any of his people had to survive would be gone.

Images of the maps around Port Royal City flashed through his mind, the hills, the spaceport, the river.

The river.

If he could get his people across, he just might be able to buy some time. He suspected the enemy would find a way to pursue, but the tanks were massive. It would take more than a portable pontoon bridge or two.

And there were forests on the other side of the river, vast dense woodlands. The kind of cover that just might help put up a defensive position to hold back the armored assault.

For a while. He was playing for moments now, thinking forward one step at a time.

"All forces…withdraw toward the river. The rally point is the forest south of the city. Pass the word along on whatever comm you've got." The chain of communications just might get the word to most of his people. At least he hoped it would…because the ones who didn't get the message were probably going to die.

* * *

"No sign of pursuit yet, Admiral."

Winters sat back in his chair, trying to hide some of the despondency that had taken hold of him. He knew what he'd done had been tactically correct, that no one could fault him for it. No one but himself. "The Sledgehammer" was not the kind of officer who ran from an enemy, any enemy…and certainly not when the withdrawal left millions of civilians behind.

He'd watched as much of the bombardment as his severely limited scanning assets could relay to him. It had been difficult to sit and stare at the screens as the planet was pounded so thoroughly, and even though he knew throwing what remained of his fleet away wouldn't have stopped any of it, it still hurt to think of how many people on the ground had been killed, wounded… and what shape the Marines and other defenders were in when the enemy had begun to land its own ground forces.

His sole solace was the realization that, whatever he might have expected, the enemy hadn't launched an extermination strike. It was hard enough to watch the limited attack…he couldn't imagine what he would have felt seeing over a hundred million people killed while his own ships hid in the dust clouds and watched.

But duty was sometimes hard, and watching the enemy, seeing the power and capability of their ships, he knew his first duty was—*had* to be—to get out the word, to make sure the rest of the Confederation was on alert. He'd already sounded the alarm, of course, the instant Barron's message had arrived, and no doubt the famous admiral was already back on Megara, doing the same. But Winters had actually fought the enemy, and for all he'd taken Barron's words as pure fact, he realized now he still hadn't appreciated just how deadly the new enemy was, or just what kind of a conflict was coming on them all.

His darkest thoughts were wild with images of great worlds burning, fleets battered to scrap, of the fall of the Confederation itself.

He'd sent three ships back through the transit point, grateful that the enemy had come in from the frontier end of the system. The way back toward the Confederation's network of transit points remained open to his ships. That made retreat a real option, and one he'd forced himself to consider. He wouldn't have thought about it for an instant if he had been alone. "The Sledgehammer" didn't run. But he was less cavalier about throwing away the lives of his people, and he'd been tortured by uncertainty for hours. He couldn't save Dannith, not with the forces he had with him. The tactical decision was clear. He should retreat, rally more forces, and return when he had some chance of victory. But he hadn't been able to force himself to issue the commands.

Not yet.

His fingers moved over his workstation, pulling up damage control reports. His crews had worked wonders on his ships, repairing far more than he'd imagined possible in such a short time…though "repair" was a strong word for most of it. The hasty fixes were mostly fragile patch jobs, and even on the bridge of his flagship, there were auxiliary cables strewn across the deck, replacements and temporary reconfigurations for comm lines and energy transmission conduits blasted in the fighting. His ships had more systems online than they had half a day earlier, but he knew they would lose them again quickly in a fight.

He shook his head bitterly. If he advanced into range of the enemy, the result wouldn't be a fight. It would be a slaughter.

He had no choice. There was nothing he could do for Dannith now…and there was a war to fight. His duty had been in the Ventica system, doing all he could to protect the beleaguered planet, but now it lay elsewhere…helping to prepare the Confederation for what looked to be the most desperate war it had ever seen.

"Commander, lay in a fleet course for the Talyon transit point." His tone was somber, despite his best efforts to hide his misery.

"Yes, sir."

He looked back to the main display, to the scans from the space around Dannith.

"I'm sorry," he said softly, to himself.

And to the millions he had to leave to their fate.

* * *

"Faster! We're almost out of time." Blanth stood on the bank of the river, watching as a column of Marines streamed across the hasty bridge his engineers had built. Bridge was a bit of an overstatement for the rickety structure, but he'd already gotten over two thousand Marines across, plus a similar number of planetary regulars and militia. That was more than he'd expected just hours before, and he knew he owed the operation's success to the five hundred volunteers out on the other side of the city, struggling to hold back the enemy advance.

The Marines weren't so much fighting the tanks as they were tearing up the landscape, doing everything possible to slow the massive things down. It had still been dangerous, and the last casualty report he'd gotten was somewhere north of thirty percent, but the desperate struggle had allowed him to regroup some of the planet's defenders.

"Planet" wasn't entirely an accurate characterization. Blanth had no idea what was going on anywhere but around the capital, having lost planet-wide communications with the destruction of the satellite network. He had positioned smaller forces in other key areas, but he'd known from the start that the fight around Dannith's main city would determine the planet's fate. If he'd had any air power, or more troops, he might have made an effort to conduct a true planet-wide defense, but without the resources, he'd put ninety percent of his strength within twenty kilometers of Port Royal City.

"Keep moving." He'd been shouting some version of the same thing for the last few hours, but now there was a new urgency. He could hear the sounds of fighting getting closer, and he knew the enemy was advancing rapidly now. His battered rearguard was almost spent, its remnants falling back on the bridgehead. It all felt almost surreal, like some army from thousands of years before, scrambling around on foot and seeing things like rivers as grand obstacles. For the hundredth time, he craved aircraft for both combat and transport, but as he had every other time he'd considered it, he realized he was better off with neither his forces nor the enemy having any. If the invaders had been able to land some kind of air support, the battle would be over already, his forces wiped out.

Of course, it he'd had any kind of air assault assets, even those giant, lumbering tanks would have been in a world of hurt…depending on how effective their anti-air defenses were.

There was no point of imagining what-ifs. He had to get as many of his people across as he could…and he had to get them organized, ready to resume the fight. He was giving the city to the enemy, and he didn't like that. But he had no hope of holding it, and if he'd dug in for a fight in the heavily urbanized areas, Port Royal would have been leveled, and many—or most—of its millions of occupants, killed.

The enemy didn't seem to be conducting any kind of genocidal operation, and that meant yielding the city was the best way to save lives.

The woods south of the river were in a virtually unpopulated area, a perfect spot for the last stand, a place where his people could unleash all that remained of their destructive capability, without killing thousands of civilians. His people would hold there for a while, but they couldn't defeat the enemy forces. It wasn't a question of if Dannith would fall, but when…and

Blanth was determined to push that time as far out as he could.

Chapter Forty-Nine

Blackstone Heights
Outside Port Royal City
Planet Dannith, Ventica III
Year 316 AC

"Maintain fire…but bursts only." Blanth had repeated the command multiple times, but he still had people firing on full auto, especially among the planetary regulars and the militias, who were governed more by fear than by his orders. He didn't mind the added firepower, but he did object to running out of ammunition in the middle of the fight…and the absolute last thing he was going to do was pull ammo from his Marines to give it to local troops who'd squandered theirs. When the planetary soldiers went through their own allotments, they were shit out of luck.

The fire wasn't doing much anyway. There were enemy soldiers out there in support of the tanks, which gave his people intermittent targets they could actually hurt. But for the most part, those troopers stayed behind the behemoths, and out of reach of the Marines' fire.

The woods had been a good choice for a defensive position. It seemed clear that the enemy had some level of restriction of the level of devastation they were prepared to utilize. He'd been afraid the attackers would unleash incendiaries on the forest, trapping his people in a conflagration and giving them the choice of fleeing out into the open or roasting alive. But they hadn't yet.

Maybe they just need to get authorization from a higher level...

There was no point worrying about it. For now, he took solace in the knowledge that the enemy war machines were tough—damned tough—but they weren't indestructible. The three artillery pieces his people had managed to redeploy had taken out four of them, before they themselves were targeted and destroyed. His people had knocked out another three with makeshift mines and similar tactics.

Blanth knew he could destroy the tanks with nukes, of course, but he didn't have any...and he was defending a Confederation world, one he preferred not to turn into a radioactive hell. Still, he wondered what kind of enemies the Hegemony had faced before. The Confederation had shied away from deploying its own tanks for the very reason he'd just considered. Offensive weaponry was just too deadly to concentrate so much power in something so large and vulnerable to fire.

Do these people fight enemies without high-yield weapons? Is the size as much for its visual and morale impact as fighting power? Or do they simply rely on adversaries not using high-yield weapons on their own worlds?

That would be a dangerous assumption. Blanth was far from sure he'd hold back himself if he'd had nuclear ordnance available.

He didn't have answers, and he didn't have time to think about it. The enemy tanks had gotten across the river, with far greater ease than he'd expected. The things were waterproof, or close to it, and most of them had simply driven across the bottom of the shallow river. The soft, sandy material of the riverbed had slowed them, for sure, but it had still taken less than an hour to get a dozen of the war machines to the southern bank.

His people had managed to inflict some casualties on the enemy infantry, though for the most part, the soldiers had remained behind the tanks. He suspected they were ready to intervene if he sent his people in to try to take the heavy weapons in the flank. He'd considered doing just that, but the dense columns formed up behind the tanks had discouraged him. Any parties he sent would be quickly surrounded and attacked.

The enemy soldiers were disturbing in their own ways. He'd seen a few bodies from the limited firefights that had occurred, and they were…different. They were human, or they had been before something was…done to them. He'd thought they were fully armored at first. He'd seen the Confederation's own experimental suits of powered armor, and he had an idea what something of the sort might look like on enemy troops. Then he realized that wasn't the case. They weren't *wearing* armor at all. It was…attached to them. There were heavy plates on their shoulders, and positioned in other places as well. It looked as though part of the armored sections were removable…but they were affixed to bolts protruding from inside the troopers' bodies. The soldiers had been surgically altered, turned into some kind of human-machine hybrids.

Blanth hadn't had time to really study the corpses, nor to develop any kind of reasonable guesses as to the combat potential such…modifications…would provide. But he guessed that when it finally came to combat between the enemy soldiers and the Marines, his people were going to find that they had encountered their deadliest enemies yet.

* * *

"Admiral, the last of Commander Covington's people have landed."

Winters nodded silently. He'd been about to withdraw when the scanners detected a force of fighters inbound. He'd belayed the earlier withdrawal order when he saw them. Abandoning Covington and her survivors would have been more than he could endure. It seemed foolish perhaps, to worry about forty-two pilots, even as millions on Dannith could be dying. But the fighter pilots had fought like uncaged devils, tearing into the enemy forces again and again. The fault for the fall of Dannith could not be laid upon them.

And they were his people. Along with a few of the pilots from the now-destroyed fortresses, no longer the green warriors they'd been hours before.

Constitution was the sole remaining fighter platform in the system. *Discovery* had survived the battle, too, but the old battleship was badly battered. There was certainly no chance of getting her bays back in operation anytime soon. His first thought had been concern about how he would get all the fighters into *Constitution*'s own battered bays. Then he'd realized there were only forty-two of them, not even a tithe of the massive strike force that had gone against the enemy in the first assault.

"Very well, Commander. Advise all ships to prepare for immediate thrust."

"Admiral...I'm picking something up on the scanners." Commander Jerome had proven to be highly capable at the tactical station. Winters knew his reputation for being hard-driving was well-deserved, and he respected any officer who could keep up with him. "Incoming ships, sir. A significant force."

Winters felt a coldness in his body. He'd already made the decision to retreat, to take advantage of the enemy's failure to pursue and finish off his last ships. He hadn't had any remaining doubts, but if he had, the arrival of fresh enemy forces would have finished them off.

He turned toward Jerome, but he didn't say anything for a few seconds. There was nothing to say. He just sat still, and finally he said, "There is nothing to be gained by delay. All ships...commence nav plan alpha. Forty percent thrust." The enemy wasn't following, and the new force was too far away to interfere. Amid the desperation and misery, Winters was grateful that he wasn't forced to abandon his cripples. Forty percent would keep his survivors together, instead of stringing out what remained of his fleet. He wasn't sure it really mattered, but it was a small mercy to him.

"Yes, Admiral...relaying command to all..." Jerome's voice stopped suddenly.

Winters's head snapped around, as much by instinct as

intent. He'd come to trust Jerome, and there was something in the officer's voice…

"Admiral…we're picking up beacons from the incoming ships." A pause. "They're Confederation vessels, sir!"

Winters heard the words, but they didn't make any sense to him. How could there be Confederation forces coming in from the Badlands?

And then he realized…

*   *   *

Sara Eaton stared straight ahead, and her eyes were cold like death. Her forces had been pursued by the enemy through several dozen systems, and then the tables had turned suddenly, and her people had become the pursuers, chasing a fleet that was faster and stronger…and was heading toward the Confederation.

She had followed, chasing every sign of the enemy, every ion trail or other clue as to the direction the Hegemony force had taken…and when she'd realized the trail indeed led back home, she'd driven her ships hard, even leaving behind those units that could not keep up…to get back to Dannith. And now, she'd arrived to find a much-depleted enemy force, one that had clearly fought a nasty battle in the system. They had faced a defense far more effective than she'd have expected just from Dannith's fortifications.

Then the scanner reports came in. There were Confederation ships there. She smiled, imagining that Tyler Barron had already managed to get some added force deployed to Dannith. But it didn't matter why they were there…what mattered was they had hurt the Hegemony fleet, weakened it significantly.

She analyzed the new information rapidly, concluding that the Hegemony forces still outgunned the combined forces of the White Fleet and the Confederation ships on her scanners. But the margin was far closer than it had been. She didn't know if her people could win the fight, but she wasn't sure they couldn't, either…and she was damned sure they could give the enemy one hell of an idea what to expect when they invaded

Confederation space.

She clenched her fists, turning toward her sister's station. "All ships…battle stations. All fighter squadrons scramble… prepare for immediate launch." There was venom in her tone, and a bloodthirsty rage began to take control of her. This was no battle fought in the endless depths of space. This was a Confederation system, and the Hegemony ships were invaders.

Sara Eaton only knew one way to deal with invaders.

It was time to show these people what a mistake they had made leaving her forces behind.

*   *   *

"It's the White Fleet, sir!" Jerome had been controlled and calm during the battle, but his excitement slipped into his voice this time. Winters had known he couldn't expect and reinforcements yet, not from within the Confederation. That had been a key component of his reluctant decision to pull out, to flee the system while he could. But the arrival of the White Fleet changed everything. Retreat became unthinkable…and there was only a single option in his mind.

"All ships, replot course toward Dannith. We're going to attack again."

"Yes, sir."

"And advise the launch bays I want those fighters refitted and ready to launch in twenty minutes." He paused, and then, with the tone that had earned him his nickname, he added, "At twenty-one minutes, I'm going to start spacing flight crew if those birds aren't blasting down the tubes."

His people knew that wasn't a serious threat, he realized that. At least they were fairly sure. But there were enough rumors about him to sustain just the slightest doubt. And that was enough to have the desired effect.

"Yes, Admiral." Jerome's voice suggested the vaguest uncertainty in the aide's mind as well.

"And get me a line to the flagship over there…we've got these bastards bracketed between two forces, and stuck in the middle of their planetary operations. We're going to take advantage of that."

"Yes, sir," Jerome said crisply.

Winters waited silently, his mind focused on the renewed fight to come…and his eyes fixed on the display, as the ships of the White Fleet continued to transit into the system.

Chapter Fifty

"Jettison the log, Atara." Barron had almost walked the two meters to her station to whisper the order into her ear. But he'd realized that would spare his people nothing. They would have known exactly what he was doing...and they were all as aware as he was just how little chance they had of surviving the incoming strike.

Barron might have ignored the log, save for one thing. It was his last chance to get the word out. Maybe when it was retrieved, after he was dead, those who listened would understand he had no more reasons to lie...and take the warning seriously. He'd sent a ship to alert Admiral Winters at Base Grimaldi, so even if the log failed, there was still some hope. And he clung to that thought. Tightly.

"Log jettisoned, Tyler." She turned and looked back at him, and their eyes connected. Atara Travis had been more than an exec to him, more than a friend. She was the sister he'd never had, and one of the few people he'd met who had never failed to be there for him. He regretted that she had to die because of what had happened to him...worse, because she'd tried to help

383

him. He'd long been prepared, on some level, to see his people die in battle, but he'd never imagined they would come to that pass not facing some enemy, but because of their loyalty to him. It was a bitter realization, but one he couldn't deny.

He felt the urge to call up the crews manning the defense grid, to rally them, work them into a frenzy…but he'd done that already. They were veterans, and they knew what to do. He had no doubt they would blast the incoming squadrons with deadly fire.

He was just as sure enough of the attack craft would get through to blow *Dauntless* to atoms.

He'd done all he could. *Dauntless* couldn't outrun the bombers, and trying to would only delay the inevitable by a few moments…and degrade his evasive maneuvers. Barron would do anything to save his people, but if they were doomed anyway, there was no reason to prolong the pain.

"Atara…set up the comm system to repeat the warning about the Hegemony." No one was listening, but he didn't want to chance his opponents ignoring *Dauntless*'s log. Maybe they would consider his words after the battle…maybe the Barron name had a last touch of magic in it. He didn't know if it would work, and he realized he would never know. But he had to try.

"Yes, sir." A moment later. "The message is being transmitted on a repeating loop, Admiral." A pause. "We've done everything we can, Tyler. If they won't listen…" She didn't finish. She didn't have to. They had both seen the Hegemony forces up close, and they knew what was coming.

Barron turned back to the display. The enemy strike force was thirty minutes from attack range. Normally, Atara would be announcing that. He knew her well enough to be sure she hadn't forgotten, and he was grateful for the simple mercy she was showing all hands by remaining silent. They could all see the display. They all knew they had less than thirty minutes to live.

Barron leaned back and closed his eyes. It seemed strange to be in so desperate a situation, and yet have nothing to do. Helplessness was the most difficult affliction for him to endure, and even as he sat quietly, his mind raced, frantically trying to think of something—anything—to do.

But there was nothing.

Then one of the lift doors opened, and he turned to see what was happening.

His eyes glistened with moisture as he saw Andi Lafarge step onto the bridge.

Another person he loved…and another who would die because of loyalty to him, because she had tried to help him.

"I hope you don't mind, Tyler," she said softly, after she'd walked across the bridge toward his chair. "I…I just wanted to be with you."

Her defeated tone struck him hard. He didn't give up in a fight, but he'd never met anyone with Andi's raw stubbornness. To see her acknowledging that all was lost almost destroyed him in an instant.

Barron had always tried to keep his relationship with Andi somewhat of a secret, perhaps the most disastrously unsuccessful effort he'd ever made. There was no point now…and he was grateful for one last chance to see her, a few final moments together, even if they couldn't be alone.

Even if they could only sit together and wait for death.

"Of course…I'm glad you came." He looked at her, and he hoped desperately that his eyes conveyed what he wanted to tell her but couldn't.

She walked up next to his chair and stood there, placing her hand on his shoulder.

"Admiral…"

Atara's voice pulled his thoughts back to the bridge.

"We've got energy readings at the Andura transit point."

Barron's head snapped around, his eyes moving toward the blue circle representing the point. Andura wasn't on any path to Megara, save the one right through Delphi. Whatever was coming, there was no way they were responding to an order from the Senate.

He knew it was most likely some kind of routine traffic, freighters or civilian passenger ships stumbling into a battlezone entirely unawares. He couldn't imagine any scenario that could rescue *Dauntless* from its impending doom.

At least it gave him something else to think about.

"We've got big ships coming through, Admiral. If I didn't know better, I'd say there are half a dozen battleships inbound."

Barron's eyes widened. Now he was totally confused. He'd have discounted the report from almost anyone else, but he'd never known Atara to be wrong about a scanner reading.

"Battleships? That's impossible. Andura leads to the Far Rim. The Confederation doesn't even *have* six battleships out there." But as he spoke, the scanner readings updated, and six massive contacts appeared in the display, right in front of the transit point. They were coming in-system at high velocities.

Barron didn't understand, but it didn't matter. If those ships were here for him, it was almost comical overkill. He waited for the scanners to update, or to pick up the Confederation ID beacons on the ships...but there was nothing.

And then, the comm crackled to life.

"All ships in the system are to power down immediately. The vessel *Dauntless* is under our protection, and any vessels firing upon it will be attacked without further notice."

Barron was stunned, and for a moment he just sat, still as a statue. He knew that voice.

Cilian Globus...leading a force of Alliance battleships. All of them were launching fighters.

It took some time for the Confederation force to receive the communique and respond, but when they did, the message was defiant. "Alliance vessels, you are in Confederation space without permission, in express violation of the treaties between our nations. You have committed an act of war, and I order *you* to stand down at once and prepare to be boarded."

Barron was impressed by the fortitude of whoever was in command of the Confederation ships. It was someone with almost fanatical bravery.

Or someone with no knowledge at all of Palatians and their ways.

"We are here to assist our friend and ally, and you are seeking to destroy one of your own ships, in violation of all tenets of honor. If the cost of standing with a friend is battle, and the loss of a treaty and ally, then so be it. Honor calls. Let us fight…and to the death."

Barron almost laughed. Globus was laying it on thick. He had no doubt the Palatian *would* fight to save *Dauntless* if he had to, but even with his honor codes and warrior heritage, he would avoid it if there was any way he could.

Not that it mattered. Barron had calculated the time until the Alliance fighters could reach *Dauntless*, and how long remained until the approaching strike force was in range. Globus's ships would be ten minutes too late, even if Barron blasted his engines at full power.

His friend might avenge him—with tragic consequences for the Rim's survival—but he wasn't going to save him.

"Cilian," he said into the comm, his voice grim. "You can't get here in time, old friend. You have my thanks and eternal gratitude for attempting to help, but heed my final request. The Confederation and the Alliance must stand together if the Hegemony is to be defeated. Do nothing here, even out of love for me, that would jeopardize that. It would be too terrible to die here, knowing I leave such tragedy behind."

The Palatian didn't respond. Instead, a moment later, he said, "Bomber squadrons…you are to veer off now. Do not attack *Dauntless*, or you will all be destroyed." Barron knew it was no empty threat…twenty-four squadrons of Alliance fighters would obliterate the spent bombers. That was almost a tactical certainty.

Barron almost sent another request for Globus to back off. But then he began to understand the grand bluff that was underway.

The stakes were high…his life and that of everyone on *Dauntless*. But it remained to be seen if the pilots would fold… or if they would call Globus's bluff.

The seconds ticked by with no response, and the bombers continued to close. The Alliance fighters were moving in too, their courses changing slightly, a vector that would put them astride the bombers' course back to their motherships.

Barron reached out and put his hand on top of Andi's resting on his shoulder. The touch of her skin helped him, somehow, gave him energy…and perhaps even a sliver of hope. He imagined the strike commander leading his bombers in, and he wondered if the officer could want to kill him so badly, he'd sacrifice his life and those of all his pilots to do it. Barron had been a comrade until just a few weeks before, and his family name had been ingrained in navy history for four generations. Some of that had to remain in any officer's mind.

Come on…come on…

Barron felt the spark of hope begin to slip away as the fighters loomed ever closer, their courses unchanged. Then he saw a hitch on the display, the bombers slowing. A few seconds later, the full readings came in. The strike force was decelerating at something that looked a lot like full power.

They were pulling back!

Globus's bluff, if indeed it had been a bluff—with Palatians one could never be sure—had worked.

Barron felt a wave of relief, and he turned and looked up at Andi, a brief smile slipping onto his lips, and matching the one she gave him.

"It's confirmed, Tyler…the fighters are pulling back. The two battleships are signaling to Commander Globus that they will remain in place and recover their squadrons." She paused, and he could hear her taking in a deep breath. "We made it. We made it."

Barron nodded. *Yes, we made it…to the far end of the Confederation, a dozen or more transits from the threatened border.* But his people had survived, for now. What future any of them had if the full strength of the Hegemony hit a naked and undefended border was another question.

Still, that was tomorrow's problem. Right now, he had a friend to thank, and that couldn't wait any longer. He toggled the comm, directing the beacon toward the Alliance flagship. "It's good to see you, Cilian…and not a moment too soon. But how did you knew we needed help?"

"We do have some spies, you know, my friend…and from the latest intelligence reports from Megara, I figured you might need help. It wasn't too difficult to convince our friends at Archellia to let us through…and there wasn't another base between the border and here that could do a thing to stop six battleships… though I fear we may left a few annoyed outpost commanders behind us." Globus paused, and then he continued, "You have good friends at Archellia, Tyler, officers I believe will listen to what you have to say. Shall we go there now, before half the Confederation fleet shows up and we find ourselves in a real fight here?"

Chapter Fifty-One

Raketh sat quietly atop his pedestal, his mood grim. The lack of commentary or discussion from his four colleagues suggested they were feeling similarly. He'd had cause for satisfaction just hours before. He had been tasked with finding the enemy's homeworlds, and the population of the inhabited planet in the system left little doubt he had done just that. The planet was a frontier world, no doubt, much weaker than the core systems that likely lay beyond, but it was a significant population center nevertheless. His forces had engaged the planet's defenses, and had the victory. The orbital forts had all been destroyed…and the enemy fleet had been battered and driven into retreat. He'd landed ground forces, and all reports suggested that the pacification of the planet was proceeding satisfactorily, despite some tougher than expected resistance.

Now, the enemy fleet he'd spared in his race to complete his mission had returned…and the remnants of the system's original force were also moving back to engage. His own forces were badly depleted, the effect of multiple battles without reinforcements or resupply. The fighting around the planet, particularly against the large force of the enemy's annoying small attack craft, had cost him many ships. He could engage both enemy forces…and most likely prevail. But the chance of victory, by his normally extremely accurate calculations, had slipped significantly below one hundred percent. There was substantial risk to remaining and fighting a battle to the end. But withdrawal would mean abandoning the ground forces.

They were, of course, almost all Kriegeri, and therefore expendable by their very nature. He'd landed six Masters to direct combat operations, but he could recover them quickly if he decided to withdraw.

Or he could load all the fleet's masters onto Danais, and leave the rest of the ships behind with the Inferiors crewing them, with orders to fight to the death. The lower orders were numerous, and the loss of some thousands wouldn't be impactful. And the ships of his fleet were but a small fraction of those his people possessed. Perhaps that was the right course, to see the enemy fleets in the system destroyed—or nearly so—while ensuring no Masters were lost.

He almost issued the order, but he hesitated. The Hegemony's Grand Fleet was massive, and the activation of even a portion of it would provide enough ships to invade the Rim. But that would take time, and until then, his forces were all the Hegemony had near the enemy. If his fleet survived and he was able to sustain operations in the vicinity of the enemy border, he could scout, capture and interrogate hostages, build logistical bases in nearby systems…and prepare for the arrival of the inevitable invasion.

He considered the options in every way he could conceive. Tactically, strategically, logistically…it made sense to withdraw. In the end, his only concern was one of perception. He would be judged on what he did, and he feared some would view his motivations as deriving from cowardice instead of strategic insight. But that couldn't be helped. He had to do what he believed best…and that was to pull back, to maintain a fleet in being.

His forces would have to pass through the newly-arrived enemy fleet, and there would certainly be renewed combat. But if his forces blasted at full thrust, the duration of the fighting would be short, and his ships would quickly reach the transit point and pass into the next system.

His analysis of the enemy suggested strongly that they would not attempt to follow.

He turned, first left and then right, glancing at the three women and one man in the room with him. "My colleagues," he said calmly, clearly. "I have considered our options, and I request your thoughts on my pending decision. As in all things, I seek your honest and most detailed analysis."

*   *   *

"They're breaking orbit, Sara!" Sonya Eaton was clearly stunned, so much that she'd inadvertently dropped the formality she usually showed to her sister while on duty.

Sara Eaton turned toward the display, confirming what she'd just been told. For a moment, she thought the Hegemony ships were simply forming up, preparing to fight the two approaching Confederation forces. But then every vessel in the enemy fleet blasted its engines at full, heading directly toward her own ships.

She swallowed hard and then took a deep breath, trying to stay calm. The fighting against the Hegemony had been some of the most brutal she'd ever seen, and even as she'd chased the enemy back to the Confederation, she hadn't fully considered what it would be like to go back into battle against the deadly vessels.

"Sonya...I want those fighters launched now. Every bird we've got in this fleet." A pause. "And tell Captain Stockton, we're going to need him like never before." If the enemy hit her line before the other ships in the system could get into the fight, she'd be at a big disadvantage...and she'd need everything Stockton could give her.

She'd received a communique from the other force. Admiral Winters was in command, and as her senior, that meant he was in charge of the battle. Their forces were still too far apart for that to have much meaning, the one minute forty second transmission time rendering real direction of the overall battle impossible. It would be some time until "the Sledgehammer" got his ships back into range, and until then, the White Fleet was on its own.

She was shifting in her seat, jacked up on adrenaline and the stim she'd just taken. But as she looked at the display, she saw that the enemy was continuing to blast their engines at what had to be full thrust. The incoming ships had already built a substantial velocity, and she'd expected them to cut their engine levels to prepare to engage. But they hadn't.

A thought crossed her mind, one she could hardly contemplate. Could the enemy be withdrawing? It was hard to believe. They'd clearly landed forces on Dannith, troops who would be doomed if the fleet fled and left them behind. She shook her head again at the coldness of the enemy. They seemed to consider most of their forces expendable, like so many torpedoes or rounds of ammunition. She'd discounted the idea at first, but as she continued to watch the enemy ships accelerating— and traced their vectors directly to the transit point—something clicked in her mind. She was suddenly sure the enemy was breaking off...and she intended to hurt them as badly as she could when they passed.

"Commander, issue a fleet order. I want all batteries at maximum power. One hundred ten percent where possible. We're only going to get a few shots at these bastards, and I want them to count!"

* * *

Blanth felt the cold wetness of the mud on his knees as his weight dug into the ground. The rain had continued for hours now, and as miserable as it had made conditions for his people, it had been a godsend. The enemy tanks, massively heavy, had gotten terribly bogged down in the marshy, low ground around the river. His lack of ordnance heavy enough to really engage the massive war machines prevented his forces from taking full advantage, but he'd sent out some volunteer teams nevertheless, and they had managed to disable two more of the great vehicles.

There had been a downside to those operations, though, at least in terms of foreshadowing for the war Blanth knew had come. The enemy soldiers had been caught by surprise by the sabotage teams, but they'd reacted quickly, and in the resulting battles, he'd gotten his first glimpse of their combat ability. His Marines had always been more capable than any of their adversaries…but the machine-assisted enemy troopers, almost cyborgs, fought his people with a savagery and effectiveness that chilled him to the bone. He couldn't admit they were better than his people—it just wasn't in him as a Marine—but he was shaken nevertheless…and he knew if the enemy tired of trying to root his people out of the woods with their armor, the enemy infantry could almost certainly do the job. They had numbers and armament, and despite his best efforts to conserve resources, Blanth's people were running out of ammunition.

He cursed all the rounds his people—even the Marines—had wasted shooting ineffectively at the enemy tanks, but there was nothing he could do about that. He had to make a choice. Stay and hold the position as long as possible…or disperse his people and hope enough escaped into the planet's wilderness to carry on guerrilla warfare. If he waited any longer, there would be no supplies left at all, and no chance to maintain even a spark of resistance around Port Royal City.

He moved forward, ignoring the heavy fire tearing through the woods all around him, and he crouched down on the edge of the wooded area. The tanks were still coming, and for all the help the rain had provided his people, it hadn't stopped the deadly vehicles, only slowed them.

Worse, he could see enemy troops forming up. From the looks of their formations, they were planning to assault his positions. He was out of time.

He started to turn, but something caught his eye. It was a flash of light, from up in the sky. He had no idea what it could be. Dannith didn't have any military aircraft, and what transport planes the planet had possessed had almost certainly been destroyed in the bombardments. Did the enemy have air assets after all? If they did, why had they waited so long to deploy them? If enemy airships had attacked his forces when they were crossing the river…

His thoughts froze as he saw an explosion around one of the tanks. The huge vehicle hadn't been destroyed, but it didn't take much of a look to confirm it had taken considerable damage.

And the shot had come from the air.

Friendly aircraft? How?

Blanth had no idea what was happening, but even as he tried to figure it out, more explosions erupted along the enemy line. His looked up, scanning the sky, but the cloud cover was thick, and he couldn't see anything in the dusky haze except for more light trails…followed by explosions.

Then, his comm crackled to life, and a voice blared through his earpiece.

"All Confederation units, this is Captain Stockton, from the Confederation battleship, *Repulse*. We have a dozen squadrons in the air now, seeking out and attacking enemy positions on the planet. All enemy space forces have retreated from the system, leaving their ground forces unsupported. There are landing craft behind us, with three thousand fresh Marines inbound."

Blanth listened, still not believing what he'd heard. He knew Stockton's voice, though, from years of service with the pilot on *Dauntless*…and he'd have bet his last round of ammunition that he'd just heard the captain's words. If Stockton was back, that meant the rest of the White Fleet had returned. Just in time to save Dannith.

He turned and raced back toward his main positions. It was time to get his people ready to attack.

* * *

Stockton was exhausted, but exhilarated as well. He'd led his squadrons against the Hegemony fleet as it fled toward the transit point, and his people had once again drawn blood, destroying half a dozen ships and sending others continuing their flight as barely functional wrecks. He'd brought his people back to their motherships, charged with excitement over the small casualty rate they had suffered, by far the lowest losses of any strike in the campaign. Whatever forces or technology the Hegemony might mass for the return engagement he knew would come, he suspected the bastards would think twice about how they'd been handled by the Confederation's fighter wings.

He shifted in his seat, moving his controls, adjusting his position. He hated atmospheric flight, and the fact that his people had been forced to fly straight through a storm to reach their targets hadn't helped at all, no more than did the fatigue growing heavy in his head and body. There had been no choice. The fleet's scanner readings of the surface suggested the ground battle was not going well, that the Marines and other defenders were on the verge of defeat. He hadn't hesitated when Admiral Eaton gave him the order. He'd only been back an hour from the battle in space, but Stara had already gotten the flight crews working, pulling the bombing rigs off from *Repulse*'s squadrons and installing the atmospheric kits. It was a tedious job, but the crews knew just what was at stake, and they'd completed it in record time, as had their comrades on four of the other battleships.

Stockton and the strike force had launched less than two hours after they'd landed, with no sleep, and nothing more than a sandwich and bottle of water to recharge themselves. But they were the best the Confederation had, and they were devoted to their legendary commander. They would have followed him anywhere.

The sleek craft had launched just outside planetary orbit, and within minutes, they were descending through the atmosphere, and targeting the massive enemy tanks.

The war machines had considerable air defense capabilities, and his veteran pilots, who rarely flew in atmosphere, suffered terribly as they pressed their attacks. By the time the strike force had launched all its missiles—and devastated the enemy forces—they had lost almost a third of their strength.

But as he stared at the damage reports, and at the landers now beginning to appear in the upper atmosphere, he knew those losses had not been for nothing.

They had saved Dannith.

Chapter Fifty-Two

Senate Hall
Troyus City, Planet Megara, Olyus III

"The measure has passed with an overwhelming majority. Gary Holsten and Tyler Barron are hereby declared traitors to the Confederation. They are to be terminated on sight. All Confederation personnel are obligated to attempt termination in any way within their capabilities, and..."

Desiree sat and listened as Ferrell read the resolution to the assembled Senate. The news of what had happened in Delphi had given her—given Ferrell, she reminded herself—all that was necessary to unify the chamber in opposition and outrage. *Dauntless* had destroyed *Titania* and the other ships sent to apprehend Barron, and worst of all, foreign Alliance ships had intervened on behalf of the renegade admiral.

She knew politicians well enough to understand their dedication to principles and ethics were utterly changeable to suit their momentary needs, but the one thing guaranteed to enrage them all was disregard for their own power and status. Barron's escape, and his destruction of the ships sent to bring him back—with foreign assistance, no less—had sent them all into fits of self-indulgent rage.

And Ferrell, for all his notable faults, had become somewhat of an expert at directing the bruised egos of megalomaniacs.

"We have done only what we have been forced to do. We

here, the members of this noble and august body, are the defenders of justice and righteousness…"

Marieles tried to pay attention—he was her creature, after all—but it was a losing fight. She'd brought Ferrell out of obscurity and thrust him into the center of things, and the formerly quiet and meek Senator had risen to the challenge. She suspected his nearly endless expression of rage would serve her purposes, at least in the immediate future, but that didn't mean she had to listen to every boring, pompous word.

"So, I say to you, my esteemed and respected colleagues, that we…"

"Senator…Senator…there is news. Terrible news!"

Marieles's head snapped around at the sound of the aide's voice, recognizing the fear in the man's tone. She knew immediately something extremely bad had happened, even as she watched the aide rush up to the podium. The news *had* to be disastrous. She couldn't imagine what else would have sent one of Ferrell's staff rushing onto the Senate floor to interrupt the politician in the middle of his self-aggrandizing speech.

"What is it, Griggs?" Ferrell snapped, holding his anger in check, but clearly unhappy at the intrusion.

"It's Dannith, Senator." The aide ran the rest of the way down, almost to the speaking floor where Ferrell stood. He turned and looked out over the assembled Senate and then back to Ferrell. "There's been a battle, a horrific battle."

"A battle?" Ferrell looked shocked, and a wave of murmurs rippled through the room. "Against what force?"

"A new invader, Senator…an enemy the White Fleet found in the depths of the Badlands."

Marieles looked away from the scene, drawing back into her own thoughts. Barron's babblings…she'd written them off as fictions intended to delay his arrest and imprisonment. Could he have been telling the truth? Had he truly come back to warn the Confederation of an approaching enemy?

And if he had…what should she do next?

AS Invictus
Outer Reaches of the Cassiopolis System
Three Billion Kilometers from Planet Archellia

"At least one power on the Rim is taking the threat seriously." Barron sat in the study, enjoying the warmth of the fireplace. It was something he'd never seen before on a warship, a perk, he supposed, of the office of Imperator of the Alliance. *Invictus* was the Palatians' new flagship, fresh out of the shipyard and on its first voyage. Barron understood the choice of the ship's name. The Confederation named new vessels after old, lost ones all the time. He didn't have to look farther than his own *Dauntless* to see that. But *Invictus* was a name that rekindled old memories—painful ones. Still, he understood why Tulus had chosen it. The original *Invictus* had been destroyed by *Dauntless*, and by all the standards of the old Alliance, such a name would be retired in disgrace, not reused. Tulus was trying to move his people forward, to retain the martial fortitude that made them strong, while shedding some of the more troublesome traits that had held the Palatians back for far too long.

"I have dispatched all additional intelligence assets at my disposal to Megara, Tyler, but I am afraid that both the Union and your Confederation are far more advanced that we in the arts of espionage." Spying had always been deemed less than an honorable career in the Alliance.

Barron owed his life to his friend, the Alliance Imperator. Without the forces Tulus had dispatched to the Confederation, *Dauntless* would certainly have been destroyed in Delphi…and the goal of preparing for war with the Hegemony would have been even less attainable than it already seemed to be.

"Thank you again, my brother. Your ships arrived just in time." Alliance ships had almost opened fire on their Confederation allies. Barron knew that was no more a cause for celebration than the fact that his own ship had actually engaged and destroyed their former comrades.

Tulus nodded.

"Your efforts to investigate are appreciated, Imperator

Tulus." It was Gary Holsten speaking. The former intelligence chief had been strangely silent since his rescue, spending most of his time in his quarters on *Dauntless*, and even sitting wordlessly for the first twenty minutes of the current meeting. But he held his tongue no longer. "There can be little doubt that Sector Nine is behind whatever is happening on Megara...and I must say, both the plan and its execution have been brilliant."

Barron didn't appreciate the skill behind whatever had so destabilized the Confederation when war was coming, and a quick glance at Tulus told him the Imperator didn't either. But neither of them were spies...and Holsten was one of the best.

"I have—at least I had—considerable contacts on Megara. I may be able to work with your agents, connect them with assets already in place, ones likely far more aware than we of exactly what is taking place."

"Indeed, Mr. Holsten...I am inclined to agree with you. Perhaps you should meet with our intelligence people. I will appoint you with vice regal powers in matters of espionage, specifically with regard to the situation on Megara and in the Confederation as a whole. All Alliance personnel will obey your commands."

"Thank you, Imperator. I am honored." There was little doubt from the sound of Holsten's voice that he was surprised by the level of assistance Tulus had so readily offered. Barron suspected Holsten didn't know the Palatian the way he did. He'd no doubt expected pride and honor to impede cooperation. That would have been true once, Barron knew, but the Alliance was changing, and if Tulus continued to be successful, changing rapidly.

And Barron suspected the Imperator understood, better than most, the grave nature of the threat faced by not only the Confederation, but by the entire Rim.

Holsten stood up. "With your permission, I will go meet with your people immediately, Imperator. At this point, I am only certain of one thing, and that is we do not have time to waste."

"No, Mr. Holsten...we almost certainly do not."

Holsten nodded toward Tulus, and again to Barron, and then

he walked swiftly out of the room.

Barron and Tulus remained, neither man speaking for a time. Finally, Tulus looked over at his Alliance friend, his brother by sacred oath, and he said, "Well, my comrade…it appears that we will fight together once more."

"Yes," Barron said, leaving it at that, but inside thinking…*I just hope we're fighting against the Hegemony, and not against Confederation forces.*

Planet Calpharon
Sigma Nordlin System

Akella sat in her chair, set on a platform above all the others present in the august gathering. The men and women around her were the leaders of the Hegemony, the most genetically perfect human beings in all of the galaxy. Yet for all their ability, for all the massive power and responsibility each of them carried, they served at her behest. She was Number One, the supreme ruler of the Hegemony, and the most genetically advanced human known. Her word was law.

She shifted, somehow maintaining her grace and confidence while she tried to find a comfortable position. She was pregnant with her first child, an event later in her life than might be expected. Her responsibilities had delayed conception several years beyond normal standards. A woman of her rank and ability was expected—no, required—to bear at least four children, and while Akella was still in her childbearing years, she'd reached the point where further delay had simply not been a possibility. There were drugs that could prolong fertility, of course, and while frowned upon to an extent, they were allowable. Unlike any form of genetic engineering or gene manipulation…or the greatest sin among those of the Hegemony, cloning. Such practices had played roles in bringing about the Great Death, the downfall of the empire that had once ruled all mankind. From the time of the Hegemony's founding, even the slightest research into such areas had always been punishable by death.

Ruling the Hegemony was a massive undertaking, even in normal times. But now her people had encountered something unexpected, a group of human survivors out on the Rim. The Hegemony had come across many pockets of survivors before and, save for the Others, had subjugated them all.

It would fall to her to lead her people into the war that now clearly loomed before them. The struggle would be nothing less than a crusade to bring right thinking to those on the Rim…and to bring their genetic material into the Hegemony's pool.

For an instant, she wished she could have been spared such a trial, that the discovery of the Rim dwellers could have come in her successor's time. For, surely, one would come soon and displace her, a Master with an even higher ranking than hers taking the role of Number One. She was proud, and she knew that would be a difficult day for her, in some ways. But it would also be a great relief in others.

Humanity had seen many governments, many struggles for power in its history. The Hegemony had been founded on the principal of avoiding such tragedies. Akella's reign had been long, and at each year's testing, she had waited to see if one of her new colleagues would surpass her. It had not happened yet, though surely it would one day. Hegemony doctrine was based on the premise of constant and continued genetic development. They had selective breeding programs, among the highest of the high as much as those subjugated for labor and combat. The child she was carrying would likely unseat her one day, if no one else did first. She had mated with Number Two, and while there remained some random factors in such pairings and the resulting offspring, it was rare for such an elite breeding to fail to produce an extraordinary child.

The discovery of survivors on the Rim presented a problem and a danger, but also an opportunity. Based on what she had seen, the enemy was resourceful, capable, and technologically advanced. They would make welcome additions to the Hegemony's gene pool. No doubt there were even a few of the survivors who would qualify to join the Master class.

The Hegemony's ways were clear, and they were followed without question. Defeated enemies, conquered peoples…they were all treated the same way once they were pacified. Those on the Rim who survived the war would be integrated into Hegemony society. They would be given the Test, and assigned positions in accordance with their resulting rankings. Most of the Rim dwellers would likely find their place as Inferiors, predominantly with the working classes of the Arbeiter. But those whose genetics qualified them for higher positions would receive them, with no discrimination at all.

Even she, the uncontested leader, was descended not from the original founders, but from a subjugated group, brought into the Hegemony by force and later cultivated through controlled breeding programs. But she had still been accepted readily in her role, the highest in the Hegemony. All of the Masters acknowledged, with unwavering commitment, the genetic rankings that gave each of them his or her power and station.

"There will be no discipline, no sanctions," she said, after a long silence. "Ninety-Six acted correctly in withdrawing his fleet. There was little to be gained by remaining to fight, and nothing that would have justified further losses. His was a scouting force only, tasked with discovering a route to the enemy's worlds, and in that regard, he has been completely successful. We must now move on, determine our strategy for dealing with these new populations, and exerting our control over the Rim."

Every eye in the room was on Akella as she spoke. There had been some debate, a few voices calling for punishment for Ninety-Six's actions, and others for an immediate strike by whatever forces could be quickly mobilized. She had allowed all to speak their minds, as befitted so elite a gathering. But she had already made up her mind, and as supreme leader, it was her decision alone.

"I appreciate the arguments of my esteemed colleagues urging for a partial strike at once, but I decline that option. This enemy will almost certainly be the strongest we have faced, the war to subdue them the most desperate conflict we have fought…save of course for our encounters with the Others."

She paused. "Though there is no doubt of our superiority or question that we will prevail in this war, I do not believe we should risk underestimating our opponents. For this reason, I am authorizing the full mobilization of the Grand Fleet, and ordering that the invasion of the Rim will commence as soon as those forces are ready to set out."

Blood on the Stars Will Continue with

Invasion

Appendix

Strata of the Hegemony

The Hegemony is an interstellar polity located far closer to the center of what had once been the old empire than Rimward nations such as the Confederation. The Rim nations and the Hegemony were unaware of each other's existence until the White Fleet arrived at Planet Zero and established contact.

Relatively little is known of the Hegemony, save that their technology appears to be significantly more advanced than the Confederation's in most areas, though still behind that of the old empire.

The culture of the Hegemony is based almost exclusively on genetics, with an individual's status being entirely dependent on an established method of evaluating genetic "quality." Generations of selective breeding have produced a caste of "Masters," who occupy an elite position above all others. There are several descending tiers below the Master class, all of which are categorized as "Inferiors."

The Hegemony's culture likely developed as a result of its location much closer to the center of hostilities during the Cataclysm. Many surviving inhabitants of the inward systems suffered from horrific mutations and damage to genetic materials, placing a premium on any bloodlines lacking such effects.

The Rimward nations find the Hegemony's society to be almost alien in nature, while its rulers consider the inhabitants of the Confederation and other nations to be just another strain of Inferiors, fit only to obey their commands without question.

Masters

The Masters are the descendants of those few humans spared genetic damage from the nuclear, chemical, and biological warfare that destroyed the old empire during the series of events known as the Cataclysm. The Masters sit at the top of the Hegemony's societal structure and, in a sense, are its only true full members or citizens.

The Masters' culture is based almost entirely on what they call "genetic purity and quality," and even their leadership and ranking structure is structured solely on genetic rankings. Every master is assigned a number based on his or her place in a population-wide chromosomal analysis. An individual's designation is thus subject to change once per year, to adjust for masters dying and for new adults being added into the database. The top ten thousand individuals in each year's ratings are referred to as "High Masters," and they are paired for breeding matchups far more frequently than the larger number of lower-rated Masters.

Masters reproduce by natural means, through strict genetic pairings based on an extensive study of ideal matches. The central goal of Master society is to steadily improve the human race by breeding the most perfect specimens available and relegating all others to a subservient status. The Masters consider any genetic manipulation or artificial processes like cloning to be grievously sinful, and all such practices are banned in the Hegemony on pain of death to all involved. This belief structure traces from the experiences of the Cataclysm, and the terrible damage inflicted on the populations of imperial worlds by genetically-engineered pathogens and cloned and genetically-engineered soldiers.

All humans not designated as Masters are referred to as Inferiors, and they serve the Masters in various capacities. All Masters have the power of life and death over Inferiors. It is not a crime for a Master to kill an Inferior who has injured or offended that Master in any way.

Kriegeri

The Kriegeri are the Hegemony's soldiers. They are drawn from the strongest and most physically capable specimens of the populations of Inferiors on Hegemony worlds. Kriegeri are not genetically-modified, though in most cases, Master supervisors enforce specific breeding arrangements in selected population groups to increase the quality of future generations of Kriegeri stock.

The Kriegeri are trained from infancy to serve as the Hegemony's soldiers and spaceship crews, and are divided in two categories, red and gray, named for the colors of their uniforms. The "red" Kriegeri serve aboard the Hegemony's ships, under the command of a small number of Master officers. They are surgically modified to increase their resistance to radiation and zero gravity.

The "gray" Kriegeri are the Hegemony's ground soldiers. They are selected from large and physically powerful specimens and are subject to extensive surgical enhancements to increase strength, endurance, and dexterity. They also receive significant artificial implants, including many components of their armor, which becomes a permanent partial exoskeleton of sorts. They are trained and conditioned from childhood to obey orders and to fight. The top several percent of Kriegeri surviving twenty years of service are retired to breeding colonies. Their offspring are Krieger-Edel, a pool of elite specimens serving as mid-level officers and filling a command role between the ruling Masters and the rank and file Kriegeri.

Arbeiter

Arbeiter are the workers and laborers of the Hegemony. They are drawn from populations on the Hegemony's many worlds, and typically either exhibit some level of genetic damage inherited from the original survivors or simply lack genetic ratings sufficient for Master status. Arbeiter are from the same general group as the Kriegeri, though the soldier class includes the very best candidates, and the Arbeiter pool consists of the remnants.

Arbeiter are assigned roles in the Hegemony based on rigid assessments of their genetic status and ability. These positions range from supervisory posts in production facilities and similar establishments to pure physical labor, often working in difficult and hazardous conditions.

Defekts

Defekts are individuals—often populations of entire worlds—exhibiting severe genetic damage. They are typically found on planets that suffered the most extensive bombardments and bacteriological attacks during the Cataclysm.

Defekts have no legal standing in the Hegemony, and they are considered completely expendable. On worlds inhabited by populations of Masters, Kriegeri, and Arbeiters, Defekts are typically assigned to the lowest level, most dangerous labor, and any excess populations are exterminated.

The largest number of Defekts exist on planets on the fringes of Hegemony space, where they are often used for such purposes as mining radioactives and other similarly dangerous operations. Often, the Defekts themselves have no knowledge at all of the Hegemony and regard the Masters as gods or demigods descending from the heavens. On such planets, the Masters often demand ores and other raw materials as offerings, and severely punish any failures or shortfalls. Pliant and obedient populations are provided with rough clothing and low-quality manufactured foodstuffs, enabling them to devote nearly all labor to the gathering of whatever material the Masters demand. Resistant population groups are exterminated, as, frequently, are Defekt populations on worlds without useful resources to exploit.

Also By Jay Allan

Marines (Crimson Worlds I)
The Cost of Victory (Crimson Worlds II)
A Little Rebellion (Crimson Worlds III)
The First Imperium (Crimson Worlds IV)
The Line Must Hold (Crimson Worlds V)
To Hell's Heart (Crimson Worlds VI)
The Shadow Legions(Crimson Worlds VII)
Even Legends Die (Crimson Worlds VIII)
The Fall (Crimson Worlds IX)
War Stories (Crimson World Prequels)
MERCS (Successors I)
The Prisoner of Eldaron (Successors II)
Into the Darkness (Refugees I)
Shadows of the Gods (Refugees II)
Revenge of the Ancients (Refugees III)
Winds of Vengeance (Refugees IV)
Shadow of Empire (Far Stars I)
Enemy in the Dark (Far Stars II)
Funeral Games (Far Stars III)
Blackhawk (Far Stars Legends I)
The Dragon's Banner
Gehenna Dawn (Portal Wars I)
The Ten Thousand (Portal Wars II)
Homefront (Portal Wars III)
Red Team Alpha (CW Adventures I)
Duel in the Dark (Blood on the Stars I)
Call to Arms (Blood on the Stars II)
Ruins of Empire (Blood on the Stars III)
Echoes of Glory (Blood on the Stars IV)
Cauldron of Fire (Blood on the Stars V)
Dauntless (Blood on the Stars VI)
The White Fleet (Blood on the Stars VII)
Flames of Rebellion (Flames of Rebellion I)
Rebellion's Fury (Flames of Rebellion II)

www.jayallanbooks.com